Low Country

Anne Rivers Siddons

Thorndike Press • Chivers Press
Thorndike, Maine USA Bath, England

This Large Print edition is published by Thorndike Press, USA and by Chivers Press, England.

Published in 1998 in the U.S. by arrangement with HarperCollins Publishers, Inc.

Published in 1999 in the U.K.. by arrangement with Little, Brown (UK) Ltd.

U.S.   Hardcover   0-7862-1424-4   (Basic Series Edition)
U.S.   Softcover   0-7862-1425-2
U.K.   Hardcover   0-7540-1214-X   (Windsor Large Print)
U.K.   Softcover   0-7240-2156-4   (Paragon Large Print)

The text of this Large Print edition is unabridged.
Other aspects of the book may vary from the original edition.

Set in 16 pt. Plantin by Juanita Macdonald.

Printed in the United States on permanent paper.

British Library Cataloguing in Publication Data available

Library of Congress Cataloging in Publication Data

Siddons, Anne Rivers.
    Low country : a novel / Anne Rivers Siddons.
        p.   cm.
    ISBN 0-7862-1424-4 (lg. print : hc : alk. paper)
    ISBN 0-7862-1425-2 (lg. print : sc : alk. paper)
    1. Large type books.   I. Title.
[PS3569.I28L6   1998b]
813'.54dc21   98-25215

For Gervais, Curry, Richard, and Hart Hagerty, the next keepers of the Ace

Nature's first green is gold
Her hardest hue to hold.
Her early leaf's a flower
But only so an hour
Then leaf subsides to leaf.
So Eden sank to grief,
So dawn goes down to day.
Nothing gold can stay.

— ROBERT FROST

Author's Note

There is no Peacock's Island on St. Helena's Sound, or anywhere else, that I know of, but perhaps there might have been, and if there had, I think it would be a lot like this one. There are no actual people like the ones in this book, but perhaps if there had been, they might have lived on Peacock's Island. There is no Gullah settlement called Dayclear, and indeed, the very name is my invention; the accepted Gullah word for dawn is "Day-clean," though I have seen "Dayclear" in one or two places. There *are* wild ponies, or marsh tackies, still on some of the Sea Islands, and there are resort developments on almost all of them, many of them called plantations, but Peacock Island Plantation is my own hybrid. There is, thank God, an Ace Basin, and it contains all the wildlife mentioned in this book and more, except a twenty-foot alligator named Leviathan and a one-hundred-dred-and-twenty-five-year-old panther — and after all, in the Lowcountry, who knows?

My thanks and love to Barbara and Duke Hagerty, who shared their friendship, their library, their house and home, and their passion for Edisto Island and the Ace Basin; to Sandra Player, whose miraculous teenage years provided Caro Venable with a provenance of her own; and to Dr. Alex Sanders, president of the College of Charleston, who once again gave me words, flesh and blood for this book. He will know which ones.

My gratitude and admiration to the creators of two wonderful books,* whose pages I have borrowed liberally and literally.

And, as always, to Larry, Ginger, Heyward, and Martha, the home team.

Anne Rivers Siddons
Atlanta, Georgia
May 1998

---

* *"Ain't You Got a Right to the Tree of Life?"* — *The People of Johns Island, South Carolina — Their Faces, Their Words and Their Songs,* revised and expanded edition, rocorded and edited by Guy and Candie Caraway and published by Brown Thrasher Books, University of Georgia Press, 1989; *When Roots Die — Endangered Traditions of the Sea Islands* by Patricia Jones Jackson, published by the University of Georgia Press, 1987.

1

"I think I'll go over to the island for a few days," I said to my husband at breakfast, and then, when he did not respond, I said, "The light's beautiful. It can't last. I hate to waste it. We won't get this pure gold again until this time next year."

Clay smiled, but he did not put down his newspaper, and he did not speak. The smile made my stomach dip and rise again, as it has for the past twenty-five years. Clay's smile is wonderful, slow and unstinting and a bit crooked, and gains much of its power from the surrounding austerity of his sharp, thin face. Over the years I have seen it disarm a legion of people, from two-year-olds in mid-tantrum to Arab sheiks in same. Even though I knew that this smile was little more than a twitch, and with no more perception behind it, I felt my own mouth smiling back. I wondered, as I often do, how he could do that, smile as though you had absolutely delighted him when he had not heard a word you said.

"There is a rabid armadillo approaching

you from behind," I said. "It's so close I can see the froth. It's not a pretty sight."

"I heard you," he said. "You want to go over to the island because the light's good. It can't last."

I waited, but he did not speak again, or raise his eyes.

Finally I said, "So? Is that okay with you?"

This time he did look up.

"Why do you ask? You don't need my permission to go over to the island. When did I ever stop you?"

His voice was level and reasonable; it is seldom anything else. I knew that he did not like me to go over to the island alone, though, for a number of reasons that we had discussed and one that we had not, yet.

The island is wild and largely undeveloped now, except for a tiny settlement on its southwestern tip, and there are wild animals living on it that are hostile to humans, and sometimes dangerous. It is home to a formidable colony of alligators, some more than twelve feet long, and a handful of wild boar that make up in ferocity what they lack in numbers. Rattlesnakes and water moccasins are a given. Even the band of sullen wild ponies that have lived there on the grassy hummocks between the creeks and inlets since time out of mind are not the amiable toys they seem. A small child from the settlement was badly kicked only last year, when he got too close to a mare nursing her foal. Clay knows that I have been handling myself easily and well on the island since I was a child, but he mistrusts what he calls my impetuosity more than he trusts my long experience and exemplary safety record.

Then there is the settlement itself, Dayclear. That beautiful word is Gullah, part of the strange and lyrical amalgam of West African and Colonial English once spoken by the handful of Gullah blacks still living in pockets of the South Carolina Lowcountry. They are the descendants of the slaves brought here by the first white settlers of these archipelagos and marshes, and some of the elders still speak the old patois among themselves. When I was a child I knew some of it myself, a few words taught me by various Gullah nurses and cooks, a few snatches of songs sung by gardeners and handymen on my grandfather's place. I know that Dayclear means "dawn." I have always loved the word, and I have always been aware of the settlement, even if I did not often visit it when I was growing up and have no occasion to do so now. I do know that it is made up now largely of the old, with a preponderance of frail old women, and that some of them

11

must be the kin of those workers of my childhood, if not the actual people themselves. I
know that there are virtually no young men
and women living there, since the young
leave the island as soon as they are physically
able to do so, to seek whatever fortunes they
might find elsewhere. There is nothing for
them in Dayclear. There are children, small
ones, left behind with the old women by
daughters and granddaughters who have
taken flight, and there are sometimes silent,
empty-faced young men about, who have
come home because they are in trouble and
have, temporarily, nowhere else to go, but
they do not stay long.

I have not been to the settlement for many
years, as my route across the island lies in the
dry, hummocky heart of it, and the house to
which I go is at the opposite end, looking
northwest toward the shore of Edisto. But
when I think of it, I feel nothing but a kind of
mindless, nostalgic sense of safety and be-
nevolence. Dayclear has never given me anything but nurturing and love.

Clay fears it, though. He has never said so,
but I know that he does. I can tell; I always
know when Clay is afraid, because he so seldom is, and of almost nothing.

"There's nothing there that can hurt me;
nobody who would," I have said to him.

12

"They're just poor old women and babies and children."

"You don't know who's back in there," he said. "You don't see who comes and goes. Anybody could come across. There are places you could wade across. Anybody could drop anchor in the Inland Waterway and come ashore. You think everybody in that little place doesn't know when you're at the house, and that you're by yourself? I don't like it when you go, Caro. But you know that."

I did know, and do. But he does not forbid me to go to the island. For one thing, Clay is not a forbidder; he would find it distasteful, unseemly, to forbid his wife anything, the operative word being distasteful. Clay is a fastidious man, both physically and emotionally.

For another thing, I own part of the island. And if there is anything Clay respects, it is the right of eminent domain.

But the main reason he does not want me on the island alone is that he is afraid that I will drink there. I do drink sometimes, though by no means often, but when I do I tend to do it rather excessively. When I am with him, at this house or the club or the town house in Charleston, he feels that he can at least control the consequences of my

13

drinking, if not the act itself. The consequences are not heinous, I don't think; I do not stumble and fall, or weep, or grow belligerent. But I do tend to hug necks and kiss cheeks, and sometimes to sit on laps, and sometimes to dance and sing, and I imagine that to Clay these are worse than staggering or tears. They might imply, to some who don't know us, that I do not receive enough affection at home. And they tend to dismay visiting Arab sheiks. So Clay, while he says nothing to me then or later and never has, stays close enough to initiate damage control when he thinks it is necessary. Perhaps if we talked about it, I could tell him that when I am slightly drunk I feel so much better than I normally do, that I am happy, exuberant, giddy, and wish to share the largesse with whomever is close. But we do not talk about it. To name a demon is to make it yours. Clay does not wish to own this particular demon, and I do not wish, yet, to give it up. So we do not speak of my drinking, though the time may come when we have to do so. Or maybe not. I do fairly well with it, as long as I have the island for refuge.

This is something Clay does not understand, and will not unless I tell him: that the island is the one place where I do not want to drink, or need to. I know that I could probably ease his mind considerably about my time over there if I told him so, but again, that would mean naming the demon, and we both know that we do not want its disruptive presence in our lives. It would be like having to acknowledge and live with an erratic, malicious relative who was apt to break the china, fart in public, insult our guests, change the very fabric and structure of our graceful lives.

So Clay goes on hating and dreading my trips to the island but refusing to discuss them, and I go on going. It is a devilish seesaw, but it provides a sort of balance.

I looked away from him and out the French windows to the lawn and the seawall, and the beach and sea beyond. When Clay first began to develop Peacock's Island as a resort and permanent home community, he decided that we must certainly live there if anyone else could be hoped to, and so he chose the best lot on the island and had this house built for us. It *is* beautiful; even now, when I cannot look at the ocean without darkness and sickness starting in my stomach, I have to admit that it is a lovely house and an even lovelier situation, a perfect marriage of shore and sea. It was the first of the famous Peacock Island Plantation houses to be built, the model for that rambling, unob-

15

trusive, graceful style of architecture that has become rather standard for beach and marsh houses in the various Lowcountry resort developments now. The architect who began it all is credited with our house, but it was Clay, all those years ago, who leaned over his shoulder for long hours at the drafting table, seeing in his mind's eye what the future homes of Peacock Island Plantation should be, and prodding until Dudley found the proper architectural metaphor for his vision. They dot the Lowcountry like beautiful fungi now, lying close along the shoreline under the twisted old live oaks and among the dark, cool thickets fringing the marshes on the landward sides of the barrier islands. They vary, of course; there is room for individual taste and interpretation, but no house is built in Peacock Island Plantation that does not meet the company's rigid design codes and so there is nothing intrusive here, nothing raw or ragged or incongruous, like you might see in other, newer and less carefully provenanced developments. Clay was adamant about that when he was young and new to the business and stood to lose a lot of money with his lofty design standards, and he has never loosened or amended them in this or any other of his projects. He likes to say that his family has loved and lived the

16

Peacock's Island life ever since its beginning. And so we have, or at least lived it, for the past twenty years, when he moved us here from the cheerful suburb full of new ranch houses and young professional families where we started out, in Columbia.

Our son, Carter, was only a year old when we came to the island. Kylie was born here. They were children of the sea and beach and marshes; it was, to them, a known world, taken entirely for granted. It was, to me, like living permanently on a kind of extended vacation. I was born in Greenville and grew up in a succession of small South Carolina towns, all long hours from the coast, and came to the Lowcountry only during the summers, to visit my Aubrey grandparents. I still feel that way about living here. Sometimes I wake up before dawn, when it is too early to see that peculiar nacreous gray morning light that the beach and sea send backward to the land, when the wind is down and the surf is so sluggish that you cannot hear it past the dune line, and I think, Have I overslept? I didn't hear the garbage trucks. I'm going to be late for school. . . .

My lucky children, I have often thought, to gauge the rhythm of their days by surf and wind and the dawn chorus of a hundred different shorebirds, not ever to have known

17

anything else. It seems exotic to me, foreign somehow. I used to say this to them, when they were very small, to try to explain this strange, suspended feeling that sometimes woke me in the earliest hours of the day, but I could never do so, at least not to Carter.

"That's dumb," he would say. "I don't see how you can still feel that way when you've been living here so long. This is better than garbage trucks and traffic any day. This is better than anything."

Carter, my pragmatist, so like Clay. To this day, I do not think anything out of his earliest childhood stalks him in the dark.

Ah, but Kylie . . . Kylie always knew. How, I don't know, but she did. She would ask endlessly for the story: "Tell about what you heard in the morning when you were little, Mama. Tell about the garbage trucks and the lawn mowers and the carpool horns . . ."

My small towns did not have noise ordinances like the island does; I realized early on that to Kylie, my childhood morning cacophony of manmade hubbub was as exotic as this profound, mystical sea-silence still is to me.

"Why do you want to hear that?" I would say. "This is much nicer. This is nature pure and simple; very few people are lucky enough just to hear natural sounds when they wake up."

But she was unpersuaded.

"Will you take me to see the garbagemen sometimes?" she would say, over and over. "Will you take me where I can hear a carpool horn?"

Kylie and Carter went to the island country day school, and were picked up at the head of our lane by a smart, quiet little school bus painted in the muted Peacock's Island tan and green.

Finally I gave in: "All right," I said. "Okay. We'll go spend a weekend in Columbia sometime soon, and you can see the garbagemen and hear the carpool horns."

We never did that, though. Somehow, we just never did. . . .

The sea at the horizon line was banked solid with angry purple clouds this morning, as it often is in autumn, but as I sat staring at it, the clouds fissured and broke and a spear of cold, silvery sunlight streaked through, stabbing down at the sea and lighting the tossing gray to the strange, stormy pewter of November. At the same moment the ocean wind freshened, lifting the fine, dun-colored sand from the tops of the primary dunes and swirling it spectrally into the air, rattling the drying palm fronds at the far edge of the

19

lawn where the boardwalk down through the dunes to the sea began, stirring the moss on the live oaks that sheltered the house. It seemed for a moment that everything was in swirling, shimmering motion: air, sea, land, swimming in diffused light, drowning in silver. I looked away, back to the breakfast table and then up at Clay. On such a day, I knew, my stomach would roil queasily with the shifting light and wind, and my heart would beat queerly and thickly with it, until the wind dropped at sunset and the benevolent golden light of sunset spilled in from the west.

It was days like these that I most needed to be over on the island.

I speak of it as if it were a different island; we all do, though it is not, really. Technically, the island is the back third of Peacock's Island, the westward third, the marsh third. It is separated from the larger bulk of Peacock's Island proper by a tidal estuary that is full only twice a day; during the other times you could wade through the ankle-deep muck in the empty, corrugated rivulet that cuts the island like a snake, though no one wants to. The mud is deep, and stinks of ancient livings and dyings. You can better cross it, as I do, on a sturdy if raffish wooden bridge just wide and stout enough to hold a truck or a Jeep; the island is never truly cut off from the larger bulk of Peacock's.

It might as well be, though. It is another place entirely, eons older, wilder by millennia. I don't think it ever had a name, since it is of course a part of the larger mass. In my lifetime, in my time here, it has always been known simply as "the island," just as the larger, more hospitable two-thirds of it has been known as Peacock's Island, usually shortened to Peacock's. I think the inept old pirate for whom it is named would have agreed with the practice. If legend is true, he had no truck with the marsh-bound back third of the island, either, except to leave some of his hapless live captives there staked out for the alligators and the wild pigs and the savage, swarming insects and to dispose of the dead ones in the black, silent tidal creeks and rivers for the nourishment of who knows what. It is shifting, unquiet land, and it is no wonder to me that the unhappy victims of Jonathan Peacock are said to be unquiet, too, stumping about and murmuring querulously in the close, still nights. The Gullahs of Dayclear are said to be as familiar with them as they are with the terrible duppies and other assorted haunts who came with them in their chains to these shores, and on the whole, perhaps, prefer them. An unhappy ghost can be cajoled, soothed, propitiated, but there is no reasoning with a duppy.

Clay was still looking at me, studying my face as calmly and gravely as he had been studying the *Wall Street Journal*. Waiting, I knew.

"I'm almost through with the studies for the new painting," I said. "I've got everything but the light on the Inland Waterway at sunset. It's different from anywhere else; it's deeper there, and the water moves a lot more. That changes the light entirely. I really want to get that. I think a night or two would do it. I'll take the camcorder and see if I can get enough of the change from sunset to full night so I can finish it back here, if you need me. Is there something special?"

At first, when I started to spend time over on the island by myself, I used as an excuse the creation of a series of paintings of the marshes in all seasons and at all times of day. It was believable, if barely; I had not, then, painted in twenty years, but I did a lot of it once, and I have two solid years of training in fine arts at Converse. I was good then, good enough so that when I quit school in my junior year to marry Clay Venable, several of my instructors begged me to wait, begged me to get my degree first and then go somewhere specialized, like the Art Institute of Chicago, where two of them had taught, for further serious study. But I did not, and after Carter was born, I did not paint anymore. I never seemed to miss it, not consciously, and yet, when I pulled it out to excuse my flights to the island and began to actually dabble once more in oils and watercolors and pastels, it felt right and easy, supremely satisfying. After a while I was spending a great deal of time there trying to catch the fey, flickering faces and moods of the marshes and estuaries; it became important to me to do it as well as I could, to give the island its full due. After a longer while, even I could tell that the work I was doing was good, and getting better. Now, when I went to the island, it was not only that I was leaving Peacock's, I was going to something that was important to me on many levels.

Clay knew that, even if he did not approve. I was good enough so that the handful of small galleries on Peacock's and a few on some of the larger islands, and even one in Charleston, carried my work. He could not argue that it was self-indulgence alone that drew me back and back to the island. And to be fair, I knew that he was proud of me.

He had another weapon in his arsenal, though, and I knew now, without his saying so, that he was about to employ it. About five years ago he had asked me, almost casually, if I would involve myself with the young families who came to the Plantation to work for the company, to act as a sort of chatelaine-hostess-troubleshooter-confidante to them, especially the young women, most of whom were wives.

"You know," he said, "give dinner parties for them when they get here so they can get to know the others. Show them around, put them in the hands of the right real estate people so they won't end up spending money they can't afford for decent housing. Tell them about doctors and dentists and schools and play groups, and such. Maybe take the wives over to Charleston once or twice a month, show them the best shops and galleries and the right hair places, take them to lunch at the Yacht Club or somewhere flossy and fun. Just listen to them. It's not an easy adjustment for some of them. Some of them have never been closer to the ocean than a couple of weeks in the summers. I'm aware that it can get sort of cliquey and ingrown here; especially if they're slated to stay here for a long time. You could be a godsend to them."

Clay's company now encompasses properties as far away as Puerto Rico and the Virgin

Islands; each project has a different management group, and he draws them from businesses and business schools all over the United States, but a preponderance of the young men and their wives come from the Northeast, from Wharton and Harvard Business Schools and others like them. No matter what property they are slated for, they all come here first. Basic corporate training in the Peacock Island Plantation way of life starts here, and the average stay for a young family is two years. Some of them end up spending three, five, and more years. To a man and woman, they know little when they get here but the theory of business. It remains for Clay and the other Peacock executives to put a Peacock shine on them. It is often a hard and daunting process; it has not been all that unusual, in the past, for young marriages to be strained and sometimes broken, for destructive habits to take hold: too much liquor, too many recreational drugs, too much time spent in the attractive company of others than one's own husband or wife. The active one of the couple, usually the husband, spends long hours away from home, living and breathing the Peacock party line, leaving the young wife adrift on a languid island in a warm sea, cut off from home and family, alone with small children and only the company of other corporate wives, who have wrestled out their own places here and are not eager to take in the newcomer and her brood, lest she be the spouse of the very one who will oust their own husbands from their hard-won places in Clay's court. Clay argued, when he put his proposition to me, that he could not afford to take the time to arbitrate this sort of thing, and that if left unattended, it could come to wreck the famous Peacock morale. I thought the whole thing tiresome, heartbreaking, and entirely thankless, but I could see that he was right. Somebody needed to take hold of the newly arrived young. I just did not think it should be me.

But Clay did, and I could hardly refuse. I had not yet found refuge in my painting when he asked, and even I could see that if I did not find something outside myself to occupy me, I was going to be in serious trouble. I have always known that he asked more for my benefit than for the cadet corps of the Peacock Island Plantation.

I knew now with absolute certainty that he was about to produce a new crop of the needy young. He had that look. "Don't tell me," I said. "Let me guess. A new crop of lambs is incoming as we speak."

I smiled as I said it, though. He was smiling again, and I would give a lot to keep hold of that smile. After all, I had agreed to this role, and I do what we call the mother-superior bit rather well. The young women who are my charges all seem just young enough so that I don't threaten them with competition, and I have both the advantage of knowing the territory and the cachet of being the supreme honcho's wife. And I never drink when I'm on a mother-superior mission. I know that Clay doesn't worry about that. I don't do the children, though. Peggy Carmichael, the warm, big-lapped, grandmotherly woman who has been Clay's director of housekeeping since the beginning, does that. It works out pretty well, all told.

"Yep," Clay said, draining his coffee cup and leaning back. There was a sheepish cast to his smile now, which is the second most appealing smile that he has. The first, hands down, is his let's-go-to-bed smile. I am fairly sure that no one else but me sees that one.

"So? I didn't know you had anything new on the books."

"I don't, strictly," he said. "There's something on the horizon, a marsh property a ways from here that's looking real good, but I wasn't going to start staffing for it yet. But these three coming in are all special, top of their classes at Wharton and anxious to get

27

started somewhere, and I was afraid if I didn't nail them down somebody else would get them. And some serious money looks like it might open up sooner than I thought. So I'm bringing them and their families on down. Just two couples and a divorced woman. I'm going to need you for this. Your light will hold a few more nights, I think. Will you, Caro?"

"So when are they coming?"

"They'll be here early this afternoon. I'm putting them up in the guest house until we can get two of the villas ready. Don't worry, they won't be staying here."

"Tonight! Oh, Clay! I can't get a dinner party ready by tonight; Estelle's got the afternoon off, and there's some kind of Thanksgiving pageant or something at school; all the others will be there with their kids . . ."

"No, no. I thought this time we might just take them over to Charleston. They'll have time to freshen up and rest some, and we can show them a little of the island on the way. Maybe you could call the Yacht Club and see if they can get us in about eight. It's a pretty impressive place, and I hear one of the wives is not at all happy about leaving Darien and New York. Thinks she's coming down here to live among the savages. It won't hurt to throw some vintage Charleston

28

at her. Let her know she can get to civiliza-
tion in less than an hour."

"Ah, yes, the Holy City," I said, getting up
to call the Carolina Yacht Club and make
reservations. Clay has belonged for years
now; and I still don't know how he managed
it. Few outsiders made it into those hallowed
halls on Charleston Harbor at the time he
joined. I know that he never tires of taking
newcomers there, just as I quail inwardly every time I know that I am going. Clay does
not understand why I feel tentative at the
Yacht Club.

"After all, this was your grandfather's
town," he said. "And your great-great-
great's, for that matter. You've got a more
valid claim on it than half the people who
live here."

I rarely answer him. It is a long way from
McClellanville, where my grandfather lived
for most of his life, to Charleston and the
Carolina Yacht Club, and the twain seldom
meet. They never did for my grandfather, or
my great-great-great, either, truth be known,
but Clay has forgotten this, if he ever really
knew it.

"Oh, wait a minute," he called after me,
and I stopped and looked back.

"There may be a problem. This woman
who's coming. She's probably the best of

29

this lot, but I don't know if it's a good idea to take her to the Yacht Club . . ."

"Why on earth? She's your guest. She doesn't have to have an escort of her own," I said.

"She's black," Clay said. "It might be a little uncomfortable for her."

"Uncomfortable is not precisely the term I would have used," I said, and went to the telephone and called Carolina's for reservations for a party of seven at eight o'clock that evening.

When Clay went upstairs to shower, I took my garden shears and a basket and went out into the yard to cut flowers for the guest house. Though it was nearly Thanksgiving, I still had some sweet, sturdy old roses in the beds behind the house, and it had been so warm that a few of the big, ruffled Sasanqua camellias had bloomed. They always do in our soft, wet autumns and winters; glowing like daystars in the grays and duns and silvers of this winter coast, then freezing and blackening to mush in the vicious little icy snaps that follow in January. We are subtropical here, and the Atlantic runs shallow and warm off our tan beaches. We have flowers long after the rest of the South has yielded up theirs to the cold. And there are

30

vast greenhouses and acres of experimental gardens in the sheltered heart of the island, which serve the Plantation's floral needs as well as supplying its ecologically correct plantings and landscaping. I could have my pick of largesse from any of those. But I like to work in my backyard garden, and it feels right to take flowers from my own house to welcome Clay's young newcomers. And he likes telling them that I brought them my own flowers. So I usually do this when we have incomings. Augmented with the ubiquitous pansies that the landscaping people blanket the public spaces with in fall and winter, I would have enough for lush bouquets in all the rooms. I would take them down later so they would be fresh.

The guest house was bought to accommodate our personal guests at Cotton Blossom, the name Clay gave our house when it was built. But we have not had many guests, not for some years, and as the guest house is at some distance from us, it works well for temporary housing for company newcomers.

Cotton Blossom . . . the name sets my teeth on edge, and I refuse to use it, or even to use the house stationery that Clay had made up for us. It sounds phony and overblown to me, a parody of every bad ol' Suthren joke I have ever heard. The rest of

31

the homes in Peacock Island Plantation do not have names, that I know of, and even the named areas — streets, subdivisions, parks — wear the names of indigenous birds or flora. But Cotton Blossom was the name of the mean little cotton plantation my great-great-great-grandfather Aubrey built over on neighboring Edisto, where he raised substandard Sea Island cotton, and Clay thought to keep the name in the family, so to speak. Great-great-great-grandfather Aubrey is my only valid link to Charleston, and a tenuous one it was and is. . . . Grandpa's town house was small and cramped and well below the salt, and his presence in the Holy City seems to have left no more permanent impression than his passing. The Aubrey town house is a garage off King Street now. Clay does not find it necessary to point out the garage to prospective investors and residents of Peacock's, as he does the crumbling ruins of Cotton Blossom over on Edisto, which look, in their vine-and-moss-shrouded decay, far more romantic than the house ever looked in the days of its ascendancy.

"Caroline's people go way back in the Lowcountry," he is fond of saying, and I don't contradict him, because I suppose, literally speaking, they do, or at least Great-

great-great-grandfather Aubrey's scanty tribe did. It's just that they didn't linger. My stake in Charleston and its environs is shallow indeed.

Clay respects my refusal to use the house's name, as he does most of my actions and decisions. He even smiles when I say that "Cotton Blossom" sounds like it ought to be wallowing down the Mississippi River, steam whistles squalling, pickaninnies dancing on the dock as it rounds the bluff. But he uses it himself, just the same, and in his soft, deep voice, it somehow manages to sound as dignified as he thinks it is. As I said, he is serious about keeping the few legitimate old Low-country names we have in the family. Not even our children escaped; Kylie was baptized Elizabeth Kyle Venable, after that same great-great-great-grandfather, John Kyle Aubrey.

"It's pretentious, that's all," I said, when she was born, trying to dissuade him. "Nobody in our family was close to the old skin-flint, or even remembered him, that I ever heard of. If you want to honor my family, what's wrong with my mother's name? Or my grandmother's?"

"Olive?" he said mildly, looking at me over the small half-glasses he had just begun to wear. "Lutie Beulie? At least they'll know who she is in Charleston. They'll know what the name means."

And I gave in, because even then I was too besotted with love and delight toward my daughter to argue about her name. In my deepest heart I knew who she was. I always did.

I put my flowers into the big, flat sweet-grass basket that I keep in the potting shed for the purpose and started back to the house. I love that basket; I love all the beautiful, intricate, sturdy baskets that the Gullah women braid from the dried sweet grass that flourishes in the marshes of the Lowcountry and sell for formidable sums wherever tourists gather. For once, I think, the tourists get fair value. The baskets are usually works of art and last, with care, for generations. The one I use for flowers we bought for Kylie to keep her toys in when she was a toddler. Carter has a larger one, a hamper, really, in his room, where his dirty clothes have more or less landed ever since he was five. It is traditional with Clay and me to give new families sets of the baskets at Christmastime, and they have always been received with what seems to me honest delight.

A flicker of red from the front of the house caught my eye as I came up the shallow steps to the veranda. It was a long way away, perhaps at the edge of the dunes, perhaps even down on the beach itself, and I felt my heart drop and pause and then start its old low, slow, cold thumping. I knew it was ridiculous, and I also knew that I was going to have to go down to the edge of the front lawn and see what it was. The sick coldness would last all day if I did not. I put the basket of flowers down on a wicker table on the veranda and went around the side of the house and across the front lawn, kept velvety and green all year by the Plantation groundskeepers, and around the tabby apron to the oval pool, and up to the little gray cypress landing that led to the steps and boardwalk to the beach. Only then did I lift my eyes to the water.

The sea was still gunmetal gray out at the horizon line, but the cloud rift that had lit the horizon earlier had drifted westward so that the beach shimmered in a wash of pale lemon light and running cloud-shadow. Strange, strange . . . somehow, even when the temperature is as mild as it usually is in November here, almost blood warm, like the water, the shifting dunes and flat beach and heaving sea seem cold to me, cold to the bone, cold to death. There is the damp, of course; the humidity of the Lowcountry is as much an element as its tepid water and low, sweet sky. The air of the Sea Islands is like a cloud against your skin in all its seasons. But it is more than that: taken in the aggregate, all that flickering, tossing, shivering, whispering pewter and silver seem to chill me to the core, and it always did, even at those infrequent times I came to a Lowcountry beach in autumn as a child. It is in this season, and in the winter that will follow, that I feel queerest, the most alien, here; there should be dark, pointed firs against the sky, not rattling, brown-tipped palms. Naked branches, wet black tree trunks, the bare bones of the earth, instead of the canopy of living green of the live oaks, the eternal fecund darkness of the sea pines. I looked at the sea and was cold in my heart.

The red turned out to be an open beach umbrella, bucking against the steady, moaning sea wind. I looked beyond it into the surf line, knowing what I would see, and did: swimmers, plunging in the lace-white edging of the breaking waves. Now that I saw them, I listened for and heard their voices: Canadians. Snowbirds. We get them every fall and winter, and we laugh and shiver when they swim determinedly every day but the very worst ones, and march up and down the empty, howling beach as if dead set on getting their winter vacation money's worth. If they ever hear the laughter and see the shivers they apparently do not care. I have seen one or two of them plowing mulishly into the ocean when one of our rare, soft, wet snows was falling. Don't laugh, Clay says. Without them the Inn and the villas and the restaurants would almost close down off season. I don't laugh. I have always liked and admired them, those tough, foolish migrants. Good sense was never a fault of mine, either.

My heart picked up its dragging pace and my breath came seeping back, and I took my flowers into the kitchen and arranged them in some of the pottery vases that I collect and keep for flowers, and left them by the door onto the veranda, and went up to take my own shower. I heard Clay moving around overhead in his study and knew that he would be bent over the architect's drafting table that he keeps there, the working drawings for the newest Peacock Plantation project, whatever it might be, permanently map-tacked in place there. Clay has a design staff second to none when it comes to attractive, ecologically sensitive Lowcountry architecture and interiors, but nothing comes off their boards that does not go directly onto his, and this morning time in his study is sacrosanct to everyone on his staff. Later he would tend to the endless rounds of meetings and conferences that made up his afternoons, and might go on until very late at night, to dinners and conferences and cigars and brandies in restaurants and drawing rooms from Savannah up to Myrtle Beach, according to where the fat new money was. But in the mornings he stayed at home and put his hands directly on his empire. It probably drove his people wild, but it had made the Peacock Island Plantation properties a name that rivaled that of Charles Fraser's Sea Pines Plantation Company in its halcyon earlier days. I smiled, thinking of him there; he would be fully dressed for his day, in one of his winter-weight tropical suits or perhaps a gray seersucker. Clay almost never wore slacks and a jacket, and I saw him without a tie usually only in bed.

I went up the central stairs, a freestanding iron staircase made for Clay by an old black ironmonger on James Island when the house was built, and whose designs now brought hundreds of thousands of dollars, and paused at the landing. The house is open on both the seaward and the landward sides, so that standing on the landing is like standing suspended in a great cage of glass. It always makes me dizzy, as if nothing lies between me and the close-pressing darkness of the old oaks and the shrouding oleanders in back, and the great, sucking, light-breathing, always-waiting sea in front. I shook my head and went quickly up to the second floor, where the bedrooms were. They are open to the sea, too, the best ones, but you can close it away with heavy curtains if you choose, and the others, at the back of the house, overlook the dark-canopied backyard and feel to me like sheltering caves. I have moved my daytime retreat there, in the back corner, away from the beach and sea, though I still sleep in the big master suite hung in the air over the lawn and sea, with Clay. But when he is away I sleep on the daybed in my den.

Instead of turning to the right, toward our bedroom and mine and Clay's dens, as I almost always did, I turned left and walked down the hall toward the children's rooms. I think I had known all day that I was going to do so. I did not hesitate, and I did not think. I walked past Carter's closed door — closed because he had left it in such a disgraceful state when he left in September for his first year at graduate school at Yale that I had refused to go into it, and told Estelle not to touch it but to let him come back and find it just as he had left it — and stopped at the big ocean-facing room on the end, its door also closed. Kylie's room.

Unlike Carter, Kylie was neat to a fault; she hated it if anyone disturbed the strict order of her things, and had insisted from her earliest childhood that no one enter her closed room when she was not in it. I had always respected that; I felt somewhat the same way about my things, though long years of sharing a room with Clay had loosened my scruples about order a bit. He is not untidy, only abstracted. I think he does not notice either order or disorder. I could still hear small Kylie, frustrated nearly to tears in her attempt to explain why she did not want me to come into her room when she was not in it: "But it's *mine!* It's not yours! You have a room of your own. Why do you need to go in mine?"

"What are you hiding in there, a pack of wolves?" I said. "Kevin Costner, maybe?"

She had fallen in love with the movie *Dances with Wolves*, and was so besotted with wolves that she was planning to be a wildlife veterinarian when she grew up, and work with the wild wolf packs of the Far West. It was a mature and considered ambition, and I would not have been at all surprised if she made it happen.

"I'm not hiding anything," she said, looking seriously at me, and I knew that she was not. Kylie hid nothing, ever. She was as open as air, as clear as water. Then she saw that I was teasing her, and she began to giggle, the silvery, silly giggle that, I am told, is very like mine, and then she laughed, the deep, froggy belly laugh that is mine also. In a moment we were both laughing, laughing until the tears rolled down our so-alike small, brown faces, laughing and laughing until Clay came in to see what was so funny, and said, grinning himself, "Ladies and gentlemen, for your enjoyment tonight . . . Venable and Venable! Let's give them a great big hand!"

And we rolled over on our backs on the floor of her room, Kylie and I, in helpless laughter and simple joy, because it was true. We were Venable and Venable. We simply delighted each other. There was nothing in either of us that did not understand and admire the other. Even when she was a baby, there was nothing childish, nothing condescending, nothing mother-to-child about it. We were companions on every level, confidantes, comrades, friends, lovers in the deepest and most nonsexual sense of the word. My daughter and I had fallen in love and delight with each other at the moment of her birth, and it was often all I could do to keep Clay and Carter from coming off second best. Because they are so ludicrously alike, and because Clay's mind is almost absurdly full of riches and Carter is a sunny, confident young man with a full and empow-

41

ering sense of himself, I do not think that either of them has suffered. Rather, they, like most other people in our orbit, simply enjoyed and often laughed at Venable and Venable.

I opened Kylie's door and went into her room. At first the great surf of brightness off the noon beach blinded me, and I stood blinking, my hand shading my eyes. Then they adjusted and I looked around and saw it plain, this place that was, of all her places, most distinctly hers.

It was not a frilly room and never had been. Like me, Kylie was born with a need for space and order and a dislike of cluttering frills and fuss. She had always been a small, wiry child, almost simian in her build, narrow-hipped and broad-shouldered, slightly long of arm and short of leg, never tall, always thin to the bone. Ruffles would have been as ludicrous on and around her as on me. She was, instead, sleeked down for action; pared to sinew and long, slender muscle; meant for sun and sand and wind and water, and that was what her room reflected. I do not think she ever drew her curtains, even at night. Kylie fell asleep with her face turned to the moon and the comets and the wheeling constellations, seeing when she woke in the night the dance of phosphorus on the warm, thick, black summer ocean, or sometimes the lightning of storms over the horizon that looked, she said, like naval battles far out to sea. Waking to the cool pearl of dawn on tidal slicks, to the pink and silver foil of a newly warming spring ocean, perhaps to the Radio City Music Hall dance of porpoises in the silky summer shallows. Kylie went as far as any human I have ever known, when she was small, toward simply using up the sea.

Her walls were painted the milky green of the sea on a cloudy day, and on them hung her posters of animals and birds and sea creatures and the big, luminous painting of Richard Hagerty's that was the official Spoleto Festival poster one year, of Hurricane Hugo striding big-footed and terrible down on a crouching Charleston. I had not wanted to buy it for her because I had thought it would come to haunt her, but she was adamant.

"Yeah, but see, Hugo didn't win," she said. "Big as a thousand houses, big as a booger, and he still didn't win."

And I had laughed and bought it for her, because I wanted her to remember that: the boogers don't always win.

On the low bookshelves were the models she had made of animal skeletons, from kits I had ordered for her from marine biological laboratories and supply houses, and three or four real skeletons we had found over on the island when she went with me to the house there: the papery carapace of an eight-foot rattler; a wild boar's skull with great, bleached, Jurassic tusks; the elegant, polished small skull of a raccoon. Estelle would not dust these herself but made Kylie do it. Clay was distinctly not amused by the skeletons, and even Carter only said, "Yuck. You're weird, Kylie." But I knew. It is important to know what the inside of things looks like. Otherwise, almost anything can fool you.

Her books were there, in a military order known only to Kylie. The old ones that I had loved: *Wind in the Willows* ("Mother! Listen! 'There is *nothing* — absolutely nothing — half so much worth doing as simply messing about on boats.' Oh, he knew, Ratty knew, didn't he?"); the *Waterbabies*; the Nancy Drew series; the Bobbsey Twins; the Lawrenceville Stories. For some reason they fascinated her. *Black Beauty. Silver Birch. Midnight Moon.* And alongside them, the handbooks and textbooks and charts and maps of the Carolina Lowcountry marshes and islands that we got for her from the Corps of Engineers and various coastal conservation and natural resources organizations.

On her desk, a small voodoo drum that Estelle's Gullah grandmother, who adored Kylie, had given her; we never knew where it had come from originally, but Estelle seemed to think it was the real thing. And the big osprey we had found newly dead on the bank of the tidal creek that cut through the undulating green marsh over on the island one summer day, still perfect except for the forever mysterious fact of its death. Clay had taken it to a taxidermist for her, and the great bird, wings spread, had kept yellow-eyed watch over Kylie and her room ever since. Of all her things, I think she loved that bird the best.

And that was all. Except for her neat, beige-spread bed and the matching armchairs, nothing else of her showed. Her clothes were shut away in the closet; she almost never left anything lying out. Her outgrown toys were in a hamper in her closet. The room did not look lonely, though. The space and order spoke of Kylie as clearly as strewn possessions would have of another child.

I walked over to the French doors that opened onto her balcony and leaned against them and looked back into the room. Something caught my eye, the edge of something blue, almost hidden under the dust ruffle of her bed. I leaned over and picked it up. A T-shirt, a small one, faded, that read PEA-COCK ISLAND PLANTATION SUMMER REC-REATION PROGRAM. You saw shirts like it all over the island; they were issued to children who joined the summer program, mostly the children of guests who wanted to enjoy the island's adult pursuits while their children went about their own, supervised activities. I remembered that Kylie liked the shirts but hated the program and absolutely refused to join, even when her father pointed out that it would be a real treat for the visiting little boys and girls to meet the daughter of the owner of the Plantation.

"Big deal," Kylie said. "You think I want to go on a nature walk with some kid who's gon' yell his head off if we see a snake?"

We did not make her attend the program. It would indeed have been ludicrous. Kylie was dealing calmly with bull alligators and rattlesnakes when the offspring of the Plantation visitors were shying at horseshoe crabs. She deigned to wear the T-shirts, though.

"That way the kids will all think I go," she said reasonably to Clay, and that was that.

I held the shirt to my face and sniffed. It smelled fresh and particular, like summer and sun and salt and Kylie herself, not at all like dust. But it should have smelled of dust; it must have been there, just under the fringe of the dust ruffle, for a long time. A little over five years; Kylie had been dead that long. I had not been this far into her room since the day we closed it, not long after her funeral, after Estelle, tears running silently down her long brown face, had cleaned it for the last time and closed the door. Sometimes I opened her door and looked in, and I knew that Clay did, too, but I did not think that anyone came all the way into it. I would ask Estelle. She must have simply missed the little T-shirt the last day that she cleaned.

I looked out at the ocean then. Kylie had died in sight of her room, in sight of our house, when her small Sunfish with the red sail had flipped in heavy surf after an August thunderstorm and the stout little boom had hit her a stunning blow to the temple, and she had gone down and not come up again, at least not until long after. None of the children she was with had seen it happen, or none would ever admit to seeing it, but then they were only ten or so, as she was, and all had been forbidden to take their boats into that stormy water, as she had been. They had been playing in a neighbor's yard after a birthday party, only three houses up the

47

beach, and had slipped off and taken their little Sunfishes out while the adults were having their own lunch on the patio, behind heavy plantings. I was off the island that day, at the dentist in Charleston. I never blamed Marjorie Bell or her housekeeper; Kylie had never disobeyed us before in regard to the Sunfish, nor had the other children disobeyed their parents. Island children have water safety drilled into their heads almost before they can toddle. We will never know what started it all, what child dared the others, who first leaped to the dare. Kylie, in all likelihood. It doesn't matter. The children were so traumatized by it that more than one of them gave away their Sunfish, or let their parents sell them, and one family moved away from the island.

I have always wondered if she looked up just before the boom hit and saw the dazzle of summer light on her window, saw the roof and trees of home.

I wondered now what she would be wearing if she had lived, what I would be picking up from her floor. What color it would be, what size. What its smell would be, the smell of Kylie Venable at nearly sixteen.

I used to have the fancy that I wore Kylie inside me, just under my skin, that I was a suit that fit exactly the being who was my child, and that she was the structure that filled out the skin that was me. Since that day there has been a terrible, frail lightness, a cold hollowness, a sort of whistling chill inside me where Kylie used to be. It makes me feel terribly vulnerable, as if a high wind could simply whirl me away. As if there is not enough substance inside me to anchor me to earth. Usually the pain of her loss is dulled enough now so that it is more a profound heaviness, a leaden darkness, a wearable miasma that is as much a part of me as the joy of her used to be. But sometimes that first agony comes spiking back, as it did now. I sank to the floor, the T-shirt still pressed to my face, feeling the killing fire flare and spring and rage, feeling the great shriek, the scream of outrage and anguish, start in my throat, feeling the scalding tears gather and press at my eyes. I opened my mouth to let it out, but nothing happened, nothing came. It never did. I screamed silently into her T-shirt, my face contorted, my throat corded and choked with the need for her, but no sound would come. I could not cry for my child. I never had, not even when they came to tell me, not even when I watched her go down into the earth of the Lowcountry, riding in a fine carriage of mahogany and bronze.

I felt a hand on my shoulder and heard Clay's voice.

"Caro, don't. You promised you wouldn't. Come on with me now, and take a shower and get dressed, and we'll have some coffee on the veranda before we go. I'll take you by the guest house; we'll put the flowers around together. They're beautiful, by the way. Those old roses, they really have lasted, haven't they?"

I did not move to get up, and after a moment I felt his hands under my elbows, and he lifted me up.

"You need to work, baby," he said. "That's the thing that will help; that's what's helped me most. Real work. This is your job now, helping with the new families, you need to come and do your job."

I looked at him then.

"She was my job," I said.

But I did not say it aloud.

2

When I was sixteen, the son of the local undertaker in the little town where we lived
asked me out on a date, and my stepfather
promptly called the chief of police, who was
in Rotary with him, and had the chief dis-
patch a deputy to follow us everywhere we
went. My friend Lottie Funderburke, who is
a painter and lives on the island (but *not*, she
is quick to point out, in the Plantation)
thinks this is the funniest thing she has ever
heard. She may be right. It was not, however,
very funny then, at least not to me. The deputy was a gangling, slouching eighteen-
year-old named Honey Cato, low of hairline
and waist and thick of shoulder and head, and
he had been whistling and making stunningly
suggestive and stupid remarks to me since we
moved to Moncks Corner, when I was
twelve. I had told my mother and stepfather
about it, but my stepfather said only, "If you
didn't run around with your behind hanging
out of those shorts, he wouldn't do it. A lady
doesn't get herself whistled at on the street."

I didn't mention Honey to him again. In

the first place, I didn't intend to give up my short shorts. Every other teenager in Moncks Corner rolled her shorts as high as they would go, and I had a horror, then, of being different. In the second place, my stepfather never would have understood about Honey Cato or boys — I purposely do not use the word "men" — like him. Honey would have whistled and made his crude remarks to Helen Keller, or a nun. It was his duty as a South Carolina good ol' boy. My stepfather was from Ohio. The difference was measured in far more than miles.

"So what exactly did your stepfather have against undertakers?" Lottie said when I first told her. "I would think an undertaker made more money than a lot of people in Monkey House, or wherever it was you lived. And you could say it's a profession. Of sorts."

"Well, you know. An undertaker," I said vaguely. "And then there was always this rumor that Sonny's father ran some kind of illegal operation out of the funeral home. Running liquor or something; I never did know what. Whatever it was, my stepfather didn't think it suited the daughter of the town lawyer. Even if he did get his law degree mail order."

"Where was your mother on this?" Lottie said.

"Well, she usually sided with him. She'd worked too hard to land him, see; she wasn't going to screw that up by sticking up for me. And I guess I was pretty hard to handle at that age. Mainly, she didn't think dating the undertaker's son suited a future Miss South Carolina."

"Oh, Christ, that's right, somebody said you'd been in the Miss South Carolina contest. I thought at the time they had to be lying. Not that you aren't right presentable, when you're all cleaned up, but you don't have a dimple to your name, and you'd look like a first-class 'ho' with blond hair. I wouldn't have thought you'd had a chance."

"I didn't. Especially after I dropped my baton."

"Don't tell me. You twirled a flaming baton to 'Age of Aquarius.' "

"Yep. Only it was 'Yellow Submarine.' I dropped the sucker before the first five bars were over."

"God, Caro, couldn't you have sung the National Anthem or something?"

"Well, I did a tap dance while I was twirling. I never could sing. It didn't matter what you did, if your boobs stuck out and you could walk in high heels. I had pretty good boobs then."

"That's the most un-Lowcountry thing I

ever heard," Lottie howled happily.

"I keep telling you, I'm not from the Lowcountry," I said. "I'm a million miles removed from the Lowcountry. I'm no more a Lowcountry native than you are. Everybody just thinks I am because Clay has made a religion of it. It's almost as strange to me right now as it was the first time I laid eyes on it. I get invited to parties South of Broad about as often as you do. It's Clay who goes to those."

Lottie is originally from West Virginia and is what Clay calls good old country stock. What he means is white trash. Hillbilly. She is nearly six feet tall, walks like she is plowing a mule, has shoulders as wide as a linebacker's and dishwater-blond hair chopped impatiently so that it will not hang in her eyes. Her skin is permanently the red-brown of old cordovan shoes, from the sun. Her voice is nasal and flat, her eyes are the faded blue of old denim, and her hands are the size and shape of coal scuttles. She is also an artist of stunning originality and talent. Her enormous, flaming primitive oils hang in galleries and museums all up and down the East Coast. Her strange, soaring iron sculptures are in collections all over America. She gets upwards of fifteen thousand dollars for her small paintings and I don't even know how much for the larger ones. She works so slowly that she rarely does more than three or four pieces a year, will not accept commissions, and still lives in the ramshackle former filling station that she moved into thirty years ago, on an undistinguished two-lane blacktop road that threads the middle of the island. My grandfather, who was intrigued with her gift and her grit, rented it to her some years before he deeded the island to Clay and stipulated that she be allowed to live there as long as she liked. Clay thinks that she was more to my grandfather than tenant, though she was only twenty when she first came to the island, and he may be right. Lottie sleeps with whomever she pleases and does not try to conceal the fact, though with no one from the Plantation, that I know of. Her gentlemen callers all seem to be from off-island, to judge from the tags on their automobiles. She built her studio herself, from random ends of lumber, and it looks like a chicken house on the outside and is glorious inside with light and space. When I asked her, when we first met, why she chose Peacock's Island, she said, "The light," and I knew what she meant. I soon found that I usually did, about everything. She is my best friend. Clay cannot stand her, nor she him. Both of them have finally worked around to a point where they simply do not discuss the other anymore.

But there are other ways of showing enmity, and Lottie's disgusted snorts and Clay's still, cold silences get their messages across. I know he thinks she is sluttish, slovenly, an eyesore in Eden, and worst of all in his primer of sins, lazy. He is probably right on all counts. She thinks he is cold, calculating, far fonder of money than me, and worst of all in her primer, a despoiler of the wild. I never thought of Clay as any of those things, not the Clay I met and fell in love with and married. But so many of the things I never thought have come about, and so many that I did think have failed to do so, that I sometimes trust my own judgment last after anyone else's. It's easier to think Lottie is wrong about Clay, though I have to admit that she has seldom been about other things.

But we all have our blind spots, don't we? Oh, yes, we do. And I figure Clay is hers. Just as he is mine.

Lord, the day I first met him! He will never seem more beautiful, more whole, more hypnotically charming than he did on the day his friend Hayes Howland brought him over to the island to meet my grandfather. Poor Clay; he would hate that if I told him, hate that in my mind, he reached his ascendancy before I even knew him well. But I never have told him, and I never will.

It was in July, just at dusk. It had been a strange, unsettled day of running cloud shadow; little winds that started up and doubled back upon themselves and then died; sudden warm, hard spatters of rain that left the earth and air steaming and shimmering. Later we would surely have a storm. I was visiting from Columbia, where we had just moved, and had brought my watercolors and easel with me and was sitting on the dock at the end of the long, dilapidated wooden walkway that led from the marsh house to the tidal creek, where my grandfather kept his Boston Whaler and his canoe, trying to catch the spectral light. I was between my freshman and sophomore years at Converse, just tasting my gift. The dazzle to the west, where the sun hung red, preparing to flame and die behind the long sweep of emerald marsh, was overwhelming; I could not look into it without shading my eyes.

I heard them before I saw them, heard the slow putt-putt of an outboard lost somewhere in the rose-gold dazzle, and turned to look toward it, squinting. The boat came out of the light, its engine silent, and loomed up almost at the dock where I sat. It bumped the rubber fender and wallowed to rest.

57

Hayes got out first; I knew him slightly, from other visits he had made to my grandfather during my own summer stays, but I stared anyway. He was resplendent in a white linen suit, with the light gilding his red head, and looked far better in both than he usually did. Hayes is substantial and sometimes engaging, but he is not handsome.

"Hi, Caro," he said. "I've brought y'all a visitor."

"Hi, Hayes," I said back. "That's nice."

A tall young man got out behind him. He wore white linen also, but you noticed the man and not the suit, instead of just the opposite, as with Hayes; it might have been his everyday garb, it seemed so right and easy on his long body. A white linen suit in an Edwardian cut, and white buck shoes. He had a great, flowing blue satin tie. It should have looked foppish but did not. The light made an old-gold helmet of his hair and slanted into his eyes so that they flamed out of his narrow, tanned face, an impossible, fire-struck blue. He smiled and the spindrift light glanced on white teeth. He had a flower in his buttonhole, a small, tight, old-fashioned pink sweetheart rose, and in his long, brown hands he held a bouquet of them.

"This is Clay Venable," Hayes said. "We roomed together a couple of years at Vir-

58

ginia. He's been a fool over the Lowcountry since the first time I brought him home with me, and I've finally talked him into moving to Charleston. He wanted to see some real, unspoiled marshland and I thought of your granddaddy's place right off the bat. I guess you can't get much more unspoiled than Peacock's. This is Caroline Aubrey, Clay. Mr. Aubrey's granddaughter. Did I tell you she was an *artiste* as well as a beauty?"

"Miss Aubrey," Clay Venable said, holding the bouquet out to me. "I thought you might like these. We've been at a fancy garden party in Charleston and I stole them off a bush on the way out. Better take them before my hostess comes after me in a motorboat."

"Her gardener, you mean," Hayes said lazily. "In a cigarette boat. We've been at Marguerite MacMillan's, Caro. I thought if Clay was going to be a Lowcountry boy he might as well start out in the virtual holy of holies. Little did I know he'd be filching roses out of her garden before the afternoon was over. Can't take him anywhere."

I put out my hands and took the roses, but I did not speak. I could not seem to look away from this tall, radiant being clothed in white and molten rose-gold light. I remember thinking that his voice did not really sound Southern; it was deep and soft and slow, but somehow crisp. There was something else about him that did not seem native, either, though I could not have said what it was then, and still cannot. Clay was born on a farm in Indiana, but by that time he had so submerged himself into the fabric of the Lowcountry that there were few traces of the rural Indiana scholarship boy left, and of course by now there are none at all. Clay is more a denizen of this coast now than someone generations born to it.

"You gon' ask us in, Caro?" Hayes said, and my face flamed at the amusement in his voice.

"Yes. Please come on up to the house. Granddaddy's having his sundowner. He'll love some company. He's always saying he'll never make a drinker out of me. Well, not that he'd really want to, of course . . . thank you," I said, remembering the roses, and caught my platform heel in a crack of the dock, and lurched to one knee. The roses sailed over the weathered cypress railing and disappeared into the sea of reeds and black water.

There was a small silence, and then Clay Venable said, "A simple 'no thank you' would have sufficed."

I froze in mortification, and then the

amusement under his words penetrated my fog of misery, and I began to laugh. He laughed, too, and helped me to my feet, and Hayes laughed, and after that it was all right. By the time he had been introduced to my grandfather and the bourbon had been poured, and we sat on the screened porch looking out over the silvering marsh, Clay Venable was as much one of us as Hayes or any of the other young men from Charleston and the islands that my grandfather was accustomed to greeting when he encountered them hunting or fishing or canoeing on the wild tidal creeks and inlets of Peacock's Island. It was common knowledge that the island belonged to my grandfather, but it was also common knowledge that he did not mind the occasional sporting visitor, so long as they did not disturb the pristine tranquillity of the marsh and woods. Indeed, he had known most of them since they were small boys and came to Peacock's with their fathers.

Dark fell, the sudden thick, furry blackness of the Lowcountry marshes, unpricked by any lights at all except the kerosene lantern that sat on a table on the porch and the citronella candles I had lit. The house had electricity, but my grandfather disliked it, and often went days without lighting an electric lamp. He had no such qualms about other appliances, and happily used his small, battered refrigerator and the old stove and even the jerry-rigged washer and dryer that sat on the other end of the porch. But he loved lamplight, and it is what I use mostly when I am at the house even to this day. I find that it calls him back to me as little else does.

I don't remember much of what we talked about: Hayes's job at one of the ubiquitous law firms on Broad Street, I think, and how restless he felt there, closed away from the beaches and marshes and rivers and creeks where so many Charleston boys spent great chunks of their boyhood. My studies at Converse, and the painting that I was doing on the island that summer. The herd of wild ponies that had chomped and stomped its stolid way around the back part of the island since I could remember. The monster bull gator my grandfather had seen the day before, and the panther that he swore he had heard scream in the deep blacknesses of several past nights. The drought that was decimating the coast that summer and how badly my grandfather's year-round property in McClellanville was suffering from it. I did not think he was unduly upset about the drought in McClellanville; since my grandmother had died several years before, he had spent more and more of his time at the marsh house, and left it now largely to look after his banking business in Charleston, or to make a run to a hardware or grocery store. He had even, the winter before, put in a big cast-iron stove in the bedroom where he slept, so that, with the huge stone fireplace in the living area, the house was habitable through the brief, icy spasms of the Lowcountry winter.

"Don't you get lonesome out here?" I asked him once.

"No," he had said in honest surprise. "Why would I? Everywhere you look something alive is slapping the water or shiverin' the bushes. And when you run out of the live ones, there's plenty of not-so-live ones, let me tell you. Many's the night I've passed in the company of somebody who left these parts a hundred, two hundred years ago."

I knew that he was teasing me, but only with the top part of my mind. The old, bottom part nodded sagely: Yes. I can see that that's so. I have always felt that there were many levels of beings on Peacock's Island, many more souls than currently wear flesh. It is not, on the main, a bad feeling at all.

Finally, that night, we got around to Clay Venable. I knew that my grandfather was as curious about him as I was, but his natural, grave good manners decreed that he make Clay feel at home before asking him to share much of himself.

"I don't think you're native to these parts, but you seem to have taken to them right well," he said mildly to Clay after a while. They were on their second or third leisurely bourbons, and off in the trees the katydids and marsh peepers had started their evening chorus. Overhead the huge, swollen stars flowered in the hot night.

"No, I come from hill country, in Indiana, around Bloomington. I'd never seen the ocean till I got to Virginia and came home with Hayes. My folks were red-dirt farmers, poor as church mice. After that . . . well, I guess I was sunk. It was like I was born in the wrong place and only just found the right one when I got down here. There's never been any other part of the world I wanted to see, not after I saw this. I went back to Indiana after I graduated and worked at an insurance agency until I could save enough to pay off my student loans and get a little ahead. Then I headed down here like an arrow from a bow. I don't know yet what I'll be doing, but I'll be doing it here. I do know that."

It was 1972, and a looming recession threatened hundreds of thousands of workers across the country. Small businesses were closing; larger ones were cutting back or at the very least freezing their hiring. Around Charleston, the strictures of an energy crisis and unavailable gasoline slowed the flood of tourist dollars to a trickle. It was a disaster of a year, all told, and yet Clay Venable sat on my grandfather's porch and spoke calmly of a limitless future in the Lowcountry that was an assured fact, a done deal. I believed him absolutely, even before Hayes Howland laughed ruefully and said, "Lest you think he's blowing smoke rings, at least three guys at Marguerite MacMillan's as much as offered him jobs tonight. I don't know what it is he's got, but whatever, this old boy's gon' do all right for himself down here."

My grandfather laughed. It was a friendly sound, a laugh offered by one equal to another.

"What would you do if you had your druthers, Clay?" he said.

Clay did not hesitate.

"I'd take all this" — and he gestured around him at the marsh and the night — "and I'd make sure that nothing ever changed the basic . . . nature of it, the sense of it, like it is now . . . and I'd make it available to a few very special people who would see it for what it is, and love it for that, and want to live here. And no one else, ever."

Hayes snorted, and my grandfather said, "You mean . . . a subdivision, or something? Develop it?"

His voice was still mild and interested, but I knew how he felt about the marshes and the islands of the Lowcountry. My heart sank. I might have known Clay Venable was too perfect; there had to be something wrong. . . .

"What I have in mind is about as far from a subdivision development as it's possible to get," Clay said, looking intently at my grandfather. In the lamplight his blue eyes burned. "In my . . . place . . . the land and the water and the wildlife would come first, people second. Not a house, not a hedge, not a fireplug would go up that did not blend so perfectly into the wild that you had to look twice to see it. Not an alligator would be relocated; not a raccoon or a deer would be run out. I would never forget who was here first. And I would have no one in my place who did not feel the same way."

We were silent for a moment.

"Never heard of a place like that," my grandfather said finally.

"There's never been one," Clay Venable said. "But there will be, and it will be mine, and it will be somewhere on this coast. I know that."

"Take more money than God's got," my grandfather said.

"I can get the money," Clay said. "If I can get the right piece of land, I can get the money."

"Don't you have it backwards?" My grandfather chuckled. "How you gon' get a chunk of prime oceanfront or marshland without any money? Not much of that left. And another thing . . . any empty land I can think of around here hasn't got mainland access. Not an automobile bridge between here and Hilton Head. How you gon' find this wild land with a bridge already built?"

"Because I've got a master plan," Clay Venable said. "It's as detailed and complete as it's humanly possible to make it. I've been working on it for three years, ever since I got out of college. Since before then, really; since the second or third time I came down here with Hayes. I've gotten two or three of the best young architects on the East Coast to work on it, strictly gratis, and city planners and environmental specialists and lawyers, and I've gotten the Sierra Club people and the Coastal Conservancy folks to put in their two cents' worth, and the U.S. Corps of Engineers. None of them would take a penny. It will work. It's a beautiful plan. It's a beautiful concept. It's ready to go. I am absolutely sure that if the right people see it, the land and the bridge and then the money will follow. I *know* that. I don't mind working at . . . whatever . . . for a few years until I can get it going."

My grandfather took a long swig of bourbon and rattled the ice in his glass.

"Where is this plan?" he said.

"In a bank vault back in Charleston. And there's a copy at my bank at home in Bloomington."

"Who's seen it?"

"Nobody yet. Except the guys who've worked on it, of course, and they're sworn to secrecy. They'll be partners, so I don't worry about them letting it out. Outside of them, nobody."

"I'll say," Hayes said. "Not only have I not seen it, I haven't heard the first word about it. Jesus, Clay . . . I had no idea! Why didn't you tell me, show it to me? I can help you with it. . . ."

"It's not time yet. When it's time, I will. I wasn't hiding it from you, Hayes."

"I'd like to see a thing like that," my grandfather said, as if to no one in particular. "I reckon that would be something to see."

"I could bring it out tomorrow or one day

soon," Clay Venable said, and smiled, a swift, transforming smile that I had not seen before. My breath stopped.

"Why don't you do that?" my grandfather said.

"Me, too?" Hayes said.

"Not yet. But soon. I promise," Clay said.

"Well, I like that! I take you to the party of the year at the numero uno hostess's house in Charleston, and introduce you to the movers and shakers, most of whom are falling all over themselves to offer you jobs, and you won't let me see your . . . village Eden," Hayes groused. I thought that he was only partly kidding.

"You'll see it before anybody in Charleston," Clay said, giving Hayes the smile. Hayes nodded, apparently satisfied.

"Would you like to see it, Miss Aubrey?" Clay said to me.

I jumped. He had not really looked at me since we had settled ourselves on the porch. His attention had been bent upon my grandfather.

"Very much," I said, and my unused voice cracked, and I cleared my throat. "I would very much like to see it. If you can do all that and still keep the land . . . untouched, as you say . . . it would be something to see indeed."

I realized that I sounded adversarial, and

started to amend my words, and then did not. I did not think what he proposed was possible, and I did not want to see his master plan and find that, after all, it was an ordinary subdivision that would clump on stucco feet through the rich, fragile coastal land and leave little of it intact.

"Then maybe tomorrow?"

"Tomorrow would be fine," my grandfather said. "You boys come out about mid-afternoon and I'll take you out in the Whaler. Let Clay run Alligator Alley and see if he still wants to save the gators."

"I'm a working man myself," Hayes said, "but I know Clay would enjoy Alligator Alley. What a great idea, Mr. Aubrey. That's just what you all should do. Only why not take the canoe? See 'em better that way."

He came at three the next afternoon in the same outboard they had brought yesterday. I recognized it now as the one Shem Cutler, over on the tip of Edisto, sometimes rented out to hunters or crabbers. I was not waiting for him on the dock — I would have died first — but I was watching from the porch of the house. It is set on stilts, a former hunting shack grown large and rambling over the years, and you can see a long way from it. He was not nearly as proficient as Hayes with

70

the boat. I could see that he was coming in too fast, and he hit the dock with a resounding smack, bounced off it, and had to balance himself with an oar when the resulting watery circles rocked him crazily. I smiled to myself. Ever since he had spoken about his impossibly idyllic Lowcountry community I had felt vaguely and sullenly resentful of him, the dazzle of his initial appearance safely dissipated. This place, this island, belonged to us, my grandfather and me, and the small settlement of Gullah Negroes over in Dayclear, at the other end of the island, and the ponies and the gators and the ghosts and all the other beings, quick and dead, who had their roots here. Who was this man, this upstart, landbound Yankee, to come down here and tell us that he was going to transform it?

I was obscurely pleased to see, as he walked carefully down the listing boardwalk toward the house, that in the full afternoon light he did not look golden at all, not impossibly slim and tipped with flame. His hair was merely brown, the silver-brown of a mouse's fur, almost the same shade as his face and hands, and he was more skinny than slender. I could see, too, now that he wore an ordinary work shirt with the sleeves rolled up and not a suit of radiant white

71

linen, that the tan stopped at his wrists, as a farmer's did, and that his legs, in a pair of faded cut-off jeans, were the greenish-white of a fish's belly.

"The mosquitoes are going to eat him alive before we've left the dock," I said with satisfaction to my grandfather, who stood beside me, and was surprised at myself. Where was this venom coming from? I had been ready to follow him to hell or Bloomington when I first met him.

"Young feller got under your skin, has he?" My grandfather grinned, and I had to grin back. It had long been a joke between us that as soon as a young man showed substantial interest in me, my own evaporated like dew in the sun. A fair number of them had, over the years; I had my mother's vivid darkness and my unremembered father's fine-bladed features, and knew that they all added up, somehow, to more than they should have. I was not particularly vain of my looks, Miss South Carolina notwithstanding; good looks had not, after all, gotten my mother very much except a young husband who left us when I was four and another who was, to me, as remote as a photograph. In my experience, a man who came in the front door was that much closer to the back one. I solved that by leaving first. I

72

could see that I was doing it again. My grandfather was right. Clay Venable had gotten further under my hide in a shorter time than anyone ever had.

Just the same I was glad that he had proved to be an ordinary, skinny, milk-pale Yankee after all. I had nothing to fear from him. And then he raised his head and saw us on the porch and smiled, and the ordinariness vanished like smoke in the wind, like a disguise that he had cast off. My heart flopped, fishlike, in my chest.

"Shit," I whispered.

My grandfather laughed aloud.

Peacock's Island is a small barrier island in St. Helena's Sound, fitting like a loose stopper in the bottleneck formed by Edisto and Otter Islands to the north, Harbor and Hunting Islands to the south, and the shallow bay created by the confluence of the Ashepoo, Combahee, and Edisto Rivers to the west. It lies in a great, 350,000-acre wilderness called the Ace Basin, an estuarine ecosystem so rich in layers upon layers of life, so fertile and green and secret, so very old, so totally set apart from the world of men and machines — and yet so close among them — that there is literally no other place remotely like it on earth. Other areas in the Lowcountry that were once this pristine have irrevocably gone over to man now, and cannot be reclaimed, but a combination of private and public agencies have set their teeth and shoulders to safeguard the Ace, and now protect sizable swatches of it.

The bottom 91,000 acres of the Ace Basin are tidal marsh and barrier islands, scalloped by dunes older than time itself and thick with unique maritime forests of live oaks, loblolly and slash pines, palmettos, magnolia, and cedar. It is possible, on Peacock's and the other barrier islands of the Lowcountry, to encounter, in a day's walk or canoe trip: bald eagles, ospreys, wood storks, an amazing variety of ducks and herons, wading birds and shorebirds and songbirds. My grandfather said that someone had counted sixty-nine bird species in the great arc of the Ace. You can also see — or rather, perhaps, see tracks of — another eighty-three species of reptiles and amphibians, including a fearsome array of watersnakes and the big, thick, brutish rattlers of the Lowcountry, and, of course, the ever-present ranks of alligators. I have seen, during my summers there, whitetail deer, bobcats, foxes, rabbits, otters, raccoons, wild pigs, possums, and some fleeting things that I will never be able to name. The ponies are an aberration; no one is quite sure where they came from, but my grandfather thinks they are offspring of the tough little marsh tackies that used to dot the interior of Hilton Head and the larger Sea Islands, themselves offspring, perhaps, of the ponies brought by the English planters to work the lowland fields. He believes that the first of the Gullah settlers over in Dayclear brought the sire and dam of this herd with them, and since no one is sure when that was, the provenance of the ponies is as misty and unsubstantial as the marshes themselves. The Gullahs can only tell you that the ponies have been there "always."

The panther that my grandfather swore he heard in the nights should not, by rights, have been on the island at all, since no one has seen or heard of a panther in the Ace Basin since time out of mind. I certainly never saw one. But I believe there was one in my grandfather's time, for in that vast, succoring basin, one-third light, one-third water, and only one-third substantial earth, life in all its abundance has evolved all but unseen for millions of years, infused twice a day by the great salt breath of the tides, and that panther was as surely a child of the Southern moon as the blue crabs and the dolphins and the eagles and the men who came so late to it. I believe that. I do.

It was out into all this that we took Clay Venable, my grandfather Aubrey and I, on a July afternoon in 1972, and none of us came back unchanged. You often don't, in the Lowcountry.

Alligator Alley is a straight stretch of Wappinaw Creek, one of the secret black-water creeks and inlets that cut the island like watersnakes. From my grandfather's dock you could reach it, in the Whaler, in a few minutes. In the canoe, however, it took about a half hour, and we passed that in near silence, broken only by the slapping of hands on mosquito-bitten flesh. They were mostly Clay Venable's hands, and his flesh. I had slathered myself with Cutter's before I left the house, and my grandfather, for some reason, never seemed to be bitten. Finally, after watching Clay endure the ordeal in silence, I relented, and reached into my pocket and brought out the tube of repellent, and passed it up to him. I sat in the rear of the big canoe, and my grandfather in front. Clay was our middleman.

He took the ointment from me and turned and gave me a level, serious look from the pale blue eyes.

"I forgot I had it," I found myself saying defensively, and felt myself flush red. I would be all right, I thought, as long as I did not get the full bore of those eyes.

Clay still did not speak, but I noticed that his head was always in slight motion, turning this way and that, as he looked at everything we passed. An osprey took off from a nest on a dead bald cypress at the edge of the creek and Clay tracked it. An anhinga dropped from a low-lying limb of a live oak when we turned from a broader stretch of creek into Alligator Alley and he noted it. He marked and measured a turtle sunning on a reed-grown bank; the flash of a whitetail far off in a lightly forested hummock; the brilliant green explosions of cinnamon and resurrection ferns; the vast, rippling green seas of cordgrass and the great, primeval towers of the bald cypresses, dwarfing all else. I had the notion that he was somehow photographing all of it, so that he would never lose it, but could replay it at will on the screen of his mind whenever he chose.

I learned later that this was not far from true. Something within him, some sort of infinite receptacle, must fix, store, catalogue, file away. It was my first experience of his disconcerting, now-legendary intensity. When he brought it into play, it precluded whimsy, idleness, pensiveness, even the sort of comfortable, unfocused dreaminess in which I and most other people pass a good deal of our time. He can suspend this thing, whatever it is, when he wants and needs to, and often does, but I know by now that it costs him something; that the effort is to drift on the moment, not to focus and record it, as it is with most of us. That, of course, accounted for the impact of those extraordinary eyes, and the force of the smile was the sheer relief and exuberance you felt when he freed you of it. The smile was his gift to you. All this I saw in one great leap that afternoon, from watching the back of Clay Venable's head. The knowledge did not sit comfortably on my heart.

The banks rise higher along Alligator Alley, as flat on top as manmade dams, overgrown with reeds and slicked with mud. Over them, far away, you can see the tops of the upland forests, but in the near and middle distance there is nothing but reeds and sky and creekbanks. Stumps and broken logs punctuate the reeds and grasses on the banks and in the edge of the black water, and more stumps protrude from the water at intervals. It looks for all the world as if heavy logging had gone on along this creek. It is not a particularly beautiful or interesting stretch of water, and the sun beats relentlessly onto the tops of heads and shoulders, and if you are in a canoe, your shoulder muscles have, by now, started to sting from the paddling. In the canoe, you sit very low in the dark water. The landscape is completely bounded by the rough, looming sunblasted creekbanks.

I waited.

To me, it is always like those drawings you used to see as a child, the one where you are supposed to find the animals in the intricately drawn mass of a forest. At first you see nothing, and then they begin to appear: a lion here, a leopard there, the ruffle of a bird's wing in a tree, the smirking face of a lamb in the tall grass. That is how the alligators come. At first you see nothing but reeds and grass and broken stumps, and then you see, as if by magic, the great, terrible, knobbed head of a gator, and then the whole gator, and then another, and then another. Afterward, you can never understand why you did not see them at once.

So the alligators of Alligator Alley came. I heard Clay's breath draw in slightly as the first gator appeared on the bank above us, as if in a developing photograph. After that he was silent, but his head tracked them as they materialized, one after another. Eventually, there were eighteen or twenty of them in sight. I can never be sure I have counted them correctly.

I have seen them every summer now since I was seven or eight, and they never fail to stop my breath and chill my heart. I know all the comforting folk wisdom about them: that they cannot bite under water, that they seldom attack humans except in self-defense, that they do not go after things larger than themselves. Certainly not a boat. I know that if you sit quietly in your craft, or stand quietly, they will disregard you, and that they have poor peripheral vision, so that if you stay to their sides you are presumably safe. Still they make the hair on my nape and arms rise and something deep within me goes into an ancient and feral crouch. They are simply such sinister, implacable things, knobbed and armored like dragons out of nightmares, seemingly formed of mud and stone and obsidian and malachite, the color of stagnant water, the color of muddy death. And as for their reputed harmlessness, every Low-country native has a story about the cat, the dog, the small child snatched from the bank by those incredible scalloped jaws. I have seen myself, on the island, the nubs of an occasional hand or foot said to have been taken by a gator. And down on Hilton Head, in the big, developed resort plantations, the shelf life of poodles and shih tzus is not long at all, not in the prized lagoon homesites.

My grandfather taught me early to be absolutely silent when we passed the alligators, and so I always am. They are not always in precisely the same place, but they do seem always to be in a cluster, and so it does not take long to pass them. These today did not move much, except to lift their huge heads lazily as we drifted past, and once or twice I heard the dry swish as a thick tail stirred in the reeds. They are usually on the bank this time of day, in the summer, taking the sun now that some of the heat has gone out of it; earlier, they would have been in the water, only their knobbed yellow-rimmed eyes showing, so that they seemed to be submerged logs, or the knots of limbs and roots. Then you cannot see their size, but when they are on the bank, of course, you can. These were big ones, mostly. I'd say they ran from about ten feet to thirteen or fourteen. One or two smaller ones, adolescent children, lay curled close to their mothers, blending into the grayish mud. If there were very small ones they would be out of sight near the nests. Even with their fearsome bulk, they are misleadingly innocent when they bask lazily like this. They look as if they could not move except ponderously, dragging that scaled hugeness on short, bent legs. But they can move like lightning, can be

81

down a bank and into the water in an eye flicker. I have seen that. I usually hold my breath until we are past them.

We almost were when one of the submerged logs in the water began to move, to glide lazily after the canoe. I drew in my breath and did not let it out again. My grandfather looked back at Clay and me and shook his head almost imperceptibly. I knew that he meant us to be still and silent. The alligator did not lift its head, but the eyes followed us, closing on the canoe, and my grandfather kept up his steady, leisurely paddling. I followed suit, but my shoulder muscles cried out to dig in, to paddle faster, to stroke with all my might. I did not look to the right or left, except once, and then I could see the gator's head almost abreast of me in the rear of the canoe. I looked back slightly farther. Just under the sun-dappled surface of the water I could see its body. It seemed, in the shifting green-blackness, to go on forever. It was like looking down into a bright summer sea and seeing, under its glittering surface, the long, dark, death's shape of a submarine, ghosting silently beside you. I shut my eyes and paddled.

After what seemed an eternity my grandfather said, in his normal voice, "I heard there was a big one around this year. Shem

Cutler saw him early one morning, taking a raccoon. Said he looked like a damned dinosaur. Shem reckoned he might be eighteen or twenty feet. I hear they've been losing pigs and a hound or two over at Dayclear, too. I wouldn't be surprised if it ain't old Levi."

"Levi?" I croaked, finally looking back. The gator had apparently lost interest in us and turned toward the bank. He did not come out of the water, though. In another stroke or two we were past the convocation of gators.

"The Gullahs tell about a giant alligator that's always been around these parts, bigger than any of the others by a country mile. They say you can hear him bellowing in the nights as far as Edisto. Every time a piglet or a dog or a chicken goes missing, they say that it's Levi. Nobody much sees him and they say you can't catch him. Gators do live to be right old, but if the tales are true, this old boy would be near about two hundred years old. *If* that was Levi, you kids have got something to tell your grandchildren. Figuratively speaking, of course."

And he grinned at Clay and me. I felt the red flood into my face again.

"Can all that be true?" Clay said with great interest.

"Naw, I don't reckon so," my grandfather

said. "Be something for Ripley if it was. All the same, the old tales don't die out. And that was one big mother of a gator. You just don't ever know, in the Lowcountry."

I felt something on the back of my neck that was like a cold little wind under the heavy sun.

"Who named him Levi?" I said.

"I've always heard that one of the first preachers at the little pray house in Dayclear did, after he was supposed to have gone off with three children in one year. It's short for Leviathan."

I felt the little wind again, stronger this time.

"God, that's marvelous," Clay breathed. "That's just marvelous."

He looked back, his face rapt and blinded. I thought at first he was looking at me, but then I saw that he was looking past me to the big gator as it lay submerged, just off the receding bank behind us. My skin prickled.

"Marvelous isn't exactly the term I would have used," I said.

But, "I reckon that's just what it is, Clay," my grandfather said, and I felt obscurely rebuffed.

We got back to the dock just as the sun was disappearing in a conflagration of rose red across the forest on the mainland to the west. The water of the creek was dappled red and gold, and the sweet, damp thickness that twilight brought seemed to drop down over us like a shawl. I have always felt that you wear the air of the Lowcountry somehow. It is not thin like other air.

Clay thanked my grandfather seriously and politely for the afternoon, but he made no move to go. He did not even look at his borrowed boat, bobbing in the settling wake our own had made. He simply stood there, tall in the falling darkness, his mouse-fur hair in his eyes, the angry splotches made by the mosquitoes glowing on his arms and legs. I knew they must itch fiercely by now, but he made no move to scratch them. A new squadron came in from the marshes, level and low, and sang around our heads. I shook mine angrily. Mosquitoes make me childish and stupid.

My grandfather swatted the back of his neck and I looked at him in surprise. I did not think mosquitoes bit him. He did not look at me.

"Let's get on in the house before they take us off clear over to Edisto," he said. "Clay, you need to put something on those bites, and then I think you ought to have some supper with us and forget about going back till the morning. We've got a guest room, such as it is, and I got a mess of crabs this morning. Cleaned 'em before you came. Some beer on ice, too. You don't want to try to feel your way back over to Edisto in the dark. Levi might get you if Shem doesn't."

I waited for Clay to demur, to say that he wouldn't think of putting us out, but he did not.

"I'd really like that," he said. "There's an awful lot I want to ask you about the island. Both of you," he said, looking at me as if remembering I was there.

"Granddaddy's the historian," I said shortly, and went to take a shower and anoint my own bites. I was annoyed with Clay Venable; he had said hardly a word to me all day. I would, I thought, have supper with them and then excuse myself and go to bed. Let them sit on the porch and gab the night away . . .

But I pulled out a new pair of flowered bell bottoms and a pale pink T-shirt that I knew would look dramatic against my tan, and sprayed on some of the Ma Griffe my stepfather had given me for Christmas. I knew that my mother had told him what to get, but still, I liked the cologne. It smelled both sweet and tart, like summer itself. I twisted my heavy hair up off my neck and pinned it on the top of my head. The day's humidity had turned it to wiry frizz, and if I had let it fall loose it would have stood out like an afro. For not the first time, I considered ironing it and then shook my head angrily at myself and simply twisted it up and skewered it with hairpins. I did put on some lipstick, though, something I almost never did on the island.

"You look pretty," my grandfather said when I came out onto the porch. He and Clay were sitting in the old wooden rocking chairs, their feet up on the rail, drinking beers. Clay smiled at me.

"You really do," he said. "Like a Spanish painting, with your hair up. Velázquez or somebody. One of the infantas."

"You like art?" I said. "As well as alligators?"

"I like lots of things," he said, "art among them. I had four years of art appreciation at Virginia. They do pretty well by you. Your grandfather tells me you're a real artist, though. I'd like to see some of your work."

"Maybe sometime," I said, and then, because it sounded so ungracious, "If you still want to, I'll show you some of the things I've been doing this summer before you go in the morning."

We feasted on boiled blue crabs, then sat while thick, utter darkness fell down suddenly, like a cast net, and the stars appeared, hot and huge and silver, and fireflies pricked the darkness. They talked of the island, Clay and my grandfather, or rather my grandfather did, mostly. He talked of many things, slowly and casually, anecdotally, spinning his stories out judiciously like a tribal bard. He talked some more about Levi and about the skeleton of the osprey someone had found on Hunting Island, with the skeleton of the great fish still caught in its claws.

"They never let go," he said. "That fish was so big it pulled that old osprey right under, and he still wouldn't let go. Drowned him."

"God," Clay breathed, as if he was hearing stories of the Holy Grail, and my own eyes pricked with tears. I could not have said why.

He talked of the pirates who had dodged in and out of the Sea Islands, and of Captain John Peacock and his ignominious career, and of the great rice and indigo and Sea Island cotton plantations that flourished on the islands from Georgetown to Daufuskie Island, and of the plantation society and economy that had shaped a slow, graceful, symmetrical, and totally doomed way of life. He talked about the Gullahs and how they came over the Middle Passage from Gold Coast West Africa in chains to work the fertile lowland fields, specially catalogue-ordered by the American planters, from Senegal, Angola, Gambia, and Sierra Leone for the agricultural skills and the strong sense of family and community that helped ensure that they would not try to run away and leave their people. He told of the strange, rich old songs he had heard in the pray houses of the islands, and of the shouts that are songs, and of the dancing of ring plays and the knitting of circular nets and the weaving of sweetgrass baskets and the cooking of fish, yams, and okra; of the tales of trickster rabbits, vain crows, and sly foxes, and the darker, more terrible things that preyed in the nights on the unwary: the duppy and the plateye and their prowling succubus kin. He told of the language that was unique on earth, and sounded in the ear like music.

"Do you know any of it?" Clay asked, and my grandfather closed his eyes and sang softly, in his rusty tenor: " 'A wohkoh, mu mohne; kambei ya le; li leei tohmbe. Ha sa wuli nggo, sihan; hpangga li lee.' "

I had never heard him sing or speak Gullah before and simply stared.

"What does it mean?" Clay Venable said.

"It means, 'Come quickly, let us struggle; the grave is not yet finished; his heart is not yet perfectly cool. Sudden death has sharp ears.' "

We said nothing. The words curled out into the night and rose and vanished.

"It's a funeral song, probably for a warrior," my grandfather said. "They were maybe the most important of the tribal songs, because the West African people had such reverence for their dead, for their ancestors."

"Where did you learn that?" I said.

"My daddy used to bring me over here hunting with him when I was little," my grandfather said. "He had a friend, Ol' Scrape Jackson, who was a hunting guide for the rich Yankee who owned this place. Scrape used to sing that. He taught it to me and told me what it meant. I don't know why I've remembered it all these years."

"It's beautiful," I said softly.

"It is that," my grandfather said.

"Your people didn't always own the island, then?" Clay asked.

"God, no." My grandfather laughed. "Rich Yankee industrialist who had a plantation over on Edisto bought it off one of the old planter families down on their luck back around 1900, for a hunting lodge. Lucius Bullock, owned some steel mills, if my memory serves. My daddy and Scrape Jackson were his guides, and then his son's, and when I was old enough and my daddy died, I took over for the son. Jimmy, that was. It was good work, seasonal, as they say, and Jimmy paid me good to do my guidin' and to look in on the property once or twice a month when it wasn't hunting season. There's not much about this island I didn't end up knowing. You could have knocked me over with a feather when old Lucius died and left the island to me, the whole damned shooting match. Of course, it's not a big island, and there wasn't then and isn't now much access to it, but still, a whole island . . . Well, anyhow, Jimmy didn't want it and he wasn't about to turn it over to the government, so I guess I was as good as anybody. It liked to have driven my wife crazy. We had a nice little place in McClellanville and I did pretty good doing some general contracting over there, and I guess she thought I'd come on home and settle down when he died. After I got it, she wouldn't spend another single night over here. This girl is the one who's kept me company all these summers. Weren't for her, it would be mighty lonesome."

Clay said nothing, and then he laughed softly.

"What?" my grandfather said.

"It's a fabulous story," Clay said. "It just goes to show you that a cat may still look at a king. It gives me great hope."

"Glad it does," my grandfather said genially, and then, "Well, I'm going on to bed. You young people set awhile. I think there might be a few shooting stars tonight. Not like the big August hoohaw, but they're something to see out over the marsh. I think there might be a bottle of that fancy white wine Miss Caro likes in the fridge, too."

It was then that I knew that he had planned all along for Clay Venable to stay over. I knew that Clay knew, too. I did not know whether to sit still and pretend innocence, or simply get up and go to bed, taking my mortification along with me. I sat still.

"If you're embarrassed, don't be," Clay said finally, out of the darkness. "If he hadn't asked me to stay I would have just stood there until he did. I wasn't going home without getting to know what makes you tick."

Somehow that broke the back of my lingering reserve. We sat in the soft darkness until very late, talking desultorily of things so ordinary that I cannot remember now what they were, finally finishing the wine, still not going in. I had lit a couple of citronella flares, so that we heard the hum of the mosquitoes but they did not come in close, and in the flickering flare light I could see the planes of his narrow face, and the flash of his teeth as he talked. At some point in the evening, aided no doubt by the wine, it seemed simply and suddenly to me that I had known the geography of that face all my life, known always the music of the voice. When the stars began to fall we stopped talking.

The last one had sunk into darkness and gone back to black, and we still had not spoken for some minutes, when we heard the scream. It rose out of the far darkness, high and infinitely terrible, rose and rose to a crescendo of grief and fury and something as wild and old and free as the earth, broke into a tremolo of despair and anguish, and then sobbed away. The very air throbbed with it long after it was gone. All the little sounds of the night had stopped. I sat stone still, my heart hammering in my throat, tears of fright and something else entirely welling up in my eyes. My fingers gripped the arms of my chair as if they alone might save me. Beside me Clay, in his chair, did not move either, did not breathe.

"My God," I whispered finally. "My God."

"Not an alligator, was it?" he said.

"Oh, no. No. No alligator on earth ever sounded like that," I said. I had begun to tremble.

Then he said, "I know what it was. That

93

was your grandfather's panther. That's what he's been hearing."

"Lord Jesus," I said, and it was a prayer. "Then it was true."

"Everything out here is, I think," Clay said, and got up out of his chair and came over and put his hands on my shoulders, and kissed me.

And that was that.

3

When I came downstairs, showered and more or less together, Clay was sitting at the round table on the back veranda making notes on the omnipresent clipboard that goes everywhere with him, and Estelle was pouring coffee for him out of the little French chocolate pot that he likes to use for his coffee. Estelle and I have both tried to persuade him that in this climate pottery or china would be more suitable, but he bought the little silver pot on our honeymoon, in Cuernavaca, and admires it inordinately. The fact that someone has to polish it after every use does not bother him in the least.

"What do we have Estelle for?" he will say when I fuss about the pot.

"Not for polishing your coffeepot every morning of her life," I say. "I've been doing it for years, if you must know."

"I do know. And I thank you," he says. "The pot makes me happy and it makes me happy that you polish it for me."

And so I do it, because I will not ask Estelle to, and it is, after all, a small thing.

He does not ask much foolishness of me. There is not much foolishness in Clay.

I knew that he had chosen the back veranda because I simply could not have looked at the sea this morning. He loves the marsh vistas, and always has, but it is the open ocean that calls to him. I sometimes think that the sheer, intense orderliness of his soul finds a kind of release in that ultimate, untamable disorder. He can sit and look at the sea for hours, though he rarely sits and looks at anything anymore for hours but whatever is on his drawing board or his clipboard. He is restless during enforced inactivity; cocktail parties are torture for him, though he goes to and gives enormous numbers of them and does the walk-through perfectly. Clay never did drink much and is impatient with the slight silliness, the looseness, that ensues after an hour or so at the best of them. He chews ice fiercely and eats enormous quantities of hors d'oeuvres, waiting to be released. When we have drinks before dinner, either at home or at a restaurant, he can go through an entire basket of bread, waiting for everyone else to finish their drinks. He sometimes waits a long time. There seems to me to be quite a lot of drinking in the Plantation. Despite the munching, I am fairly sure he has not put on an ounce since we married. I never see him weigh himself, but the contours of his long, angular body do not seem to have changed.

Estelle poured out a second cup of coffee and plonked a plate of sticky buns down in front of me. They were still warm from the oven. The rich cinnamon rose to my nose and I sniffed appreciatively, though my stomach heaved at the thought of food.

"They smell wonderful, Estelle, but I think I'll just have coffee," I said. "Will you put some aside for me? I'll eat them with my tea this afternoon."

"You eat them now," she ordered. "You looks like the hind axle of hard times. You been up in that room, haven't you?"

I looked over at Clay, and she said, "Mr. Clay didn't tell me. I seen the door still open. And I know that look on yo' face. You ain't got no call to be broodin' in that room, Miss Caro. It don't do nothin' but stir you up. She ain't in there. She in a better place than this, and happy as a little lark. You try to rejoice in that an' leave her po' things be."

I bent my head over my coffee so she would not see the unsheddable tears gather. Estelle's faith is earth-simple and granite-hard. Not for the first time I felt a profound ache of pure envy. I had ceased negotiations with God on the day that my daughter died.

I felt no anger at Him, only a dreary and cell-deep certainty that whether He was there or not, that door had slammed shut for me. There was a kind of peace in it.

We drank our coffee in silence. I was grateful for it. Clay knows that I cannot abide hovering when I am feeling out of sorts. Even if I could, I don't think it is in him to hover. He deals with his deepest feelings by snapping them firmly into the steel grid inside him and going back to work. The night that Kylie died, he stayed at his board all night, working furiously, while I slept in a thick swamp of barbiturates. The master plan for Calista Key Plantation, on the south coast of Puerto Rico, was conceived almost in its entirety that night. It is thought by most critics to be by far Clay's most innovative and attractive property. I have never been there. He does not go often, either. Neither of us can forget what terrible fuel fed the fire it was born in.

Finally he lifted his head and said, "You ready? I went ahead and put the flowers in the car."

And we went out into the misted morning to get the guest house ready for the new nestlings.

The Heron Marsh section of the Plantation is, except for the seaside neighborhood, the oldest. It was Clay's thought to offer to the first venturesome investors and home buyers the choice waterfront lots on the ocean and the marsh tidal creek that separates Peacock's from "the island." In between, he devised lovely neighborhoods of single-family and cluster homes bordering man-made lakes, lagoons, and a golf course, each with its own pool and tennis court. So, theoretically, everyone who lives in the Plantation has his own bit of waterfront. But it is the great dazzling vistas of sea and marsh that are the prizes, and they were gone almost in the first year of the Plantation's existence. I have always loved the Heron Marsh homes. They sit so deep in lush ocean forest that they are all but hidden from the road, and the contrast of coming out of that dark cave of green into the light that seems to pour like sour honey off the wide marshes is stunning. All the Heron Marsh homes have long back lawns and gardens that slope gently down to the reeded marsh's edge, and the deep, swift tidal creek that is the belt on the island's midsection is studded with docks at which cheeky outboards and slim sailboats bob. From this part of the creek you can reach the harbor and open ocean in a five-minute sail. The water is almost unfailingly calm and shining; even our fierce summer storms can't reach their clawing fingers here. I remember that I wanted to build on Heron Marsh when I first saw it, because it looks straight over into "my" part of the island, the secret green heart where I spent so many summer weeks with my grandfather. But Clay was in love with the ocean even then. It does not bear thinking that we might still have Kylie if we had come here, and I try hard not to. I really do. I have always known that there was simply no blame to be assigned, except perhaps to my child herself. Certainly not to Clay. I sensed even in the depths of my very earliest grief that that way lay the death of our marriage.

The house Clay uses as a guest house is the largest of twelve on the marsh. It was built for a very rich family from Spartanburg who had eight children and innumerable grandchildren, and so it sprawls octopuslike among its azaleas and oleanders and great ferns and overhanging live oaks, harboring a staggering number of smallish bedrooms, each with its own bath. There is an enormous family room and a kitchen and dining room that can accommodate an emerging nation, a wraparound veranda that steps down one step to a huge pool, and two Har-Tru tennis courts at the fringe of the water. It is made of our tradition-hallowed tabby, a mixture of sand and crushed oyster shell that dates back who knows how many hundreds of years in the Lowcountry. I always loved the thick, pitted surface of tabby; it looks as if it could stand for millennia, and may well do so. The tabby and the now-matured plantings are, to me, the only things that save the guest house from a rather daunting institutionality, which may be why the rich Spartanburgers sold it after the first year, though local legend says that it is because an alligator came out of the creek and ate the wife's Yorkie and was going for the youngest child as dessert before the screams from the children drove the sensible beast back into the water.

I always try to cram as many big, loose, rowdy bouquets as I can into the bedrooms and common areas, to soften the look of an upscale Elks Hall. Today the back of my Cherokee was almost full of them.

Clay helped me take the pails and vases into the kitchen and did not make a move to leave, but I knew that he was at least an hour past his customary time for going to his office, so I said, "Why don't you go on and catch up? I'll finish this up and then I think I'll walk over to Lottie's. She's starting a humongous new thing of the lighthouse that I want to see. I'll probably have some lunch with her, too. What time are your chickens coming in?"

"The two couples should be in about two. I think the woman . . . you know, the black woman . . . is getting in an hour or so later. Hayes is going over to Charleston to pick her up; the others are renting a car. Did I tell you that she's got a child with her?"

"Oh, Clay, no, you didn't. How old a child? She's surely going to need a sitter, isn't she? Or do you think she'll even want to go out and leave it? What is it, by the way?"

"A boy. I think she said he was five or six. Yeah, I guess she'll want a sitter. Can you leave them with sitters at five? I don't remember . . ."

"Just," I said. "But she may not want to. I'll pick up a few things for a light supper for her and the little boy in case she wants to stay here and bring them over after lunch. I want to put some breakfast things in the fridge for everybody, anyway. Lord, I hope I can get somebody at this late date. There's an awful lot going on around the island this time of year. . . ."

"Don't you bother with that; I'll get somebody in human resources to do it. There's a list over there. It's what they're for."

"No, I'll do it this time. I know how I'd feel if I was coming to a new place with a small child. If all else fails maybe I can heavily bribe Estelle to do it. She was saying the other day she missed having her grandchildren at home now that Emily has moved to the mainland."

He kissed me on the forehead.

"You okay now?"

"Yes. I'm sorry about that."

"Don't ever be sorry. Just don't do that to yourself. That's all I ask. Estelle's right. It doesn't . . . get us anywhere."

"I know."

He got into the Cherokee and drove away, and I filled vases and pitchers and set my riotous roses around, watching the stark rooms catch flame with them, and then I went out back and sat for a time on the low wall that bordered the veranda, looking west into the dull-pewter noonday dazzle toward "my" part of the island. From the dark line of the distant woods a pair of great, gawky birds rose into the air and lumbered away into the sun. Wood storks, I thought. They had been homing into the Ace Basin for some years from their historical habitats in Florida, because extensive development there has left them no home. Now, in all of the Carolina Lowcountry, they come only to the Ace. These, I thought, had been fishing one of the small freshwater ponds on the island and might be headed back to one of their rookeries. My grandfather had said, just before he died, that he thought there were perhaps three of them.

He had died seven years earlier, suddenly, because, as Kylie said seriously when we told her, "His heart attacked him." He died on the porch of the marsh house, his empty coffee cup overturned beside him, sprawled half out of one of the old green-painted rockers. He had not been dead long; I had gone over because he had not answered the telephone that morning when I made the daily eight A.M. call that was as much to hear his voice as to check on him. His heart had been ailing slightly for so long that we no longer really worried about him. When I found him, and touched his face, it was not entirely cooled and his hand was still flexible.

"Don't go," I whispered, tears starting down my face, but of course he had. All things considered, as Clay pointed out later, it was the place and the way he would have chosen, and after all, who of us could ask for more than that?

" 'I know,' " I quoted at him, trying to smile, " 'but I am not resigned.' " Clay was my husband and my love, but my grandfather had been the armature of my life. For a time after that, I felt tremulous, too tall on the earth, vulnerable to all the winds that blew. I think I feel so secure on the island now because it seems to me that part of him is still there.

We married in 1974, almost two years after we met. I think if I had not accepted Clay's proposal my grandfather would have seen to it with a shotgun. There was never a time, even after the Plantation was in full development over on the shore and Peacock's Island was alive with homeowners and guests, that he did not admire Clay. He probably loved him, but in his world men did not speak of that, and so he never said. I know that he loved me, and Carter, and most of all Kylie, for he said so once or twice, shyly and gruffly, usually after a shot or two of Wild Turkey. The only time I ever saw him in a suit was at our wedding, in the Presbyterian church in Columbia that my mother and stepfather attended. That he wore the suit surely spoke of love; that he came at all to Columbia, a city he loathed, to attend a wedding grandiosely funded by a man he loathed equally but silently, spoke more of it. He never mentioned his own son to me, the father I did not remember, and somehow I never asked him. I know that my father died well before I met Clay Venable, of the familial coronary disease that later killed my grandfather, in a small town in southern Colorado, but no one thought to tell me much more than that. My mother would not speak of him, either. By the time I felt that I should pursue the other half of my biology, if only for the appearance of things, it hardly seemed worth the effort. Shortly before she died, my mother gave me some letters from him to her that she had saved for many years, but I have not yet read them. My main men, as the kids say, are both here on this island. My grandfather's ashes are now a part of the ancient salt blood of the Ace; I scattered them from the dock on a still gray morning in early spring, when the marshes were just greening up.

On the day that we married he deeded the entire island over to Clay.

"It's really yours," he said to me, "but I didn't want you to have to worry about taxes and all that stuff. Clay will take the kind of care of it I would, or you would. I've seen the plan for the development over on the ocean, and I got to say it looks good to me. No sense thinking we could keep this island to ourselves much longer, and I'd rather Clay looked after opening it up than anybody I know of. He's going to keep what he calls the spirit of it, and that's all I care about. I ain't a fool; I put a line or two in the agreement that says if he's ever stupid enough to run off with his secretary, or if he kicks the bucket before you do, it reverts to you. But if that doesn't suit you, he and I will redo the agreement."

"No, it's perfect," I said, weeping into his neck with love for him and the magnificence of his wedding gift to us. "I don't want to change a thing."

But I found that ultimately, I did. I found that for a long time after he died I simply could not cross the flimsy little bridge from Peacock's to the island without getting a great, cold lump in my throat, and I could not bring myself to stay in the marsh house very long, or go with Clay in the Whaler out into the heart of the marshes. I could not go over to the little settlement of Dayclear without crying silently, and the sight of the obdurate, mud-encrusted little marsh ponies bolting noisily over a hummock moved me to sobs. The void my grandfather left on the island whistled in my heart, the emptiness filled and choked me.

After a time Clay grew impatient with me.

"What good does it do for us to own it if you never want to go over there again?" he said one night, as I moved silently around the kitchen getting dinner. We had tried again with the island, taking the two children over for an afternoon, and once again I had stayed behind, huddled silently on the sunny dock. "What would make it all right for you?"

And without thinking at all, without even realizing I spoke, I said, "I want the island. I want that part of it. I want it to be mine, in my name. I don't know why, but I do. It's like . . . he'll come back, then."

He hugged me silently, and two days later he came back from a trip into Charleston and said, "Now it *is* yours. I had it transferred to you. Come on by the office and I'll have Linda witness your signature. You now own fifteen thousand acres of swamp, a herd of mangy ponies, and a town full of Gullahs."

"Oh, no," I said in horror. "I don't own Dayclear! I don't want it; that's awful! You can't own a town! He never owned Dayclear; he's told me a thousand times that he thought old Mr. what's-his-name deeded those houses over there to the Gullahs way before he left him the island."

"Well, there's not a scrap of paper anywhere to that effect that I could find," Clay said, "but it may be true. Trying to get clear title would be a nightmare, but then I don't guess you're planning to sell it, are you?"

"Of course not," I said, running into his arms. "Thank you, darling! I know it

shouldn't matter, but somehow I just . . .
needed it. And you've still got by far the biggest part, the part you really wanted, don't
you?"

"Of course. If you're happy, I'm happy.
Now, you think you can go back over there
without crying on the dock?"

"Yes," I said, and from that day, I could.

I went back over the next day, by myself,
and it was as if my grandfather had never left
it, was simply off somewhere in the canoe,
and I could move as easily about the house
as I ever had. I drifted through it, straighten-
ing up, sweeping, dusting, making mental
notes of everything that needed repairing
and brightening, and then I went back out to
the Cherokee and drove over to Dayclear.

I had not gone to the village often without
my grandfather. He was scrupulous about
according the villagers their privacy, and I,
spawn of the sixties and seventies, had the
Southern liberal's horror of appearing condescending to anyone with skin darker than
my own. But I knew most of the old men and
women living there, because I ran into them
when I went with my grandfather to the
scrubby little mom-and-pop store at the
bridge or to the tiny post office. I knew
which house Scrape Jackson had lived in,
and that his son, elderly himself now, and ill

109

with diabetes, still lived there, with his old wife and a rotating assortment of small grandchildren. Toby Jackson was usually to be found sitting out in front of the little unpainted house in an old armchair, covered with a paisley shawl that looked as if it might have once graced the shoulders of a fine lady or a grand piano on Tradd Street, weaving sweet-grass baskets and watching his chickens forage in the dusty yard. He was there that morning, and I stopped the car and got out and went over to him.

"It's Toby, isn't it?" I said, smiling foolishly and wishing I had my grandfather's natural ease with the Gullahs.

He nodded his head slowly. I noticed that his eyes were filmed, as if with cataracts, and realized that he probably could not see me well, if at all.

"Yes'm," he said.

"Toby, I'm Caroline Aubrey. Mr. Gerald's granddaughter. We've met, but you probably don't remember. I knew your daddy, though . . ."

"I remember," Toby said.

"Well, I guess you know Granddaddy died not too long ago . . ."

I paused, and he nodded.

". . . and I just wanted to let you know . . . let all of you know over here, I mean, that

110

nothing's changed, and nothing's going to. This part of the island is mine, across the bridge over here, and I'm not sure what you all's arrangement about the property here is, but I didn't want anybody to worry that anyone would, you know, bother you about it or anything. It belongs to you all, just like it always did. It always will."

He did not speak but only nodded slowly. After a while I said, "Well, that's all I wanted to say. It's nice to see you again, Toby."

I had started back to the Cherokee, cheeks burning, when he called after me, "Miss Caroline?"

I turned. "Yes?"

"Thank you for telling us. I guess we been kind of wondering ever since Mr. Gerald passed. Couldn't none of us prove we owns our houses, I don't think, but they's been ours for a long time."

My heart smote me.

"Somebody should have come right away and talked to you. I'm so sorry."

He smiled for the first time. He had a large gold tooth in front, and his smile looked festive and sweet.

"We figured you git around to it sooner or later. You his granddaughter, after all. We all thought a sight of Mr. Gerald. We sure did."

I sang in the Cherokee all the way back over the bridge to Peacock's.

After that, I was at the marsh house at least twice a week. After school and in the summers, Kylie and sometimes Carter came with me, though, like Clay, Carter gravitated eastward to the ocean like an iron filing to a magnet. It was Kylie who became my eventual companion on the marshes. They sang to her as they never did to Clay and Carter. She was especially enchanted with the ponies. One, a cobby, dun-colored mare of astonishing stupidity and passing equine sweetness, took to following her around, doglike, for the lumps of sugar Kylie kept in her pockets.

"You'll ruin her teeth," I used to say, and we would laugh, because the mare's long yellow teeth seemed impervious to everything from sugar to dynamite. We named her Pianissimo, for obvious reasons. I still see her sometimes, though never again so close as when Kylie came with me to the island.

At nine-thirty that evening I sat at a round table in the quiet patio room of Carolina's, listening to the conversation between Clay and his new cadets and sipping on my third glass of Merlot. Ordinarily I do not drink at these shakedown cruises, as Hayes Howland calls them, but tonight's was going so badly that by the time our appetizers came I could not bear the slogging tedium and the Herculean effort of trying to draw the young wives of the anointed into the conversation, and when Hayes, who had joined us, ordered a bottle of Merlot and put it down on the table between us, I simply gave up and drank each glass he poured for me. Clay was still toying with his first glass of wine when we waited for dessert, and the young men were sipping matter-of-factly and moderately, as if they did not realize they were drinking wine at all, hanging on to Clay's words, but the two young women were not drinking at all, and simply would not be either assimilated or consoled. After an hour of trying himself, Hayes had raised an eyebrow at me and murmured, *"À votre sante,"* and settled silently into the wine, and I had given up and leaned back and joined him. Clay passed me a level look or two, but when I lifted my shoulders in an almost imperceptible shrug and raised my glass to him, he did not look again. I knew that I had broken my end of the bargain — to engage and draw out the women while he began spinning their husbands into the cocoon of the company — but I was bone-tired and annoyed with them all, and wished suddenly for nothing so much as to be safely in the marsh house on the island

and not required to speak another word until tomorrow. The morning in Kylie's room had bled me more deeply than I had thought. And my afternoon encounter with the young black woman Clay had hired had made me both angry and bored, a combination unbeatable for sheer enervation.

I had stayed too long at Lottie's studio, and by the time I got back to the house I barely had time to run out again to the little supermarket in the Plantation's chic, lushly planted little mall for provisions for the guest house. When I got back to the Heron Marsh house it seemed as empty as when I had left it, and the kitchen was in its same pristine state, so I put my grocery bags down on the counter and was unloading them when a cool voice said, "I beg your pardon?"

I looked around as guiltily as if I had been caught rifling the silverware. A tall young black woman stood in the door to the hallway. She wore a severely cut ivory linen pantsuit and simple gold jewelry, and was utterly beautiful; her skin was the color of coffee with a great deal of sweet cream in it, and her face looked like something on the wall of a highland African cave, newly come to light after millenna. She was not smiling. Her delicate brows were lifted high over almond eyes.

"I'm sorry," I said, smiling. "I didn't know anyone was here. Your plane must have been right on time."

"Are you the baby-sitter?" she said.

I laughed.

"No. I'm Caroline Venable, Clay's wife. I wasn't sure what you would want to do about dinner, whether or not you'd want to leave your little boy with a sitter, so I brought some things over for supper in case you wanted to stay in tonight. I know how it is the day you get in from a long trip . . ."

"Mark is fine with sitters," she said levelly. "Mr. Howland said the company had them available. I'm sorry, I thought you must be someone he sent. He's gone to the office to see about it . . ."

"Well, I'm afraid we weren't able to do much on this short notice. This time of year is crammed full of things for the children. But my housekeeper said she'd be delighted to sit. She's wonderful with children; she practically raised mine, and she has a raft of grandchildren herself. . . ."

"That will be fine," the woman said, and then, putting her slim hand out, "I'm Sophia Bridges. I'll be doing research and development for the new property eventually, but right now I suppose there'll be indoctrination and that sort of thing. It's kind of you to bring these things for us, Mrs. Venable, but I mustn't keep you. I've got Mark down for a nap, so I'm going to use the time to get unpacked before we leave for dinner. What time could your housekeeper be here?"

Her hand was chilly in mine, and firm, but it did not linger. The slim fingers disengaged hurriedly.

"Please call me Caro; everyone does," I said. "I hope I'll be seeing a lot more of you, and of course I want to meet Mark. Estelle can be here around five, I should think. We'll probably leave for Charleston about a quarter of six. It takes an hour or so to drive it. We'll be taking two cars over, so I'll pick you up, or perhaps Clay will. Somebody, at any rate. You needn't change, what you have on is lovely. . . ."

But I was talking to her slender back as she turned and went back down the hall toward the bedroom, where her son presumably slept a cool and orderly sleep.

"You're welcome," I said under my breath to her back, and only then wondered if there was a Mr. Bridges, and if so, where he might be.

There probably never was one, I thought nastily. He's probably a test tube somewhere in a fertility lab. I can't imagine any living man getting close to her long enough to accomplish conception.

I picked up my keys and started out of the kitchen, then stopped as I heard her voice behind me. I looked back. She stood in the door, poised like a royal coursing hound, perhaps a saluki.

"Your housekeeper . . . is she African American?" she said.

"Why . . . yes. She is," I said in surprise.

"Then I'm sorry, but I think I'll stay here with Mark this evening. He's never had a woman of color for a baby-sitter. I don't want him to get the idea that African-American women are subservient or take servants' roles. He's never seen that. I realize that may be a little problem down here, but Mr. Howland . . . Hayes . . . thought we could get around it. I'm going to want white sitters for Mark."

I drew a deep breath and let it out slowly.

Then want shall be your master, I thought, but aloud I said only, "Well, it could be a problem. So many of the black women on the island, or within commuting distance over on Edisto or St. Helena's aren't trained for much else, and the baby-sitting and housekeeping jobs they have are very important to them. They do them wonderfully well, and they know how much we appreciate and depend on them. We'll see what we

117

can do, of course, but African-American women in white homes is simply a fact of Lowcountry life. I think your son is going to see a lot of it no matter who sits for him. Maybe when you see the reality of it you'll feel differently. These are warm, wonderful, skilled women; they are more partners than servants . . ."

"I have made my own reality for Mark," she said without smiling. "It has cost me a great deal to keep it intact. Thank you, though. I'm sure the company's human resources people will get to work on it for me."

And she turned and went back down the hall with the stride of a big cat. All she lacked, I thought, was a great, switching tail. Obviously Ol' Massa's wife wasn't required to deal out her largesse here. Ol' Missus slunk back to her car and jerked it into gear and screeched back off across the island.

When Hayes Howland and I had decanted our two passengers and gone back outside to wait for Clay, he said, "I presume you've met Mrs. Bridges and the crown prince?"

"I have indeed," I said. "They've gone into voluntary exile until a pale enough courtier for the prince can be found."

"Uh-oh," Hayes said, grinning his gap-toothed grin. "I'm afraid I dropped the ball, too. I could only think of that Filipino waiter at the Island Club, and that didn't suit, either. Maybe an American Indian? I hear the new teller at Palmetto State is half-Seminole. Maybe she's got a sister."

I have never really managed to like Hayes as much as I thought I would when I first met him, or as much as Clay wishes I did, but he can be bitingly funny. Tonight we burst into laughter, and could only stop when Clay pulled up in the Jaguar with the second of the two new couples in tow and raised his eyebrows at us and said, "Want to share the joke? We could use a laugh; the drawbridge was up for twenty-five minutes and I never could see why."

"Nothing worth repeating," I said, and took his arm, and we went inside, the seven of us, to begin the interminable business of assimilating four disparate strangers into the Plantation family.

We had stopped first for drinks at the town house Clay keeps in Charleston. Hayes had had his family's cook go over and open and air it, and set out the cocktail and appetizer things. Mattie sometimes does that for us when I cannot get over ahead of time, and often stays to serve drinks and pass around almonds and benné seed biscuits. Clay likes that. Mattie has a sure, unobtrusive dignity I cannot muster. Many guests think she is our employee, and neither Clay nor Hayes disabuses them.

The town house is on Eliott Street, a short, shady cobbled alley off Bay Street lined with dollhouse Charleston single houses. Clay bought the house years ago, when it became obvious that Plantation business was going to keep him in Charleston a great deal of the time. I know that even if it hadn't, he would have found an excuse to own a Charleston house. He has never stopped loving Charleston, as much, I think, for what it will not give him as for what it will. Clay has made a great deal of money, but there is a small core of old Charleston that does not care about that and will not admit him into its inmost bosom no matter what civic endeavor he underwrites. He will never, for instance, belong to the St. Cecelia Society, for the simple reason that membership is inherited, and he has come to ridicule it, but he never gave up on the notion that Kylie might come out there.

"You could cultivate Charleston," he said. "You've probably still got kin around here you don't know you have."

"You remind me of Groucho Marx when he said he wouldn't belong to any club that would have him as a member," I said once. "You scorn it, but you want your daughter to make her damned debut there. What kind of message do you think that gives Kylie?"

"That there are some things worth having that aren't easy to get," he said. "That real quality is rare."

"And that exclusion by policy is the Amurrican way," I said. "I'm no more going to 'cultivate' Charleston than I'm going to let her go to St. Margarets's. She doesn't live over there, Clay. I'm not going to have her in a car for two hours every day of her life just so she can go to a silly dance. Country Day is as good a school as there is in the Low-country. You've seen to that. What's it going to say to these newcomers you hire if your child goes to school in Charleston while theirs are expected to go on the island?"

"That rank hath its privileges," he said, but he did not push it, and of course, as it turned out, it did not come up.

But Clay still loves Charleston with the single-minded passion of a man for a lost first love, and when Hayes found out that the little house was being put up for sale by the old couple who were moving to the carriage house of a child's home, he called Clay immediately. This was just before the first of the wealthy Northerners discovered Charleston and began buying up historic properties at prices the natives could not afford; Hayes,

121

though never much of a lawyer in many respects, has the native's nose for real estate and knew that such properties would soon triple and quadruple in value. It was still early days in the Plantation, but Clay got the money together and bought the house sight unseen, as much for its street address as for its attractiveness or livability. It lies in the heart of the hallowed area "South of Broad," which in Charleston means more than the words might imply, and fortunately it is a prettily proportioned house that had been well cared for, needing only cosmetic attention. I have to admit that I am charmed by the little house and its walled garden, too, though I do not spend much time there. It never seems quite real to me, never seems to be our house at all, and when Clay refers to it as our pied-à-terre, as he often does, I can only look at him.

Charleston is as lovely in this soft, misted pre-Christmas dusk as it ever is, with gas carriage lights lit in the old district and warm lamplight shining from the shuttered windows of the old pastel houses and fingers of mist curling off the harbor up through the live oaks on the Battery and down the little side streets South of Broad. We walked the short distance over the glistening cobbles to Carolina's down on the waterfront. The streets were full of people walking slowly, looking into shop windows, laughing, talking. There are never many cars on the streets at night in the old district, though parking is at a premium, and walking is a good way to get your initial feeling for the city. I watched the two young couples as we walked. The men were so absorbed in Clay and his words that they might have been walking in downtown Scranton. They would have, after tonight, no feeling for Charleston at all. They followed him like ducklings, having imprinted upon him instantly and totally.

I have seen this before many times with the young who come to work at the Peacock Island Company. Just out of the pure ether of their Ivy League business or liberal arts schools, heads pounding with abstractions, newly adrift in a world so alien to the one they have just left that it might be in another geological epoch, they find Clay to be hyper-real, the Word made flesh, the only solidarity in a great mist of strangeness. He plies them like a Pied Piper. Nobody does it better than Clay.

Almost everyone does it better than me. The young women who clicked along on their sensible heels beside me in the soft, wet night, stumbling every now and then on a cobblestone, knew very well they were sacrificial lambs in an alien land, knew that they were here almost on sufferance, to be petted and cajoled while their husbands were courted; knew that sooner rather than later they would be on their own in this wilderness, while their men received the keys to the kingdom. They had a keen, if terrible, sense of Charleston; I thought they might never alter it. I felt an unwilling stab of sympathy. I suppose all the new company wives go through something like this unwanted epiphany, but some seem to relish it, and others at least to try to put a gallant face on it. These two did neither. Sally Bowdon-Kirkland looked straight ahead, neither smiling nor responding to anything Hayes or I said, simply gone away behind her long, narrow New England features.

Barbara Costigan cried.

When we picked up her and her husband, Buddy, at the guest house, her blue eyes were swollen almost shut and her little porcine nose was pink and raw. Allergies, she said; something in the air down here that they didn't have at home in Old Greenwich. But I know the stigmata of tears when I see them. Later, on the way to Charleston, I would hear an occasional rattling sniff from the backseat, where the young Costigans sat, and a murmur of concern from the stolid

Buddy. In the restaurant Barbara's slitted eyes leaked almost continually.

"Wow," she said over and over. "I hope you've got some good allergists down here."

"Oh, yes," I said. "Some of them, I think, from Connecticut."

She and Buddy were a pair: both square and short and tanklike, though I rather thought that Barbara's flesh was newly acquired. Her short-skirted silk dress fit her like the casing of a sausage and was obviously a size or two too small. It was also a delicate shell pink, which might have suited her fair skin and flaxen hair if the former had not been splotched vermilion and the latter sprayed into a helmet against our all-pervasive humidity. Buddy was blond, too, but a lighter shade, near-white. His skin was red. His smallish features sat in the middle of a large face as if someone had drawn them on a balloon, and radiated self-confidence and benignity. I'd have thought him the archetype of the young German burgher but for the last name. Clay had said that his IQ was off the charts. They looked, all told, like a little couple on the top of a wedding cake. I winced, thinking of the twin sunburns they would sport from April to October.

The Bowdon-Kirklands were of a piece, too, though I thought that it was a spiritual twinship instead of a physical one. She was tall and very thin, almost six feet in her Ferragamos, and he was perhaps a half-inch shorter, and wiry. Tennis, I thought, for her and golf for him. It was obvious both of them were sports people. Their smooth tans spoke of good private grass courts and deepwater sailing and golf somewhere like the Maidstone Club, where both had been members since birth. Both were lank-haired, long-featured, and awesomely collected. Both were polite. Both were as distant as Uranus. He spoke pleasantly in a New England honk but seldom to me. She spoke hardly at all. There was no sign of tears in her slightly protuberant gray eyes. I imagined that she probably wept only when her favorite hunter had to be put down, and then a good grade of English toilet water, the kind with a number instead of a name.

Peter Kirkland had been first in his class at Wharton. Sally, I remembered, had done something at a museum in Boston.

I tried at first.

"Do you have children?" I asked the young Costigans on the way over.

A great sniff from Barbara, a hearty "Yes, we do, a daughter," from Buddy, followed by more whispering and sniffling. I wondered what was wrong there. Postpartum depression, perhaps? A child somehow flawed?

"She's only a month old," Buddy said. "Our parents thought it would be better if she stayed behind with her granny and a nurse until we know where we'll be living. She's a little beauty; her name is Elizabeth Sloan, but she's already Sissy, just like her mama was. We miss her a lot, don't we, Barbs?"

A sob, disguised as a little cough.

No wonder, I thought. Dragging that poor child all the way down here and leaving her new baby behind. What could he have been thinking of?

Turning around, I said, "Well, there are wonderful things for children to do in the Plantation. The children's program is famous, and of course the weather is almost always nice, and the beach is perfect for small children almost all year round. Sissy will love it. Summer is paradise for kids."

"We'll be spending our summers on Fire Island," Barbara Costigan said in her little-girl whisper. "My parents have had a house in Point o' Woods forever. We always go there. I went there every summer of my life. I met Buddy there. The house was my grand-parents'."

"Now, Barbs," Buddy said heartily. "I bring you down to one of the most famous beach resorts in the world and you go on about Fire Island. Just wait till you see the beach in the Plantation; you'll change your mind in a minute."

Barbara was silent. There would be, I knew, no mind-changing there, about beaches or anything else. I could almost see the fine, tensile steel filaments that bound her to her family back up North.

Still, she tried, too.

"Do you have children, Mrs. Venable?" she asked politely.

"My son is twenty-two," I said. "He's in graduate school."

It is what I always say, when I am asked.

"Well, that's nice. I always thought boys must be so much easier to raise," Barbara said, in the tone of one who thought no such thing. "You're lucky you never had to put up with the wiles and the flirtiness of a little girl. Even one as little as mine — ours. They're just shameless. Sissy has Buddy wrapped around her little finger, and my father —"

She made a small noise and fell silent, and I knew that Buddy had heard about Kylie and pinched or poked her.

Another sob. I sighed.

"She'll have a lot of company," I said cheerfully. "There are several new babies in the staff family this year, and it seems to me

128

that most of them are girls."

"That's nice, isn't it, Barbs?" Buddy said. She did not reply. I felt real joy when we saw in the distance the spires of the bridge over the river into Charleston.

Toward the end of the evening, when neither young woman had spoken for long minutes and I was considering asking Hayes to order another bottle of Merlot, he suddenly roused himself from the contemplation of his wineglass and said, "You'll have to go and see Caro's paintings sometime, Sally, you being in the art game yourself. She's really good. She shows all over the place: Charleston, the island, you name it."

Sally Bowdon-Kirkland turned her fine mare's face to me.

"You paint?" she said, as if she thought I might perhaps have an example of my work with me, and she would be required to examine it.

"A little. Nothing special. It was my major at school. Tell me about your museum work; I've been meaning to ask you. Are you a docent?"

"Actually, I own the museum," she said, smiling a little for the first time and revealing long teeth. I felt as if I should offer her a sugar cube.

"Well, goodness . . ."

"It's a very small museum, really. We show mainly American minimalists who worked after 1980. I'm hoping to make it one of the tops in its field, though; and I'm having some luck with acquisitions. Or rather . . . I did have. I turned it over to my cousin when we . . . knew we were coming here."

I thought, not for the first time, how hard the life of a Plantation corporate wife is. They are not permitted by policy to work for the company, and the families are required by policy to live where the husbands work. That limits career opportunities to primarily resort areas. There is not a real estate position left in the Lowcountry, I don't think. Commuting to Charleston is almost out of the question, in drive time. Some of the young marriages do not survive it; some wives with esoteric degrees and formidable skills find that, after all, they cannot live in such air. Those who do not leave adjust, I suppose, make their separate peaces, but it seems to me that there is a good bit of drinking around the club pool in the afternoons. I know that human resources is kept busy with references for counselors, of one sort or another. There is a list of them posted in the corporate office, alongside the baby-sitters.

"Well, it's no substitute, but some of our

galleries are really good, and there are about a million museums in Charleston proper. I should think any of them would carpet your path with palm branches, if you'd like to keep busy," I said.

It was not the right thing to say.

"Keeping busy is really not my first priority," she said. "Finding a new American idiom to nurture is. My family has been instrumental in that for a long time. A distant kinswoman of ours founded one of the great American museums. It's in Boston. The Gardner. Perhaps you know it."

"Yes," I said. "I know it."

I did not think that Sally Bowdon-Kirkland would be one of the ones who made a separate peace. Looking at Peter Kirkland, oblivious, as he had been all evening, to anyone but Clay, I wondered if he would notice.

A moment later Barbara Costigan suddenly jumped to her feet, clutching her napkin to her chest, and fled, knocking over her water glass. We watched, open-mouthed, as she floundered around the corner toward the ladies' room.

"Oh, no," Buddy said. "I'm sorry, folks. She's . . . it's been hard on her, leaving the baby. I think she's got all kinds of hormonal things going on . . ."

I looked over at Sally Bowdon-Kirkland. She was studying her newly arrived crème brûlée judiciously. She looked up at me.

"Do you think you ought to . . . ?" I began. She lifted her shoulders.

"We just met this evening. I'm sure she'd rather have you," she said.

I got up and went into the ladies' room. It seemed empty, but I could hear alternating sobbing and flushing coming from one of the stalls.

"Honey, it's Caro Venable," I said. "Please don't cry. Come on out and let's talk about it. There's nothing so bad that we can't fix it, I promise. . . ."

She sobbed steadily for a time, but gradually she stopped. There was another flush and then she came out, rubbing her eyes like a child and scrubbing at the front of her dress. It was stained almost to her chubby waist.

"I'm so sorry," she whispered. "They leak; almost every time it's time to feed the baby, they leak awfully, even though she's not here, and I . . . I thought I had enough Kleenex in there but I don't . . ."

I looked at her in the harsh fluorescent light and felt an actual pain in my heart. I also felt a sharp, cold pang of anger at her husband and Clay and the company. Poor, bereft, sodden, frightened little soul.

"I remember that," I said. "It's awful, isn't it? But it stops. Before you know it it will have stopped, and then you'll have your baby with you and everything will be better. This is a hard time. I know it is. Come on, let's get your face washed and some fresh lipstick on you, and I'll just drape my cardigan around you . . . like this . . . and nobody will ever know. We'll say you spilled your wine."

"She'll know." Barbara Costigan hiccupped. "She'll know I was sitting there leaking like a cow and crying like a fool. You can just bet she's never leaked anything in her life, or even cried . . ."

I knew that she meant Sally Bowdon-Kirkland, and did something I virtually never do. I ridiculed one corporate wife to another. I did not feel one iota of guilt about it, either.

"If she leaked anything, it would be ice water," I said. "Come on. You won't have to see much of her at all, once this night is over. Being friends with every woman down here is not in the company policy manual. You'll find your own, and so will your little girl. I did."

She managed a watery smile, and we got her fairly presentable again, swathed in my scarlet cashmere sweater, and went back to the table. Clay was holding up his hand for the check. All of a sudden I did not think I could bear the drive back to Peacock's Island in the company of this forlorn child and her little Prussian husband. I simply could not bear it. Riding with the Bowdon-Kirklands seemed even worse.

"I think I'll stay over at the town house," I said casually, not meeting Clay's eyes. "There are some things for the garden I want to pick up in the morning, and I want to bring the summer linens back with me and pack them in mothballs. Clay, you can get everybody in the Jaguar, can't you?"

He looked at me. I knew that he thought I was going to go back to the town house and drink alone. Or perhaps stay and drink wine with Hayes Howland; I did not know which he would think more unseemly. I realized, too, that I was on my way to being quite drunk. There was a shimmery distance in the air around me, and though I did not and hardly ever do stagger, still, I was walking carefully in my unaccustomed high heels and talking very properly. Poor Clay. Twice now tonight I had broken our bargain. If we talked about it, I could have told him that I did not want to drink, did not even feel like it. I simply did not want to be with these aw-ful, doomed children anymore. I did not want to be with anyone.

But we do not talk about it, and I did not tell him.

"Suit yourself," he said neutrally. "Be careful of your car, though. Lot of traffic tonight."

I knew that he realized that I was not sober. For some reason, that made me angry.

"I'll drive her back to the town house and walk on home," Hayes said. "The air will do me good."

We stood on the cobbles outside Carolina's, Hayes and I, and watched Clay drive away in the Jaguar with the two captive couples. No one spoke for a moment and then Hayes said, "You want to go back in and have a nightcap? That was pretty awful."

"No, I really don't. Thanks, though," I said wearily. "I think I'll just go on back to the house and turn in. You're right. It was awful. I feel very bad about it. I really didn't do much to keep things going."

"Wasn't your fault," Hayes said. "You tried. We both did. There wasn't any way those two were going to let you draw them out. You were doomed before the night even started."

"Why?" I said, surprised.

"Christ, Caro, look at them," he said.

"And look at you. One of them looks like a fat little brewer's wife in a too-tight Sunday dress and the other one looks like Seabiscuit, and there you sit looking like . . . I don't know, a Persian princess or something in that red silk, with all that black hair down your back, and you twenty years older at least than either one of them, and a million times richer . . . What do you think?"

"I never thought about it that way, Hayes," I said honestly. "I really never did."

"Well, it's true. You're something special, Caro. Time you knew that, if you don't already. Clay ought to tell you."

"Well . . . thank you," I said.

The car came, and we got in and drove the short distance to the town house in silence.

"Would you give me a nightcap if I came in for a minute?" he said, not looking at me.

What is this? I thought. This is Hayes. I don't know what this means.

"Lucy would kill me," I said lightly, and then, "And I'm really tired. Why don't we make it one night soon when Clay and Lucy can join us?"

"You got it," he said affably, and saw me to the door. I shut it behind me, but then I went to the front bay window and watched as he walked away down Eliott Street toward Bedon's Alley, where he would cut over to

136

Church Street and home. In the light of the corner streetlight he stopped and looked back at the window, and I stepped back involuntarily, as if he could see me. But, of course, he could not.

For an instant, it was as if I had never seen him, was seeing him now for the first time. Only then did I realize that, whenever I looked at Hayes Howland, I had been seeing the young man who had been Clay's friend when I first met him, the irrepressible roommate from the University of Virginia, broad of shoulder and flaming red of hair, freckled of snub face and irreverent of tongue, a kind of sprite, an elf, an Ariel of sorts.

But now I saw that Hayes was middle-aged. It was funny; I did not see that in Clay, nor really, even, in myself, when I looked into my mirror. But it was true of Hayes Howland. He seemed older by far than any of us, older than he should by rights be. I saw that the broad shoulders were a little stooped now, with the beginning of a roundness to the back, and the red hair dulled and streaked with iron gray and worn away on top so that it was almost like a monk's tonsure. It made his pale face seem longer, and the glossy mustache he cultivated, which made him look, as Clay once said, like he was eating a chipmunk, was thinner and gingery. Even from my window I could see that the freckles on his face had run together in places, and the ones on the top of his head, so that he seemed splotched with darkness here and there. His raincoat had a rip in the lining, and part of it hung down below the hem. That meant nothing; Hayes wore wonderful clothes, but they invariably looked as though he had slept in them. But somehow tonight, the draggled hem and the bleaching lamplight and the rounded shoulders all added up to something else. Hayes looked . . . defeated. Seedy. I thought of Willy Loman.

I went upstairs and undressed and crawled into one of the pretty rice beds in the master bedroom. The sheets smelled a little musty but were smooth and cool. I turned off the bedside lamp and lay in the darkness, thinking about Hayes. The thought came, unbidden and as whole and complete as an egg: What does he get out of all this? What's in it for him?

He had been with Clay now almost since college. Day by day, closer than any brother, he had cast his lot with Clay at the very beginning of the Peacock Island Plantation Company, leaving without apparent regret the job with the Charleston law firm and coming on board as Clay's legal adviser, as-

138

sistant, and general factotum. Hayes did everything. He advised, he traveled for the company, he ran errands, he oversaw personnel, he haunted building sites and construction crews, he sat in on marketing and advertising meetings, he scouted universities and graduate schools for the kind of young man or woman Clay wanted, those with the invisible but unmistakable stamp of the company upon them. Most of all he was Clay's link to the Lowcountry. There was not an old family or a cache of old money from Litchfield to Savannah that Hayes did not know, or his family did not. Hayes brought Charleston to Clay. In turn, Clay took Hayes with him on his trajectory straight into the sun.

And yet . . . and yet. Somehow it did not seem that Hayes was a terribly successful man, much less a contented one. I could not have said precisely what I meant by that. It was just that Hayes had a restlessness, a kind of chronic discontent that his general affability and foolishness sometimes did not hide. He was court jester and confidant, but sometimes he was moody and bitter, too, and then Clay wisely let him alone. The moods rarely lasted more than a day, but they were real.

For one thing, I don't think Hayes and

Lucy ever had quite enough money. He had married Lucy Burton the year after Clay and I had married; they had known each other since infancy, and were out of the same tiny, dense gene pool. Lucy's parents, like Hayes's, were an old Lowcountry family, though, as Hayes himself said cheerfully, poor as a cracker's pisspot. Hayes did not marry money, but he did marry Charleston, and that, from what I could see, was what always mattered to him.

But I thought now that it must have been a struggle at times for them. Hayes was officially listed as number two man in the company after Clay, but he had no financial interest in it, for all the joint venture money he sniffed out for Clay, and I knew that his salary, while better than any other in the company, even the one Clay allowed himself, was not spectacular. Clay puts most of the Plantation's money back into the company. Hayes and Lucy must have stretched his salary very thin to maintain her family's beautiful old Federal house on Church Street and give the parties that they did, and educate two daughters in the bargain, much less keep them in Laura Ashleys. I could not think there was much at all left over.

Once, I remembered, I asked Clay when he was going to give Hayes some sort of property of his own, a partnership or something.

"I guess when the right one comes along," he said. "Though if you think about it, can you imagine Hayes running one of the Plantations?"

"Why not?" I said.

"Well, for one thing, it would probably mean leaving the Lowcountry, and he'd let you cut his throat before he'd do that. And then, frankly, I think he gets off on being my sidekick. Who else thinks he's as funny as I do? Who else would let him fool around and goof off as much as I do? Hayes is a born second banana, and I think on some level he knows it. He's never asked me to let him have a crack at anything else."

I thought about that conversation now, as the night stilled and quieted outside my drawn curtains. Something was missing; something did not equate. Hayes was more than he seemed, had to be more . . .

But the thought eddied away on the spiral of thick wine-sleep that took me under, and when I woke, only short hours later, with a cottony mouth and the beginning of a dull headache, it was gone from my mind. I sat up abruptly, as if summoned by an alarm clock, slid out of bed, splashed my face and scrubbed my teeth, ferreted out some old jeans and a sweatshirt of Clay's from the bureau, and was in the Cherokee and on the road south within an hour.

By the time dawn broke, red as the apocalypse to the east, I was on the bridge from Peacock's over to the island, and by the time the sun touched the tops of the live oaks that leaned over the marsh house, I was fast asleep again in the small iron bed that had been my first in the Lowcountry.

4

The five rules of sleep according to Kylie Venable:

1. Don't draw the curtains. God can't look after you if He can't see you.
2. Face the door. You need to be able to see what's coming.
3. Pull your knees up to your chin. It'll get your feet first that way.
4. Keep your ears covered up. You won't hear it calling you.
5. Never let your hands hang over the side of the bed. There's no telling what might take hold of them.

She made those rules for herself when she was about five, after a series of screaming nightmares that dragged us out of sleep night after night, hearts hammering. We wrote them down for her and pinned them on her bulletin board. If she followed them scrupulously, she dropped right off to sleep. If she omitted one, or fell asleep before she could complete her ritual, she would have the dreams. We were never sure why it worked. A child psychologist who was visiting on the island later told us that it was the instructive power of ritual, and that Kylie had, in effect, healed herself.

"But should we just let it go?" I said. "I don't want her getting the feeling that there's nothing between her and danger but some kind of magic ritual she thinks up. On the other hand, I don't want her to think she can prevent all kinds of harm just by doing the same thing."

"If it ain't broke, don't fix it," the shrink said. "It was about time for the nightmares, and it's about time for them to go away. Kylie has a good sense of her own needs, I'd say."

And she did. The nightmares faded, and she was never so afraid of anything incorporeal again. Or if she was, I never knew it. And I think I would have. But all of her life, she put herself to sleep at night by following her Five Rules of Sleep, and I often do it, too, to this day. It does help. I don't know why, but it does.

On this morning, I lay still in the tiny room that had always been mine, that looked out through a great, twisted, moss-shawled live oak to the marsh proper and the creek, and for a moment I did not open my eyes. I knew that it must be late morning or even early afternoon, for I had the cleansed, heavy-wristed feeling that you get when you have finally had enough sleep, but there was no sense of the strong overhead sunlight that should have fallen on my lids. I opened my eyes and looked out my uncurtained window into a solid wall of white. Fog. The dawn conflagration had told it truly: red sky at morning, sailors take warning. It was odd, though. We usually get those heavy, solid, still fogs in winter and very early spring.

I rolled over and stretched luxuriously, feeling each separate vertebra pop, feeling the long muscles in my legs pull. I lay still, smelling the peculiar island smell of damp old percale and salt mud, listening. But I heard nothing; not the songs of the migratory birds who often lingered on their way farther south; not the busy daytime rustle of the small communal wildlife in the spartina and sweet grass; not the faraway tolling of the bell buoy off the tip of Edisto; not the low throb of engines on the inland waterway. Nothing. The fog had swallowed sound as it had sight. I knew if any noise did penetrate, it would sound queer and displaced, without resonance. Fog bounces sound about like a ventriloquist.

I knew that I would take no photographs

145

until it lifted, and toyed with the idea of simply burrowing back into the old piled, limp pillows and going back to sleep. But I did not need sleep; I needed to be out on the island, to let it slip its green fingers into my mind and draw out the sad silliness of the night before. Watercolors. That was what this day called for. Watercolors of the intimate, ghostly body parts of the island as they emerged from the whiteness and were swallowed again: a live oak arm with its sleeve of fog-covered moss, a cypress knee, the bones of the dock, the red hull of my grandfather's canoe, bumping against the rubber tire fender. I thought of John Marin and his watercolor *Maine Islands*, so much more powerful and evocative for what it hid in the fog than what it showed. Yes. A day for vignettes and glimpses.

I got up and showered in the rusted stall in the bathroom, letting the brackish, sulfur-kissed water sluice every knob and crevice of my body. I was, I thought, one of the few people on earth who liked the paper-mill stink of the island's water. I kept big drums of spring water at the house, both for drinking and cooking and for washing my hair, as I knew Clay hated the smell of it after I washed it in island water. Like a chemistry experiment gone wrong, he said. But I liked it. Today I would be totally a creature of the island; I would smell of it and taste of it, as well as see and touch and hear it.

I put the jeans and sweatshirt back on and made coffee and found a rock-hard bagel and zapped it in the microwave, then took my breakfast to the table before the long windows that faced the creek. I ate staring into the shifting wall of the fog. After breakfast I rooted out my watercolor block and the tin box of colors, filled a plastic two-liter cola bottle with water, and started out the sliding door onto the deck. Silence and wetness smacked me in the face. I stopped and closed my eyes and breathed it deeply into my lungs.

I heard the hoofbeats while I stood, eyes still closed. It did not frighten me; I knew that it was the ponies. They had undoubtedly seen my lights and smelled my bagel, and were hoping for a handout. The Park Service maintained them nominally, but the Gullahs in Dayclear fed them biscuits and corn bread and whatever they had at hand, and so had my grandfather, adding grain in the winters, and the ponies had grown particular. I heard the stamping of hooves and an occasional snort and whicker, and I knew they would be grouped about the bottom of the steps up to the deck, waiting to see whether they would dine or would be forced to bolt. No one on the island mistreated or shooed them, that I was aware of, but sometimes they made a great, eye-rolling, hysterical show of fright and persecution, and went lumbering off in a pod as if ringmasters with chains were after them. There seemed to be no pattern to it. My grandfather always said, when they spooked and scattered like that, that they were simply bored, but Clay maintains that their brains are somehow smaller than those of normal horses, or that their synapses do not meet, or some such arcane genetic glitchiness. He does not care for the ponies. They trample grass and gardens and keep the shallow banks of the creek slick and muddy. And they leave their excrement everywhere.

I inched my way down the steps, talking softly all the while so that they would know I was there. I finally saw them when I had almost reached the bottom step. A small puff of breeze, the little wind off the mainland that usually comes up in the afternoon, blew aside the curtain of fog, and there they stood, perhaps seven of them in a loose knot, staring patiently at the steps where they knew I would materialize.

I do not know what they looked like originally, but they mostly look alike now, distinguishing characteristics blunted and buffed away by generations of inbreeding and the years in the subtropical wild. Now they are almost all a kind of taupish dun color, shaggy of coat and tangled of mane, with fat, hanging bellies from the rich marsh grass and the largesse of the islanders, and splayed, untrimmed hooves. Their coats are caked with the dust of their mud wallows in hot weather, when the slick odorous black mire is an effective fly and mosquito deterrent, and long and tattered like beggars' coats in winter. Their heads are large in proportion to their stumpy legs, and there is usually some sort of rheumy effluvia stuck in the corners of their large, feminine brown eyes. They have long eyelashes, ridiculously like cocottes in a French farce, and pretty, curly mouths like a fairytale illustration of an Arabian stallion. They are a very long way from being handsome creatures, but there is a kind of tough, cocky competence to them, a chunky briskness, that pleases the eye. They have attitude. For some reason, the sight of them always makes me smile. When the group shifted and I saw emerging from its middle the little goblin shape of a colt, I laughed aloud. I had not seen a baby in the herd since I myself was small.

One of the adults ambled out of the herd

and stretched a stubby neck out toward my hand, and I opened it so that the sugar cube was visible. Long yellow piano-key teeth closed over the sugar and raked it none too daintily into a black-lipped mouth. Pianissimo. Nissy. And then the colt came scampering out, too, and bobbed its head against her flank and looked around her shoulder at me with huge, black-lashed eyes, and I both heard and felt my breath come out in a little puff of wonder and delight.

"Oh, Nissy, you have a baby," I breathed. "How pretty he . . . she? . . . is. What shall we call it? Oh, wouldn't Kylie love this, though!"

I fished in my pocket for more sugar and Nissy came closer and so did the colt, stretching its miniature neck out like its mother, ever so slowly, its head actually trembling with shyness and curiosity, and finally, delicately, it took the cube from my palm and crunched it, then wheeled and galloped away on its long, still-slender legs. Nissy swung her big head around to watch it, but she did not follow. The colt disappeared back into the body of the expectant herd. I threw a handful of cubes down on the ground and stepped back. Solemnly, not jostling and pushing as dogs or children would have done, the marsh tackies lipped up the sugar cubes, crunched them reflectively, waited awhile until no more were forthcoming, and then, as if one of them had given a signal, wheeled and scampered clumsily away in one of their mock-panic attacks, snorting and whickering. The fog swallowed them almost immediately, and in another moment swallowed the sound of them. I was left standing on the bottom step surrounded by swirling white, with nothing for company but the memory of them and another memory that bobbed to the surface of my mind like a cork, bobbled there tantalizingly for a moment, and then lay still and whole in my head.

Another day of such fog, long ago, almost the only time I remembered a fog like this one, for we did not come to the island so often in winter. There was too much going on on Peacock's for the children then. But for some reason we were here, Kylie and I, in a chilly, silent white fog like this one, she perhaps five or six, still tiny in her yellow slicker, waiting for my grandfather to finish whatever he was doing in his bedroom and come and take us crabbing over on Wassimaw Creek. I would not have taken the boat out in such weather, but he knew every inch of all the island's waterways by heart, and knew that almost no one else would have a boat out. It was, he had said the night before, a fine day for crabbing. So we waited, and Kylie chafed. I usually let her run free on the island, but not in fog like this.

Kylie had no fear. You needed a little, sometimes.

The phone rang, and I went into the kitchen to answer it and talked for quite a while to Clay, who was leaving on a trip to New York and could not find his cuff links. When I hung up, Kylie was gone.

My grandfather came out then, and together we went out into the white nothingness, groping our way down the steps and across the grass to the edge of the marsh, which dropped a half-foot or so down from the hummock on which the grove and the house sat. Scarcely six inches, but the difference in terrain was dramatic. On the high ground, the earth was firm and level. On the marsh, it was ephemeral, trembling, not quite solid underfoot. Not precisely watery, or outright bog, but . . . not solid. When you could not see, as we could not on this day, the feeling was eerie, unsettling, as if you stayed on the surface of the earth only by its capricious sufferance. We called and called for her, hearing our voices stop short against a wall of fog, hearing nothing in return but the dripping from the old live oaks and the slap of the creek against the distant pilings of the dock. For the first five minutes or so I was very angry with her. On the sixth the fear came. By the time we had groped our way to the edge of the hundred-foot plank walkway that wound across the marsh to the creek, I was weak-kneed and nearly sobbing with fear.

"She can't have gotten far," my grandfather said over and over. "She can't be in any real trouble. If she'd fallen or something, we'd hear it."

"You can't hear anything in this fog," I quavered. "You can't even hear the fog buoy. . . ."

"You'd hear if she fell into the water," he said sensibly. It did no good at all. I was halfway down the walkway when we did hear a noise. I stopped. It was the muffled thundering of the ponies coming up over the hummock from the opposite direction, behind the house on the high ground. Above it I could hear Kylie's laughter. In the distorting fog, it seemed to come from everywhere around us and from far away, from nearby and nowhere.

I was back on solid grass by the time the ponies materialized out of the mist, running hard. One of them was a good half-head in the lead. It was Pianissimo, and Kylie was on her back, bent low over the thick neck, hands woven into the straggly mane, clinging like a yellow-clad monkey. Kylie, laughing as hard and joyously as I have ever heard her laugh in her life.

While I stood there, speechless with relief and anger, the pony set her stumpy legs and stopped abruptly, and Kylie half slid, half fell off her back, still laughing. By the time I reached her, Pianissimo had lumbered away, back into the fog with the other ponies. I could hear them as they trotted along the line of the hummock toward the distant maritime forest that often sheltered them, but I could no longer see them.

Kylie was properly chastened when my grandfather and I finished with her, but she was not repentant. She had, she said, seen the herd off at the edge of the copse while I talked on the phone and went to give them sugar, and they were so friendly, especially Pianissimo, that she just wanted to see if she could ride. Nissy, she said, had stood like a statue while she climbed onto her back, but then had taken off as if she had heard a shot.

"I rode her all the way down the old deer path, Mama," she said. "She can run like the wind, for a fat little old pony. It was . . . it was neat. Just me and her and the fog . . .

154

and you could hear the others behind us. It was like we were leading them on a charge."

"Didn't you hear us calling you?" I said.

"Yeah," she admitted. "I did."

"Kylie, you know you have to come when I call you. That's not negotiable. You agreed to that. How can I let you out of my sight if you don't keep your word about that?"

"I was, Mama," she said. "I was coming faster this way than if I was on my own two legs. Lots faster."

She was right, technically, but I was not prepared to argue the point. I cut our visit short and we forwent the crabbing expedition and went back home to Peacock's. She was disappointed, but she did not whine or cry. If Kylie deliberately disobeyed me, or did something she knew I would not have permitted, she took the consequences without a murmur. She simply fell in love with an idea, weighed the pleasure against the cost, did the deed with relish, and paid the price uncomplainingly. It was a very adult way to live a young life, all told. Except that the final price had been more than she could have imagined. More than I could have, too.

I stood still on this morning, in the fog, thinking of that day, hearing again the thudding of the hooves of the herd, seeing again the flash of my daughter's yellow slicker in the cottony nothingness. Fog and ponies and Kylie . . .

Before I went out with my watercolors I called Clay at his office. Shawna, the office's forty-year-old receptionist who has never married and thinks that she is married to Clay, said that he was out of the office until after lunch. She did not know where he had gone, but she had an idea it was into Charleston.

"I hope he's seeing a doctor finally, Mrs. Venable," she said in the honeyed twang that puts my teeth on edge. Shawna is originally from New Jersey. The Lowcountry got her about the same time Clay did. She sounds as if she is chewing cape jessamine.

"What on earth for?" I said, surprised and faintly alarmed.

She was silent a moment, and then she said, "Well, nothing, really, I guess. It's just that none of us think he's been himself lately. You know, he's just so distracted, and abrupt, and it's as though he doesn't really see you when you talk to him . . . We just thought he ought to get a checkup. But of course if you haven't noticed anything, then there's nothing . . ." She let her voice trail off. My own blindness and neglect were implicit in the dying syllables.

"I think he's just fine, Shawna," I said

briskly. "But thank you for worrying about him. If there's anything amiss, I'm sure he'll let us know. We had a pretty late night last night, with the new people coming in and all. . . ."

"Of course," she said. "He's just tired. I keep telling him he ought to let somebody else take over those dinner things for the new people, but you know how he is. . . ."

"Yes, I do," I said, and thanked her and hung up smartly.

Did I, though? Had Clay really been all those things — distant, abstracted, tired, unseeing — and I had not noticed? I thought back. He had been working very late in his home office for the past month or so, but he frequently did that when there was a new project in the wings. And he had been silent and gone away behind his *Wall Street Journal* or his clipboard in the mornings at breakfast, and to some extent at dinner, but when wasn't he? Clay was not gregarious, not loquacious, not a mealtime gossip. He never had been, especially not since the Plantation companies had taken off like they had in the past four or five years, with new properties coming on line in half a dozen states and the Caribbean. Not since Kylie.

Both of us had been, to some extent, gone away since then. I had been content to have it so. I could not have borne the weight of a hovering, demanding relationship in those first few precarious months and years. I did not think he could have, either. It was as if we had had an agreement: when the time is right, when the healing is further along, we will come all the way back to each other. We will know when. There is no hurry.

But there had been no agreement. I had just assumed he felt as I did. I shook my head and went on out into the day. I would call again after lunch, and tonight at dinner we would talk about it. Finally, we would talk. I could not abide the thought that he was unhappy and alone with it.

The fog lifted about noon, and the sun fell so heavily on the windless marsh and creek that I was soon hot and sweat-slicked, and shucked my jacket and tied it around my waist. With the fog gone, my morning's pursuit of fog-sculpted vignettes vanished, too, and the glare off the water began to give me a headache. I trudged back to the house and put on a T-shirt, exchanged the watercolors for my camera, made myself a peanut butter sandwich, and took everything out to the Boston Whaler that bobbed at the dock. We had not yet put it away for the winter; there had been no real winter on the island, and there probably would be none. I could remember days in January and February out on the water, with the sun burning face and forearms and only a chill edge to the wind to remind you that the soft Lowcountry winter had teeth and could bare them if it chose. But it rarely did. Only occasionally did we get a slicking of sleet or ice, and only once in my lifetime did snow fall on Peacock's and the island. But it had been a spectacular snow, drifting up to eight or nine inches and lingering for three or four days. Snow on palms and Spanish moss . . . everyone had taken photos of it, to send to family and friends off-island.

I took the boat down Alligator Alley to Wassimaw Creek and over to the inland waterway, to photograph the steel winter light there. But the sky was too milky for much contrast, and there was a softening in the distance that spoke of returning fog. So I cut the motor and threw out the little anchor and let the Whaler drift. I ate my sandwich and drank the Diet Coke I had brought along, and then I stretched out on the backseat and pulled the Atlanta Braves cap that belonged to everyone and no one over my eyes and drowsed. There must have been virtually no traffic on the waterway; I saw none, and heard none, for the entire time that I was there. But for much of that time I was fast asleep, and when I woke, the fog was just reaching its succubus's fingers out to pat my face, and the heat was gone from the day. A solid white bank lay over the Inland Waterway, and I knew that it would drift up the creeks and estuaries until it swallowed the entire island. I pulled up the anchor and started the engine and putted for home. I was not worried about the fog, but I was cold in just the T-shirt, and I had a neck ache from sleeping with my head tilted forward against the stern. I wanted hot coffee and a shower before I left for Peacock's. More than that, I wanted not to leave for Peacock's at all. The island had done its work while I slept, and I felt washed and lightened and eased. There would undoubtedly be some sort of additional welcome ceremonies for the new people this evening, and I simply did not feel like wasting this beneficence on them.

"Please let them all have previous engagements," I whispered to the whitened sky, though what engagements they might have there among the alien corn I could not imagine. But when I got back to the house the answering machine light was blinking, and I picked it up to hear Clay's voice telling me that he and Hayes had to go to Atlanta on the spur of the moment and that the human resources people were baby-sitting the new-comers tonight.

"So stay another day or so, if you want to," he said. "I don't know how long we'll be. There are some money people who made some time for us earlier than we thought. I'll call you either there or at home when I know where we're staying and when we'll be back. Or I'll let Shawna know. Take care."

He did not say, "I love you," as he some-times did. He was using his flat, intense, strictly business voice. He did not use it for endearments. I would not have had it so. I thought that the money people must be pretty important. My heart lifted. I could stay on the island. Clay would not miss me in this mood.

I had my shower and built a fire and put on a tape of Erroll Garner's *Concert by the Sea*. It was an old recording; it had been my grandfather's. Oddly, he had loved the cool, improvisational West Coast jazz of the late fifties and sixties, and I had transferred a lot of his old records to tape for him. I loved this one, too. Perfect fog music. I made a pot of coffee and rooted around in the bookcase among the yellowing, damp-warped books and magazines for something I had not read recently. I settled on *Kon-Tiki*, another fa-vorite of my grandfather's, and curled up on

161

the spavined sofa to lose myself at sea.

An hour or so must have passed when I heard the ponies again. The fog-flattened sound of their hooves pulled me back from the wastes of the Pacific, and I shook my head for a moment, not quite knowing where I was. Then I smiled and got up and went out onto the deck to see if I could spot Pianissimo and her colt again.

The fog was blowing, spinning fast in the circle of yellow light from the overhead porch light. A brisk wind from off the ocean meant that it would be clear later tonight, and there would be a sky pricked full of icy stars. In the swirling skeins I caught glimpses of the herd, moving restlessly around the support posts of the house. It was not full dark, but it would be in fifteen or twenty more minutes.

I went back for sugar cubes and then walked slowly down the steps, clicking my tongue.

"You here, Nissy?" I called softly. "Want some sugar? Come on, bring that baby up here and let's have a look at him. Or her."

A dark shape came out of the fog: Nissy, sure enough, with the colt close on her flank. I stretched out my hand with the sugar cube, and that's when I saw the child.

She stood off at the edge of the pale orb of

porch light, perhaps thirty feet away, still as a statue, staring at me. Her head and shoulders were fairly distinct, but from her waist down she was lost in fog. I got the impression of a small brown face and great dark eyes that fastened intently on me, and a headful of dark curls with fog droplets clinging to them. She wore a yellow rain slicker. She looked to be about five or six, maybe seven. A small seven. She made no noise at all, and she did not move.

I did not, either. I could not have. My heart began to thunder, pounding so hard that I could hear only it and my blood, roaring in my ears. If she had spoken, I could not have heard her. But she did not speak. My knees and thighs and wrists turned to water. It seemed to me that only the powerful heartbeat held me up, that I hung from it like a marionette.

Nissy whickered and stamped her hoof, and I held out my hand toward the child as slowly as if to a wild creature.

"Who are you?" I meant to say.

"Is it you?" came out of my mouth, a crippled whisper.

The child turned and bolted. The fog took her before she had gone four paces. I could hear her footsteps for a bit before they were lost in the cottony whiteness. I thought she ran back around the house and toward the dirt road leading into the hummock where the house stood.

I could not make my legs go after her. In the space of a minute, I was not sure she had been there at all. I felt sweat break out in huge, cold drops on my forehead and at my hairline, and sat down heavily on the bottom step. I sat there until the ponies moved away, and then there was nothing but fog and silence and the yellow pool of light from the porch. And still I sat there.

Presently I got up and went up the steps, as stiffly as if I were very old or had been badly beaten, and into the house. I went to the closet where the cleaning supplies were kept. From behind a cardboard grocery carton of toilet paper I took a bottle of Wild Turkey. There were three of them there; they had been there since my grandfather died. I would not have thought I even remembered them. But my fingers did, and my blood. I took the bottle and a glass and sat back down before the dying fire and began to drink. I drank, not moving from the couch, until I passed out. It was not the first time that had happened, but it had not happened many times, and never in this place. One of the last things I remember thinking was, I've broken all my covenants now.

The first waking moments of a bad hangover are a time when all things are possible.
Reality is canceled; it does not yet prevail.
There is only, for the first instant, a purity of
being, an utter, bodiless awareness. The
body will get its licks in almost instantly, of
course: the dry, knife-edged throat and lips,
the pounding sinuses, the first roilings of the
abused and mutinous stomach. Hard on
their heels will come the sickly, slithering
feet of the great shame and fragmented
memories of the night before, sliding in like
dirty water under a shut door.

But that first moment: that is pure Zen.
Nothing is closed to you. Nothing is past and
nothing is ahead; everything is now.

When I woke on the sofa in front of the
dead fire the next morning, there was only
me and the child I had seen the night before.
That was the great, ultimate reality of my life
in this moment. It remained only to decide
what to do about it.

I lay without moving, eyes still closed, letting sensation seep in bit by bit under the
great, white knowledge that enclosed me:
stiff, cold limbs, pounding head, killing
thirst, a great pressure on my bladder, a
great pressure waiting to crush my soul. I
pushed them all back; they could and would

wait. Until I opened my eyes, until I moved, the child from last night was the one real thing, the one true thing, in my universe.

I remember clearly thinking: Madness is waiting for me. I can choose it or not. If I choose the child, I choose the madness. If I don't, I can have my life back like it was. I don't have to decide until I open my eyes. But I will have to decide then.

I lay still, eyes closed, not moving, reaching out to her with my mind and my heart and all of my being. I heard the morning wind start up in the live oak that hung over the deck and the first grumpy twitter of the anonymous little songbirds that lived there. A part of my mind noted that it must be very early. The light felt pearly on my lids. Everything in me called to her. I did not move.

I heard the ponies then. They came chuffing and trotting over the hummock from behind the house; I could hear them clearly. Their hooves had depth and resonance. I knew that the fog had gone. I waited.

And I heard her. I heard her small feet thudding after the ponies, coming closer, coming from the east, the direction of the road. I heard her laugh. It was a giggle: silvery, delighted, unafraid. And I heard her voice. It was the pure, generic piping of childhood: it could have belonged to any child.

Any child at all.

"Here, baby," she called.

Choose, my heart said, and I chose. I opened my eyes. I got up and ran lightly across the floor and out onto the deck, tip-toeing, heart bursting, lips curving in a smile that was only a remembered shape on my mouth. If this was madness, I thought, then I embrace it, now and forever. Oh, if this is madness, let it never lift. . . .

I started down the steps and stopped. She was there, looking up at me as she had last night, still wearing the yellow slicker. She did not move.

She was not my child. She was no one's child I had ever seen. In the clear, opalescent light of early morning a stranger's child stood there, poised for flight, dark eyes wary but not frightened, feet and legs bare under the too-big slicker, taking my measure as handily as she took my heart and turned it to frozen lead. She did not speak again. From behind the house, I heard the ponies begin to move back toward the road.

A man came around the side of the house then. He was not tall, but he was stocky and heavy-shouldered, tanned almost black and with a great bush of wiry, gray-streaked black hair. He stopped and looked at me; his eyes were hers, the child's.

"I'm sorry, I didn't know anybody was here," he said. "My granddaughter was chasing the ponies and got away from me. I hope we didn't scare you."

I simply looked at him. It seemed to me, in that dead moment, that no one and nothing would ever scare me again.

5

I sat down abruptly on the steps and looked at him. My legs and arms and, when I looked down, my hands, were trembling, a shivering so fine that it was hardly visible, but profound for all that. I was as weak as if I had been ill for a long time. It struck me that I had spent a lot of time, all told, sitting on these steps. The thought might have made me smile another time. I could not have smiled now, with my trembling lips and numb face. It was all I could do to focus on him.

He came closer, frowning slightly.

"We did scare you. You're shaking all over," he said. His voice was rich and deep, plummy, almost a theatrical voice. There was a note in it that was somehow foreign, though he spoke with no discernible accent. There were deep grooves in the leathery brown face, between his heavy, gray-spiked eyebrows, running from his brown avian beak of a nose to his wide mouth, radiating from the corners of his eyes. A well-used face. His crown of wild hair would have brushed the collar of his blue work shirt if it had fallen straight, but it foamed and frizzed in the heavy fog-humidity into an exuberant afro. It made his head look too large even for the thick torso. I thought distractedly of a portrait of the Minotaur I had seen in a book of Greek legends once. I thought also of an aging hippie. The work shirt was knotted at his waist and exposed a tangle of gray chest hair with a medallion of some sort on a chain buried in it, and there was a flower in the top buttonhole, a drooping camellia. His blue jeans were bleached nearly white and frayed at the hem, and his feet were bare. Unlike the rest of him, they were neat and small.

He was no one I had ever seen and bore little resemblance to anyone who ordinarily came to Peacock's and the island, and it occurred to me that perhaps I should be afraid of him, but I was not. I was sick, depleted, utterly numb, and vaguely angry at him. Or, at least, I knew that I would be angry, when I could feel much of anything. Mainly, I simply wanted him to be gone, him and his intruding granddaughter.

"You didn't scare me," I said dully. "I thought for a minute the little girl was someone else. But you should know that you're on private property. I own this house and land. And I'm not feeling very well, so if you wouldn't mind I really think —"

"I wanted to see the horses," the child said in a clear treble voice. "There is a baby, Grandpapa."

He did not move, but his face went bone white and then flushed a dark red. He drew in a great breath and let it out again on a long sigh. He turned his face to the child, and tears welled in his black eyes, and his face seemed almost to crumple.

"Tell me about the baby, Lita," he said very softly. He was still staring at her; he did not turn to me. I thought at first he must have had some sort of an attack, a stroke or something, but then I could see that he was flooded with strong emotion of some sort, almost to the point of open weeping. I opened my mouth to ask them to leave. Slowly, I shut it again. The thought of this massive, dark man weeping on my doorstep was somehow more than I could bear to even contemplate. I hoped that, if I were still and silent, he would regain his control and go away and take his changeling with him. Then I could sit in the pale lemon sunlight of a Lowcountry autumn and see if there was a way to go on with this day and this life.

The child did not speak again. He turned his head to me finally. His face was relatively composed now, though the tears had overflowed his eyes and ran down his face into the chasms on either side of his mouth.

"She has not spoken in a very long time," he said. "The doctors weren't sure that she ever would again. I hope you'll forgive the sloppy tears. It's a happy moment for me." His face *was* happy, incandescently so, almost foolishly so. It was the face of a large, giddy child, rapt and open. I had seen no faces like this on any man I had met before. Most men learn early to shield the force of their loves from strangers. A tongue of sympathy and interest curled in my heart in the midst of all the aridity, infinitely small and alien.

"She spoke this morning, too, before you came," I said. "I heard her. She said, 'Here, baby.' And last night I heard her. I think maybe those doctors didn't know what they were talking about."

He looked from me to the child. She looked solemnly back at him. She had a strange little face, very brown and sharply triangular, with a small pointed chin and enormous dark eyes. Under the cap of lustrous black curls, it looked almost medieval, the face of a Florentine child on a triptych.

"She was not here last night," he said to me, still looking at her. "She was asleep in our house. I put her to bed myself. You must have heard something else."

"I don't think so," I said, smiling at the child. "It was you last night, wasn't it? With the horses, in the fog?"

She smiled a tiny, formal little smile, but she did not break her silence.

"Were you here last night, Estrellita?" her grandfather asked her, very seriously. "Did you slip away and come looking for the ponies?"

She looked at me, and then down at her bare dirty feet, and then up at him.

"*Sí, Abuelo,*" she whispered.

He did not say anything for a long time, only looked down at her. I saw that he was once again struggling to contain the tears, and turned my face away. I was very tired, and once more wished that they would go, whoever they were. I wanted no part of their epiphanies.

He turned to me then, briskly, and took the child's hand. "We'll be on our way," he said. "We didn't mean to bother you. She thinks the ponies hung the moon, but she's never run away after them before, and she's certainly never spoken of them. I'll see that she stays closer to home from now on."

They turned to go.

"Wait," I said. They turned back.

"Who are you?" I said. "Who is she?

Where do you live? How did you get all the way out here? Why has she not spoken for so long?"

He laughed aloud, a raucous, unfettered sound. Across the copse in the thick pine woods a flock of crows answered him, making almost the same sound. The child laughed, too.

"My name is Lou," he said. "Lou Cassells. This is Estrellita Esteban, my granddaughter. We're living at the moment over in Dayclear, up at the other end of the island. I'm working around there, and she's spending the summer with me. She has not spoken since her mama died three years ago. That was back in Cuba, where our family comes from. Her mama died in their house in the mountains, in childbirth. There was no one with her but Estrellita. The new baby was born dead, and Estrellita's mother died after two days. Lita was still at their side when they found her. It was almost too late; she was badly dehydrated, and she had not had food for days. She did not speak after that until . . . now. That we know of, anyway."

"My God," I whispered. It was literally incomprehensible to me that there was still a place in the world, especially so close to my world, where women and babies died alone in childbirth and small children starved be-

174

side them, waiting for help that did not come. How could this be? An old pain, sharp and terrible, that I thought I had buried forever, tore at my heart. I put out my hand jerkily, as if it moved by itself, and touched the black curls, then dropped it at my side.

"How did that happen?" I said softly and fiercely. "How in the world could you let that happen?"

His face closed. It looked like a Toltec mask, severe and blunt and empty.

"Her father was dead. Her mother stayed on at the farm in the mountains because the baby was so nearly due; she could not travel. There were no close neighbors. Everyone had gone. It is very poor back in those mountains. Most of Cuba is very poor. I could not prevent it. I have not been back to Cuba in almost forty years. I cannot go back. I would be arrested."

"I'm sorry," I said miserably. "I spoke out of turn. It must have been awful for you. Was her father your son?"

"Her mother was my daughter."

We were both silent then. I looked at him across a sea of troubles that for once were not my own. It looked uncrossable. I was ashamed.

"Please come into the house and have some coffee with me," I said. "And I think there's a jelly doughnut in the freezer. Maybe by that time the ponies will come back and we can see the baby."

I smiled at the child and she smiled back, a fuller smile this time.

"Her mother's name is Pianissimo," I said. "My daughter named her when she was about your age. It's because she has big yellow teeth like a piano."

The child laughed aloud, a liquid gurgle of pleasure, and her grandfather smiled. I did, too, surprising myself.

"If she comes back maybe you can help me think of a name for her baby," I said. "Meanwhile, let me show you my house. I used to come here to the island to visit my grandfather, too, and this is where he lived. My name is Caroline Venable, but you can call me Caro."

The little girl made the shape of my name with her lips, but silently, "Caro." The man stopped and stared at me, and then laughed again, with surprise and, I thought, pleasure. This was a man, obviously, to whom laughter and tears and who knew what else came naturally and were not reined in.

"Mrs. Venable," he said. "I've heard of you, but I thought you'd be . . . older, I guess. I knew we'd meet sooner or later, though. I'm working for your husband."

I stopped and looked back at him, surprised. He was definitely not the sort of man who usually came to the Plantation to work for Clay.

"You work for the company?" I said. "For Clay?"

"Not really," Lou Cassells said. "This is a one-time-only deal, I think. I'm doing some landscape consulting for him. For the project over at Dayclear."

I stared at him.

"It's named for the Gullah settlement up at the other end," he said, mistaking my silence for ignorance. "You know, where the little houses are, and the old people. That's to be the center of it, so that's what your husband is calling it for now. Clay, yes. Privately I call him Mengele. I'm hoping to charm you thoroughly enough so you won't tell him."

Still I did not speak.

"If that was out of line, I apologize," he said, his face changing. "More than one person has told me my tongue is going to get me into bad trouble. Again."

I held up my hand, shaking my head.

"No. I mean, no, I don't mind you calling him Mengele. Well, I do, I just . . . I wasn't aware that there was a property planned for Dayclear. It's way back on the river, in the

177

middle of the marsh . . . Why would anybody want to make a . . . project . . . of it? How could they, if they did?"

He shrugged. "I thought you would know about it. I hope I'm not the bearer of bad news for you. Actually, it will make a beautiful . . . ah, property, as you say. The river is deep and wide and navigable there. Good natural basin for a marina. It would be simple to dredge the rest. I don't know, I only work there. Mengele . . . Clay . . . hired me to do a landscape workup, see what would grow there, what plants to keep, what to take out, what to import. It's my specialty. I have a master's degree in subtropical botany from Cornell. Please don't bad-mouth me to your husband; this is miles above working as a disc jockey in a twenty-megahertz rock 'n' roll station out Wappoo Creek Road. That was my last job."

I turned and went on up the stairs. They followed me. The hangover bell jar of detachment and torpor descended again. I pushed the thought of the development at Dayclear outside it. I would deal with it later; there was, of course, some mistake. This man had his facts wrong. It would be easy for a casual employee to do that. He probably meant that Clay was using the settlement and the land around it as a model for a marsh property he was developing some-where else. The vegetation would be virtu-ally the same. I would straighten this out with Clay when he got back from Atlanta. There was simply no sense borrowing trou-ble. Sufficient unto the day the evil thereof. It was something I had learned, and learned well, in the long days after Kylie died. I was good at it.

I sat them down on the sofa before the fireplace and lit the half-burned logs, and they leaped into life. The fire felt good. With the clearing of the fog had come fresh, sting-ing cold air from the west. I thought that we were done, now, with the last soft, wet traces of the Lowcountry Indian summer.

The child sat quietly while I made coffee, but then her curiosity got the best of her and she got up and began to roam around the house. She picked things up and examined them and set them down again, very gently, looking at me as for permission. Her grand-father said something to her in soft, rapid Spanish and she stopped and clasped her hands behind her, but I said, "No, let her look. There's nothing here she can hurt. It's all childproof. I did the very same thing, and so did my daughter . . ."

He spoke again, and Estrellita went back to her solemn examining. He got up and came into the kitchen, where I was getting mugs down from the rack beside the stove and pouring milk, and leaned against the refrigerator.

"This is a good house," he said. "It feels lived and loved in, and it looks just like it should. It honors the marsh."

I smiled.

"That's a good way of putting it," I said. "I think it does, too. My grandfather would have liked to hear that."

"He's gone then."

"Yes. For several years now. But sometimes it seems to me that he's still here, in this house and in the marsh . . ."

I fell silent, reddening. Now he would think that Mengele's wife was some sort of New Age fruitcake, though why I cared what he thought I could not have said.

"Yes, it's odd, isn't it?" he said. "Odd and good, how our dead stay with us sometimes, if we are very lucky. I often feel my daughter close, though I did not see her after she was very small, smaller even than this one here. I wish I could feel my wife, but she does not come. Ah, well. She never did want to leave Cuba. Why should she leave it now?"

I shot him a swift look. He was smiling gently, as if the memory of his wife was a warm, quiet one.

180

"She's gone, too?" I said.

"She died two years ago, in Havana. She had been raising Lita. One of my Miami relatives was able to arrange to get the child out for me. I don't know what would have happened to her otherwise. I'm very grateful."

He spoke so matter-of-factly of his unimaginable life that it put me at ease. Somehow I thought he had learned to do that so that his American friends, so unused to this sort of tragedy, would not be smitten with guilt and pity. It was a graceful thing to do. I liked him for it.

I handed him a cup of coffee.

"I'm not going to pry into your life, but I wish you'd tell me how you got to the South Carolina Lowcountry. That trip must be some kind of story."

"One day," he said, smiling so that the crinkles fanned out from his eyes. "One day I'll do that. But I want to hear about you now. You already know a lot about me. Turnabout is fair play."

We sat down on the sofa in front of the fire. Lita had gone out onto the deck and was swinging on the low branch of the live oak that curved over it, shawled in silvery Spanish moss. I knew that it was sturdy enough for her slight weight. It had borne mine, and later Carter's, and Kylie's.

"It's awfully tame compared to yours," I said. "I'd bore you to sleep."

I did not want to talk about myself. In fact, now that I had invited them in and settled them down, I wanted, perversely, for them to be gone again. The hangover and the shame and the accompanying uneasy fatigue surged back full bore. I wanted simply to lie down on the sofa and go back to sleep.

He seemed to sense my hesitation.

"Another time we'll meet and swap stories, maybe," he said. "I think you're tired, and you said you weren't feeling well. We need to get back, anyway. I don't think my hosts know where we are."

He started to get up. A thought struck me.

"Wait a minute," I said. "Why do you call him Mengele? Clay?"

He grinned. It was white and wolfish, framed in the dark skin. It was also the grin of a havoc-minded, completely unrepentant small boy, and I had to smile back.

"Well, number one, I'm Jewish, and I have a very well-developed sense of both paranoia and history. When somebody threatens me, I automatically think of Josef Mengele. Number two, those amazing blue eyes. They look at you as though he's wondering what would happen if he connected your liver up to your kidneys, whether you'd piss bile or what. No other reason. He's been a perfect gentleman to me."

"But he threatens you . . ."

"Not so much me. Just . . . oh, shit, I don't know. Maybe nobody. For all I know he raises Persian kittens and butterflies in his spare time. It's just that I've seen eyes like that in photographs from Nuremberg. Haven't you ever thought how . . . extraordinary they are?"

"They are that," I said. "But I never found them threatening. Intense, maybe."

A stronger surge of nausea flooded through me, and the fine trembling came back, and I leaned my head back and closed my eyes for a moment. When I opened them he was looking at me gravely and the smile was gone.

"This is none of my business," he said. "But I think you ought to let me put a drop of bourbon in that coffee. I know a hangover when I see one. You feel like death. It'll help, if you don't have any more."

I started to protest, and then simply did not. I felt too badly, and there was something disarming about this man. He did not intimidate me in any way, despite the piratical skin and hair and the big Chiclet teeth. I suddenly did not care what he knew about me.

"How'd you know bourbon was my drink?" I said dreamily.

"Well, for one thing, I smelled booze on you when we first met. For another, there's a half-empty bottle of it just under the coffee table. And for still another, it was my drink, too, and I'd know the smell of good bourbon anywhere, even if I haven't tasted it for eight long years. I've been where you are. It feels damned awful. A little hair of the dog is not a bad thing, if you stick to one. After that I think you ought to go home. It doesn't do to be by yourself with a bad hangover. Is there somebody there to look after you?"

I thought of my vast, beautiful, empty house in Peacock Island Plantation.

"That's a good idea," I said. "I'll do that. I think I'll skip the hair of the dog, though."

He was silent for a moment, and then he said softly, "I think you're lying, but I've been there and done that, too. Just promise me you'll go on home and we'll be on our way. Your daughter, is she in school? You want to be there when she gets home . . ."

"My daughter is dead," I said, still wrapped in the peace of the bell jar. "She drowned five years ago. She would be fifteen now. I thought your granddaughter . . . for a minute, last night, she looked very like my daughter at that age. She used to chase the ponies, too."

"*Ay, Dios,*" he said softly after a long while. "I'm sorry. Lita must have been an awful shock for you. I'll see to it that she doesn't come again."

"No. She's a nice child. And the ponies are obviously helping her. Later, maybe, another day, you can bring her over and I'll tell you where to find the baby and her mother. I think I know where they're hanging out this fall. I can't stop living. I don't want to. She's welcome here."

He got to his feet and went to the door and called to Lita to come in, it was time to go.

"You are a very nice woman, Mrs. Caroline Venable," he said. "I'm sorry if we brought any pain at all into your enchanted hideaway here. I think that you didn't know about Dayclear, and I've shocked you badly, and as I say, I wish I could bite my tongue out, but I'm sure it would simply go on flapping. Your husband should have told you about it. You must talk with him about it now."

Anger flared from somewhere under the hangover. How dare this man, this perfect stranger, this hired employee of my husband's, this trespasser, tell me what I must and must not do, or what Clay should have? I recognized the anger for what it was: a

185

mask for fear, but that did not lessen it. I sat up abruptly and glared at him.

"I find that arrogant beyond belief," I said coldly. "My . . . relationship with my husband is absolutely none of your affair. It never will be. And you are dead wrong about the new project. You've got your facts confused. There is no way Clay would start to develop this island without telling me first. There's no way I wouldn't know. For one thing, he doesn't own this part of the island, I do. All of it, except for the settlement itself. And I'd never in this world permit such a thing. He knows that."

He looked at me silently for a long time, a level look suddenly as cold as my own. All the small-boy charm was gone from the brown face. I could almost feel the impact of the opaque black eyes. Uneasiness crept in over the anger. I did not know this man. How could I have forgotten that?

"They'd like to know that over in Dayclear," he said finally. "They're really upset. They're sure they're going to lose their homes. It's all they talk about, the old ones. There's not anywhere else for most of them to go."

"They do know that," I retorted. "Right after Clay deeded this part of the island over to me I went over and told them. I told Jackson. He said he'd tell the others. Toby would do what he said. I told them they'd never have to worry about losing their homes. My God, I love this marsh as much as my grandfather did, and all of them knew how he felt about it. . . ."

"Well, perhaps you'll pardon them for being a little confused," he said. "They've got surveyors over there, and people in pink Izod and LaCoste shirts thunking around in their little deck shoes with no socks, making notes on clipboards, and every now and then Mengele himself pays a royal visit and chats everybody up, and his trusty sidekick Goebbels is over there every other day, and then I come poking around in their bushes and sticking tags on their live oaks . . . you can see why it might look to them like something's up. And for the record, I'm not mistaken. I've seen the master plan."

I felt my face whiten.

"You are definitely mistaken. I don't care what you think you've seen. And even if you weren't, Clay does not own Dayclear, nor do I. It belongs to them, the people who live there. My grandfather always said that it did. . . ."

"Actually, nobody knows who it belongs to," he said. "There's no way you could establish clear title to those homes. I imagine they'll be offered a handsome cash buyout. That's the way it's usually done."

"And how can you possibly know that?"

"A friend of mine told me. Someone who lives in Dayclear. Perhaps you know of him. Ezra Upchurch? I gather he's rather well known in the Lowcountry. . . ."

"Ezra Upchurch! Living in Dayclear? I thought he was on John's Island," I said. "Of course I know of him. I know him, too. I used to play with him when we were both about eight, but then his mother came and got him and they moved. . . . What's he doing back in Dayclear? I wouldn't think things were lively enough for him over here."

"He thinks otherwise," Lou Cassells said, smiling a new, cold smile. "He's decided to come back to the humble village of his birth and stay a spell. Rediscover his roots, so to speak. As a matter of fact, I'm staying at his house, his and his old aunt's. He'll be happy to know that according to Mrs. Mengele, Dayclear is safe as a baby's butt in a cradle."

Ezra Upchurch. Bastard child of a mother who fled Dayclear at fifteen, leaving him behind with his young grandmother. Changeling child possessed of a quicksilver mind and a steely will, so gifted that he graduated from the county high school at sixteen and went on to Morehouse College in Atlanta on a full scholarship, and from there to Yale Divinity School and then Duke Law. Full scholarships all. Then he came back to the Lowcountry and began a rich, glinting career that included preaching at the smallest, most time-lost pray houses in the marshes and woods, taking the smallest and most impossible pro bono legal cases for the remaining Gullah Negroes, playing piano in a number of scabrous, deep-woods roadhouses where few white faces were ever seen, disc jockeying for black jazz stations up and down the coast, racing his Harley-Davidson, and lecturing at colleges and universities all over the country for astronomical fees, most of which went to support the various drives, funds, and marches that he organized to improve the lot of his people. He was almost magically successful at these; the media adored him, as did what he called "my little folks" everywhere. A great many white Lowcountry people, particularly the gentry and those who aspired to be, called him an agitator. His supporters called him a savior. No one called him humble. His fat, flashing ego preceded him, to paraphrase Cyrano de Bergerac, by a quarter of an hour. To hear him speak was an unforgettable experience. I never had, not in person, but I had heard him on television; the fine hairs on my arms had risen at his words and voice. Ezra Upchurch, in Dayclear.

What must I think about that?

I shook my head slightly. It had begun to throb.

"Well, since you know him so well, you go back and tell him that none of it's true and I'm not going to let anything happen to this part of the island. And that includes Dayclear. And let that be an end to it. I don't want to hear any more about this . . . silliness. Do you understand me?"

He nodded his head and tugged at a forelock in an elaborate parody of a servant with his mistress.

"Yes, Miz Mengele," he drawled. "I understand, I sho' does. You have, by the way, read *Lady Chatterley's Lover?*"

I stared at him, speechless.

"Ah, so you have. Well, then, doesn't it give you the least little pang of fear, or whatever, to realize that you're out here all alone in the wilderness with your husband's greenskeeper? You know what came of that for Lady Chatterley."

I got up off the sofa and marched to the door and opened it and stood beside it, speechless with anger. Beyond the glass windows I could see that Estrellita's mouth was open in a little round O and her black eyes were huge. She stared in at us.

He turned and went out the door.

"Go on home, Mrs. Venable," he said, without looking back.

"Go to hell, Mr. Cassells," I said, my voice shaking.

After they had gone I stood for a long time, staring out over the marsh and the creek, across it to the distant line of trees that marked the river. All of a sudden I could see it: a jumble of masts and flying bridges and antennas soaring over the rippling green marsh grass, villas and homes clustering around manicured lagoons that did not yet exist, golf carts crawling like beetles over the green hummocks where now the ponies cropped.

The ponies . . .

I would, of course, go to Clay about it the instant he got home. Of course I would. But that would be a while yet; I knew that he could not possibly be home yet from Atlanta. Usually his money trips lasted several days. So there was no need to leave the island and go back to Peacock's. No need at all.

I got up and straightened up the coffee table and plumped up the sofa pillows and gathered the spilled magazines and newspapers from the floor where I had left them. I pulled the bottle of Wild Turkey out from under the sofa and carried all of it into the kitchen. I tossed the magazines and newspapers into the trash basket and set it beside the back door, ready to carry over to the big Dumpster on Peacock's.

And then I poured myself another small drink and took it out onto the deck, and sat down in the old twig rocker, and put my feet up on the railing, as my grandfather and I had done a number of times before.

There was all the time in the world.

6

This time it was Lottie who woke me.

I know that I did not have more than the one drink, but when you have drunk as much as I did the night before, and when you are as small as I am, it doesn't take much to drag you under again. It's as if the alcohol still in your system is like a banked but living fire; it only takes the touch of a match and it's off and roaring again. I fell asleep sometime around eleven in the morning, in the rocker, and only woke when the sun was slanting toward midafternoon, my head hung cripplingly over the back of the chair. I heard myself give a great, gargling snore as Lottie shook me awake.

I snorted and gaped and blinked, licking my lips. They were dry and chapped, and the sick-sweet taste of bourbon was strong on my tongue. She came into focus as I squinted at her, seeming in the painful dazzle of light off the creek to loom over me like a colossus. She was leaning against the railing, scowling at me and rolling my empty glass back and forth with her toe.

"What are you doing here?" I rasped.

"Better still, what are you?" she said. Her voice was the familiar twanging growl, but there was something in it I did not recognize, or rather, something not in it that I missed. None of the usual fudgy, tolerant warmth was there today. Her leathery face was closed and scowling. Her muscular arms were crossed over her chest.

"You look like Daddy Warbucks." I giggled, and then hiccupped loudly. "Oh, shit," I said. "I think I fell asleep. My neck is killing me."

"I think you passed out," Lottie said. "I hope it *is* killing you. What the hell do you think you're doing, out here by yourself dead drunk?"

"I am not dead drunk," I said with what dignity I could muster. It was not much. "I had one little drink sitting out here, and I fell asleep. I hardly got any sleep at all last night . . ."

"No wonder," she said. "It must have taken you all night to drink half a bottle of bourbon. This is bad stuff, Caro. I thought you didn't keep booze out here."

"Well, *'scuse* me," I said indignantly, trying to sound righteously affronted. "How many times have I rooted you out at noon with a hangover that would stun an army mule?"

"That's me," she said. "That's what I do. I've been doing it since I was fifteen, and I never do it unless I mean to. It's fun and I like it and when I don't want to do it I don't. It's different with you, and you know it."

"And why is that?"

"Because there's something in you that won't stop until you're dead," she said matter-of-factly. "I've always known that. There's something in you that doesn't have any limits. And you can't let go of all that precious pain, or you won't. It's a shitty combination, and I'm not going to sit around and watch you self-destruct."

"So who asked you to?" I said, shame and anger stinging in my throat. "I don't remember asking you to be my own private temperance society. And as for my pain, as you call it, what do you know about my so-called pain? When have I ever mentioned it to you?"

"You don't," she said, shaking her head slowly. "We all know you're too brave to mention that you're in mortal pain almost every waking minute of your life. God, everybody who knows you tiptoes around scared to death they're going to slip and mention death or daughters. You don't know how many times I've wanted to just ask you if your daughter was still dead."

I felt the blood drain from my face.

"How dare you?" I whispered. "How dare you talk to me like that? I've never . . . I don't . . . you talk like I use Kylie or something, like I . . . hug it to me, like I cherish it . . ."

"Don't you?" she said, and then shut her eyes. "I'm sorry. That was rotten. But I hate to see this, Caro. I always thought of this place as somewhere you could come that was safe, where you didn't feel hustled or threatened, or need to drink. I didn't worry about you when I knew you were out here. I don't want to have to start now."

"So don't," I said snippily. "How did you know I was out here, anyway? For that matter, how did you know I drank half a bottle of bourbon?"

"Didn't you?"

"Yes."

"Well, then. As for how I knew, a little bird told me."

I saw it clearly, with one of those swift, untutored leaps of connection that you make sometimes, for no reason at all.

"He told you, didn't he? That awful Cassells man . . . Lou, or whatever his name is. Okay, Lottie, so how do you know him? As if I had to ask."

She grinned. It was her old grin, full and

gleeful and lewd.

"I know him just the way you think I do," she said. "And I'm damned glad I do. He's as good a lay and as good a man as I've met on this island in a coon's age, and as long as he wants to drop on over of an evening, I'll leave the light burning for him. He's not a bad art critic either, among his other more obvious talents. I purely love fucking a man who can talk about something afterward beside his orgasm. I thought you all would meet eventually, but I can't say I had anything like this morning in mind."

"He told you all about it, undoubtedly."

"Of course. He has no secrets from *moi*. He was worried about you, incidentally. He doesn't go around gossiping about the boss's wife just to be doing it."

"Oh, I'm sure not," I said nastily. "Did he happen to mention that he insulted me? And that he calls Clay Mengele?"

She gave a whoop of laughter and doubled over.

"Oh, God! How perfect! I'll never be able to look at him with a straight face again. . . ."

"God*damn* it, Lottie!"

She held up one hand, palm out, gasping for breath.

"Okay," she croaked. "All right. Truce. I'll lay off Men— Clay if you'll go take a shower

197

and toss the booze and let me feed you lunch. When did you eat last? Never mind. Shem just brought a mess of crabs in. I'll boil if you'll crack."

And because it was Lottie, and because I felt shamed and diminished and out of control and frightened by that, I did as she said. I climbed, shaking, into the shower and let the reeking hot water wash the agues and wobbles out of my head and muscles, and she tossed the liquor. I heard her ferret out the remaining bottles of Wild Turkey, heard them clink into the trash sack, heard the back door slam and a bit later her car trunk, and knew that she would haul them out to a Dumpster someplace. I felt better after that, as if a loaded gun had been taken out of my house. She was right. I had fouled my own nest last night and today. I did not intend it to happen again.

A little later we sat at the scarred old picnic table out behind her gas-station studio, cracking open the hot boiled blue crabs and picking the sweet meat from the shells. My hands and face were sticky with crab juice, and I could feel my forehead and scalp stinging from the spurted juice of an errant lemon. I imagined that I smelled about as bad as I looked, but I felt much better. Fresh crabs and Lottie have that effect on me.

Somewhere during the late lunch we had arrived at a tacit agreement not to speak of my drinking again, or of Clay, and I felt lulled and warmed by the sheer, rank, earthen force that was Lottie. The hangover was all but gone. So was the residue of last night's eeriness, and the near-madness. I could even speak lightly of it, and found that I wanted to.

I told her about seeing the child in the fog, and about sitting there in the firelight, drinking and waiting, and about waking to the laughter, and then running down the steps to meet not a revenant Kylie, but a strange, near-mute Cuban child and her black-furred grandfather. I even laughed a little, at myself and my lunatic, fog-fed fancies.

She did not smile back. Her eyes were dark with pity and something near fear.

"You want to stick a little closer to the world for a while, Caro," she said seriously. "I feel like this is a dangerous time for you. I don't know why, but I do feel that. Maybe you ought to lay off the island for a spell."

"Well, I will, I think," I said. "It's so close to Thanksgiving now, and there're a bunch of new kids in, and Clay's going to want to do that ghastly Lowcountry Thanksgiving thing for them and all the others who don't go home, so I'm just about out of time. Besides that, I don't want to run into Mellors the gamekeeper again. He could ruin a place for you in a New York minute."

She leered at me.

"I see the sexual aspect of the man has not escaped you. It's pretty powerful, isn't it? For an old man and a grandpa, he flat reeks of it. I gather he pointed out the similarity of your — ah, situations, yours and his and Lady Chatterley and company. He laughed like a hyena when I mentioned it."

"It was your idea, was it? I might have known he'd never think of it by himself. What, a little pillow talk or something?"

"Or something. I did tell him about you, for what it's worth. He was curious about Clay, about what sort of wife he would have, what sort of children. Don't worry, I didn't tell him about Kylie. That's for you to do or not, as the friendship progresses."

And she smiled at me again, a wolflike baring of her big teeth.

"There's no friendship to progress and there isn't going to be," I said. "He's arrogant and insufferable, and if it weren't for his granddaughter I swear I'd try to get Clay to fire him. She's crazy about the ponies, though. She talked for almost the first time since her mother died when she was with them. It's the saddest thing, Lottie. . . ."

"I know the story. You're right. It's awful. Well, I don't think you need to worry about him hanging around. He's pretty busy over in Dayclear, from what he says. He also said he has no intention of bothering you again, said for me to be sure to tell you that. He was only there today because the kid ran away. But you're cutting off your nose to spite your face. He'd make you a good friend. You don't have so many of those around here that another one wouldn't help. Come to think of it, he'd make you a good . . . whatever else, too. A tad of Lady Chatterley would do you a world of good, no doubt about it. And I sure don't mind sharing. There's enough there to go around."

"I'm going home if you're going to talk like that," I said, face and neck burning. The thought of those dark hands and arms, those heavy shoulders, that black hair . . . would it be coarse? Silky? How would it be?

I got up and ran water from the outdoor spigot over my sticky hands and hot wrists, letting my hair fall over my face so that she could not see the flush. I heard her chuckle. To divert her, I said, "You know what he said? He said Clay's going to put a property, a resort community, right smack in the marsh where the river and creek meet, where Dayclear is. He says Clay hired him as a consultant about subtropical plants and land-scaping for it. I think he must be really crazy. You know that's my land. You know I'd never let anything like that happen on the is-land. And you know Clay knows that, too. Next time you see old Babalu or whatever you call him, you might enlighten him about that. I certainly didn't get very far trying."

When she did not respond I straightened up and looked around. She was looking at the ground, and her face was very still. Lottie's face is many things, but almost never that.

"Lottie," I said tentatively.

"I don't know anything about that," she said. "You ought to talk to Clay about that."

"Well, of course I will, but don't you think it's the craziest thing you ever heard?"

"I've heard lots of crazy things, Caro," Lottie said. "Somehow that's not the crazi-est."

"But, my God . . ."

"Ask Clay. I don't know. I try to know as little about what goes on in his mind as pos-sible. You know me. Just a little ol' trailer tramp, only interested in fuckin' and drawin'. Speaking of which, I've got a paint-ing drying up on me in the studio where I just walked out and left it when I heard you were on a private toot on your private island.

I need to get back to it and you need to get on home."

"Lottie . . ."

"Home, Caro. Not the island. Home. Okay? I'm going to call you in an hour and see if you're there, and if you're not I'm going to call the sheriff to go out to the island and get you. Now go on. Git."

She turned and stomped back into the studio, leaving the litter of crab shells and paper napkins reeking in the sun. I got, fuming at her high-handedness. Under it all there was a small, cold curl of fear, like a worm.

It was close to five when I got home. I knew that Estelle would be gone, but she had left the kitchen and downstairs sitting room lights burning against the darkness that comes early off the ocean this time of year. I was glad. The wind had picked up and I could hear the surf, usually flaccid and sullen, booming hollowly on the shore beyond the house, and the palms rattling fretfully. It is the time of day that I like least in winter, and I went into the house singing loudly simply because I hate to be answered by nothing but wind and sea.

" 'Trailer for sale or rent, rooms to let fifty cents,' " I wailed in my frail soprano.

I would light a fire in my little upstairs sitting room, I thought, and take a supper tray up there, and find an old movie on TV, and drift off to sleep on my quilt-piled daybed, and when I woke it would be to the sound of Estelle singing gospel down in the kitchen and the smell of coffee. And then I would find out where Clay was staying and I would call him, and he would tell me when he was coming home, and the free fall of the past two days would stop, and the orderly quadrille of my life on Peacock's Island would resume again. I realized that I was missing Clay very much. I missed Carter, too. Maybe I would call him tonight. Except that I almost never caught him in, and for some reason that depressed me. Oh, well. He would be home for Thanksgiving, and that was less than a week away.

There was a note from Estelle on the counter. It was sitting under the steam iron. I walked over and looked at it.

"It have play out," the note said, and a fat black arrow pointed to the iron. I felt a smile twitch at my mouth, and then banished it. Clay thought Estelle's notes to us were wonderfully funny, but I did not, and I usually threw them away before he saw them, lest he take them to the office and show them around. More than once Hayes Howland had quoted an Estellism at a party, and I resented it sharply. Illiteracy in any permutation is not amusing to me. I was about to pick this one up and throw it away when I noticed that another arrow directed me to turn the paper over. I did.

"Mr. Clay be home tonite," it said. "He coming by privet jet. Home by midnite."

I did smile then, both at "privet jet" and the fact that Clay would be home by midnight. I wondered whose private plane he might be taking. He was adamant that no such amenity be purchased for the company, except for a small twin-engine Cessna that was virtually a necessity for island-hopping among the company's properties. When he traveled he was scrupulous about flying coach, and he insisted that everyone else on company business do it, too. He even turned his frequent flyer mileage back to the company. Hayes ragged him incessantly about it.

The house seemed to settle in around me all at once, fitting like a sweet skin. The dark night stopped pressing against the windows and wrapped them tenderly. I lit the logs in the big sitting room so that the house would smell of apple wood and peeked into the oven. Estelle had left a pot roast there, ready to be heated. Clay's favorite. That and some of the Merlot he had brought back from Atlanta the last time he went, and the last of the key lime pie we had had the weekend before . . . or, no, I would make something for dessert. It would pass the time, and please Clay, and I suddenly wanted very much to be in my own kitchen, making something wonderful with my own hands. I looked into the refrigerator. Crème caramel; we had everything I needed. When I went upstairs to our bedroom, I was nearly dancing on the steps.

He was late coming. At one A.M., I gave up and went upstairs and turned on my little television and found a rerun of *Pillow Talk* and fell asleep before Doris Day even had time to get pertly angry with Rock Hudson. I don't know how much later it was when a sound from the kitchen woke me. I got up and ran my hands through my tousled hair and shrugged into the nicest negligee I had, and hurried downstairs. I was not afraid. I knew it would be Clay.

He did not hear me coming in my bare feet. He was sitting at the kitchen table with the platter of cold, uncarved pot roast and vegetables in front of him, hands in his lap beneath the table, staring into space. I had never seen him look so old, or so tired, or so . . . ill? I was afraid suddenly, so afraid that for a moment I could not get my breath to speak. I remembered Shawna's words the day before . . . or was it the day before that?

. . . and that I had brushed them aside impatiently.

Then I said, "Honey?" and he looked up, and his face was Clay's again, with only the normal fatigue of a late night home from a business trip on it.

"Hi, sweetie," he said, and got up, and came over and hugged me. His face against mine was cold, but his arms were tight and hard around me, and he held me for a long time. I hugged back, eyes closed, my face pressed into his shoulder.

"You hopped a ride on a jet," I said, still close against the fabric of his coat.

"Yep. The guys we went to see were coming to Charleston anyway, and I talked them into staying over a day or two with us. Well, not with *us*. I put them in the guest house, now that the new kids are in their own places. It saved me a bad three hours in the Atlanta airport."

"Clever," I said, kissing the side of his face. I felt stubble there, and was surprised. He hardly ever allowed a trace of growth on his chin. He must have skipped shaving that morning. I had never known him to do that in all the years we had been married, and the anxiety came nagging back.

"Are you okay?" I said, leaning back to look at him. "You looked awfully beat up there for a minute, and Shawna was carrying on the other day about being worried about you. Your health, I mean. I blew her off; I thought she was just being Shawna. Should I have?"

He made a small, disgusted noise.

"You should have. She drives me nuts with that sweet-concern business. I'm thinking about assigning her to Hayes. He can't stand her. Yes, to answer your question, I'm okay. I just hate Atlanta. And I'm getting really sick of this money-raising business."

"Why don't you let somebody else take that over?" I said, picking up the platter and putting it into the microwave. "Surely Hayes could do it by himself by now; he goes with you every time you go."

"Most investors still want to see the honcho do his dog and pony show," he said, rubbing his eyes. "Makes 'em feel like they can jerk him around. Which of course they can. You want a glass of wine while that's heating?"

"No," I said, perhaps more forcefully than I meant to, and he shot an oblique look at me but said nothing more. He poured himself a glass and sat back down at the table.

"So tell me about the island," he said. "I assume you stayed over there? Shawna said you hadn't called in when I called the office."

"I was going to call her in the morning and find out where you were and all that," I said. "Yes, I did stay over. It was awfully foggy, but I got some nice watercolors started, and one morning of photographs. Oh, and I saw Nissy and she has a colt! Wouldn't . . . isn't that something? You remember, we've never known how old she is, so we thought maybe she was too old to have a baby, but apparently not. I'd love to know who the daddy is. Oh, and I met that new man of yours. That Lou Cassells person. He came over looking for his granddaughter. She'd run away after the ponies and ended up at the house."

"Cassells . . ." he said reflectively . . . "Oh. Yeah. The plant guy, the Cuban. His granddaughter was at the house?"

"Yes. Apparently she saw the ponies and had been chasing them around for a while, and sneaked out early yesterday morning and followed them over to our place. I'd been feeding them, so they're hanging around. She's a nice child, about five, I guess. There's a sad little story about her I'll tell you sometime, but right now you need to eat and then I need a snuggle, and there's just no telling where that could lead."

I smiled at him and he smiled back. I did

not mention seeing the child the night before, in the fog, and wished that I had not
mentioned Lou Cassells, and wondered why
I had. That could have waited for morning.
This was not the time for that. Perhaps there
would not be a good time for it. Perhaps I
would, after all, just let the whole thing lie. I
did not want to tax my tired husband with
that can of worms. It all seemed, suddenly,
so absurd as to have been a fairy tale, something I had heard long ago.

The microwave dinged and I took out the
roast and carved him a couple of slices and
spooned the browned vegetables onto his
plate. He took a big mouthful and smiled appreciatively around it.

"Estelle never forgets, does she?" he said.

"Never." I smiled back. "I don't, either. I
made crème caramel. We can eat it in bed."

"Well, you hussy," he said, grinning a little. It was the grin I loved most. I had not
seen it in some time. "Can't you even let a
man get his nourishment first?"

"Be quick about it," I said.

An hour later we lay tangled together in
the big bed in our "real" bedroom, the one
that faced the sea. The drapes were closed
against the darkness, and they muffled the
sound of the waves. The palms still
scratched and rattled, though, and banged

against the wrought-iron railing of the balcony that lay beyond the French doors. I burrowed my ear deep into the hollow of Clay's naked shoulder and heard, instead of the palms, the roar of my own diminishing blood and the pulse of his. If I moved my head slightly I could taste the sweet salt sweat on his neck. I did that, tasted the essence of Clay after love, and hugged him hard with the other arm that was flung over his chest. He hugged back.

"Not bad for an old bag," he said drowsily into my hair. His breath tickled.

"Or for an old crock," I said. "The only trouble is, I know all your tricks. Why don't you get some new tricks to amaze and delight me?"

"And just where do you suggest I get them? Shawna? Some daughter of joy from the mean streets of Atlanta?"

"You could get a book," I said. "Or we could rent a video. I bet Hayes knows some good ones."

He laughed and shifted me slightly in his arms. We lay still for a while, I listening to the regular cadence of his breathing. I kept thinking that I would get up and bring the comforter and spread it over us, but I did not move, and before long I began to think that he had fallen asleep. But he had not.

"So what do you think of him? My new guy?" he said, when I was just thinking that I would disengage myself and get up. My stomach gave a small squeeze of anxiety. I did not want to speak of this. I was done with this.

"Oh, who cares?" I said. "Go to sleep. It's almost three."

"I'm not sleepy," he said into the dark. "No kidding, what did you think of him? His credentials are good, but I don't know . . . there's something about him. I realized after I hired him that I really don't know anything about him."

For some reason, I felt a stab of perversely proprietary protectiveness toward Lou Cassells. I said, "He seemed fine. Like I said, he had his little granddaughter with him and he's certainly crazy about her. He's apparently had a pretty rough life; he just lost his wife, and his daughter . . . died . . . having a baby, back in Cuba. He takes care of the child now. You've got to admire that."

"I suppose," Clay said. "I just don't much like the idea of him hanging around the house over there, or knowing when you're there and when you're not. I'm going to have to make that clear, I think."

"No, don't. He wouldn't have been there if the little girl hadn't come there. He told

Lottie he didn't plan to bother me."

"Lottie . . . oh, terrific. I guess he's shagging Lottie Funderburke like half of the rest of my staff, huh?"

"Well, you don't have any rules about that, do you? Let him be. He was . . . nice. And apparently he's highly educated. He was telling me a little about himself."

Clay lay in the darkness for a while, and then he said, "What else did you talk about?"

"Oh . . . nothing. Everything. About Dayclear. He's staying over there, and you know who with? Ezra Upchurch. Isn't that something? Ezra, back in Dayclear?"

"There goes the neighborhood," Clay said neutrally. "So . . . did he say what he was doing over there? Ezra, I mean? Him, too, for that matter. I thought he lived on John's Island. I thought they both did."

"He's visiting his old aunt, apparently. She's the only one he's got left, Lou said. Ezra, I mean. As for Lou, he's there because he knew Ezra somehow or other on John's Island and I guess this is a lot closer to his work. He didn't say."

"Lou, huh?"

"It's what he said his name was, Clay."

"He told me Luis."

"Well, what's the difference?"

"It's just . . . familiar, that's all. I don't like

213

the idea of him being familiar with you. I want you to tell me if you see him over there again. As a matter of fact, it might be a good idea if you gave the island a rest for a while."

"Why, for pity's sake?" I could not keep the exasperation out of my voice. This was not at all like Clay. Not at all.

"Oh, for Christ's sake, Caro, because I said so, okay?" he snapped. "Is it a terrible great lot to ask, just for a little while?"

I raised myself up on one elbow and stared at him.

"I think you're jealous, and I think it's absolutely ridiculous," I said.

He raised himself up, too, and glared at me.

"Jealous of you and a . . . Cuban Jew gardener? Not hardly," he said, and there was something cold in his voice.

I was stung.

"Well, maybe you ought to be concerned, though not for the reason you think," I said, trying to match his coldness with my own. "He seems to know an awful lot about your business. He seems to think you're about to put a resort over there in Dayclear. In fact, he's awfully sure about that. If he's telling me about it, who knows who else he's telling? If you have to make anything clear to him, that's what you ought to clear up. It made my hair stand on end."

The cold sickness did not start until the silence had spun out so long that it was obvious that he was not going to answer me. Then it flooded me and took me deep under, so that I could not move or get my breath to speak. Over it, very gradually, came not anger, or fear, but a terrible desolation that was the sum of every bad thing I have ever known was waiting ahead for me. It was not anxiety or even terror; that presupposes a catastrophic event still ahead of you. This event was here. I knew as certainly as I knew it was I who sat here in the dark with Clay that what Luis Cassells had said was true, and that my husband lay beside me pregnant with a great betrayal.

Presently I said, wondering that my voice was not cracked and choked, leaking life, "So it's true. I thought he was a liar and a fool. I guess the fool was me."

And the liar was you, I did not say. But it lay between us.

After another long moment of silence, he sighed, a thin, tired sigh, and said, "There's a lot I have to tell you, Caro. None of it's good. I didn't want to do it yet, and I didn't think I had to, until after Christmas maybe. And I guess I thought there was just a chance that I wouldn't have to tell you at all. But

215

Cassells has put the kibosh on that. Maybe it's just as well. I just wish it had been me and not him."

"I wish so, too, Clay," I said, feeling the pain inside so deep and viscous that it felt like blood pooled in my chest. "You just don't know how much I wish it had been. So. You're going to tell me now, right?"

"I . . . Caro, Christ, I'm so tired I think I could die from it. Couldn't we just . . . sleep? Get some sleep, and talk about it in the morning? It won't seem so bad then. It's not so bad, come to think of it. It's nothing that can't be fixed. But I'm so tired . . ."

"I don't care," I said, and found that I didn't. "I don't care how tired you are, Clay. I hear it now, whatever it is, or I'm getting up from here and going back to the island and I don't know when I'm coming back. Or if. You can't just . . . Listen, you tell me. Sit up and tell me."

And so he did. He turned on the bedside lamp and pulled on a T-shirt and sat up in our bed, half turned away from me toward the hidden sea, and he told me that things were so bad financially with the company that unless he got an infusion of cash very quickly, he ultimately stood to lose it all. All of it. The scattered island properties, even Peacock Island Plantation, the flagship of

216

the line, the mother church, the first and still best thing he had ever created. He would lose it all. Everything.

I could not understand. I could not comprehend what he was saying. My head felt as empty as if my brain had atrophied. I simply sat in the lamplight, still naked and not noticing at all, and looked at him. Or rather, at the side of his face.

Finally I said, "You mean . . . we wouldn't have a place to live? We wouldn't have any money?"

"Well, it's not that bad," he said dully. "We could keep this house, of course. We own it. I'd keep some company stock. We have a few other personal investments. Carter's almost through school. We could live. It's just . . . that all this wouldn't be mine anymore. Ours, rather. I . . . Caro, I can't let that happen. I can't. This is everything, all this . . ." He gestured, his hand taking in the sweep of beach and sea and land that spread out from the epicenter that was our bed.

"Oh, Clay . . . is it really?" I said, feeling the pain flare up until I thought I would die from it. This will be mortal, I thought. Those five words are what will kill me now.

He turned and looked at me wordlessly. His face was flayed, burned, scoured. I did not know this face.

"After you, it is," he said, eyes closed. "After you and Carter, it's everything. There isn't anything else. Not for me, anyway."

I lay back against my pillows, knowing that in some vital, visceral way I would never sit up whole again.

"I need to know about it," I whispered. "I need to know."

A great, indrawn breath. Then he said, "Remember Jeremy? Jeremy Fowler, at Calista Key?"

I nodded. Who could forget Jeremy? The golden boy, the chosen one, the flaming comet that had come streaking out of Texas when he was only twenty-two, just out of the University of Texas Business School, shining with youth and charm and intelligence and energy and Texas oil money, begging Clay to hire him, to let him do anything for the company, let him tend bar at one of the plantation clubs, let him trim shrubbery, let him answer the telephone or sort the mail. I'll make you glad you did, Jeremy Fowler said, and his voice held all the promise of the new millennium in it.

Of course, Clay hired him. And Jeremy did what he said he would. Within a year he was second in command at one of Clay's oldest resort communities, an established mountain family resort in Tennessee. In two years he was back on Peacock's, heading up the elite forward planning team. A year later Clay sent him down to Puerto Rico, to head up the just-borning Calista Key Plantation. He was by far the youngest project manager Clay had ever had, and his trajectory took him and Calista straight into the Caribbean sun. The first two years' reports out of Puerto Rico were stunning. Advance sales were unprecedented. Jeremy didn't come back to the States often; he made it a point to be a hands-on manager. But when he did, with his fey, beautiful, haunted wife, Lila, he trailed a kind of glittering aura that was nearly palpable, and he received a hero's welcome.

"He . . . Calista's bankrupt, Caro," Clay said. "The figures that came in were . . . not true. There's hardly any occupancy. The project is way behind construction schedule; he hasn't paid any of his suppliers in months. Nobody's been working since summer. Whoever went down there from the home office got shown a great bustle of activity and dozers and workmen, but they were free-lances he hired for the day. The photos he sent . . . Christ, I think they were the same few units, in the various stages of construction, with different paint and plantings. From what I hear, morale is so bad that half our kids down there are drunk most of the time, and the other half are on drugs. Seven marriages have broken up. Lila Fowler has left and gone back to her folks in Philadelphia. The construction engineer split for Arkansas last month. Hayes says Jeremy is living in a broken-down hotel in Humacao with a Puerto Rican woman, drinking like a fish. He says there are chickens walking around in the courtyard."

He stopped and scrubbed at his eyes with his hands, as if the chickens were the worst of it.

"How could that happen?" I said. "How could that be?"

"I don't blame Hayes," he said. "I should have gone down there myself. Hayes is new to this kind of stuff. He's never overseen a project before. Jeremy always did have Hayes in his back pocket. He's not the only one, either. Hayes had no reason to doubt the figures or what he saw with his own eyes. And I didn't butt in because I wanted . . . I thought it was time for Hayes to have something of his own. And I thought Jeremy could handle it. I didn't go down there on purpose. I didn't want to hover . . ."

"Hayes," I said leadenly. "Of course. It would be Hayes, wouldn't it? I thought Hayes didn't have a project of his own. I thought he was a, quote, perfect second banana, unquote."

"He didn't want anybody to know until he got the hang of it," Clay said.

"Well," I said, "so we lose Calista Key. Why does that mean that everything else . . . what does that have to do with the island? With Dayclear?"

"Because," Clay said, "I've . . . we've . . . things have not been so good for resorts in the last few years, Caro. I've kept expanding because I didn't think I had any choice. I could pay the Alabama Gulf investors, for instance, with the money we made when we opened up Biloxi. And we paid the Biloxi guys when we opened up Georgia. And so on. But Calista . . . we owed a ton of money on that one. That one was a money pit from the beginning. There's not enough cash in all the others put together for me to pay off the Calista folks unless I sell Peacock's. And when that goes . . . it all will. Eventually, it all will. Or . . ."

He fell silent. I waited. Then I said, "Or you could open up a new property, right? Get some more joint venture money. But you don't have enough cash to buy one, so you'd have to use land you already had. Like the island. My friend Mr. Cassells says it's a natural, that site. The only thing is, Clay, it's not your land, is it? It's mine. Did you forget that?"

"No," he said in a low voice. "I didn't forget that."

"Clay, isn't all this a pyramid scam or something? Isn't all this illegal? Who knows about this?"

"Not strictly, no," he said. "It's done often, and done quite successfully, if you can keep all the balls in the air at once. I thought I could. There was nothing to make me think I couldn't. Nobody said anything; none of the company money people ever said a word. Hayes has always been a wizard at finding properties and investors. He's the one who just might save us now. And to answer your question . . . nobody knows about it, I don't think. Not outside the Plantation family, anyway. I mean . . . they know about Dayclear coming on line, but not the reason for it. Yet. I don't think too many of our people know about Calista . . . yet."

He lay back against the pillow and closed his eyes. He might have died, he was so still, so white, his face so emptied of everything that had ever meant Clay to me. I waited for my heart to twist with pain, but it did not. My heart felt as cold and hard as a cinder, dead for eons.

"Remember how my grandfather felt

about that land?" I said finally, feeling as if I were going to collapse from the effort to talk. "Remember what he said about the Gullahs in Dayclear always having their homes, about the wild things, the birds, the fish, the things that bloom and grow there that don't anywhere else? Remember the panther? Would you really . . . could you really just doze all that down and put up a . . . a . . . what? A golf course? A lagoon community? A marina? What? Cluster housing, condos where the old houses are now?"

"It can be done well, Caro," he said in the new, dull voice. "You know it can. I've got studies, a master plan, that leaves so much of the land and marsh in place that it almost looks as if it hasn't been touched. There's plenty of wild habitat still provided for, over where your grandfather's house is. I wouldn't . . . we wouldn't disturb that. This looks like an award winner; the joint venture people are crazy about it . . ."

"I gather that's what you were doing in Atlanta," I said. "Peddling it. Who is it this time, Clay? Texas money? Los Angeles? Arab?"

"Local Atlanta," he said. "Fellow Southerners who know land like this. A long track record, lots of experience, solvent as all get-out, plenty of cash. I'll tell you about them later. They'd respect that land, I think. They've been crazy to get down here for a long time, but nothing's really pleased them till they saw the marsh property. If it's got to be done, I'm glad Hayes knew these guys."

"Clay. Listen to me. I'm sorry about . . . everything. But that land . . . that land is mine, Clay! Weren't you even going to ask me? Couldn't you at least have leveled with me before . . . before it got this far? Don't I matter? Doesn't my grandfather? Were you *ever* going to talk to me?"

"I haven't been able to talk to you for a long time, Caro," he said. It was almost a whisper. I opened my mouth to protest, and then did not. It was true. He had tried. Maybe not about Dayclear, but about other things that were important to the two of us. I had not refused to discuss them, but I had not talked back. My very silence had been his answer.

"What were you going to tell the people in Dayclear?" I said. "What were you going to do about clear titles and all that stuff? Providing that I agreed, which I cannot imagine doing?"

"Well, we'd do a substantial cash buyout. It would be more than enough for them to relocate, and we'd do that for them, too; find them homes, or maybe build some for them off-island. They'd be better off financially than they've ever been in their lives . . ."

"Except that they wouldn't have their homes. Can't you understand what that means? It seems to me you should, if you're about to lose yours . . ."

"There are other things we can do. Hayes thinks we might leave the settlement as is, maybe make a sort of cultural attraction of it. You know, a preservation center for the Gullah culture, with the Dayclear people doing the things their people have always done, planting and harvesting rice and cotton, spinning, dyeing, growing vegetables, making sweet-grass baskets, telling the old stories and doing the old dances, teaching visitors the songs and legends . . ."

"My God. A theme park. Gullah World. That's just extraordinary, Clay," I said fiercely. Anger was beginning to raise its snake's head. It felt good, like scalding hot coffee when you are frozen and exhausted.

"It's not like that. It could be done with great taste and dignity. Sophia Bridges . . . you know, the young black woman with the child . . . she has an undergraduate degree in cultural anthropology, and she did her thesis on the Gullahs. She's going to do a great deal more research down here. She thinks it's fascinating, and that it could be an important cultural asset to the whole region . . ."

"Sophia Bridges wouldn't know a real Gullah if one tackled her and held her down and put her hair in cornrows! This is not an experiment, Clay! Those are real people over there! My God! And the ponies . . . what about the ponies? Are you going to open up a Wild West exhibit with them?"

"The ponies are ultimately the responsibility of the government," he said. "The Park Service. We've been talking with them for months about the ponies. They've given us at least six months to relocate them or to cull . . ."

"*Cull?*"

He looked away again.

"They're not healthy, Caro. They're so inbred that their genetic weaknesses are going to kill them in another generation or two. They don't get enough food, or at least not the right kind. They've just about grazed out the available hummock grass on the island. You can't let them starve. They'll be much better off on one of the undeveloped islands, where the grass is strong and new."

"They're not starving, they're fat as pigs," I cried. "Clay, this is . . . I won't do this, Clay. Not to the people, and not to the ponies. I will not give you that land."

He did not speak. I watched him, my chest heaving with rage and anguish. Finally he nodded.

"Then, as you say, it's your island," he said.

There was another long silence, and then he said, "Caro, I have to sleep. I'll die if I don't sleep. You should, too. I'll talk to Hayes in the morning, tell him it's off. The Atlanta people are still here; we can wrap it up before noon. But right now I'm just plain done for."

He turned over and reached up and pulled the chain on the bedside lamp. The room swam back into its comforting darkness. I heard him settle into his pillow and give the small sign that meant he was poised at the edge of sleep. I felt my heart contract slightly with the first frisson of pity. He had never before said he was too tired to talk to me. This must have taken a terrible toll on him. I remembered how it had been with him when he was first learning the island, in the summer days after Hayes had brought him over from Charleston the first time. I remembered the sheer enchantment on his face, the wonder in his blue eyes. You wouldn't lose that, not entirely.

I lay still, staring at the drawn curtains. A faint line of pale, colorless light had appeared under them. Dawn. The dawn of a day I wished I might never see.

"Clay . . ." I said softly into the darkness.

"Yeah."

"Isn't there any other way? I mean, anything you could do so that the people at Dayclear and the . . . the ponies and all . . . could stay, wouldn't be disturbed? Put it somewhere else on the island, or scale it down, or something?"

After a long time he said, "We could try. If you'd agree to think about it, I'd agree to go back to the drawing board and see if we can't do better for the people and the horses. We have until spring before we have to give the earnest money back. That money would keep the Calista investors off my back for a long time. Maybe long enough. I think we could . . . Caro? If we could show you how much better it could be? If we could show you it would really benefit the people at Dayclear?"

"I . . . if you could really show me, I guess I could . . . think about it. I guess I could do that. But oh, Clay . . ."

"We'll talk about it in the morning, baby. I promise you we can make it work. I promise you it won't be anything you'd have to hate . . ."

"Will you promise me something else?"

"Anything."

"Will you promise me not to talk about it anymore until after the holidays at least? I don't think I could stand it, Clay. I don't think I can talk endlessly about this thing, or hear about it. Let's just get through the holidays. It's going to be bad enough, looking at all those poor, silly little new people and knowing what you brought them down here for . . ."

I should not have said it. No matter what, it was a gratuitously cruel comment, designed to hurt, and it did. I knew even before he answered that I had hurt him.

"That shouldn't be too hard," he said in the chill, neutral voice I fear most. "We don't talk about anything else."

I lay still, wrapped in my own pain, until I heard his breathing slacken into sleep. I meant to get up then, and go to try to sleep some more on my daybed, but before I could gather the energy I fell asleep, too, and when I woke, the sun was high and straight over the sea, and he was gone.

7

It's funny how a night's sleep can change the complexion of things. I couldn't have slept more than five hours, but when I finally got showered and dressed and in some sort of forward motion, the terrible night before had faded and bleached itself down to a kind of half-memory, half-dream that lacked the poisonous immediacy of the night itself. I knew it was something I had done myself, while I slept, in order simply to survive and go on; I had done it sometimes when the pain of Kylie got too overwhelming. It was a kind of interior litany that threaded my troubled sleep and bore me up when I waked: Well, it was awful; it was the worst thing in the world, but here it is the next day and we're still here. The sun is still shining, the birds are still singing. It isn't going to kill us, and what doesn't kill us can only make us stronger. There's still Clay and me, the fact of us. There's still that.

I was so proficient at it that it was buried deep in my subconscious now, and I knew only that a night had passed and a day had been born and we were still intact. As long as we were, we could work this out. He had said so, hadn't he? He had said they'd go back to the drawing board with ideas for Dayclear. He'd said we didn't need to speak of it again until spring. It would take at least that long to come up with a better plan. I didn't have to do anything at all about this until then. The light would have turned to pale, tender gold and the marshes would be greening up before I ever had to think of it.

I ran down the stairs two at a time, eager to be out in the crisp, clear light that flooded the back garden. I would have coffee there, and then cut the last of the roses and bring them in. Then I would go back over to the island. There was one more thing I had to do before I could pack the enormity of Dayclear away.

An hour later I stopped at the little unpainted cabin that had served the settlement as a general store and community center since I was a small child, to ask where Ezra Upchurch's house was. I knew that Janie and Esau Biggins, who had kept the store almost that long, would know. They had served the settlement's needs and wants and its deepest aches for forty years. And they were Gullahs, too, originally from Edisto. There was little

231

about the people of Dayclear they did not know.

The vertical planks of the little house were blackened with age and weather, and several had rotted through. The roof was rusted tin and missing many squares. The listing porch held a long-defunct metal Nehi cooler that squatted stolidly in a corner, like an abandoned god. Usually someone sat on it, or a group played checkers or cards on its pitted surface, but the day was sharp, and I knew that everyone would be inside, clustered around the black iron stove that would surely, as my grandfather always said, burn the place down one day. A few chickens pecked and scratched in the swept dirt yard and under the porch. They were Domineckers; I had always admired their precise tweed dress and vaguely African demeanor. They seemed to me so much more exotic than the fat, complacent Rhode Island Reds, almost as picturesque as the beautiful, witless, pin-head guineas that sometimes foraged alongside them. These did not stop their noshing as I walked through them and up the steps.

Inside, the thick, rank semigloom smelled of smoke and licorice and the dusty peanuts in their shells in a big barrel by the counter, and something else darker and older: dried blood from the carcasses of the chickens that were slaughtered out back and sold. I felt a little uncomfortable, for I knew that mine would be the only white face, but I had been here before, many times, and I was known. I would be treated with courtesy because of my grandfather. He would have been treated with affection.

Janie was behind the counter this morning. She smiled her gold-toothed smile and nodded but did not speak. That was for me to do first, and I did.

"I'm looking for the house Ezra Upchurch is staying in, Janie," I said. "He's got someone staying with him, a Mr. Cassells, that I need to see."

"Ezra, he stayin' with his auntie down at the end of the row, but he ain't to home," she said equably. "Seem like he say he goin' to town today."

I did not know if "town" meant the village on Edisto or Charleston or what, but it did not matter, since it was Luis Cassells I wanted. I was glad that I would not have to say what I had to say to him in front of Ezra Upchurch. The great wind of Ezra's presence would, I knew, overwhelm me. This was going to be hard enough.

"That's okay. I'll just walk on down there and see if Mr. Cassells is there. Thanks a lot," I said.

"I'm here," a masculine voice said from somewhere in the gloom behind the stove, and I peered into it. Luis Cassells was sitting in a spavined old rocking chair in the shadows, drinking coffee and smoking a large black cigar. Both smelled good, rich and masculine. They reminded me of my grandfather. There was a cardboard box beside him on the floor, and I heard a scuffling and scratching from it. Walking back, I peered in. There were three small black and tan hound puppies there, curled around one another. Luis was scratching their heads with the hand that held the cigar. He smiled up at me, his teeth flashing white in the murk.

"Pull up a chair," he said. "I'll buy you a cup of coffee. Or maybe you'd prefer a puppy. Esau's trying to find homes for them. Their mama got run over on the bridge."

"I wish I could," I said. "If he can't place them, I'll put a notice in the office. Where's Lita this morning?"

"Ezra's auntie is teaching her how to wrap her hair. She's been after me for a week to let her. Says that way I won't have to comb it for days and days, and she won't have to cry. She has a point. Combing hair is not one of my long suits."

I smiled. Then I said, "Mr. Cassells . . ."

He raised an eyebrow at me and I felt myself blush, and was glad of the darkness.

"Luis," I said. "I came to apologize. I was pretty crappy to you yesterday. And . . . you were right about Dayclear. There are some plans to develop it. I didn't know about them. But that doesn't mean it's going to happen; I *do* own this part of the island, and if it seems to me that the property would harm the settlement in any way, it's not going to happen. Clay and I have an agreement about that. I thought you might pass the word along. Nothing at all is going to be done until spring, and then only with their blessing."

He studied me for a space of time.

"I see," he said. "Well, that's good to know. Why don't you come on back with me and tell them yourself?"

"Because they'll be more apt to believe it if it comes from you," I said, knowing it was true. "They're nice to me because of my grandfather, but I'm whitey all the same. We don't have a great history of truth-telling in these parts. But you're one of them. They'd trust you."

He laughed, the big, rolling laugh I remembered.

"You're right about that," he said. "Nobody would confuse me with whitey."

I blushed again, hard.

235

"I meant that you're Ezra's friend, staying in his house. That would be enough right there."

"I know what you meant," he said, still chuckling. "You're right. They've taken me and Lita in like family, God bless them. I think it's because I've traveled such a long road. These are people that know a thing or two about journeys."

"You said you'd tell me about that road one day," I said.

"I did, didn't I? Well, since you honored me with an apology . . . completely unnecessary, by the way . . . the least I can do is honor you with the absolutely fascinating, never-equaled story of my life. Capsule version. That is, if you'll quit hovering and sit down and drink coffee with me."

I sat. He held up a finger and Janie brought two more cups of strong black coffee, smiling her gold-toothed smile as she did. It tasted strong and fresh and bitter, odd but good on this stinging day. I told her so.

"I puts a big ol' lump of chic'ry in every pot," she said.

Luis drained his second cup, set it down, and said, "Okay. Here we go. I was born . . ." And he grinned his pirate's grin. "Don't worry; it's the abridged edition. I was born in Havana in 1939, or just outside it. My family

236

was rich. My father was third in a line of doctors and gentlemen farmers, and we had what you all would call a country estate here. The finca, we called it. I was supposed to follow in the family tradition of medicine, but I hated everything about it, and by the time I was ready for college I knew that plants were going to be it for me. The old man was furious, but he had my younger brother already in the fold, so he paid for me to go to the university and start studying tropical botany. That was in 1957.

"I got married the same year. We do that in Cuba, or did, especially in the wealthy old families. She was the daughter of a neighbor; just as rich as we were, and I'd known her since we were in diapers. Her name was Ana, and she was little and round and soft like a dumpling, with the most wonderful giggle. All she ever wanted was to be married and have children and live exactly like the women in her family had lived for generations. And we got a good start on it; our daughter, Anita, was born the next year, 1958. Anita, little Ana. God, she was a pretty little girl. She looked like a Christmas angel.

"The next year Batista packed it in, on New Year's Day, 1959, and the world we knew turned upside down. The revolution was supposed to be for all of us, but it was clear very soon that that didn't include the quote, aristocrats, unquote. I could see what was coming, but my family never could, and Ana's couldn't, either. And her folks did a real number on her; when I begged her to bring the baby and come out with me, she wouldn't do it. It was all going to blow over in a few months, she said. She would stay with her family on the estate and wait for me to get it all out of my system. Then we'd go on just as we'd planned. She wasn't a stupid girl, but she was totally of her time and class, and she couldn't imagine that anything could ever change, even after it did.

"So. I got out with a young uncle on a commercial fishing boat out of Miami, and I stayed with some relatives there. There are Cassells all over the place. These didn't have half the money my folks did, but they were realistic about Cuba under Castro. They knew I couldn't go back. They found a job for me in a little Cuban radio station and I sent home what I could. I never knew if any of it got there or not. I didn't hear from Ana and the baby for almost a year, and by then things were pretty bad for all of them, my folks included. There wasn't a prayer of Ana getting out while the baby was so small. She wouldn't, anyway. Her family was in terrible shape, trying to do farm work for one of the cooperatives and dying from it. She wouldn't leave them. I knew in my heart that I wasn't going to see them again, though I wouldn't admit it to myself.

"I went back to Cuba in April of 1961 with the invasion forces that the CIA trained in Florida and Guatemala. I was captured almost before I put a foot on the beach and spent a year and a half in prison down there. I try not to talk about that year and a half. They let me out just before Christmas of 1962, and I was going to go and find my family, but I was met at the gate by a friend of my family in Miami and taken straight to the harbor at midnight, and put in the hold of a sailing sloop that belonged to some rich German dude who knew my uncle. That was the last time I saw Cuba.

"In 1963 my uncle sent me to Cornell and I got a graduate degree in tropical botany. I finished in 1966, with about as much chance of making a living in my specialty as if it had been sword-swallowing. But I'd met some people and learned some things at Cornell, and those months in that prison made something of me I'd never been before. There was a guy in Miami then, a fantastic man named Jorge Mas Canosa, sort of the legendary king of the anti-Castro exiles. The word 'charisma' might have been invented just for him. He founded the anti-Communist Cuban American Foundation, headquartered in Miami. It was the daddy of all the anti-Communist movements. He modeled it after your American political action committees, and he raised a ton of money for the movement, and got out the exile vote for the Republicans year after year. He was the most alive human being I ever saw. I would have followed him into hell. In a way, I did.

"He couldn't use a botanist, but he could a radio-TV announcer. He got me into Radio and TV Marti, his propaganda voice, which was nothing if not controversial in those days, and I just ate it up. I did everything. I read the news and played the music and kept the station logs and sold airtime and even had my own slot singing once, when we ran out of money and he couldn't get anybody else. But then I started to drink, which was almost endemic in the exile community in those days, especially among the ones of us who'd been in the invasion and in prison. Big man stuff, you know. I was one of the ones who couldn't handle it. It didn't take me long to go the whole way down. I was born to be an alky. I make a better drunk than I do anything else, probably. I got so bad on the air that he didn't have any choice but to fire me. Even I knew that. So I drifted around, doing landscape work and whatever radio and TV I could get. I didn't hold on to any of it. I never remarried and I never stayed with any woman long enough to settle down. I was married to the bottle, and that's no joke. I've done essentially that from the late seventies until now, only I've done the last eight years of it sober. I met Ezra in Charleston when he was speaking there, and he had this afternoon jazz and talk program on a station out on Wappoo Creek Road, and he put me on with him, and we played music and needled the Conservatives and he let me help him with some of his organizing. I helped organize the sanitation workers on John's. It was as big a thrill as I've ever had. But mostly I just do the radio program and what landscaping and consulting I can pick up.

"Like I said, I never went back to Cuba. There wasn't anything to go back to, really. My parents tried to run a little shop in Havana, but of course they knew nothing about that. They checked out with sleeping pills and rum one night about the time I discovered booze over here. My wife's folks ended up on one of Fidel's biggest agricultural co-operatives, doing field labor until they dropped from it, and my wife worked in the

241

fields, too. I only found this out later. She never would come out, not even when I found a fairly safe passage for her and Anita. Ana always thought things were about to change. Always did. Anita married a young man from the cooperative and went with him into the mountains to start a new agricultural colony there, but it failed after the first year. It's hard to tell anybody just how bad things are up in those hills. Everybody was checking out right and left, but she was nine months pregnant and spotting, and she didn't want to risk the baby. Her husband left with the others, saying he'd be back in a day or two with food and supplies, and after the baby came they'd go back to Havana and start over. I don't know if Anita had any sense or not, but she was Ana's child to the core, and she believed him. I don't know what happened to him. I guess she didn't, either. Dead, probably, from liquor or a fight, a lot of them died young. Anyway, he didn't come back and she went into a long and awful labor alone in their little shack, and the baby was born dead. She lay there bleeding to death with Lita beside her. I never even knew I had a grandchild until after they were all dead but her. She was not quite five. She wouldn't leave her mother and the baby. She just lay down beside them and waited. It was days before the Red Cross found her. They located my wife back in Havana and brought Lita to her, and that's where she's been until I could get her out, after Ana died. She wouldn't let me bring Lita out before that. Still waiting for things to get back to normal, she was. I have no picture of my daughter but the one made at her christening, and I cannot remember what my wife looked like, except for a picture I have that was made on our wedding day. Well, you know the rest of it; I told you yesterday. So. Does that earn me the right to hear the story of Caro Venable, from gestation up to now?"

"One day," I said, my eyes stinging with tears. "One day, maybe. My God, what a life. How could mine compete with that?"

"Are we having a competition? I tell you, Caro Venable, for all its comings and goings and ins and outs and so forth, the best thing I can say about my life up to now is that I beat booze and I have Lita. It doesn't seem very much for the amount of energy expended, does it?"

"If that's all you think a life like that adds up to, you've got a problem," I said.

"It was a selfish life," Luis said briefly. "When all's said and done, I did just what I wanted to. Anyway, I have a feeling things are about to change."

And he gave me such a showily exaggerated Latin leer that I could only laugh helplessly. If he had had a long, waxed mustache, he would have twirled it.

"I have to go home now," I said. "I've hung on breathlessly to your every word, but now, alas, my own duties call me."

"And are you impressed beyond words and moved almost to tears?"

"I'll think upon it and let you know," I said lightly, but inside I was both those things, and not ashamed of it, though I would never tell him so.

When he walked me to the car, he said, "Will you be staying out here? Lita is wild to see the ponies again."

"I've got to do Thanksgiving for about a million homeless lambs," I said, "but I'll try to come out after the weekend, and we'll track them down. How will I let you know?"

"I'll know," he said, bowing from the waist and kissing my hand. "I assure you, I'll know."

I shut the Jeep's door a little more smartly than was necessary, and he went back into the store. As he walked away, I could hear him laughing his hyena's laugh. I laughed, too. It felt good.

Two days before Thanksgiving, Jeremy

Fowler walked down to the sea in Puerto Rico at four o'clock in the morning, sat down, and blew his brains out with a police .38 nobody knew he had. By noon we had the news on Peacock's Island. By six o'clock that evening the company was in deep shock and full mourning.

Clay and Hayes flew down from Charleston that afternoon as soon as they could get a plane out. I went to the office and put a note on the front bulletin board and told a weeping Shawna to pass the word to everybody: our house was open for whomever wanted to come. There would be drinks and some supper, if anybody wanted it.

Almost everybody came. Most of those who had expected to go to their respective homes for Thanksgiving canceled their plans and drifted in, distraught and aimless. The two new couples had both left earlier in the week, but Sophia Bridges, who had not planned to go back to New York until Christmas, came. I was a little surprised at that. She had not known Jeremy, and knew few of the others; I had heard that she kept pretty much to herself and did not attend the formal and informal social occasions the company provides its employees. Shawna said, sniffling, that she seemed to prefer the company of her son to anybody else's, and that that was probably a good thing, since nobody could find a baby-sitter that suited. The child was in the company's modern day-care center when his mother was at work, but the rest of the time he was in her company. I wondered what she had done with him this evening. She had obviously come to our house in haste; her sleek black hair was disarrayed, and she still wore the slim jeans and sweatshirt she had obviously changed into when she got home that evening. Whoever she found for the boy would have to have been a last-minute solution.

I had asked Estelle to stay, and she had ordered groceries and made sandwiches and cheese straws and baked a ham while I went to the liquor store and picked up deli potato salad and a couple of carrot cakes from the little specialty pastry shop in the mall. Clay's youngsters picked at the food, but they lit into the liquor as if they were dying of thirst. By eight that evening more than a few of them were slurring their words, and some were weeping aloud. I didn't blame them. If it had not been the time and place that it was, I would have loved to have drunk bourbon and cried along with them. I had known Jeremy, too, and loved him, as they did. It had been impossible not to. I knew that the tears were not only for his death but for the sad, shocking trajectory of failure and waste that led up to it. The word flies fast in a close, ingrown company like Clay's. Everyone there knew about the collapse of Calista Key. Most knew that it would be a severe blow to the company, although few if any could have known just how severe. Under the grief and incredulity was fear. Fear of what the catastrophe might mean to both the company and to them personally, and a deeper and older fear: the fear of the golden, vital young when the first and the best of them falls.

I moved among them, patting shoulders and kissing cheeks and hugging whoever held out their arms. Some of them are only ten or so years younger than I am, but they have always seemed like my children to me, or rather, like young kin that I do not see often but still feel a vague responsibility for. With the exception of Sophia Bridges, I have known them all for some time, and many for years. It was as easy and natural for me to mop tears and exchange funny or bittersweet fragments of remembrance about Jeremy as if we had all been students together or denizens of the same small town. The only thing I could not seem to share with them was the tears. Mine lay, clotted and swollen, just at the base of my throat, and would not fall. I remember wondering if I could not cry for Jeremy Fowler, who on earth would I ever weep for again?

In a way I was glad it was just me on this first evening. In deep distress Clay goes still and silent, and sometimes seems cold and correct but little more. This is not true, of course; inside he suffers and bleeds like everyone else. I have often thought of Emily Dickinson's "After great pain, a formal feeling comes" — when I think of Clay in grief. It is his only armor, and I bless it for whatever ease it may afford him, but others, the young especially, need to be wept with and held. I could do that or, at least, the latter. Clay could have done neither. Later was when his iron and stillness would serve them. And as for Hayes, it seemed to me that he could only gibe. This night was not the time for that.

By nine o'clock most of them had gone home to drink some more or drive the baby-sitters home, to sit up into the small, cold hours of the morning talking about it, to cry again, and finally to sleep. I poured myself a cup of coffee from the big silver urn and went over and sat down beside Sophia Bridges. She was sitting where she had been for most of the evening, alone on the white sofa beside the fireplace in the big living room that looks out to sea. I had forgotten to draw the curtains, and, following her gaze, could see the distant line of white lace that was the surf curling in on the dark beach. The fire had burned itself nearly out.

"I'm sorry I haven't had more time to spend with you," I said, sitting down on the arm of the sofa. "This has just about done us all in. Jeremy was something special. I wish you had known him."

She smiled up at me faintly. Her face under the untidy hair seemed younger this evening, and softer. I thought perhaps it was because I had never seen her smile before.

"Oh, but I did," she said. "I've heard nothing but Jeremy since I got here. By now I feel like I know him like I would know my brother. I think maybe it wasn't such a good idea to come tonight, but I thought it would be worse if I didn't. He was obviously a powerful icon. I didn't want to seem to diss him."

She smiled again, as if to show me that her use of the slang was intentional. Two smiles in one evening, back to back. Through the fatigue that suddenly swamped me, and the numb, dumb desire just to go to bed and sleep, I felt a small sting of sympathy for her. It is not easy in the best of circumstances to walk into the Peacock Island Plantation

Company and be instantly accepted. How much harder it must be if you were black, alone, and known to be "the best of the lot." I knew that I had seen no one in conversation with her for any length of time all evening.

"It was just the right thing to do," I said. "They'll all appreciate it when they've got a little perspective on this. I know it's not so easy at first, getting your feet wet down here. It must seem like the other side of the moon from . . . where was it? New York?"

"New York; right," she said, stretching her long arms and rotating them in their sockets. Even in the sweatshirt she looked as elegant as a Modigliani.

"We've lived in the Village since . . . for a couple of years. On Bleecker Street. A fabulous little carriage house; I was so lucky to find it. There was a woman next door . . . a lovely Swedish woman; she got to be a real friend . . . who came in and stayed with Mark every day. I wouldn't have been able to finish my doctoral degree otherwise. I guess you can see why I was so hesitant about having an African-American woman stay with Mark. He's never had one. For a long time I didn't realize that he's actually afraid of people with dark skins. Now I see that I was not only foolish to insist on that, but I was doing him actual harm. I need to apologize to you about that little remark, Mrs. Venable, among other things. When I'm scared I get snotty."

"Call me Caro, please," I said, liking her, all of a sudden, very much indeed. I could see precisely why she pulled isolation around her and her son like a cloak. She probably had few peers. How many young black women could imagine being where Sophia Bridges was in her life? How many young white women could imagine the life itself?

"You have absolutely nothing to apologize to me for," I said. "As I said, there are a million things easier than walking into a tight little society that has existed quite nicely without you for a long time. They'll come to you eventually; I've seen it happen over and over again. Though not many of them came here with reputations like yours preceding them. That may be part of the problem. Clay thinks you're awfully special."

The easy smile vanished and the remote Ibo princess was back. I knew that there would be no easy victories with this one. But it was good to know, too, that there were chinks in her armor.

"I'm glad to have his high opinion," she said formally. "I've worked very hard for a long time to be special. It's what I have now in place of friends or a nice house in Connecticut or a husband. In the long run, I've always known that when you're black you'd better be special, because you can't count on the rest of it. It's something I want Mark to learn young. But you were right that first day; he has to live in the world he finds himself in. My baby-sitter tonight is an African-American woman, and he was doing fairly well when I left him. He'd almost stopped sniffling. She's as old as his grandmother, and she's lighter than me."

"Well, good," I said, unsure whether it was the right thing to say or not. Was that going to be her criteria? Black women might tend her son only if they were mulatto matrons? I wondered if she had ever seen the movie *Six Degrees of Separation*.

She made no move to leave, and declined coffee or a bite to eat or another glass of wine. So I hauled myself up by my mental bootstraps and said, "How is your work going? Clay said you had a degree in cultural anthropology; are you finding it useful here?"

"Yes, that was my master's," she said. "Up to now I've mainly been doing orientation, and you know of course that that's the same for everybody. I'm starting now to research the Gullah culture, though. I'm going into Charleston to the library next week. It should have something. I understand that there are several neighborhood units in this area, almost intact. It would be interesting to tie that in with the new development some-how; I think a lot of prospective homeowners would find that sort of ethnicity an attractive part of the whole picture. It would give such texture and resonance to the package . . ."

I thought of the dilapidated little gray houses in Dayclear, warm with pine and ker-osene lamplight against the winter twilight, and the sweet, liquid, and nearly incompre-hensible music of the Gullah tongue that was still sometimes spoken over on the island, and about the immense dignity and beauty of the old faces I knew from there. They would be amazed to know that they could be considered texture and resonance. My liking for her faded. I realized that I would love nothing more than to take her out to the set-tlement and fling her into the middle of it and leave her floundering there among her theories and pretensions.

"Then you should really come with me someday soon to my part of the island, back on the marshes," I said. "I spent most of my summer vacations there, in my grandfather's house, and the house is still mine . . . ours. There's one of the oldest Gullah . . . ah, units in the Lowcountry near there, a little settlement called Dayclear. Why go to the library when you can go to the source?"

"Clay mentioned something about Dayclear," she said. "I didn't realize it was actually part of the island. That would be a real opportunity for me, Mrs. Venable . . . Caro. I could take my tape recorder and a camera, and I'd love for Mark to see something like that *in situ*. Could we take you up on it soon?"

"Oh, yes," I said, baring my teeth in a smarmy smile. "We can go early next week, if you like. I'm tied up with this Thanksgiving oyster roast thing, but maybe the Monday or Tuesday after that?"

"I'll put it down," she said. In another five minutes she was gone and Estelle and I put the kitchen to rudimentary rights, then I sent her home and went up to my little study and fell asleep almost before I hit the daybed.

It was nearly a week later before I got Sophia Bridges and her son, Mark, over to the island. Late on Thanksgiving evening our crisp weather gave way to a long spell of fog and murk, with occasional fretful spatters of rain. Despite the company's advertising brochures, our late fall weather is seldom anything to cheer about; it is the start of our tenacious fits of sulking humidity that the Gulf exhales all across the deep South. Lingering leaves and moss hang sodden and sticky at eye level; doors swell and shoes go furry gray-green in closets, for the temperature is not cool enough for heat and too cool for air-conditioning. The air is the color and consistency of veal stock. If we are lucky, this climactic tantrum will run itself out a couple of weeks before Christmas, and those holidays will be bright and crisp and mild, the stuff of rhapsodic letters home from vacationing Canadians. Christmas is the true time of the snowbird, the season of the blue-fleshed but determined ocean bather, but we had a few of them even over our soggy Thanksgiving weekend. I saw them from the living room windows and was doubly grateful that Clay had canceled the Thanksgiving oyster roast. The weather, coupled with the painful knowledge that it was on a Peacock Island Plantation Company beach that Jeremy Fowler had made his final exit, put paid to any notion that a seaside revel could be enjoyed. Instead, we had everybody back to our house and used the oysters as on-the-half-shell appetizers, and Estelle and her niece and I cooked four turkeys and panfuls of corn bread and pecan dressing and made enough gravy to float a catamaran. By the time the last of our guests drifted home, I was drooping and stupid from fatigue. Clay kissed me on the top of the head, sent Carter to take Estelle and Gwen home, and pointed me upstairs to bed.

"I owe you for these past four days," he said. "You've fed and succored my flock twice now. I'm going to start cleaning up. Carter can help me when he gets back. You sleep in tomorrow. Don't get up till you wake up."

"You're walking on your knees yourself," I said, and it was true. His narrow face was actually sunken with fatigue and strain, and his crystal-blue eyes were dull. I knew the trip to Puerto Rico had been terrible for him. Jeremy's shattered parents had come from Texas, savagely seeking somewhere to lay the blame for their pain, and word had come that Lila Fowler had collapsed back in Philadelphia and been hospitalized at a discreet and prodigiously expensive private institution that specialized in treatment for substance addiction. Lila, it turned out, had been eating Percodan like after-dinner mints and washing them down with 150-proof Mount Gay rum. Her parents were threatening legal action. On top of his very real grief for Jeremy and the specter of the company's collapse, I wondered how Clay could bear it all.

But he insisted.

"I couldn't sleep," he said. "I'd just toss and turn. Let me do this. I need to talk over some things with Carter, anyway."

"Does he know . . . about the company?" I asked.

"Yes. I told him when I went to pick him up in Charleston. He took it better than I thought. In fact, it seems to be a challenge for him. He had some pretty good ideas right off the bat. He wants to stay here after this semester is over and help out, and I think I'll let him. He might as well get his feet wet now as later, and a real crisis is not the worst way to learn a business. Everything after it will look awfully good."

"Well . . . if you think so," I mumbled, hoping that there would be an after. "I'd like for him to go on and finish school, but it's nice that he wants to come home and help you show the flag. It'll be wonderful to have him around."

"Well, actually, he's going to be in Puerto Rico," Clay said. "There's a lot of mopping up to do, and I thought he could take care of some of that for Hayes and me. We've got our hands full here and in Atlanta."

"Have they . . . have the Atlanta people gone back?" I said, not wanting to talk about it but feeling that I must ask. It was, after all, his future. His and mine.

"Yep. They weren't very happy about us wanting to go back to the drawing board, but they want this project awfully bad. They're willing to give us a couple of months to come up with something else. Then we'll see where we are."

"Clay . . ." I said, going to him and laying my head against his shoulder, "thank you for that. Thank you for trying again. Thank you for . . . not making me the heavy in this, and for not making me deal with it quite yet. I'll do better about it a little later, I promise. I just . . . I can't . . ."

"I know," he said, sighing into my hair. "Go to bed."

And for the next three days, I slept, off and on, as though I had been drugged. When I finally did wake up enough to know that I was slept out, it was the following Sunday evening, and the rain was still falling. So it was not until the Wednesday after that that Sophia and Mark and I set out in the Cherokee to see the Gullahs of Dayclear, as Sophia had said, *in situ.*

It had faired off clean and crisp, but the ground was still waterlogged, and I knew the marshes would be a virtual soup. I wore the oldest jeans I had, and an ancient waxed cotton waterproof jacket, and the over-the-ankle L.L. Bean rubber boots that had been my winter marsh footwear for a decade. They were so salt-bleached and mud-caked that it was impossible to tell what color they had been. When I picked the two Bridgeses up at their smart little condominium in the harbor village, Sophia wore a linen safari suit almost the precise color of her skin and a smart felt Anzac hat. She was strung about with expensive leather cases holding cameras, a tape recorder, and a bottle of Evian. She looked, I thought, like Ava Gardner in *The Snows of Kilimanjaro*.

Her little boy looked like a miniature Michael Jackson.

"I'm not kidding," I told Lottie later. "He's so sort of carved and delicate and perfect that he doesn't seem alive, and he's paler than most white children; if it weren't for a slight crinkle to his hair, you'd think he was Norwegian or something. And his eyes are this strange ice gray. I'm sure his father is white. But the real thing that stops you is this incredible air of . . . I don't know, fragility. Otherworldliness. He reminded me of Colin in *The Secret Garden*. He looks like he might have been ill most of his life. And he's so shy it seems like outright fear. He stood behind his mother the entire day, almost, and he

259

didn't speak a word until it was almost time to leave the island. And I saw him smile exactly once. I'd love to know what's going on there. If he's that frail, no wonder she guards him like a lioness. I keep looking for the right word for him, and I almost have it sometimes, but it gets away . . ."

"Fey," Lottie said.

"Fey . . . yes. But, Lottie, that means . . ."

"Doomed. Soon to die. I know."

"Well, I didn't get that impression; I don't think he's sick. He just looks like he might have been. But yes, that's the word. . . ."

It was a long time before I could think of little Mark Bridges in any other terms but "fey."

He sat silently and correctly on the backseat of the Cherokee as I drove us over the bridge to the island, and got out at the house when his mother told him to, but he stuck just behind her, and his eyes, as he took in the old gray and silver live oak grove the house stood in, and the vast sweep of the lion-colored marsh, and the tangle of silent green that was the river forest beyond it, were wide and white-rimmed. I did not think he had often been in places like this. Nor, it was apparent, had Sophia.

"It's stunning," she said. "Primeval, really, isn't it? We've been to several beaches around New England, but there are no marshes there, and nothing as wild as this. Look, Mark, see that big white bird? I'll bet they have birds like that in Africa." Turning to me, she said, "We plan a photo safari to Kenya when Mark is a little older. This will be a good start for him."

But I did not think Mark Bridges would be ready for Kenya anytime soon. The marshes of Peacock's Island seemed to intimidate him thoroughly. He took hold of the edge of his mother's jacket and did not let go until we had gone into the house. Then he sat on the sofa that faced away from the glass window wall, sipping the apple juice his mother had brought in one of her assorted leather pouches, and did not look at the marsh.

Sophia did not prod him to be more adventurous, or try to explain his timidity, as many other mothers might have done, and I liked her for that. This kind of fear, I thought, could only be healed by the boy himself. He would find his own talisman against it, or not.

"The place where we're going isn't so wild, Mark," I said to him. "It's a regular little village, where people have lived for a long, long time. There are little houses, and a store, and a tiny little church they call a pray house. I don't think there are many children, but I know of one who might be around. She's about your age, and she's a little Cuban girl, from a country way down south in the ocean below Florida. She may not be there, though; she goes out with her grandfather a lot. He's a very special kind of gardener, and he works all over the island. But the old people there know some wonderful stories and songs. Maybe they'll sing some for you. And there's a little herd of ponies somewhere close by, and one of them has a baby. Maybe we'll see them."

Mark edged a little closer to his mother. Apparently ponies were not a part of his special reality.

"We had a rather bad little scene with a horse in Central Park," Sophia said matter-of-factly. "I'd rather Mark didn't experience horses again until later."

"Well, these are very small horses, and quite shy," I said. "But I doubt we'll see them. They don't hang around the village much. How about chickens? Is he okay with them? They're all over the place in Dayclear."

"He's seen them at the Central Park petting zoo," she said. "I think he'll be fine with them, if nobody talks about eating them. He gets upset when he thinks he's eating anything that was alive."

"Well, I hope we don't come across anybody wringing a hen's neck for the pot," I said more crisply than I intended. I was getting a bit weary of this pair and their strange, self-constructed universe.

"Surely they don't do that," Sophia said, clearly disapproving.

"Sophia," I said carefully, "this is a real Gullah settlement, one of the longest-standing that I know of. They are quite isolated. They still live much the way they did a hundred years ago. They sing the old songs that originally came from Africa, and do the old dances, and tell the old stories, and raise their food and prepare it much the same way as they always have. They are quite poor by our standards, but they are self-sufficient and they do very well with what they have, all told. Their lifestyle is not the sanitized one we live. They kill chickens and they trap rabbits and they eat them. If that's a problem for Mark — and I can see why it might be; that's not a criticism — then maybe we should do this another day when he's in school or something. You can let him experience it gradually and it will probably be okay."

She stared at me, as if to determine whether or not I was, indeed, implying criticism, and then shook her elegant head. Her hair today was sleeked back and tied with a leopard-printed chiffon scarf. The hat hung down her back from a cord.

"No. It's an authentic ethnic culture, and I don't want him to be afraid of that," she said. "We'll talk about it all, he and I, when we get home and make a little parable of it. We do that a lot."

We finished our coffee and Mark his apple juice, and went down the steps toward the Cherokee, to set off for Dayclear. Just as we reached the bottom one, a great grinding roar burst into the clearing, and a spuming cloud of fine black mud swept, tornadolike, down the sandy drive, and we heard, over the roaring, shouts and catcalls and huge, raucous laughter. A hurtling shape burst out of the mud spray and I saw what it was: a great black motorcycle with two men astride it. They were shouting and beating on the sides of the machine, and laughing, looking for all the world like demented gods on a terrible *deus ex machina*. They were singing, too; under the bellowing motor I made out the roared words to John Lee Hooker's *Boogie Chillen*: " 'I was walking down Hastings Street/I saw a little place called Henry's Swing Club/ Decided I'd stop in there that night/And I got down . . .' "

We stood frozen on the steps. The motorcycle swept into the yard and past us, missing us by what seemed inches. It roared out of the yard, made a circle, and came burring down on us again. The two men called greetings and laughed loudly. I could not make them out for the fantail spray of wet black mud.

Mark Bridges made a high, strangled sound like the squeak of a rabbit caught in a snare and threw himself down on the steps and rolled into a ball. Sophia hurtled off the bottom step like a missile. She ran into the path of the motorcycle and stood there, fists balled, screaming with fury. I could not seem to move.

"Stop that, you sons of bitches!" she shrieked. "Can't you see you've scared my child to death? Stop it this second or I'll get the police on you!"

The motorcycle skidded to a stop. The silence rang like a brass gong. Sophia did not move. The two men dismounted and came toward her slowly. I recognized Luis Cassells first, mud-spattered and windblown, his big, dark face crestfallen. Then I saw that the other man was Ezra Upchurch. He was even more mud-slimed and wind-savaged, but one would have known that squat, tanklike build and the massive, overhanging brow and the perfect blue-black of his skin almost anywhere. Practically every man, woman, and child in America had seen it in newspapers and on television since the late seventies.

"Jesus, lady, I almost hit you," he said, and the beautiful, coffee-rich voice seemed as familiar as a neighbor's, because I had heard it so often over the air.

"You almost hit my son, too, you complete, capering asshole," Sophia spat, and I gasped, simply because the words were so at odds with her chilly elegance.

"What's the matter with you that you think you can come roaring in here on that thing and run children down? Mark is a sensitive child; it's going to take me *days* to get him calmed down! I'm of a good mind to report you to the authorities *and* to Clay Venable. If you aren't aware of it, this is his land you're trespassing on. I happen to work for him, and this lady happens to be his wife."

Ezra Upchurch looked down at the crouched ball on the steps that was Mark Bridges. I had sat down beside him and put my arms around him, and I could feel the profound trembling that shook him like an ague.

"I'm sorry," Ezra Upchurch said. "I didn't see the boy. I know whose land this is, ma'am.

Hello, Caro. Haven't seen you since you were in training bras. Come a long way, I see. Ma'am, my name is Ezra Upchurch—"

"I know who you are," Sophia said. "It doesn't make you any less an asshole."

Luis Cassells laughed.

"She's got you pegged, Ezra," he said. "Caro, I apologize. This is my fault. Shem was crabbing under the bridge when you came over and when we stopped to talk to him he said he'd seen you come this way with a . . . real fine-looking young lady. He didn't say anything about the boy. We wouldn't have scared him for the world. We were just . . . having fun."

"Oh, God, Luis," I said, my heart still hammering. "You could have killed somebody. Mrs. Bridges is new with the company, and I was about to bring her over to Dayclear. She's doing . . . some research for Clay. But I think maybe we ought to get the little boy home . . ."

Ezra Upchurch walked close to Sophia Bridges. His coal-black eyes, lost in ridges of pouched flesh and a network of fine wrinkles, lingered on her, taking in the exquisite carved face and the long, slender body and the safari outfit.

"I do apologize," he said. "Let me make it up to your boy . . ."

He started for the steps, where Mark had begun to sob. He did not move to uncoil himself from the anguished ball. Through the silky fabric of his little Shetland sweater I could feel his heart going like a trip-hammer.

Sophia Bridges moved like a cat. In a split second she stood in front of her son on the bottom step.

"If you touch my son I'll scratch your eyes out," she said in the cold, pure voice I had first heard at the guest house. "That's before I call the police."

He stopped and studied her. Then he smiled. It was a lazy, insinuating, completely sexual smile. I felt its sheer wattage even though it was not directed at me.

"Unnnh . . . *uh!*" he drawled. "What we got here?"

The lapse into street black was as deliberate as a pinch or a leer. Sophia Bridges's face blanched with fury.

I stepped in then.

"Sophia, there are chocolate chip cookies and fresh milk in the fridge, and the coffee's still hot," I said. "Why don't you take Mark in and give him some, and I'll just say good-bye to these two . . . gentlemen. I agree with you, they were foolhardy, but I know they didn't mean any harm. Mr. Cassells here has a granddaughter that he dotes on;

you know, the little Cuban girl I was telling Mark about. And Mr. Upchurch was born and grew up in Dayclear. If you can find it in your heart to forgive him, he can tell you almost anything you might want to know about it. You couldn't have a better tour guide. He knows things I never will."

She said nothing but lifted her child up and carried him bodily into the house. I would have thought his weight, frail as he was, would be too much for her slender arms, but she carried him easily. I could hear Mark still sobbing into her shoulder, but it seemed to me that the sobs were growing fainter. Sophia did not look back.

"I thought maybe the little boy might like a nice, slow ride on the cycle," Ezra Upchurch said, pitching it just loudly enough for Sophia and Mark to hear. "The kids in Dayclear love it."

"Over my dead body," she flung back over her shoulder.

But Mark lifted his strange, tear-drowned little face for a moment and looked at Ezra Upchurch, and then at the motorcycle, before lowering it again to his mother's shoulder. Ezra made the old peace sign with his fore and middle fingers and smiled broadly at the boy. That smile had bent tougher spines than Mark Bridges's. Just before he tucked his face back into its nest of expensive Armani khaki, I thought I caught the faintest ghost of an answering smile.

I stood looking at the two men.

"Good work, guys," I said. "Maybe she won't call the police, but she's going to tell Clay, sure as gun's iron."

"Not Mengele! Oh, no," quavered Luis Cassells, and I glared at him.

"I'll take my chances," Ezra Upchurch said equably. "Look, I *am* sorry, Caro. I guess she's got a right to be pissed. What's the matter with that boy, anyway?"

"I don't know," I said. "I think maybe he's been sick. And he's a long way from home, and he probably misses his father. They're divorced. She's pretty protective of him."

"She's pretty, period," he said, grinning. "But that mama is way too much mama for me. Whoo-eee!"

Then he fell back into the perfect, Harvard-inflected English that was one of his hallmarks.

"I hope you'll persuade her to bring the boy on over to Dayclear," he said. "I'd like to make this up to both of them. If it's . . . ah, research I believe you said . . . that she's after, I'd be delighted to play cicerone for her. You, too. I'd like to catch up with you. I know what you've been doing since I saw you last, but not how you feel about it. Will you try to change her mind?"

"I will, but don't count on it," I said.

But to my surprise, Sophia Bridges decided to go on to Dayclear. When I got inside she was sitting with Mark at the kitchen counter drinking coffee while he finished his milk and cookies, and both of them were neatened and brushed and face-washed and composed again.

"Mark has decided he wants to go," she said. "So we will. We'll leave now. But I'm adamant that I don't want that motorcycle anywhere around. I must insist on that, Caro."

"I'm sure Ezra can hide it in the swamp or something," I said, amused and not a little annoyed at her peremptoriness.

She stared at me hard.

"He better do that," she said without smiling, and I sighed, and we left for Dayclear.

8

In fact, he had done just that. When we got to the general store, I saw the motorcycle deep in the tangle of scrub and kudzu out back, hardly showing at all. Only its crusted headlights were clearly visible. But I was looking for it, and had no trouble spotting it. I do not think that Sophia Bridges saw it. She had begun photographing when we reached the sand road that led in through the woods to the settlement, leaning out the window and imploring me to go slower. When we rounded the last curve and the general store was in sight she was intent on capturing a back view of an old man leading a spavined mule down the road. Both wore straw hats. Mark may have seen the cycle, though. I heard a soft gasp from the backseat that I somehow did not think was alarm, but whether he was intrigued by the motorcycle or the chapeau-clad mule and its owner I did not know.

As we approached the old man and the mule I put a hand lightly on Sophia's shoulder and said, "I wouldn't photograph them head-on. Not right now. They're very shy about strangers until they get to know them, and they don't like cameras. Later on, after he gets used to you, he'll probably pose for you all day."

She turned a glowing face to me.

"They don't by any chance think the camera steals their souls, do they?" she breathed reverently.

"Not since they got here from Africa a couple of hundred years ago," I said acidly. "It's just not considered polite. I think the soul thing was that tribe in New Guinea that had never seen a white man, anyway. Maybe you ought to leave the camera and tape recorder here the first time out."

She did not want to do that.

"I want to be very clear about what I'm doing," she said. "Really up front with them. I don't want to seem as if I'd just come to gawk."

But I thought that without the tools of her trade she felt uncertain, somewhat at sea, and perhaps afraid that the people of Dayclear would not perceive her authority and expertise at first.

"You're with me, and they know me a little," I said. "That's the only entree that's going to work, believe me. You better hope Ezra *is* around. That's the best way, by far. Next to being long-lost kin, to be known by a native to the village is the most acceptable way to come into a Gullah community. Their sense of family is tremendous; we don't have anything like it in our culture, not really. The family structure, the ancestors, the tribe . . . it's everything. Mark will be a real draw, too, even if he doesn't want to say a word. They won't care about that. Children are almost magical to the Gullahs. Back in Africa they were the responsibility of everybody in the village. Hillary Clinton's right about that."

In the end she left the camera and the recorder in the car, but she was more ill at ease than I had ever seen her when we walked into the little general store. I could not imagine why. Surely her fieldwork in cultural anthropology had led her into stranger and more threatening places than this. Mark lagged behind her, clutching the hem of her jacket.

Janie Biggins was at the store counter again today. She wore, over a shapeless black cotton dress that looked as if it might have been a maid's uniform once and probably was, a man's heavy wool cardigan missing its buttons. The little store was chilly. There was no heat except for the iron stove in the back, but that was glowing red against the nip of the bright, cold day. Several old men sat in chairs around it. They stopped their talk when we came in and stared at us.

Janie Biggins did, too. There was no cheerful welcome for me today. I knew that it was partly because I had brought strangers with me into the fortress of Dayclear, but I thought, too, that they had all probably heard by now about Clay's plans for the settlement and the land surrounding it. I knew that they would wait, now, to see what I would do about that. I felt a twist of pure misery, and a stronger one of anger. I hated being in this position.

"Good morning, Janie," I said politely. "I've brought some friends of mine to visit Mr. Cassells. Do you happen to know where he is?"

She shook her head slowly, not looking directly at me.

"I seen him a while ago, but I don't know where he got to now. I sho' don't."

I knew that she did know, though. Janie knew where everybody in the settlement was most of the time.

"We saw Ezra over at my grandfather's place, too, and he asked us to come over and meet his auntie," I said. Sophia shot a look at me, but I did not return it.

Janie met my eyes and I knew I had found the key.

"Ezra, he down to Miss Tuesday's," she said. "I 'spec Mr. Cassells be there, too. They generally both there roun' lunchtime."

And this time she did smile, just a bit. Ezra Upchurch was a powerful totem.

I thanked her and we walked out of the store and down the sandy road that led through Dayclear. The little houses — shacks, really, leaning badly and unpainted and tin-roofed — were none of them more than two or three rooms large, and many had only one. All sat up on stones or bricks or rotting wooden posts. There were broken-down chairs on the small front porches, and a few under the great live oaks in the neatly swept white-sand yards, but they were empty on this sharp day. The usual cacophony of chickens and the sleeping yellow and black dogs were absent, too. The dogs would be inside, in front of fires along with their masters. Perhaps the chickens were, too. Seeing the look of clinical interest and faint distaste on Sophia Bridges's face, I hoped that they were. Some of the panes of the windows that faced the road were missing and had been replaced with cardboard and newspaper, but the ones that remained were sparkling clean. I knew that many pairs of eyes watched our progress through them.

On the other side of the little road there were cleared fields and small garden patches, neatly put to bed now for the winter, where the villagers raised their own food and the produce they sold to the truck farmers around the Lowcountry. Fanciful scarecrows tilted in the bare fields, doing nothing at all to dismay the flocks of cheeky black crows, and smartly mended rail and wire fences enclosed each plot. We could see the little lean-tos that housed goats and pigs and a few cows and the prized mules, but their occupants were inside like their owners, out of the strong wind. In all of Dayclear, we saw no one during that walk, but I felt the eyes of everyone. I wondered what they made of the elegant Sophia Bridges and her pale princeling.

Janie had said that Ezra Upchurch's aunt's house was the last one in the row before the forest started again. It looked just like the others, except that there was a new paint job in progress; the dingy gray boards were turning a sharp blue-white. Ezra, I thought. From under the porch a pair of wicked yellow eyes regarded us.

"Look, Mark, it's a little pet goat," I said before he could see the malevolent gaze and be panicked again. I hoped it was indeed a small goat, and a pet. Whatever it was, it did not leave its shelter to investigate us, and Mark did not shy at it. During the entire time we had been here, he had been silently drinking in Dayclear with his gray eyes, and they were as large and lucent now as small frozen ponds.

The front door opened before I could knock, and Ezra Upchurch stood there. He was clean, and dressed in a tweed sports coat and gray flannel slacks, and looked in his shining, tailored blackness like the president for life of some ancient, affluent African state. Behind him, Luis Cassells stood, holding a tray of something so hot that it smoked. Both of them were grinning hugely, near-identical, feral white smiles.

"I would have bet the farm you wouldn't show," Ezra said, "but Auntie said you would. Said she saw it in the dishwater this morning. She sent me out to pick collards and dig yams, and I went without a murmur. Auntie's dishwater seldom fails her. Come in and meet her."

Ezra's Aunt Tuesday Upchurch was so tiny as to be almost a dwarf, bent nearly double with arthritis and nearly blind with cataracts. I wondered how she could see the dishwater or much of anything else through the fish-scale films on her eyes. But she trained them on me intently when Ezra introduced me and smiled. She had few teeth, and one of those was gold. I thought she must be ancient beyond imagining.

"You be Mist' Gerald's gran'girl, I 'spec," she said in her tiny, piping wheeze. "You has the look of him, yes. Who you bring to see me this cold day, child?"

I thought Ezra had probably told her about Sophia and Mark, but I presented them as formally and politely as was due her great age.

"This is Mrs. Sophia Bridges, who is working for my husband, and her son, Mark. They've just moved to Peacock's from New York, and wanted to see all there was to see in the Lowcountry. Thank you for letting us come, Mrs. Upchurch."

She cackled.

"Hush, girl, I know you come to see this bad Cuban hire and my big ol' nephew, but never you mind, you welcome in my house, and yo' company, too. Come here, girl, and let me look at you, and bring that boy here," she said, turning the silvery eyes on Sophia and Mark. They came forward, Sophia pushing Mark ahead of her. Mrs. Upchurch put out her withered little claw, and after a moment Sophia took it.

Mrs. Upchurch held Sophia's hand for a long time, looking silently into her face.

Whether or not she saw I could not tell, but I had the impression that she was taking Sophia's full measure.

"I'm glad to meet you, Mrs. Upchurch," Sophia said in her cool, clipped New York voice, and the old woman cocked her head. Sophia made as if to withdraw her hand, but Mrs. Upchurch held it fast.

"What your maiden name, child?" she said finally.

Sophia was silent for so long that I thought she was not going to answer, but then she said pleasantly, "McKay. Sophia McKay."

The old woman nodded slowly, and then looked down at the boy. He stared back, a fledgling mesmerized by a snake.

"I'm glad you bring this boy to Dayclear," Mrs. Tuesday Upchurch said. "We don't see many younguns here anymore. This boy be welcome. You bring him back."

Still Mark stared.

Just then Estrellita bounded into the room, followed by her grandfather, who had also changed into a jacket and slacks, though not so natty or well-tailored as Ezra's. The child skidded up to me and threw her arms around my waist and hugged me hard. I went still. I had forgotten the feel of small arms just there.

"Caro, Caro, can we go see Nissy and her

baby?" she cried. There was nothing hesitant or unused about her voice today. I looked at Luis, and he laughed.

"She hasn't stopped talking since that day," he said, ruffling the glossy black hair. "Either you or those horses are powerful magic. Not today, *cara*. Today is too cold for the ponies. We'll go soon; it'll warm up again, you'll see. Maybe Mrs. Venable will take us. Meanwhile, say hello to Mark Bridges. He and his mother have just moved down here from New York City, and I bet you anything he doesn't know any little Cuban girls yet."

Lita swung around to Mark. He edged back behind his mother. I could sympathize with him; on this strangest of days, in this strangest of places, surrounded by this eldritch old woman and the two big men, this small, dark dynamo must simply be one elemental force too many.

"Let Mark get his bearings," I said softly. "It's hard to come to such a new and different place all of a sudden, when you're still small yourself."

"I know," she said sympathetically, and I winced. She did know; she of all people knew. "You'll get used to it soon," she said kindly to Mark. "It doesn't take long at all. This place is *paradiso*."

"That means she thinks it's a wonderful place, Mark," Sophia said, and her son merely looked at her. Who was kidding who here?

Mrs. Upchurch had cooked collards in a big black pot on the rusty old iron cookstove and baked sweet potatoes — she called them yams — in the ashes of the banked fire. We ate them at a rickety, immaculate, oilcloth-covered table, and the greens, redolent of smoky ham, and the potatoes, their jackets still dusty with ash, were as good as anything I have ever tasted. We ate hot crackling corn bread with them and drank strong coffee made in a spatterware pot on the stove. Mark had a glass of milk that, Mrs. Upchurch said, had come fresh from the cow that morning. His eyes bulged at that, but he drank the milk, glancing at his mother for approval. She nodded, but I could tell she would far rather it had come fresh and dated from the supermarket. She herself only picked at the sweet potato and left the grease-shimmering greens and the fat crackling bread untouched. She drank a lot of coffee. Ezra and Luis and I finished off two helpings of everything. I would have, even if I had not been hungry. Mrs. Upchurch nodded serenely, smiling a little, as if she were falling asleep, in her rocking chair by the stove, and did not seem to notice that two of her guests did not seem enthusiastic about her lunch. I would, I thought, speak to Sophia Bridges about this in no uncertain terms. She could not hope to accomplish anything in Dayclear if she did not observe the rudimentary rules of etiquette.

After lunch I could tell Sophia was eager to be gone, but Mrs. Upchurch had moved over to a big armchair before the fire, and Ezra took his place at her side in a straight chair. We were obviously expected to stay, at least through whatever came next. Luis settled himself into a chair beside mine and Lita crawled into his arms and promptly fell asleep in the warm, dim room. Her small head lolled back onto my arm. Across from me, Sophia perched on a milking stool in her militant Armani, looking like a peacock in a henhouse, poised for flight. Mark, his eyes still huge and translucent, stood straight and still at her knee.

Ezra cleared his throat.

"Luis and I have a little business in Columbia, but before we go, Auntie thought you'd like to hear a story. In a Gullah home" — and he looked at Sophia and then at Mark — "the host or hostess wouldn't think of letting a guest leave without a story. How about it, Mark? You know the story of Ber Rabbit in the peanut patch?"

I saw Sophia frown and thought, If she says a word about not wanting Mark to experience the stories told in black dialect, I'll snatch her baldheaded right here, but she fell silent. Her eyes were cast down, though.

Mark's shone. He nodded his head, staring up at Ezra.

"Well, then. Here we go. Auntie, you're on."

The old lady closed her eyes and began rocking, a gentle, hypnotic movement. Her lips curved in a beatific smile. She rocked and rocked. Then she said, "I gon' tell a short story."

"Uh hummm. Tell 'em." Ezra Upchurch chanted. He was rocking, too, and the bright black eyes were closed.

"Tell about the rabbit and the . . . the man . . ."

"Uh hummm! Ber Rabbit! Ber Rabbit!"

"Now one day the man catch the rabbit in his peanut patch. Trap 'im in the peanut patch. And he say, 'Now, Ber Rabbit, you always sharp! You always got a lot of scheme! But now, you know what I gon' do with you? I gon' punish you! I gon' throw you in dat fire!' "

"Yeah, the fire!"

"Ber Rabbit, O Lord! I tell you what he do. He say, 'Old man, throw me in the fire!'

284

"And the man say, 'No, you too free!' Say, 'I ain't gon' do that! I tell you what I gon' do with you. I gon' throw you in that river!' "

"Yeah! The river!"

"Ber Rabbit say, 'I tell you what you do. You throw me in that river. Let me drown in there. Just throw me in the river. I want a dead anyhow.' "

"Uh hummm!"

"Man say, 'No-o-o. I ain't gon' throw you in there 'cause you too free! You too sharp!' And he say, 'I know! You know what I gon' do with you, Ber Rabbit?'

"Rabbit say, all unconcerned-like: 'What you gon' do? What you gon' do?'

"And the man, he carry 'im to the briarwood patch. And boy! That briarwood been about high as his head.

"Say, 'Ber Rabbit, I gon' throw you in that briarwood patch.'

" 'OOOOoooo Lord!' say Ber Rabbit. 'Pleassseee don't throw me in there! Dem briarwood stick me up!' "

"Ummm hummm! Stick 'im up!"

"And the man take Ber Rabbit, say, 'Oh, I got you now, Ber Rabbit!'

" 'Ohhhhhh, don't throw me in there! I rather you kill me!'

"So he take the rabbit and throw 'im in the briarwood patch. The rabbit say, 'You fool you! This where I born and raise!' "

"Born and raise! Ummm hummm!"

They both fell silent. Mrs. Upchurch's head nodded down on her chest. I thought she slept but could not be sure. No one moved or spoke. I looked over at Sophia Bridges. Her face was closed and still, and she had pulled her body slightly backward, as if to remove herself as far as possible from the story and the storyteller. I looked at Mark. He was rapt, his mouth in a perfect O.

Ezra Upchurch was looking at him, too.

"Good story, huh, Mark? You'll have to come back soon. She knows all the old stories there are to know. All the old games, too. Lita knows some of them; she can teach them to you."

Sophia Bridges stirred and started to speak, but he broke in over her.

"Now, before we all go, I want to sing you my auntie's favorite song. She always sings it for visitors before they go, but she's a little tired, I see. She'll jerk a knot in me if I don't sing it for her, though."

And he stood, as easily as if he were alone in the room, shining like a basalt cliff in the gloom, and threw back his head, and began to sing. His voice rolled and caromed in the little room, as full and complex as deep winter water.

"Honey in the rock, got to feed God's children.
Honey in the rock, honey in the rock.
Honey in the rock, got to feed God's children,
Feed every child of God."

Luis Cassells came in with him:

"Oh, children, one of these mornings I was
    walking long.
I saw the grapes was a'hangin' down.
Lord, I took a bunch and I suck the juice,
It's the sweetest juice that I ever taste."

The deep male voices climbed in the frail afternoon light slanting through the little panes, filling the house up to the rafters, spilling out into the clear air.

"Satan mad and I so glad.
He missed the soul that he thought he had.
Oh, the devil so mad and I so glad,
He missed the soul he thought he had.
Honey in the rock, honey in the rock
Got to feed God's children now."

When they had finished there was no sound but the gentle bubbling snore from Mrs. Upchurch, and the song seemed to spin on and on. I felt my hands and feet tingle, and my face burn as if I were blushing. It had been inexplicably, incredibly beautiful. Across from me Sophia Bridges seemed as still and empty as someone in a coma. Mark looked from one adult to another, as if waiting for whatever would come next.

Mrs. Tuesday Upchurch shook herself and came back to us. She hauled herself to her feet and tottered over to Mark and Sophia. She put her bleached, wrinkled old hand on the boy's head and smiled down at him. He did not move. She picked up Sophia's limp hand and peered up into her remote face.

"You remember about Ber Rabbit, girl," she said softly. "When you born and raised in the briarwood patch, the briars can't hurt you."

Then she turned and shuffled out of the room, through a dusty old velvet curtain hanging in a doorway, and was gone.

"Auntie needs to sleep now," Ezra said. "How about I take you all on a little tour of Dayclear, let you meet some of the other old-timers?"

"We have to go. We've stayed much longer than I intended," Sophia Bridges said abruptly. What was it in her eyes? Not just distaste. Fear? But how could that be?

She turned to me.

"Mark has a French lesson at four. We'll have to hurry if we're going to make it."

I stood, holding out my hand to Ezra.

"Ezra, please thank your aunt for us," I said. "It was a wonderful lunch, and we loved the story and the song. I hope —"

"No," said Mark Bridges clearly.

"What?"

His mother looked at him. We all did.

"No, I don't want to go home in the car. I want to go home on the motorcycle," he said. His voice was a papery whisper, like the wings of a dead wasp.

"Mark, for heaven's sake! I'm not about to let you get on that thing; it scared you to death this morning," Sophia said. "Get your things now."

"No. The motorcycle."

He did not have a tantrum. He did not cry or beg. He did not even speak again. He merely looked at his mother with all the force of those enormous, extraordinary eyes. They seemed to spill pure, liquid light out into the room.

"It'll easily carry three," Ezra said quietly. "I can wrap you both up in my sweaters and scarves. We can go real, real slow. It hardly makes any noise at all that way. It'll only take a few minutes, just a little longer than the car would."

Mark stared, unblinking, at his mother. His face was suddenly heartbreakingly beautiful. Why had I ever thought it strange?

She raised her hands and shoulders and dropped them helplessly.

"All right. Okay. But if you miss your French lesson, you're going to pay for it yourself, out of your allowance," she said.

Without moving at all, his face shone like the young sun. Hers was cold and shuttered. Ezra Upchurch merely smiled, his big, genial wolf's smile, and left to get warm wraps. Sophia would not look at me. She did not again, that day.

Luis walked me up the road to the car, carrying the sleeping child in his arms. He put his head into the open window after I had shut the door.

"You going home now?" he said.

"Yes."

"Going to have a drink with Mengele?"

"He's out of town. Don't call him that. I asked you not to."

"Good," he said, as if he had not heard me. "You drink too much."

"How do you know how much I drink?"

"I know about you."

"How? Why?"

"Research. I always know my territory."

"You're a tough cookie, aren't you?" I said.

"No. If I was a tough cookie I'd be back in Miami practicing pro bono law."

"So why *are* you here?"

He did not answer. Suddenly, I thought I knew.

"You're one of them, aren't you? You're with Ezra; you're one of his activists, or whatever it is he calls them. That's why both of you are in Dayclear right now. You knew all about the project before you even came to work for Clay. I could have you fired, Luis Cassells. You're a mole."

He shifted the child in his arms and looked at me levelly.

"You going to?"

I shook my head slowly, suddenly so tired I could hardly hold it up.

"No."

"Why not? It's the only loyal thing to do, Caro. You know you're going to go along with him in the end. . . ."

"I don't know anything of the sort. I just said I'd think about it. They're going to re-design everything and get back to me. There's all kinds of time yet . . ."

"There's never time," he said, and pulled his head out of the window, and carried his sleeping granddaughter back down the sandy road toward the house of Ezra Upchurch's aunt.

9

Ever since I was a small child I have had the fancy that, between Thanksgiving and New Year's Day, time somehow stops. I knew then and know now, of course, that each day wheels past at its appointed pace, but it has never seemed to me that it is real time that passed. That strange, glittering, suspended time seems swung between two realities: it belongs to no sober workaday chronology that I know. It is, in effect, the Washington, D.C., of the calendar year. And so it was with this holiday season. I walked lightly and carefully in that bubble of timelessness and thought neither behind me nor ahead, and was for the interval oddly happy.

I did not really forget what had happened to the company and more particularly and terrible to Jeremy Fowler, but I found that I could put it away for the nonce. And there was no forgetting the heavy sword that dangled over Dayclear and my island, but I did not have to remember it until after the holidays were over. This gift of suspended time was one of the sweetest and most unanticipated that I have ever received. I was as awed and delighted with it as a child with a wonderful, unexpected present. And for that period I behaved, I believe, more like a child than I have since I was one myself, or my children were. I was sometimes shamefully silly when Carter and Kylie were very young, but the silliness went, as did so much else, with my daughter, down into the sea. Now it was back. I indulged it gratefully. I would, I promised myself, shape up and buckle down to my real life on the second of January.

I dragged home an enormous Frasier fir tree from the island nursery and put it up in front of the glass windows in the big living room and spent an entire day decorating it with the cartons of ornaments and lights we had stored when I took to having smaller, more understated trees and putting them in the small library that overlooked the back garden. After Kylie I could not seem to bear the thought of those tender, annunciatory lights shining on that black sea. No one had ever mentioned it, but when Clay saw the tree, and when Carter came home from Puerto Rico and first spied it, their faces lit in a way that told me the loss of the big tree had been hurtful. My heart smote me. Selfish; I had never even thought of that.

And since we had the tree up anyway, I

had an open house and asked everybody we'd ever known in the Charleston area, or almost, and was surprised and gratified that almost all of them came. It was an old-fashioned party; I had eggnog and Charleston Light Dragoon Punch and benné seed cake and my grandmother's fruitcake, and Estelle made divinity and peanut candy, but there was little on my buffet that was sophisticated or clever. Looking over my food list, I saw that I was indeed having a children's party, and so I moved the time to four in the afternoon and invited the children of my guests, and a great many of them came, too.

The party was such a success that many people suggested we make it an annual occasion.

"Of course," I replied, and "Why not?"

Next year was so far outside my bubble of now that it need not even be reckoned with. In the meantime, the assorted children darting and shrieking around the tree and through the living room and out onto the lawn gave our house the air of a Lord & Taylor Christmas window, and that is how I chose to regard it. We had recordings of the traditional carols, and small presents for the children, and there was enough laughter and singing to fill the vast cave of the living room, for once, to its eaves. When dusk fell and the lights of the tree swam in their underwater radiance against the darkening sea and sky, only living children were reflected in my wall of windows. If a small shade joined them, I resolutely did not see.

I was truly moved to see how much Clay enjoyed the party. I did not realize until I saw him laughing with his guests and their children how quiet he had become, how far into himself he had drawn. I was accustomed to Clay's going away inside his own head when there was a new project on his drawing board, but only when he emerged into our Christmas world, blinking and smiling, did I see that there had been a quality of somberness, almost of mourning, in his abstraction. Of course there was Jeremy, and the great peril that hung over the company, but I knew this was more, and I knew what it was. But I did not have to deal with it for the time being. It was enough that I had Clay back. I was determined to keep him as long as I could.

So we became social butterflies, something I, at least, had never been. We went to every party we were asked to; there was hardly a reception or open house or cocktail or dinner party from Georgetown to Beaufort that we did not attend. Sometimes, if the drive was long, we stayed over, either with friends or at an inn. We had done that so seldom in our marriage that it was festive and somehow erotic to me to wake up beside my husband in a pretty eighteenth-century bedroom that was not mine, with breakfast made by someone else waiting for us when we chose to come down. We slept late, ate heartily of shrimp and grits and oysters in every imaginable style and creamed seafood in patty shells and crab cakes according to the receipts of a dozen Charleston grandmothers, and we danced, and we even sang a little when someone played a piano in the late evenings or with the car radio, riding home on the black, deserted roads, with the cold Christmas moon silvering the marshes alongside us. I had not heard Clay sing since we were young marrieds; it simply did not seem to occur to him. He smiled often, now, and laughed outright more than he had in what seemed to me years. Whenever I glanced over at him, at a party or on one of the moon-flooded drives home, I caught him looking at me with something in his eyes that had not been there in a long time.

I never wanted those suspended days to end.

On impulse we spent Christmas in Key West, meeting Carter there when he came in from Puerto Rico, and it was an eccentric, sweet, indolent time. I had a heady, sweet-heart-of-the-regiment feeling the entire three days, with the two tall blond men on either side of me everywhere I went, and the hot sun beating down on my bare head and shoulders. It was strange and funky and so tropical as to be safe, for there was no shard of Christmases past to sting and cut me. For the past five years, Christmas Eve and Christmas Day had been dead times for me. But this one was raffish, excessive, and totally alive. I thought that this would be what we must do each year from now on, though the thought of future Christmases seemed entirely unreal to me.

In the week between Christmas and New Year's we went to a party at Hayes and Lucy's house on Church Street. It had been Hayes's notion to invite his oldest friends, those who had grown up with him and gone to Virginia with him and Clay, and so we were surrounded with many of the people I had first met even before Clay and I married, the handful of couples who had been my first real "crowd," and who had remained so until our children started to come and we moved away from one another. Almost everybody came, for everyone loves to visit Charleston, and Hayes had taken a block of rooms at a nearby inn and footed the bill as his Christmas present to his guests. If I wondered how on earth he could afford it, I did not wonder long. Hayes's finances belonged outside the bubble. Inside there was only room for the funny, lost young Hayes who had brought Clay to me on a hot summer day, out of a blinding glitter of dying sunlight.

Hayes and Lucy's house is one of the big old Charleston double houses, which means that it is two rooms wide instead of one, and very long. Its upstairs and downstairs piazzas were hung with garlands of smilax and holly, and tinsel and tiny white Christmas lights studded the crape myrtle trees and the lower branches of the live oaks that hung over the garden. It was a crisp night, too chilly to be outside, but we went out at midnight to sing carols, and the sound of our whiskey-sweet voices climbing into the night sky over the old vine-covered back garden walls of Church Street, and the clouds of frosty breath on which the songs floated, and the yellow flames of candlelight from neighboring windows all made that night as enchanted as if it had fallen in Avalon. I stood in a circle with these people who had been my first friends as a married woman, who had been young with me, our arms around one another's waists and shoulders, and thought that if I should have to die suddenly, I would not be sorry if it was on a night like this. It was a seductive enough thought to frighten me, and I went back into the house and asked Hayes for another old-fashioned. Looking back, I see that I drank a lot in those days of the bubble, but it was not as it was in other times. I never seemed to get tipsy at all.

We stayed over with Hayes and Lucy that night, and made hilarious and silent love in their high-ceilinged old guest room, under an embroidered coverlet that had come, Lucy said, with one of her forebears from England in the time of the Lord Proprietors. I think, though, that she exaggerated; Clay and I gave the coverlet a rather muscular workout and it was still intact in all its silky shabbiness in the morning. We laughed a great deal that night, silently, with our hands over our mouths, for our bedroom was just down the hall from Hayes and Lucy's, and neither of us felt like listening to Hayes's sly insinuations at breakfast. It was very late when we finally lay still and sliding toward sleep, and Clay said, "I wish this night would never end."

I traced my finger along his bare chest. It was slick with cooling sweat.

"I do, too," I said, feeling tears prick my

eyes and blinking them back. "Oh, I do, too."

In all that spangled and fragile country there was one place that I could not go, and that was to the house on the island. I did not even try. I was afraid, and knew it clearly, and knew what I feared: both that in the long, still nights I would hear the laughter and voice of my dead child, and that I would not. The mere thought of sitting alone all night in that darkened living room overlooking the creek — for I knew that I would not sleep — made me break out in a cold sweat at my hairline. One way or another, the island house was haunted for me now.

Oh, I could go in the daytime for a little while, and did once or twice, but soon I stopped even that. The winter dark came down too soon. The silence that I had so loved waited too breathlessly for sounds that could not come . . . or could, and bring madness with them. I knew this notion of mine was not rational. I would, I resolved, deal with it as I could with all the other things that bumped like sharks at the aquarium wall of my bubble, after the holidays. But I missed the island, and I found that I missed the ponies and Lita and even Luis Cassells in some unexplored way. So I filled the days that remained to me inside the bubble with activity, from first light to long after dark. I polished silver, washed windows, cleaned out long-neglected closets, took curtains and drapes to be cleaned, attacked the neglected winter garden with a vengeance. It pleased and soothed me, somehow, to feel with my fingers the lares and penates of my marriage and my life with Clay, to tend them, to put them away renewed and shining. I sang as I tended and counted my treasures.

One morning toward New Year's I was preparing to leave the nursery with a trunkful of new rose cuttings and ran into Luis Cassells. It was a raw day, with wisps of the morning's fog still curling among the ocean pines and clinging in heavy droplets to the moss, and he wore a hooded sweatshirt and thick-soled boots caked with the black mud of the marsh. He had two enormous sacks of fertilizer in his big arms, and he grinned around them when he saw me.

"Miz Mengele!" he yelled across the parking lot. "Happy holidays to you and yours!"

Heads turned toward me, and my face reddened. I could feel it. At the same time I felt the corners of my mouth tug upward, and a laugh start low in my throat. He was outrageous and incorrigible, and I had missed him.

"And to you and yours," I called back, and

went over to the Peacock Plantation pickup truck, where he was storing the fertilizer. "Have you had a good Christmas?"

"You ask a Jew that?" He laughed. "Oh, hell, what chance does a poor lone Jew have down here? We had an old-fashioned Dayclear Christmas, and that, my lady, is some kind of Christmas indeed. A combination of Southern Baptist and Kwanza and Hanukkah, with a little Anglican and Disneyland thrown in. We cooked and ate for three days, and went to a Christmas Eve watch service and shouted and sang until dawn, and Ezra cooked a wild turkey somebody shot illegally and gave him, and Auntie Tuesday made hoppin' John and cooked seven thousand pounds of yams, and I made black beans and rice to go with it, and Sophia ordered bagels and lox from the H&H deli in New York for Christmas breakfast, and Lita and Mark threw up three times apiece on Christmas Day. It was totally satisfactory."

I lifted my eyebrows.

"Sophia and Mark?"

He grinned; with only his face showing under the tight-drawn hood, I thought that he looked like a werewolf.

"Well, nobody else asked her for Christmas. Ezra thought it was the only neighborly thing to do."

"Oh, Lord," I said, aghast. "I thought surely she'd be going back to New York for the holidays. I should have checked; it's sort of my job to see that all the office crowd has somewhere to go for holidays. I just got busy, and then we went to Key West . . . I'll call her this morning and apologize."

"I wouldn't bother," he said. "Looked to me like she had a great time. Oh, she showed up in some kind of suede jumpsuit thing and high-heeled boots that cost more than Auntie's house, and she still isn't used to brushing a chicken off wherever she wants to sit down, but she's learning. She's learning. She makes careful notes on everything that happens in her little leather Day-Timer, and she's about to run everybody crazy with that tape recorder and camera, and she still talks about 'the Gullah experience' and 'the oral tradition' and a pile of shit nobody can understand, but she's Ezra's guest and they're getting used to her, and nobody gets ruffled up about her much anymore. And they love the little boy. He used to cry whenever somebody touched him, and it took him four or five visits to start talking, but he's jabbering a blue streak now. Lita has taken him under her wing. In another month they'll both be little Gullah younguns."

"Four or five visits . . . she goes over there often then," I said. Somehow I simply could not see it, remote, elegant Sophia Bridges spending her days in the hardscrabble clutter and the warm, smoky funk of Dayclear.

"She's come almost every day," Luis said. "She's taking her assignment from Mengele very seriously, whatever it is. She says only that she's studying the culture under his auspices and with his blessings. I don't ask her anymore what she aims to do with her new-found knowledge, or what he does. You'll notice I'm not asking you, either."

"I really don't know," I said, feeling the walls of the bubble quiver perilously. "And I'm not going to ask Clay. You know what I told you, about them coming up with a better plan . . . for everything. I'm sure Sophia's research is part of that, but beyond that I just —"

"— don't know," he finished for me. "Ah, yes. Well. Come and have a cup of coffee with me and tell me what you do know. I promise not to ask you anything else about the island except why you haven't been over there lately. We've been looking for you almost every day. Lita is driving me crazy about the ponies, but I'm not going to take her to see them without you along, and besides, I haven't seen them or their calling cards for a while."

I hesitated, but then I went with him to the chic little coffee shop on the traffic circle nearby. We took our cups to a corner table and he pulled the hood off his big head and was the Luis Cassells I knew again, half mythic creature and half lowland gorilla. His hours in the winter sun had kept him walnut brown, and his teeth flashed piratically in the dimness of the little shop. I saw a face I knew at a table across the room and sighed. Shawna would be in Clay's office within the hour, smiling archly and twittering about seeing me having a little coffee date with the hired help. I did not care if Clay knew, but I hated the smirk on Shawna's proprietary face and hoped devoutly that Hayes was not around when she told Clay.

"So why haven't we seen you?" he said matter-of-factly. "What's the matter?"

"Why does something have to be the matter?" I said, annoyed. "I've just been busy. Christmas is always a zoo down here, and then we went to Key West over Christmas Eve and Day, and there have been a bunch of parties in Charleston . . ."

"Ah, I forgot. Miz Mengele is a social lioness. Of course. The Charleston parties."

His grin widened evilly. I could not remember if I had told him how I hated parties or not, but I knew that he knew somehow that I did.

"It's the only time of the year I go to them," I said defensively, and then laughed aloud. "Though why I'm explaining myself to you I do not know."

"Why, indeed?" he said, and then his smile faded. "What *is* wrong, Caro?" he said, and the softness in his voice startled me so that I told him.

"And you're afraid you'll hear your daughter in the night? Or see her?" he said, when I fell silent.

"I'm more afraid that I won't, I think," I said helplessly, at a loss as to how to make him understand and wishing I had not spoken of it. "Or that I will, and that she'll just . . . fade away then. That would be worse than not seeing her, but either of them just seem like more than . . . I could bear right now. I know it's stupid. I know I need to get myself over this."

"It's not stupid. But you do need to get yourself over it. Not only does it hurt you in more ways than I think you know, it dishonors your child. She should not be the agent of your fear. She would not want to drive you from the place you and she loved so."

"I know," I whispered, feeling tears but

knowing dully that they would not, could not, fall.

"I feel responsible," he said presently. "It was Lita, after all, when she came that night after the ponies. I know that you thought . . ."

"I did, for a minute, and finding that I was wrong was one of the worst moments that I have ever had in my life," I said. "But that was scarcely your fault, or Lita's. And it's not that I'm afraid of my child. Oh God, of course not. If I thought she could truly come to me there I would go and never leave. I guess I'm afraid . . . of the long nights alone. I'm afraid of being afraid. Franklin Roosevelt would not be proud of me."

"Perhaps you should go and spend a night there and see that it does not happen," he said soberly. I was grateful to him beyond words that he did not laugh at me, or try to tell me that I was really being silly and hysterical. I knew that I was.

"I would be glad to stay with you," he said. "I would not even speak if you didn't want me to. I'd just be there. Do you think that would help? Or maybe your husband . . ."

"No," I said. I did not tell him that I would rather die than tell Clay I was afraid that our daughter would come to me in the night on the island and even more afraid that she would not. It would be a knife in his heart. Worse.

He nodded as though he knew.

"I think . . . that I'll have to do it by myself," I said. "And I will. Maybe in the spring, when it's light longer and everything's green again . . . I don't know. The thing is, Luis, I think that I can't stay there all night awake, waiting . . . and not drink. And somehow to drink over there is abhorrent to me. I hated it that time I did it. It feels as if it might finish me off somehow, just kill me. And . . . I don't know. Poison the island somehow."

I took a deep breath and looked up at him. I had never even admitted that to myself, and there it lay, out on the little marble-topped table between us, pulsing like a beating heart.

"It's a first step, Caro," he said, and covered my hand briefly with his own. It was enormous, and so callused that it felt like a leather glove that had dried in the sun. It was very warm.

"If you're going to start that twelve-step business with me, I'm going home," I said, annoyed that I had told him and near panic that I had actually named the beast. And not to Clay, but to Luis Cassells.

"No. It's not time for that. It may never be," he said. "I agree with you. The island house is no place for you to drink. And I also think you're probably right about doing it by yourself. Let me think on it."

"It's not your problem, Luis," I said, gathering up my purse and keys. "I didn't mean to burden you with it."

"You are no burden, Caro," he said, and he was not smiling. "I have burdens, but you are not one of them. I have an idea, though; why don't you come and spend a whole day there, and I'll bring Lita and perhaps we'll find the ponies, and maybe Ezra would come and bring Sophia and Mark, and we could just sort of . . . have a day at your place. Live a day in Caro's world. You've had one at ours, after all. It would be wonderful fun for the children, and who knows? It might start to give you back your island. . . ."

"Maybe," I said slowly, thinking of it. The sun on the greening marsh, and the quiet lap of the water against the dock, and the ponies, and the lazy banter and laughing, and maybe a picnic lunch . . .

The shadows that had lain thick over the house and the island in my mind lifted a bit.

"Maybe I will."

"Name a day."

"Well . . . after the holidays. Maybe a little

later, when the marsh starts to green up?"

"You don't want to let it go too long," Luis said.

And as it turned out, I did not.

Two days before New Year's Eve Clay came home to dinner and said, "How would you like to spend New Year's in Old San Juan?"

I looked up from ladling the Portuguese kale soup that he loves on winter nights.

"Puerto Rico?" I said.

He read my face.

"It's a long way from Calista. And it's beautiful. A lot like Key West, in the oldest parts. Or vice versa, I guess. I thought you like Key West so much . . ."

"Oh, Clay . . ."

I did not know how to tell him that, for me, the very earth of Puerto Rico would always be stained now with Jeremy Fowler's blood.

I did not have to. He sighed.

"I know. I don't want to go, either. I swore I never would again. But Carter has a buyer, I think, and he won't talk to anybody but me. It's not going to do the company much good; the payments are spread out too far. But it'll get the investors off us for a while, and it's the only offer we're apt to get. The main man is spending the holidays in San

Juan on his yacht, doncha know, and he insists that we do this right now or not at all. I think it's another case of jerk-the-CEO, but right now I'm not in any position to argue. I thought you just might want to come. You're apt to be lonesome here by yourself. I mean, you're not painting much anymore, are you? I didn't think you'd been over to . . . the other house for a while."

"No, I . . . well, maybe I will start again," I said, not wanting to get into my reasons for avoiding the island. "The weather's wonderful. And I need to give the house a good cleaning . . ."

"Take Estelle for that, for God's sake," he said, lapsing into his pre-Christmas abstracted irritablility. "You don't need to be humping out houses yourself."

"I think it might be just what I do need," I said stubbornly. There was no reason on earth to quarrel with Clay about who cleaned the island house. I could simply do it myself and not tell him, if I wanted to. The fact was that I felt the walls of the bubble beginning to erode badly, and it frightened and angered me. Had it been so much to ask, this period of giddy peace?

"Suit yourself," Clay said coolly, and went upstairs to his office. Thus it was that when he left for Puerto Rico two days later, the

311

kisses we gave each other were cheek kisses only, and glancing ones at that. I hated it but did not know how to get the past three weeks' intimacy back, and he gave no sign that he wanted to.

When he was gone, I sat down in my shining, empty house and suddenly could not bear it. I dug out my battered Day-Timer and consulted it, and then dialed the number I had written down for the little nameless store in Dayclear.

Janie answered.

"Sto'."

"Janie, it's Caro Venable. Could you get a message to Mr. Cassells for me, do you think?"

"Reckon so. They outside playin' football right now."

When he came to the phone, I said, "Don't you ever work?"

"Ah, if only I could," he said lugubriously. "But instead I must hang around this store waiting for you to call. I'm weeks behind. Mengele will gas me. Or connect my ear to my fat *Cubano* butt."

I laughed; I could not help it. The fragile sorcery of Christmas came drifting back.

"Do you think you could take your fat *Cubano* butt over to my house today? I'm going to be around, and we're not apt to get a better day to show Lita the ponies. If I can find them."

"My butt is yours," he said. "As a matter of fact, I think the ponies are around your place somewhere. Ezra was out on the creek yesterday and saw them hanging around under your porch."

"Lord, I hope they're not chewing on the supports again," I said. "They aren't pressure treated, and I've found enough teeth marks on them so that one day they're going to gnaw through them like beavers. Granddaddy said it was the salt that soaked into the wood that they like."

"I think it's more apt to be the six tons of windfall apples I've been lugging over there every week, at Lady Lita's direction," he said.

"You've built a pony trap under my porch," I said, grinning into the telephone.

"*Sí, senora,*" he said in a dreadful Latino whine.

"I'll be over directly," I said. "I'll bring a picnic lunch. You bring whatever you want to drink for the two of you."

When I got out of the Cherokee there was no one in sight, and I stopped still and looked up at the weathered gray house on its stilts, dreaming in its shroud of silvery moss and the mild sun. It was a warm, sweet morning, so much like the spring that was still six weeks away, that I could almost hear the little liquid sucking sound that the wet earth sometimes makes in spring, as the dormant roots come alive again and drink in the standing rain. Out on the creek the water danced and sparkled, and the sky over it was the pale washed blue that March brings. The sun was already warm on my forearms and the top of my head, and I took off the hat that I had worn. I waited. Nothing happened, nothing broke the silence except the distant cacophony of the returning ducks and waterbirds in the big freshwater pond across the river and the tiny rustlings of small things that should, by right, still be sleeping in the mud. Well, I thought, what did you expect to hear? But I knew.

Anxiety crawled out of the pit of my stomach and closed around my heart. I shook my head and walked briskly up the steps to the house. I would not have this. Not on this most beneficent of days. Not here. Not now.

There were baskets and grocery bags piled at the door, and a small sack of the tiny, gnarled Yates apples that lay everywhere in the long grass of the island, the last spawn of centuries-old orchards. I knew they would be as sweet as smoke and honey, but that you were quite apt to meet half a worm if you

314

bit into one. Pony bait, I was sure. So Luis and Lita were already here. But where? I saw no vehicle, and there was no sign at all of the herd.

And then there was. The familiar, half-spectral sound of their hoofbeats in soft, wet earth came bursting down the road that led into the hummock. My breath stopped. Then the herd itself swept into view, still looking like clumsily made toys. They were not galloping, as they sometimes did, but trotting phlegmatically along in a messy knot. At the rear, I saw the awkward sprite's shape of Nissy's colt, capering on longer legs, and then Nissy herself. Lita was on her back, sturdy little legs clamped around Nissy's fat, shaggy stomach, hands inter-twined in the scabrous mane. Beside them, Luis Cassells trotted, breathing hard but keeping up. I put my hands to my mouth, my heart pounding. I had seen this before, in another, distant lifetime. I did not know if I could handle it again.

Nissy set her splayed hooves in an abrupt, skidding stop and Lita slid off her back, crowing with joy. She ran straight to me and threw her arms around me and buried her head in my stomach.

"*Ay*, Caro! The *jaca*, she let me *montar . . .*"

"English, Lita," Luis said, puffing and laughing. *"Ingles, por favor."*

Lita threw her head back and looked up at me.

"Nissy let me ride her! It's the first time! Abuelo . . . Grandfather said I could surprise you. Are you surprised, Caro?"

I reached down slowly, almost reluctantly, and touched the damp curls on top of her head. It was all right. They were springy and a bit wiry, not like Kylie's at all. I ruffled them.

"I *am* surprised," I said. "You must be a witch. I didn't think the old lady would let anybody near her."

Not again, my heart said.

Luis pulled sugar cubes out of the pockets of his blue jeans and offered one to the nervously pawing Nissy. She looked at him, the whites of her eyes showing so that she looked wall-eyed and stupid, and then took it delicately. The colt came skittering up and nosed at Luis's hand, and gobbled his sugar so fast that he choked a bit, and coughed, and tossed his big goblin's head. We all laughed. He would grow up to be an ordinary, homely little marsh tacky like the rest of his herd, but right now he was an enchanting mixture of grace and caricature.

"He really does need a name," I said.

"He has one," Lita said shyly. "That is, if you like it. I call him Yambi. It means 'yam' in the Vai language. Ezra told me. He eats all the yams we bring him. Auntie Tuesday lets Abuelo take the leftover ones and put them under your porch, and they're always gone when he comes back. I know it's him that eats them. Abuelo found one that had little tiny teeth bites in it."

"Yambi it is then," I said. "Hello, Yambi. Are you an honorary Gullah like Lita?"

The colt cocked his head at us, saw that no more sugar was forthcoming, wheeled, and fled away on his still-delicate hooves. In a moment the entire herd had one of its feigned panic attacks and went thundering back down the road toward the line of the woods.

Lita's small face screwed up with dismay, and Luis said, "They'll be back after a while. You wait and see. They'll come back for lunch. There's not a marsh tacky alive that can resist the smell of . . . what, Caro?"

"Ham sandwiches. Egg salad. Tuna fish on hoagy rolls. Potato salad I made myself. Estelle's fruitcake. Chocolate chip cookies. Oh, and taco chips."

"Taco chips," Luis said triumphantly. "Marsh tackies never get enough taco chips. They'll be back begging and pleading."

We stowed the groceries and my picnic basket and Auntie Tuesday's big plastic jug of lemonade, and went back out into the sun. As if by previous agreement, though there had been none, we drifted across the wet grass to the edge of the marsh and stood looking across it toward the creek. The grasses waved in the soft, fish-smelling breeze like the sea that lay beyond, and I saw for the first time the faintest tinge of gold-green, just at the tips, so that they looked as if they were haloed. That suffusion of new green meant the coming of the spring in the Lowcountry.

Please, no, something inside me whispered. It is not time for the spring yet. It's much too early for the green-up. It's merely an aberration. We have weeks of winter yet.

And we did; I knew that. This haze of green *was* an aberration; it happened sometimes on the marshes, when there had been a lot of rain and almost no cold. I was still safe there in the bubble of winter.

The weight of the sun on us was palpable, and the smell of salt and clean mud and the billions of things growing and dying deep in the black silt was mesmerizing. Small white clouds that looked like washing hung out, sailed across the tender blue sky. Songbirds set up their choruses in the small knots of myrtles and scrub trees on the little hum-mocks that dotted the sea of grass. We stepped onto the creaking wooden board-walk over the marsh and strolled out toward the water that glittered in the noon sun like crumpled foil. No one spoke. Sun and sleep-iness lay heavy on my eyelids.

We sat silently for quite a long time on the little dock, swinging our legs over the edge toward the water. The Whaler and the canoe had been put away in their cradles under the house, but I had forgotten the salt-faded old oilcloth cushions, and we laid them on the uneven old boards and stretched out on them in the sun. I closed my eyes under its red weight. I could hear the water slapping hollowly against the pilings below and smiled slightly. It was the sound of all my summers in this place.

Beside me, Luis said quietly, "How is it for you? Is it all right?"

"Yes," I said, not opening my eyes. "So far it's all right. It seems that so long as the sun is out, it's okay."

"Then we shall stop the sun," he said in the tone of Moses commanding the Red Sea to part, and I smiled again. Pretty soon the slapping water faded, and I think that I slept for a while.

A great splashing and shrill shouts from

Lita woke me. She and Luis were standing at the very edge of the dock, looking back toward the shore. I scrambled to my feet, sweating and confused, and staggered over to join them.

Dolphins. A school of them, huge and rubbery and silvery, so close that you could see their silly, cunning smiles and hear the wet, breathy little noises of their blowholes. They were churning straight for the marshy banks of the creek, silvery thrashing ahead of them. And then, incredibly, they drove a roiling school of small fish into the reeds and floundered, slapping and blowing, out of the water and onto the bank after them. Each of the six or seven huge dolphins managed to eat a fair number of the fish before they half rolled, half flapped themselves back into the water. They frisked for a moment, flashing tails and fins, and then were gone.

I began to laugh.

"My grandfather told me about them," I said. "I never believed him. He said there was a . . . what? A group, a pod . . . of salt river dolphins that actually drive the fish on shore and go after them and eat them. He said they only exist from about Seabrook down to Hunting Island, and that they taught themselves to do that ages ago, and it's almost a genetic thing with them by now.

But only with this particular group. Any visiting schools have got to do it the old-fashioned way. They work for it."

"Ah, *Dios*, how perfect," Luis said softly. "They know so much better than we do how to use their world, and they do not need to either destroy it or leave it. They're very smart fish, dolphins. Do you know that some of the old Gullahs call them horsemen?"

"Horsemen? Why?"

"I'm not sure I understand. It's a tale one of the old men told around the stove at the store one night. I think it's because the fishermen used to know a trick: they'd go out to where they knew the dolphins liked to hang out, and they'd bang on the sides of the boat underwater, slow, heavy bangs, and for some reason that attracted the dolphins, and they'd come swimming toward the boat, driving the fish before them. So there was fish for everybody then: the fishermen and the dolphins alike. I made out that they call them horsemen partly because they work for men like intelligent horses do. The 'men' part I think has to do with certain . . . ah, bodily parts that apparently are quite like . . ."

"I get you," I said, feeling myself redden.

He leered.

Lita came running back from the bank,

flushed with excitement.

"I touched one!" she cried. "I just reached right out and touched him on his head, and he let me! It was like touching wet rubber!"

"They're pretty tame," I said. "The ones around here, anyway. You know, sometimes they sleep right off this dock, just sort of drift suspended in the water and sleep all night."

"How do you know they sleep?" Lita said. "Maybe they're just fooling. I do that sometimes."

"You can hear them snore," I said. "No kidding, I'm serious. I've heard them snoring in the nights in summer, when the windows are open, so loud that you can't sleep. It's a funny, snorty, bubbling sound, but it's definitely snoring. When eight or ten of them are doing it, you can kiss your slumbers good-bye."

"I don't believe you," Luis said, obviously wanting to.

"Scout's honor. My grandfather said they'd been doing it since he was a young boy out here. If you don't believe me, you just come spend the night sometime and listen yourself —"

I stopped, reddening again.

"I'll do that," he said.

"Isn't it lunchtime?" Lita said from the end of the dock, where she was watching in case the dolphins came back.

"Can you wait a little longer?" Luis said. "We're having company for lunch."

"Who, Abuelo?"

"It's a surprise."

"Not much of one," I said, as the menacing growl of the Harley-Davidson curled into the still air. It grew rapidly until it and the machine burst into the clearing at the same time. I saw that three people rode astride, one sandwiched between the other two.

"It's Mark!" Lita shrieked in an excess of joy. "It's Mark the nark and Ezra Shmezra!"

"And Sophia, of course," Luis said dryly, giving her a long look.

"Yeah. Her, too. Okay. I know. I'll be polite."

I lifted my eyebrows at Luis over her head.

"Competition," he mouthed silently, and I laughed.

"It starts young."

"Does it ever. Of course, she is one fine-looking lady, you must admit."

"Yeah," I said. "I guess I must, at that."

"Just not my type." He grinned. "I like 'em down and dirty."

I bridled, and then looked down at myself. I was all black mud up to the knees of my blue jeans, and my rubber Bean shoes were caked with it. My T-shirt was spattered with marsh water. My hair hung around my face and stuck to it with noonday sweat, and I could feel twigs and bits of moss caught in it. In disgust I twisted it up off my neck and secured it with the rubber band I carry with me always, for just such a purpose.

"That's pretty," Luis said. "You look sort of Spanish like that."

"Like one of Velázquez's *majas?*"

"Yeah. Like that. I'll bet you've been told that before."

"Only once," I said.

Mark and Lita rushed to meet each other, shrieking in the ear-piercing treble of small children everywhere; I had almost forgotten it. They rushed off together down to the edge of the creek, where, from her extravagant gestures, I gathered that Lita was telling him about the dolphins. Ezra and Sophia came down the little rise to the edge of the boardwalk. He wore blue jeans and a red T-shirt and looked, Luis said in my ear, like a brick shithouse. Sophia, to my surprise, wore skintight, faded blue jeans spattered with black mud and a large, flapping man's blue work shirt with an elbow out and filthy, wet sneakers. She still managed to look like an Ibo princess, though. Just a slightly grimy one. She was carrying the smart Louis Vuitton tote that I never saw her without, and I saw the outline of the ubiquitous camera and tape recorder inside it, as well as several small, plastic-wrapped bundles and a long, pale brown baguette.

"Brothers and sisters," boomed Ezra. "Let us break bread. Since we brought it, that is."

"We did, too. Caro brought enough for an army," Luis said, clapping Ezra on his massive shoulder. In the sun that poured straight down, Ezra Upchurch shone almost blue. It was a beautiful color, rich and virile and somehow royal. I thought that he would match Sophia Bridges in elegance any day, as long as he stood in sunlight.

"Caro," Sophia said coolly. She looked levelly at me. Her face was calm and courteous, but closed.

"Sophia," I said back.

We lapsed into silence, and the men stood quietly, too, watching us. What is the matter with everybody? I thought in irritation, but still I did not speak, and still we regarded each other, Sophia Bridges and I.

What are you doing here? her long almond eyes said to me as clearly as if she had spoken. You are not a part of this company. You belong on the other side of that bridge. You belong with Clay Venable. Where do you stand in this?

I might ask you the same thing, my eyes

said back to her. So do you belong with Clay Venable. So do you belong on the other side . . . of the bridge and the fence. Where do you stand in this?

We were silent for another moment, and then, just as Ezra drew a breath to speak, we burst into simultaneous laughter, and the day slid smoothly into afternoon, wrapped in sunlight and the sweet false spring. Only then did I remember that it was New Year's Eve.

We ate lunch late, and we ate for a long time. I didn't remember being so hungry for weeks, months. We ate most of my sandwiches and a great deal of Estelle's fruitcake and divinity, and we finished off the silky truffle pâté with cornichons and the baguette Sophia brought.

"Where did you get this gorgeous stuff?" I said, licking a smear of truffle off my fingers. You could probably get pâtés in Charleston, but I knew that the closest Peacock's Island had to them was liverwurst.

"She ordered it from this little bistro she knows, around the corner from her house in the Village," Ezra said, drawing out "beee-stro." "She sent to Charleston for the baguette. You could have fooled me. All this time I thought I was eating French bread."

Despite his disreputable clothes and

shuck-and-jive demeanor, I knew that he was no stranger to truffle pâté and baguettes. Ezra had a town house in Washington, D.C., that I had heard was as spare and elegant as he himself was massive and shambling. Lottie had told me in amusement that *Architectural Digest* had been after him for years to let them do a spread on it, but he always told them that the hens were laying good and he didn't want to disturb them, or other of the down-home nonsense that so charmed the national media.

"I happen to know that you have a charge account at Zabar's," Sophia retorted. She was lying with her back against the railing of my porch, as indolent in the slanting sun as a jungle cat. After our explosion of mutual laughter, things between us had been comfortable, if not intimate. I enjoyed the comfort, knowing that intimacy with me or many other people was probably beyond this beautiful, tight-drawn creature. I saw her smile fully and often only at Mark — and once or twice at Ezra.

"Wouldn't *that* be something," I murmured to Luis, when they had gone to the Harley to stow the plastic pitcher and the disposable champagne glasses they had had, Ezra told us, to go to the Edisto Wal-Mart for.

"A veritable mating of titans." He grinned. "But I wouldn't count on it. I'd just as soon woo a totem pole as Miz Sophia Bridges, and Ezra has at least six women in every port. I don't know how he's standing his enforced celibacy down here."

"Maybe he isn't," I said.

"Yeah, I think he is. He doesn't cross the bridge to Peacock's that I know of, and he's around Dayclear practically all the time."

"What does he do?"

"Hangs out, mostly. Talks to the old folks. Visits. Listens to the tales. Tells some of them around the stove. He's preached once or twice. You forget he's a preacher sometimes, but you should hear him in the pray house. It's something to make your hair stand up. And he's with Sophia and Mark a lot. He's showing them all sorts of stuff, and she's writing it down in the goddamned little book of hers, or poking that recorder in his face. And Mark is just drinking it in. That kid has bloomed like kudzu. I don't think he had any idea he was black. Now I think he wishes he was as black as Ezra."

"That's a switch for her," I said. "I think all their friends in New York were white as a field of lilies. I'm surprised she allows the exposure."

"Yeah, I am, too. There's something going

on there, but I don't know what it is. Sometimes she gets the oddest look on her face, and sometimes she just . . . turns her head. Or walks away. But she's always back the next day. If I didn't know her for the little Mengele-ite she is, I'd think her interest was more than anthropological. But leopards like that don't usually change their spots."

The sun slanted lower, and was so beneficent on our faces and arms that no one moved off the deck for another hour or so. The children, worn out, napped on the living room sofas. We four talked, but it was not the sort of talk that demands or receives intense attention. It was as drifting and desultory as the talk between the oldest of friends, only we weren't that. I put it down to the cockeyed magic of this strange, displaced spring day that had fallen into our midwinter.

Presently, into a lull, I said, "Why do you come back here, Ezra?"

He did not answer for so long that I thought perhaps I had offended him, and looked over at him. But his big face was calm, and his eyes were fastened off on the creek, where the glitter was turning from hot white to gold.

"I think . . . to remember who I am," he said. "And to remember who they are. I don't think we're going to have all this" — and his big arm made a sweeping motion that took in everything my eyes could see and all that they couldn't — "very much longer."

I said nothing. Neither did Sophia Bridges. We carefully did not look at each other. I felt a bolt of complicity leap from my mind to hers, though. Shame and unease followed it. No fair. My bubble time was not up yet.

"Nothing seems to have changed in Dayclear in a hundred years," Luis said sleepily. "It's like Brigadoon."

"I wish it was," Ezra said. "The fact is, a lot has changed just since I was here last, and lots more since I left to go to college. The old ways are going. The old stories are being forgotten, and the old dances, and the old ways of making things . . . baskets, circle nets. None of the young folks come back often enough to learn the shouts or hear the histories and mythologies of their own families. In another generation, nobody is going to understand the language, much less speak it, and no kids are going to play 'Shoo, turkey, shoo,' or sing 'Sally 'round the sunshine.' Nobody's scared of the hags and the plateyes anymore. We'll even have lost our ghosts, and that's when you know you're a poor, sorry-assed people."

I felt rather than saw Luis Cassells's eyes on me. I would not look up.

"And you're here to try to preserve the old ways? To see that they go on?" I said. I realized that I sounded like an elementary school teacher talking to her class, but I wanted to get off the ghost business quickly.

"Oh, no," he said, and laughed richly. "I leave all those fine endeavors to Miz Bridges here. She a cultural anthropologist atter all." He gave it the rural black pronunciation. Sophia's mouth tightened.

"No, I'm just here to . . . bear witness, I guess. Oh, I do what I can. When I preach I talk about the real world, of course, because they live in it, after all, but I always end with one of the old songs, and I use the rhythms of the old shouts. For one thing, I love them. They come right up out of my gut. For another, no preacher is going to survive in these little communities who doesn't tap into those deepest feelings.

"It's not that all the old ways are gone," he went on. "I could take you all right now and walk you not three miles from here and show you a graveyard that's completely surrounded with woods, just buried in them. Some of the graves are new, too. They're hidden in the woods so the poor spirits of the dead can't get out and get lost and roam away. And you'd be apt to find an alarm clock on lots of those graves, an old rusty drugstore windup job, with its hands stopped at the moment of the deceased's death. And pictures, photos, in fancy frames. Family shots, mainly, but always what the dead loved most. I know of one fine picture of a mule in that graveyard.

"All the old Dayclear names are there. Some of mine are. My mama and grandmama are there. So is my uncle, Auntie Tuesday's husband. Peters. Miller. Cato. Bullock." He paused a moment and looked intently at Sophia, who was digging for the tape recorder, to catch the scholarly words.

"Mackey," he said.

She put the recorder down and turned her head away. But before she did, I thought I caught the glisten of tears in her dark eyes, and then wondered if I had, after all. It did not seem possible.

The silence that followed was no longer comfortable. He seemed to realize that he had broken a spell.

"And I painted my front door blue, in D.C.," he said in a bantering tone. "Everybody admires it as a creative touch. They don't believe me when I tell 'em it wards off evil spirits. But I haven't had a plateye since I moved in."

We laughed, but we could not get the sleek skin of the moment back. I looked around restlessly. The heat was going out of the afternoon, and the sun was nearly level with the tops of the trees far across the marsh, on the verge of the inland waterway. The sky was turning gold. The old anxiety came stealing back, rising in my throat, marching up my vertebrae one by one, like stair steps.

"I need to get back," I said. "This has been . . . wonderful. I can't tell you. But I've got . . . stuff I need to do."

"Me, too," Sophia said briskly. "Mark and I have been invited to a little New Year's Eve party with some of his kindergarten friends' parents. Let me go get those children on the road."

"Can I persuade either of you to stay and listen to me preach at the New Year's Eve watch service tonight?" Ezra said. "I can promise you more shouting and singing than you ever heard. I am amazing when I get going. You could get a whole chapter out of this thing, Sophie Lou."

"I really can't. Thanks, though," she said crisply. She got up and went into the living room to wake the children. In the darkening gold of sunset, she looked suddenly very small and thin. What was it he had said, to drive her away from us like this?

He looked after her, and then at Luis.

"Losin' my fabled touch," he said, and grinned, but there was no warmth in it.

He settled Sophia and Mark on the Harley and eased off down the driveway, slowly now, to take them back to Dayclear, where Sophia's car was. Luis and I sat on the steps, watching the night come in from the west. It was not coming fast, but it made me want to leap to my feet, to run for my car, to be away and gone. Lita slept on in Luis's arms. He looked down at her, and then at me.

"I left the truck a half-mile or so down the road where we saw the ponies," he said. "If you need to go, maybe you could drop us off there. I think I've lost the princess for the night."

"I will in a minute," I said. I sat, listening to the night wind that was ruffling the water far out, to the sleepy twitters of the birds as they settled down off in the hummocks. To the soughing of the great oaks over our heads. To the tiny scratchings and rustlings that meant the small night creatures were waking up, to hunt or be hunted. There was nothing untoward, nothing I had not heard a thousand times before out here. And still I listened. . . .

"Let her go, Caro," Luis said softly. "Just . . . let her go."

I turned my face to him, feeling the color drain out of it.

"You mean . . . just forget her? Just . . . throw her out?"

He shook his head.

"Of course not. You won't forget her. How could you? I mean . . . stop calling her back with your need and your hunger and your pain. It's too big a burden for one little ghost to carry. Send her off with your love and pride and all the things you laughed at and all the tears you cried together. You won't lose her. It's like the old saying, 'Hold a bird lightly in the palm of your hand and it will always come back to you.' And maybe then there'll be some room inside you for . . . other things. Other people."

I started to protest that there were other people in my heart, many of them, but then did not. There was a great grief rising in me, like a storm.

"How will I live without her?" I whispered.

"I'll tell you. It's a game I know. It works for me. Just close your eyes and think of what you'd be willing to die for, and then — live for it. It's very simple, really."

I just looked at him.

"The only rule of this game is that whatever you choose has to be alive," he said very gently.

I dropped my eyes. The heaviness of tears was near to overflowing.

"Go on," he said. "Try it. Close your eyes. Say to yourself, 'What would I die for?' and grab the very first thing that comes into your mind. No thinking about it. The very first thing."

I closed my eyes. Behind them, red and white lights arced and pinwheeled.

"What would I die for?" I said soundlessly to myself, and saw, not Clay's face, not even that of my lost child, or Carter's . . . but today. The day just past. The island, the dock, the low sun on the water, the dolphins, the ponies pounding down the sandy road, a small child who was not my child clinging in joy to one of the stumpy necks. My house on its stilts, its head in the moss and live oak branches. The island. My island.

I looked back at him.

"Yes," he said, and now he was smiling.

"Well, let's get you going," he said, struggling to his feet with the sweet, limp weight of the sleeping child in his arms.

"No. I'm going to stay," I said.

He studied me gravely.

"Are you sure? There's lots of time for that. Today was . . . a very full day for you."

336

"I'm sure. You said it yourself, not long ago. There's no more time. Now is it, for me."

He stood quietly in the dusk for a moment, and then he shifted the child to one shoulder. She mumbled sleepily, but did not really wake. I leaned over and kissed her swiftly on the top of her head.

Luis Cassells put out his hand and touched my hair, very lightly.

"Don't drink, Caro," he said.

He turned and went down the steps with his granddaughter, and in a moment was lost to my sight in the darkness under the trees.

Presently, I heard the distant motor of the Peacock Island Company pickup catch, and then it faded, and the great quiet came down again.

And I did not drink. I sat sleepless before my fire all through the night, and I saw the dawn of New Year's Day born red behind the live oaks, but I did not drink.

10

It was a curious time, the first hours of that new year. I should have been bone-tired, but I was not. I felt, instead, light and hollow and empty, but in no hurry to seek whatever it was that would fill me. I was content to sit on the dock in the little wind off the ocean, warm and heavy with the fragrance of things blooming far to the South. I felt that I was waiting there for something to come, but I did not know what, and was not particularly threatened by its prospect, not even curious. I was just . . . waiting.

Quite clearly my heart told me that it would not be my child who came, not again to this place, and somehow that was all right. I still had her at the core of my being. The morning was still new. Whatever was coming, it would emerge.

It was Hayes Howland who came. I was surprised by that. I had not seen Hayes at the island house since the days just before Clay and I married. But here he was, in his growling little Porsche, dressed in his customary disheveled but well-tailored khakis and ap-

338

parently-slept-in cardigan sweater. He picked his way through the wet, mossy grass as if to spare the Gucci loafers, but they were already beyond salvation. He wore sunglasses and had his hands thrust in his pockets, and grinned up at me, the old Hayes grin.

"I thought you might be out here," he said. "Got a hair of the dog for a sinner?"

"Nope. Got coffee, though," I said. "Come on up. Did you sin egregiously last night?"

"I did. I sinned so grotesquely that I may not be able to put my head back into the Carolina Yacht Club again until the millennium. But if I can't, at least sixty other people can't, and I don't think the club can stand the loss of revenue."

He took off the glasses, and I saw that his eyes were indeed reddened and pouched, with bluish shadows in the thin, scored skin underneath. Like most redheaded men, Hayes was aging early. The punishing Lowcountry sun was not kind to him. There were splotches and raised patches on his face and forearms that would need medical attention before long, I thought. The little white circles of scar that mean treated skin cancers are a hallmark of the Lowcountry male.

"Who all was there?"

I did not much care, but this was obviously a social call, since he showed no signs of having business to transact or news to relate. He leaned against the deck railing, his eyes shielded against the glitter of the sun off the creek, and drank the coffee I brought, and looked around, sighing appreciatively.

"Oh, the usual crowd. You know. This is really something out here, isn't it? I can see why you run away from home so much. It's a pity more people don't realize how beautiful the marshes are. They only want ocean-front."

"Well, let's hope they never learn," I said, annoyed by his remark about running away from home. "You know I don't run away out here, Hayes. Clay knows where I am. He's out here with me when he can be. And I'm really serious about this painting, whether or not you think it's worthwhile."

He lifted a propitiatory hand.

"Badly put. I know you're serious. You ought to be; you're really good. I was just admiring your view. It could make people change their minds about the ocean."

"Yes, well," I said shortly. I was not going to be baited into a discussion of the Dayclear project. My bubble time was not up yet. Technically I had until tomorrow. And when I talked of it, it would be with Clay, not Hayes Howland.

"So, did you see the New Year in all by yourself?" he said, dimpling at me. I thought I knew where he was going with this.

"I did. Absolutely nobody but me and a gator or two. Best company I've had in ages."

"Not what I hear," he said in a schoolboy singsong that made my jaw clench.

"And just what do you hear, sweetie pie?" I said, grinning narrowly at him.

"I hear that you're getting boned up on subtropical landscaping, if you'll pardon my pun."

"You didn't have to explain it, Hayes," I said, rage running through me like cold fire. "I get the allusion. And where on earth did you hear a thing like that? The only person I can think of who would know is our friend Lottie. You been calling on Lottie, Hayes?"

He flushed, the ugly, dull brick color of the redhead. Hayes disliked Lottie Funderburke even more than Clay, so much so that I often wondered if he'd made a move on her and been rebuffed. Lottie would not have had Hayes on her property. He kept the grin in place, though.

"Okay, truce," he said. "I was out of line. I didn't come to pick on you."

"No? Then why did you come?"

"I came to give you a message," he said. "And to put a proposition to you."

I looked at him wearily.

"Hayes, if this has anything to do with . . . you know, the new project, I don't want to hear anything about it now, and when I do, I will hear it from Clay. He said it was going to be spring at least before we were ready to talk again."

He studied me for a moment, and then set his coffee cup down with a thump.

"Well, things have escalated," he said crisply, and I knew that our pleasantries were over and the skin of my bubble had burst. I wanted to howl with desolation and betrayal.

"Whatever it is, I want to hear it from Clay."

"Clay is somewhere so deep in the wilds of Puerto Rico that they don't have phones," Hayes said. "And it can't wait. If it could, do you think I'd be here? Do you think this is my idea of a terrific New Year's Day? I'm missing four Bowl games and a brunch."

I sat staring at him. He returned the stare for a long moment, and then he dropped his eyes. Two hectic red patches of color bloomed on his cheeks.

"Okay. Here's the deal. The government is washing its hands of the horses. They had a ranger out here in December to try to make some kind of assessment about their condition, and he couldn't get close enough to the herd to even see them, except for an old mare and a colt. The mare kicked him. They're not going to maintain them anymore; not that they've been doing much for the past five years or so. I don't know what they're eating, but it can't be much of anything. The guy said the hummocks are pretty much grazed out. Caro, they're going to starve if you don't let the company step in and do something about them."

I was having a hard time keeping the glee I felt at hearing that Nissy had kicked the ranger off my face. I straightened my twitching mouth and regarded Hayes with as much intelligence and interest as I could muster.

"What is it that the company wants to do, Hayes?" I said.

"Well, it all fits in with the proposition," he said. "If I promised you that we weren't going to try to round them up and . . . cull them . . . would you listen?"

"I'll listen to anything except the idea of anybody shooting them. I promise you I'll shoot the first person I see near them with a gun."

He shook his head impatiently.

"No. There are a couple of options. One,

we could round them up and capture them and sell them to some sort of wildlife preserve outfit, seeing as they're bona fide marsh tackies. There'd be some interest in them. Two, we could sell them to people for their kids, or whatever. Then there's three. They can stay here and be maintained in comfort, some might even say luxury . . ."

"If."

"Right. If. If you'd be willing to entertain the new proposal for the Dayclear project that we've come up with."

I sagged down slowly onto the top step of the deck and looked out over the sunny marsh to the creek. Over it a line of ungainly, prehistoric shapes lumbered against the sun. The wood storks, out fishing in the mild morning.

"Tell me about Dayclear, Hayes," I said dully.

He sat down beside me.

"I'm going to leave it to Clay to tell you the whole thing," he said. "The nuts and bolts. He knows how to talk about densities and site usage and such better than I do. But what I want you to know especially is that, with this new plan, the settlement is virtually untouched. It stays just like it has been for . . . oh, a hundred years, I guess. The bulk of the project's . . . amenities will be downriver about two miles, nearer the waterway. We've ditched the idea of having the harbor there completely. All that, and the housing and the tennis complex will be sheltered with berms and heavy new planting. The Gullahs won't see anything when they look out their windows but what they've always seen. And the golf course will be a nine-holer, and it will be near the bridge, so it's isolated from the settlement, too. There'll be a quarter-mile of untouched woods around it."

"Wonderful. No idiot in a full Cleveland yelling fore and driving a Titleist right into the middle of your supper or your prayer service."

He frowned.

"It's a hell of a lot better from your standpoint than it was the first time, Caro," he said. "And that's just the beginning. We can divert the creek a little just where it swings close by your house and deepen the new tributary, so that boat traffic in and out to the ocean won't come by your dock. You shouldn't see a thing from here. You'll scarcely hear it. This place and the settlement will be completely isolated and set apart with plantings and earthworks."

"And the ponies? Do they get a berm of their own?"

He took a deep breath.

"What we're proposing is this. Not only will we preserve Dayclear itself, but we'll restore it. We've got some wonderful stuff from Sophia Bridges and there's a lot more coming; we'd re-create a Gullah settlement of a hundred years ago, with authentic clothing and housing and the old crafts, and young men and women plowing and harvesting and making baskets and circle nets and growing a little specimen cotton and indigo and rice, and the old folks telling stories and singing songs, and the children playing the old games. We'd have a sort of educational complex, with a little rustic building for films and dioramas, and a little crafts and artifacts museum, and shops, and docents to take people on tours, and special seasonal activities. Sophia has some great stuff about Christmas and New Year's services, and songs and shouts and such. A regular story program for kids, with a Gullah bard to tell the old ghost stories. A petting zoo. Maybe a simple little cafe, with ethnic specialties like yams and hoppin' John and crabs . . ."

He stopped and looked at me expectantly. When I did not speak, he went on.

"We'd buy out the village and pay each family a handsome annual salary to stay and take part in all this. We'd provide the clothes and the tools and craft materials, and of course we'd offer insurance and health coverage, maybe get them on some kind of regular medical and dental services from the county. Oh, and we'd electrify the houses that didn't have it . . . Sophia says some of them don't . . . and keep the houses and outbuildings in good shape, and see that everybody has plumbing and heating and television . . . it's more than they could aspire to in their lives, Caro, and the best part is, they won't have to move and they won't have to scrabble for a living anymore. How can they lose?"

I looked at him. Black spots wheeled before my eyes.

"The ponies . . ." I whispered.

"We'd like to make a kind of wild, natural island out in the river where the two creeks run into it, dredge it there and build it up and landscape it and put some picturesque little lean-tos on it for shelter, and keep it planted in grass, and put the ponies there. They'd be fed grain and hay on a regular basis, and we'd have a vet look them over periodically, and if they tame up a little, maybe even curry them once in a while."

"You think they'll go for condos?" I said. My ears were buzzing. "I think they're more the time-share types myself."

He ignored that.

"We thought we might have a kind of monthly pony swim, from the new island over to Dayclear and back. Like they do when they bring the wild horses in from Chincoteague and Assateague, on the Outer Banks. They're a big favorite with families. That way the ponies would be healthier and better cared for than they've ever been in their lives, and they'd be a real asset, instead of parasites."

"I thought Clay was kidding," I managed to whisper through lips that felt blanched and swollen. "I thought he was teasing me. He laughed when I called it Gullah World. . . . It's a theme park, Hayes. How can you even think of it?"

"I can think of it because it's what your husband thought it would take to get you to agree to this, Caro," he said. There were mottled white spots on his clamped jaws now. "I can think of it because it's the only way either of us can see to save that goddamned flea-bitten settlement and those goddamned mangy horses, and Clay says we do that or we forget it. I wonder if you know what would happen to all of us if we forgot it, Caro?"

"Clay's told me about all that . . ."

"I wonder if he's told you just how bad it could be? But the important thing is that

SouthWard loves it, and we took an awful chance by insisting on revising the first plan. They didn't even want to listen to any changes at first. If you knew what Clay and I and everybody else has gone through to work this thing out for you . . ."

My hand flew to my mouth.

"SouthWard! My God, Hayes!" I cried.

"They're going to save your ass, Caro," he said. "All our asses, plus some black ones and some hairy horse ones. Nobody else would even listen. Clay and I have been all over the country with this. Nobody else even gave us an appointment."

SouthWard . . .

Once, when Clay and I had been newly married and the children had not yet come, we took a driving trip through the lower Southeast, so that Clay could show me other resort communities and tell me how his vision for the Peacock Island Plantation Company properties differed from anything yet in existence. We saw some well-done properties and some merely rather ordinary, and a few that I thought were ghastly in concept and execution. Of these, one or two were unique to me in their sheer bizarreness of taste.

One of these was in the mountains of North Georgia and was called Hillbilly Hollow. I would like to think that the name was someone's idea of tongue-in-cheek, but after we had driven through it, I abandoned that idea. Hillbilly Hollow was a caricature of every bad joke anyone had ever heard about the Appalachian mountains and the people thereof. By the time we left it I did not know whether to laugh hysterically or simply cry.

At the gate was a security guardpost gotten up like a miniature log cabin. Artificial chickens, pigs, and dogs dotted the little backyard. On the leaning front porch a guard sat in a rocking chair, dressed in tattered overalls and with a torn felt hat pulled down over one eye, holding a shotgun in his lap. A rustically lettered sign on a piece of knotty pine said, STATE YO' BIZNESS POLITE-LIKE. This particular guard wore wraparound yellow sunglasses and was reading *Rolling Stone*, but the effect was hardly diluted.

Inside the gates was a sales office in the same cabin style, but much larger, dripping with calico and gingham and more rustic sayings burned on pine. A woman in a calico dress and apron, with breasts like, as Clay said in wonder later, the bumper of a 1953 Studebaker, gave us literature about the different styles of resort homes and rentals available, and the amenities enjoyed by the future residents and visitors to Hillbilly Hollow. They included a general store for vittles, a brush-shrouded "still house for wines and likkers," a large, supervised playground and activities cabin for little billies, a lake with paddleboats and motor rentals for when you needed to make a fast water getaway, a miniature golf course for when the city cousins came to visit, a shuffleboard and hoss shoe complex, Ping-Pong and bowling facilities, and an RV campground and mobile-home theme park with hillbilly rides and attractions for the rugrats. A senior citizens cabin community was planned for "when grandmaw and grandpaw need a place to hang their hats," and a shooting range and gallery were under construction, so that "Bills and Billies could keep their shootin' eyes sharp against the revenooers." A smaller sign in the office said that if you required tennis or handball or regular golf or equestrian facilities, Atlanta was ninety miles south thataway.

The Studebaker lady told us that Hillbilly Hollow was already at ninety percent occupancy, and the waiting list stretched into the next year.

"You folks better get your names in the hat right quick," she said, smiling broadly.

Hillbilly Hollow was the first resort property to be developed by SouthWard of Atlanta.

Over the years, SouthWard prospered, and no one could quite figure out why. All of its properties were themed, and none of them with much more innate taste than Hillbilly Hollow. Soon they covered the inland southeast like kudzu, and became a joke to the developers and residents of newer, more restrained and upscale communities and a near-bottomless source of income to their shameless and canny young developers. They were cheap to build, cheap to buy or rent into, and cheap to maintain for the simple reason that SouthWard did very little of that. After about ten years stories and news reports began to seep out about equipment breakdowns, failed inspections, sewage and gas leaks, pollution of nearby streams and rivers, and lawsuits against the company by residents and neighbors alike. SouthWard invariably settled. There was always a new theme community sprouting somewhere else to pay the freight. SouthWard was flush and fat.

They had never managed to get a toehold on the Southeastern coast, though. Waterfront land was at a premium by the time they looked seaward. Almost all of it was either under development, about to be, or privately owned. In the few instances that they saw a window of opportunity, local consortiums shut them out before they could even make an offer. They had almost resigned themselves to looking to the Texas coast for colonization, which did not suit nearly as well, since Texas itself often seemed to be a theme park and was therefore less receptive to their novelties.

Until now.

Hayes had the grace to redden.

"This is altogether different, Caro," he said. "For one thing, we're maintaining design control. For another, they realize they can't come into this market with anything like their others; Charleston and Low-country people would laugh them out of business in a month. This is going to be a new direction for them, a move into serious, substantial resort development, with all the responsible environmental concerns met, the whole ball of wax. Dayclear would give them the kind of dignity they want to project now . . ."

He stopped. I did not think even he believed his words. I did not reply. I was trying very hard not to see it: fishnets and plastic crabs and black people dressed in aprons and head kerchiefs and faded overalls, plowing marsh tackies and picking cotton and singing. An RV village where the dense Florida maritime forest, untouched for eons, stood now. Miniature golf on the secret green hummocks.

But Hayes gave it a valiant try.

"If you saw the site plan and the density studies and the environmental proposals, saw that they were mainly Clay's and his strictest to date, and you had our promise in writing about the settlement and the ponies, would you be willing to take the proposal about Dayclear to the folks there? Just run it past them, see how the wind blows from that quarter? We thought they'd rather hear it from you than one of us. You're known to them, and they know how you feel about the island."

"Hayes," I said slowly, around the nausea and incredulity, "in the first place, what makes you think SouthWard would honor Clay's plans for two seconds after they owned the property? And in the second place . . . who is 'we'? You and who thought they'd rather hear it from me? Does Clay know you've told me all this?"

He puffed out his cheeks and blew a gust of air, like a man who must now do something distasteful to him. He looked away toward the dazzling creek, and then back to me, his hands in his pockets.

"There's something else I came to tell you. I don't want you to get upset, because it's all right now, I promise. But . . ."

"But what? God, Hayes, what?"

"Clay's in the hospital in San Juan. He had some kind of collapse or something last night; Carter called me early this morning. He wanted me to tell you. But Clay's okay now . . ."

He raised his hands toward me as I scrambled to my feet. I could feel the blood running out of my face and hands.

"No, listen, Caro, he really is. Carter's taking him back to the hotel right about now. They just kept him overnight as a precaution. He's coming home in the morning. Carter say the doctor thinks it was exhaustion and stress plus maybe a mild heat stroke; apparently he was out all day on a boat, and then spent the late afternoon tramping around the Calista property with that guy who was looking to buy it. In the end the guy nixed the deal. Carter said he offered so low that they told him to eat shit and hit the road. It must have been the last straw for Clay. A decent sale could have changed things. There wasn't anything wrong with Clay's heart, though, or anything like that. They did find a duodenal ulcer, though. He's been asking for that for months; the strain of the business with Calista, and then the enormous stress of trying to get this Dayclear thing up and going . . . he hasn't been eating right, and the hours he's keeping are criminal. He's traveling way too much, too. Well, you know all that. Maybe now he'll cut back some and let me take some of the load. I've been trying to do it for a long time, but you know Clay . . ."

I sank down on the top step, weak and trembling. Clay had always seemed to me simply . . . invulnerable. Put together from sinew and steel and powered with an inexhaustible energy, driven smoothly on the current of his extraordinary intensity. Clay in the hospital? Clay with an ulcer? What did this say about me?

"Why didn't someone call me?" I whispered.

"What could you have done? By the time Carter heard from the doctor, Clay was almost ready to leave the hospital. Neither he nor Carter wanted to scare you, and Clay'll be home before you could get down there. They called me because they didn't want that motormouth Shawna to get hold of it somehow and blab it to you. Carter says to tell you that if you really want to do something, pick Clay up at the airport in Charleston tomorrow and take him somewhere nice and relaxing for lunch, and then make him go home and rest for the rest of the day. I told him I'd tell you. And when I couldn't raise you at the house, I knew I'd find you here."

"Did Clay ask you to tell me all this, Hayes?" I said, my voice trembling. "Does he want me to take this proposal over to Dayclear?"

Hayes looked at me soberly, and then shook his head.

"No. He doesn't know I've told you about our needing to move things up, and he didn't ask me to ask you to go over there with it. I took that on myself. It might have been the wrong thing to do, and he'll probably be pissed as hell at me, but I just couldn't dump anything more on him right now. And this has got, repeat *got,* to be done and done soon. You can tell him I told you if you want to. You know better than any of us what he can take and what he can't."

"I wonder if I do?" I said so softly that I did not know if he heard me or not. Oh, my poor Clay . . .

"You really do love him, don't you?" Hayes said. "Your face looked like you were seeing ghosts."

"I was," I said drearily. "Yes, Hayes, I really do love him. I always did. Did you ever doubt it?"

"Then . . . are you going to tell him I told you?"

"I don't know. I just don't know. I'll have to wait and see how he is when I pick him up tomorrow. I'm not going to have him collapsing in the airport or something. You'll just have to trust my judgment on that. Eventually I will tell him, of course."

"Eventually I hope you will, or I will," he said. "It's just that right now he needs for things to let up a little. It's a damned shame that the project has got to go forward right away; I wish we did have those three months he promised you. I just thought you might be willing to take some of the load off him by talking to them over at Dayclear."

"You always did know which of my buttons to push," I said to him, and he smiled a little.

"I guess I did," he said. "You don't try to hide them, do you? Well, will you do that at least? Will you go over there and give them the proposition? If that hurdle could be behind him when he gets back, it would be a bigger help than you know."

"Hayes, I . . . yes. Okay. I'll do that. I may or may not tell Clay you came to me with this, but I'll go over there and tell them what you propose for the property. I may tell them I hate it, but I'll wait till they've heard the whole thing before I do that."

"When will you go?"

I shook my head.

"Don't push me on this. I'll get to it. I want to think it out first. You know I'm never going to find it acceptable. But it should be up to them, and I'll leave it like that."

"Fair enough," he said, turning to get into the Porsche and go back to his brunch and his Bowl games. "Don't leave it too long, though, Caro. It wouldn't do Clay any good at all to lose this offer. Not at all."

"You let me be the judge of what's good for Clay, Hayes," I said, but he had started the big, soft engine and did not hear me. I stood on the porch watching the Porsche race off through the trees, leaving a rooster tail of black mud-mist behind it, thinking it looked like blackness and misery and meanness on four wheels and very glad indeed that it was leaving my part of the island.

When I picked Clay up at the airport in Charleston late the next morning, he looked like a man returning from a funeral, and I hugged him hard and we went to lunch at a crab shack on Edisto and had crab cakes and beer, and then I drove us home and bullied him into taking a nap, and he slept far into

that night, and I did not tell him what Hayes
had come to ask of me.

Time enough for that.

11

I didn't tell him for over a week. For the first part of that time I was afraid that he was seriously ill. For the middle part of it he slept. During the last of it he was gone again. By the time I got to him, almost everyone on Peacock's Island knew what my decision was but my husband.

By that time, everything had changed.

I got him to the doctor the day after he got in. He did not even argue vigorously; he was too subdued for that, and his stomach was hurting him rather a lot. He did not tell me this, but he did voluntarily ask for an antacid. I had never known him to take one before. When he went to get water to wash it down, I called Charlie Porter in Charleston and he worked us in late that afternoon.

Charlie had been at Virginia with Clay and Hayes, and they had remained friends as well as doctor and patients. He had a lucrative practice in the new medical complex over on Calhoun, and he and Hayes played tennis a couple of times a week, or sailed from the Yacht Club. Clay saw him less often, but regularly, usually when he was in Charleston overnight. Charlie and Happy sometimes had him to dinner at their house on Tradd, or he and Charlie went to the club. Charlie was tall, thin, bald, and laid-back to the point of seeming asleep much of the time you were talking to him. But he wasn't.

"What you need most is a solid month at one of your own resorts," he said at the end of the day, when he had come with Clay back to the town house on Eliott and was having a drink with us. He stood in front of the fireplace, where I had lit the little fatwood fire that was kept laid there, his hands in his pockets, rocking back and forth.

"I don't feel tired," Clay said restlessly. "I never did. I just got too hot and got dizzy for a minute. You never got too hot?"

"I never move that fast," Charlie said affably, and took a swallow of his scotch. "I don't care how you feel. You don't know how you feel. That's your problem. You've been running flat out on empty for a long time. You need some rest and I'm not kidding about that. What do you think an ulcer means? What do you think passing out in the middle of a parking lot means? I know about that; Hayes told me. Carter told him. You're lucky there's not any permanent damage.

Your heart and your blood pressure are basically okay, though I'd like to get the pressure down some. But there are other indicators and you've got all of them. God knows what your blood work will show. What are you eating? *Are* you eating? You say you're not sleeping very well . . ."

"I never slept a lot . . ." Clay said, not looking at him.

"You slept more than two or three hours a night or you'd be dead," Charlie said.

"Can you do anything with him, Stretch?" he said, looking over at me. He has called me that ever since we met. I come about to Charlie's shoulder when we stand together.

"Nothing short of drugging him," I said lightly, to mask the concern I felt. I was glad to hear that Clay's heart was not faulty, but I did not like the sound of the passing out or the insomnia. Not at all. I could not remember a time when Clay had not simply functioned physically like a well-made machine.

"Then that's what we'll do," Charlie said.

And that's what we did. Charlie wrote a prescription for Halcion and Zantac, and I went to the big Eckard's on Calhoun and had them filled. On the way home I looked at the dense little city unrolling outside my windows. It was still balmy and there were people on all the narrow streets in the historic district and around Colonial Lake, strolling or jogging or riding bicycles or in-line skating. The twilight was clear and green, the kind of late winter light that speaks of coming spring and blooming things, and indeed, the big camellia bushes in the gardens of most of the old houses were full to bursting, and whenever I got in and out of the car I caught the breath of the Confederate jasmine that is January's gift to the Lowcountry. I was caught and pinned with a sudden, overwhelming sense of sheer community, of the presence all around me of my fellow species. It was a benevolent presence, and I did not feel it as a weight but as a lifting.

Could I live here? I thought, turning off Meeting Street onto Tradd. Lights were coming on in the streetside windows. Through the sheer blinds and curtains that people in the shoulder-to-shoulder district South of Broad affect, I could see beautiful rooms swimming with lamp and firelight reflected off polished old wood, and the gleam of silver and china, and the dark chiaroscuro of gilt-framed ancestors on paneled walls.

If the worst happened, like Clay says it might, and we could not live on Peacock's anymore, could I come and live in the little house on Eliott, and be a part of this?

I could if I still had the island, I thought. But then the image came, of masts and antennas and aerials and putting greens and golf carts, and of the silent pewter creek "redirected" so as to fool me into thinking that there was no water traffic outside my windows. A lump formed in my throat, and when Clay asked if I wanted to stay over at the town house, I said no, that I thought we should go home. I did not think that anything but the dark marshes would cleanse my mind of the pictures there.

When we got home I gave him one of the Halcions and he went to bed in our big bedroom. He was sleeping quietly when I came to bed a couple of hours later. But when I woke up, he was asleep on the little daybed in my sitting room across the hall.

"I got up to get some water and just wandered in there and fell asleep," he said. But the next morning I awoke and found him there again.

"Okay. Tell me," I said, when he woke, cramped and stunned, to find me sitting in the wing chair beside him.

"I . . . Caro, do you dream about Kylie?" he said, and my heart stopped and then jolted forward again. Clay had not spoken of Kylie since before Thanksgiving when he had found me in her room.

"Sometimes," I said after a while. "I didn't know you did, though."

"I never have," he said, and his face was slack and grayish in the early morning light, and his voice empty. "But for the past two nights I've dreamed about her, and they're . . . not good dreams. It has something to do with the ocean. It seems louder than it has, or something . . . it keeps getting into my sleep. I always liked that sound before, but now . . . Listen, would you care if I slept in here for a while? Just until I get caught up and back to the office?"

He had promised Charlie that he would take a long weekend off. I had thought it was a wonderful idea, but now I was not so sure. Maybe, in this new vulnerability of his, the structure and discipline of the office would serve him better than this utterly alien, unformed time. Then I thought, My poor lost Kylie. First I bind her with my own need, and then her father, whom we thought had let her go a long time ago, calls her back with his delayed grief, or whatever this is. I had assumed that he had dealt with his own pain in silence, but perhaps he had merely buried it, and it had found a weakness in the wall only now and broken through. Old sorrow and an obscure anger welled; I can't even handle my own need for her, I thought. Don't ask me to shoulder yours.

"Of course I wouldn't mind," I said. "It's probably a good idea. Didn't Charlie say that Halcion sometimes caused increased dreaming?"

Clay sighed and rubbed his eyes, and turned over.

"I guess he did. I think I'll nap just a little longer. Don't wait breakfast on me."

He slept for most of three days and nights. Sometimes I came and sat beside him and simply looked at him. In the dim light his Christmas tan looked bleached, and his sun-streaked hair was simply a lightless brown, dull, rough. He looked thinner and smaller under the light duvet I had put over him, and his face was naked and somehow blurred, hollow at the cheekbones and temples. He looked at once much younger and quite old. I remembered how he had seemed to me the second time I saw him, when he had come alone to the island in Shem Cutler's boat, and I had seen that he was not golden and radiant after all, or limned in light, but merely a too-pale, too-thin outlander with no magic to him. Until he had smiled.

I wished he would wake up now and smile, but he did not. He simply slept, and slept, and slept, and I watched him as I had my children.

"Let him," Charlie said on the third day, when I called him, alarmed. "It's what he needs. It's what I hoped he'd do."

"He looks dead, Charlie."

"Who looks good when they sleep, Caro? Except you, of course. Find yourself something to do and let him sleep. He'll wake up when he's ready, and you'll see a big change in him."

And so, on the afternoon of the third day, I got into the Cherokee and went at last to Dayclear, to do, finally, what I had promised Hayes I would do.

In the days after Kylie, I became skilled at living on the very top level of my mind. Part of this process consisted of a conscious, on-going dialogue with myself about the things I saw in the world around me. I was aware that I was doing it; I even came to call the process my little class trips, as in, "Oh, look, class, there's the first robin of spring," or "Class, notice particularly how pretty Mrs. Carmichael's tulips are this year." Even when the nethermost core of me was screaming with pain and loss, even when foreboding loomed in my subconscious like an iceberg, I was able to take my class trips and keep myself in the moment. The amount of focus and single-mindedness it required was astonishing. If I could have harnessed it I might have lit leaves and paper to fire with the sheer force of my concentration. It is a talent I have yet to find any real use for, beyond the numbing of pain.

So even as I drove over the bridge onto the island, passing over the rippling marshes and the tranquil black water of the slough, I did not think, as I might have, of what I would see here if Dayclear became the epicenter of another Peacock Island Plantation property or, rather, what I would not. And I did not see in my mind the face of my depleted and diminished husband as he slept, or wonder what might become of him if I could not, after all, bring myself to deed the island back over to him. I only thought that if the mild weather continued we would have one of those rare, perfect, attenuated springs where everything reached its absolute optimum early and balanced there, shimmering with life and perfection, long after the savage young summer should have been born.

"A perfect spring for painting; I'll have to get back to it," I said chattily to myself.

But the other thoughts, the older, darker ones, were there. I felt them, bumping like sharks, down deep.

When I came into the settlement, it seemed that everyone in it was out renewing themselves in the sun. Old men sat on the porch and steps of the store, wrinkled old turtles' faces turned up to the light, drowsing or nodding among themselves. I knew that, barring a deadly cold snap, they would sit there now until late next fall. A ritual herd movement had taken place.

A few of the younger men and women were scratching in the bare garden plots across the road from the cabins, turning over the rich black soil, perhaps to ready it for planting — though that lay a month or so ahead — or perhaps just to see what they could see. Old women hung laundry on sagging lines behind the houses; in the soft, fresh little wind sheets and underwear and overalls billowed like sails, and would, I knew, smell fragrant beyond words when donned, sweet with salt and sun. A couple of old women sat in chairs set out in front of the houses, watching children toddling and stumbling after thin black dogs and chickens in swept-out dooryards. In a dooryard near the end of the line of cabins, old Toby Jackson, near-blind and smiling, looked into the sky. I wondered what he saw behind his useless lids. Perhaps he smiled because it was wonderful beyond the telling; wouldn't that itself be wonderful? His hands were busy with the coils of a sweet-grass basket, as they almost always were, and the grand paisley Legare Street shawl lay loosely on his shoulders, more decoration than protection on this soft day.

I went into the store and found Janie behind the counter, as usual. She had opened both the front and back doors, and light that did not reach the fusty old interior all winter flooded it, picking out the astounding clutter and shabbiness and dust. The iron stove was cold. All the old men were outside. Janie was propped, elbows on the counter, flipping through a book of lottery tickets. Out back I could hear garbage cans rattling. Esau, hastily tidying up for the spring that had come before he was ready for it.

"Hey, Caro," Janie said, flashing her gold-toothed smile. "It's God's day, ain't it?"

"It is indeed," I said, smiling back at her. "You fixing to win the lottery?"

"From yo' lips to God's ear," she said. "Shoot, why not? Lady over to John's Island won fifteen thousand dollars last month. Never had a pot to piss in before, neither."

"What did she do with it?"

"Got her boy to buy her a double wide over to Edisto. Gon' start a beauty parlor over there."

"Wonder why she didn't stay on John's?" I said.

"Oh, most of the folks around where she live is old. They either wears head rags or does hair wrappin'. Not much business in the old places."

"What about you, Janie? Would you stay here if you hit the jackpot?"

She looked at me out of the corner of her eye.

"You handin' out money today?"

"Well, I wish, but no, I was just curious."

She sighed.

"I don't know. That's God's truth. There ain' much over here. Never has been. But the spaces, they're easy on the eyes, you know. The marsh and the woods, they don't confuse the mind like the cities do. When I go over that bridge I always come home with my head achin' and my eyes wo' out from things and stuff. Look like I can't look at but one or two things at a time. I might feel different if I was younger, but I 'spec it's too late for me to move now. This old place, this is a good place for the old folks. We don't need much, but what we do need is right here."

I dropped my eyes. I had thought I might go from one villager to another, the ones I knew, anyway, and tell them what South-

Ward proposed merely as part of an idle conversation on a spring day, but I saw that I could not do that. I could not say it but once.

"Is Ezra around?" I said. "I need to talk to him."

"He and Luis gone over to the old cemetery with Auntie Tuesday to clean up the family plots. They took the chirrun and that Sophie with 'em. She want to make pictures of the markers, she say. I don't know if Auntie gon' let her do that or not. Ain't too many white folks seen that graveyard."

"Sophia's not white," I said in confusion.

"Yeah, she white. She might be black in her blood, but she white in her mind," Janie said. "Least she used to be. Look like she changin' some these days. Ol' Ezra, he talkin' his trash to her all the time now. Not many gals stand up to Ezra's trash."

I laughed, surprised at the acuity of her words. "White in her mind." It was just what Sophia Bridges was.

"You know when they'll be back?"

"I git 'em in here now if you really need 'em," she said, and turned and went out onto the rickety little back porch. I followed, protesting that I could wait.

But she had already taken up a weathered old wooden mallet, and with it she struck a mighty blow on a huge, age-blackened bronze bell that sat at the foot of the back steps. It was as big around as an oil tank, and rose above her waist. I thought it must be centuries old, and hand cast. It spoke with a great, ponderous boom that rolled away through the drowsing woods like summer thunder, echoing and echoing until I lost it among the farthest trees back to the west, fringing the inland waterway.

"My lord," I said reverently. "That's some bell."

"Sho' is. Used to be a quittin' bell on one of them big indigo plantations on Edisto. Called folks out of the fields five miles away."

"How did it get over here?"

"Esau's great-granddaddy took it when they 'mancipated him, instead of money or a mule. Took him three weeks to git it over here by oxcart. Said from then on he was gon' to be the only one to ring that bell, and while he was alive, he was. You listen now."

I did. From far away came the thin shriek of what I first took to be a hunting osprey, or perhaps even an eagle, but did not sound quite right for that.

"That's Ezra," Janie said. "He got him one of them whistles ladies in the city carries to keep from gittin' jumped on at night. They be on in here terreckly."

374

And in ten minutes or so I saw them, trudging up the sandy white road that led away into the scrub and the forest. Mark and Lita capered in front, with Sophia just behind them. I could see the easy swing of her stride even though I could not make out her features yet. Then came Ezra's great bulk with the tiny figure of his aunt on his arm, and behind him, carrying what looked to be hoes and a rake, came Luis Cassells. I realized that I would know his great-shouldered slouch anywhere. Auntie's rangy yellow dog trotted at his heels.

When I had hugged the children and greeted everybody and they had settled Auntie Tuesday into a chair on the porch, Janie brought opened Mello Yellos and Mountain Dews for us, and we sat down on the porch steps. The old men nodded and smiled and dozed. No one spoke. Ezra and Luis looked at me keenly, but I simply could not get my tongue working. I wished I was anywhere on the face of the earth but here, about to propose this monstrous indignity to these dignified people.

Finally Ezra said, "I think you've got something to say to us, Caro."

And I sighed, and took a deep breath, and said, "I'm only here because I promised I would tell you this. I want you to know that it is not my idea. I still feel the way about this island that I always have. But I promised."

He nodded, not speaking. I could not read his eyes. Luis was not looking at me but out across the cleared field to the edge of the forest. Sophia Bridges looked at her feet. They were shod in muddy old tennis shoes and she wore filthy blue jeans and a sweatshirt whose message had long since faded. Her narrow, beautiful head was wrapped in a kerchief in the manner of the other women in Dayclear. She looked as near as Sophia could look, I thought, to belonging here.

Auntie Tuesday nodded her head and made a sort of hypnotic humming sound: "MMMMM hummmm, Mmmm hummmmm . . ."

I realized she was singing to herself, but I could not tell what the song was.

And so I told them. About the dilemma Clay found himself in — though I could not have said why I did that — and about his and Hayes's long search for something that would save the company and the jobs of so many people, and finally about SouthWard. I did not think that the name would mean much to most of the villagers, but Ezra looked away from me, and Luis made a soft little sound of disgust, and I knew that they knew of it. I also knew, somehow, that they were not surprised to hear the name on my lips. I felt my face color, but I went on.

I told them everything Hayes had told me. I was very careful about that. I told them just what SouthWard proposed to build on this land, and also how they proposed to mitigate the project so as not to disturb the settlement or my house too much. I told them about the dredging and the rerouting of the creek, and about the berms and the greenbelts and the careful indigenous landscaping. I saw a few eyes go to Luis Cassells then. And finally I told them about the plans for the settlement, ending with the offers of health insurance and steady salaries and central heating and television and indoor plumbing for everybody, and about the catch-up tutoring for the children. Finally I fell silent. I was standing so that to look at them was to look into the sun, and I could not do it, and was glad. I pulled my sunglasses out of my pocket and put them on. In the dark green world the people of Dayclear stood silent and still, looking at me with polite, closed faces.

"You may want to talk about this among yourselves," I said finally. "You probably will. I don't think you have to decide one way or another right now, but I do think the company wants to move pretty quickly on it, so I guess I'll go on and let you talk. Maybe

Ezra can come and tell me when you've made some decision. I'll let the . . . right people know. And I'll answer any questions you have right now, if I can."

I waited again. Nothing. Only still black faces, looking at me.

"Anybody?"

"I think everybody pretty much agrees that it's up to you, Caro. Not us," Ezra Upchurch said. His voice was as soft as the breath of a sleeping tiger, but it was still a tiger's breath.

"Oh, no," I said, distressed. "Of course it's not up to me. It's up to all of you; that's the whole point. I'm only relaying the message. It's entirely up to you all. . . ."

"Ain't us owns this island," a cracked old voice said. I did not know whose it was.

"I know that, but I'd never go against your wishes. You must know that. I promised my grandfather . . . I never would . . . I only thought that this new thing might make things better for some of you. I know how hard it is to get good medical and dental care sometimes, and how much plumbing costs, and heating . . ."

But I did not know those things and fell silent. I should not have come. I should not have let Hayes talk me into this. He had used my fallen husband to get me to do this; I saw

378

that now. I took a deep breath and started to speak, but then Toby Jackson spoke. I had not seen him join the group on the porch. I supposed that his old wife must have guided him up the road.

"Miss Caro, is people gon' come over here and pay to look at us?" he said.

Something cold and rock-hard around my heart cracked and broke open. I almost stumbled with the release of it.

"No, they are not," I said as clearly as I could pitch my trembling voice. "They are not going to do that because I am not going to turn this land over to the Peacock Island Plantation Company. Not now and not ever. I'm sorry I even let them talk me into telling you about it, and we will not speak of it again unless you all bring it up."

I waited awhile, my breath coming fast and shallow, to see what they would say. A few of them nodded, and one or two smiled a little at me, as they always did, but still no one spoke, and I wondered if I had made myself clear. I started to speak again, and then did not. I stood a minute longer.

"Thank you for your time," I said idiotically, and turned to go.

"Wait a minute," Sophia called after me. "If you'll give me a ride back it'll save Ezra a trip."

"Of course," I said automatically. My ears were ringing with the silence of the people of Dayclear.

She left to get her things together and call Mark from the backyard of the store, where he and Lita were chasing a platoon of squawking Domineckers.

Luis Cassells came down off the porch and fell into step beside me. He did not speak, either, until we had reached the Cherokee. I got in and he put his hand on the rim of the lowered window and looked in at me.

"How are you feeling about all this? It was a tough thing to do and a brave one," he said.

"It was a stupid thing to do," I said. "I never should even have mentioned it. It should not have come up. Luis, do you think they understand that I mean to keep the island? That they're okay; they're safe?"

"They understand everything," he said. "They're grateful to you, even if they aren't ready to show it yet. You don't have to worry about that. They've always known where your heart was, Caro. They just haven't been sure whether you would follow it."

"I've tried to do that," I said tremulously. I wanted to cry, to howl aloud. I had just doomed my husband's company.

I said as much to Luis Cassells.

"It was the right choice," he said.

"I just did in my husband's entire future," I said, trying to smile. "You'll excuse me if I can't feel too confident about my choice."

He shook his tangled dark head. "Your decision about Dayclear isn't the agent of your husband's future's tailspin, Caro, much as people might like you to think it is. And it's not the only one for him. He could have others that don't cost so much. You could, too. . . ."

"No," I said. "Not Clay. For him, I think the company has been the only one."

"Then you don't know anything, *carita*," he said, and pulled his head out of my window and went back down the hill. It was not until Sophia and Mark were in the car and we were headed back down the road toward the bridge that I realized he had said not *Carita* but *querida*.

The Spanish for "dear."

We were across the bridge and back on Peacock's before we spoke. Sophia sat in the front seat beside me, her feet propped up on the Cherokee's dashboard, her head thrown far back against the seat. The sinews in her long feet stood out as she wedged them for support, and her eyes were closed. She still wore the headwrap. Her feet were dirty;

somehow I liked that. In the backseat, Mark's sleepy grizzling had subsided into the real thing.

Finally I said, "I know you'll have to tell Clay about this, but I wish you'd wait until after I do, okay? He's not in good shape. It didn't go well in Puerto Rico."

"I'm not going to tell him," she said, eyes still closed.

"Sophia . . . where are you on all this?"

She opened her eyes and looked over at me.

"I don't know. I just . . . don't know. You going to turn me in to headquarters, Caro?"

I laughed.

"For what? Disloyalty? I'm really the one to do that, aren't I?"

" 'Then there's a pair of us! Don't tell! they'd advertise — you know!' " she said, and her voice had a rich hill of laughter in it.

"When I first read that, in junior high, I thought it might have been written for me," I said, laughing at her laughter. "It was just the way I felt. 'I'm Nobody! Who are you? . . .' "

" 'Are you — Nobody — too?' God, if you thought that was you, just imagine who I thought it was. A little black girl in Brooklyn Heights with a rich mama and daddy who raised her white . . . I didn't fit in anywhere.

They left it up to me to decide which world I would live in. As it turned out, neither one wanted me very much."

"And which did you?" I asked. It seemed suddenly that I could ask her anything. We had been through a great deal together, Sophia Bridges and I, whether we had perceived it like that or not. We had both lived for a time with one foot in a near-alternate universe.

"Oh, white," she said. "You get lots more stuff white, and you get it easier and faster. I couldn't really pass myself; I know I don't look white. Just real classy black. But I rammed my way into the white world at school. And I married white. You probably guessed that. You can also probably guess it didn't last long. After the novelty wears off, white really wants white."

"Are you bitter about that?" She did not sound so, particularly. Not now.

"I was, certainly. When I got down here I was bitter about almost everything that smacked of either really, really white or really, really black. I can just imagine the message I was giving Mark."

"Why *did* you come? The Lowcountry . . . under the surface, it's about the blackest place I know," I said. "You surely must have had a world of choices about a career and where you would live."

"I had plenty," she said matter-of-factly. "The thing is . . . my people come from here, Caro. I didn't know that; I had no idea where our family originated. If my parents did, they never said. I think, in their minds, they just sort of invented themselves and me. But when I started in cultural anthropology one of the first courses I had involved the Gullahs of the Southeastern Lowcountry. I felt an immediate . . . I don't know, a connection, I guess you'd say . . . and I started sort of surreptitiously researching names. I know my father's family's was McKay. Eventually I found what looked like a link to some Mackeys on Edisto. Peacock's was mentioned. All this time I was either pretending none of it existed or that I was merely doing fascinating research. I never told Chris . . . my husband . . . what I was studying. He loved telling his little liberal white law partners that his wife was a cultural anthropologist. I don't think he would have loved telling them she was a Gullah Negro whose ancestors came over in the hold of a slave ship from Angola. Come to that, I had a fine time pretending mine didn't, either. Christ, I don't know where I thought they came from. Certainly not on the *Mayflower*."

She looked over at me obliquely.

"You could special-order us, did you know that? I didn't. But you could. A lot of the Charleston and Edisto planters did. Our people were known to be good agriculturists, and we were so ancestor and family besotted that we weren't likely to run away and leave our families over here. Made to order to the rice and cotton fields, wouldn't you say? You could specify how many of us, and what sex and what age, even what height and weight. I wouldn't have made a good field worker, but I would have done well as a house nigger. Skinny; not a big eater. Presentable enough for the front rooms. Light enough so if the massa knocked me up the kid could probably pass . . ."

I made a soft sound of pain, and she shook her head impatiently.

"I'm not trying to lay a guilt trip on you," she said. "I know you're one of the good ones. It's just that . . . it's my first experience with blackness. I don't know how I feel about it yet. I don't know what it's going to mean to Mark. I don't know where the next step will take me, or what it will be. I don't know if I can make being black work; I was white too long. And I don't know if white will ever work for me again. I don't even know what's important in the long run, in the big picture. Except that I know that is, over there." She gestured back toward the island. "I know that somehow that's awfully important. I know that it . . . needs to stay whole, over there, whether or not I ever set foot there again."

"So, are you a double agent or what?" I grinned.

"Or what, I guess," she said peacefully. "I don't seem to be in any hurry to make lifetime decisions. I don't feel like I have to, right now. It's been a great month or so, just *being* . . . just teasing along on the moment."

"Ezra's good company," I said.

"Ezra's a pain in the ass." She smiled. "But he's sure a whole piece of cloth, isn't he? I never met anybody like him. He's more things in one skin than I thought was possible."

"Maybe that's what we're all meant to be," I said.

"Maybe. Who knows? I guess it will emerge. For now I'm going to just let it carry me. You know, Caro, I guess I was waiting to hear what's going to happen to Dayclear, waiting to see . . . what Clay will do. If he goes ahead with it, I know now that I'll have to resign. If not . . . well, I'm not likely to get another job that lets me write my own ticket in my specialty and pays me like Clay does. It's the kind of job that makes a reputation early, and that means big bucks. I want Mark to have the kind of education I did. He's no more apt to want to live in Dayclear than I do, even if his ancestors' names are on those gravestones, but he needs to be able to walk back and forth between worlds as easily as he crosses a street in Manhattan. Or as easily as you go back to . . . wherever it is you go back to."

"I haven't been back to my hometown in twenty-five years," I said. "But I see your point. There's nothing stopping me if I wanted to. I always meant to; my daughter, Kylie, always wanted to go so she could hear the garbage trucks in the morning. To her, that was about as exotic as you can get."

She put her hand over mine briefly. It was cold and rough with the dried mud of her ancestors' resting place. I rather hoped some of it stayed under the perfect ovals of her nails.

"You've never mentioned her name," she said.

"It's hard to talk about her," I said. "I'm trying to learn to make her a normal part of my life now. I think maybe I've enshrined her too long."

"I cannot even imagine what would happen to me without Mark," she said. "I cannot imagine who or what I would be. I don't see how you've gone on."

"Well, I have other people I love, other things," I said. "All of us do. It's hard to see that at first, but . . . we do."

And then I remembered that, so far as I knew, she did not, and muttered, "Sorry. I assume a lot."

"Oh, I have them, too," she said. "Even if most of them are dead. I just found them. It's a powerful feeling."

"Maybe not all of them are dead," I said, thinking of Ezra's black eyes on her.

"Maybe not," she said. "Maybe not."

We were silent again until I pulled up in front of her condo in the harbor village. Despite the balmy weather, it was still winter, and the darkness had swept in suddenly and completely from the west. There were a number of big white yachts in the harbor, their portholes radiant with the lights of cocktails and dinners being celebrated, and the flagstone walkway around the harbor was full of tanned, sun-bleached people strolling to the shops and restaurants, or from one boat to another. In the old live oaks the tiny white lights that always reminded me of Christmas twinkled in the skeins of silvery moss. Soft rock music drifted from somewhere. It was festive and rich and quite lovely, and about as real as cotton candy. I knew suddenly that if I ever saw this over on the island I would have to leave. That day. That moment.

We made a date for lunch the next week — I was not going to let this accessible new Sophia go — and I drove slowly back to the house. It was dark except for the light I had left in the kitchen. As I pulled into the driveway, I saw a man come out of the back door and down the steps. Before I could even feel uneasy, I saw that it was Hayes Howland and felt a sharp sting of resentment instead. I did not want Hayes going in and out of my house when I was not there. I supposed, with weary resentment, that I would have to start locking my doors after all. It was ironic to think that when I finally capitulated to that, it would be Hayes I was locking out, and not the occasional random robber or rapist.

I met him at the back steps.

"Are you stealing the silver?" I said, trying for lightness.

"Looking for Clay. I haven't been able to raise anybody on the phone all afternoon, and I got uneasy. I saw Charlie at lunch, and he said Clay was not in such hot shape. You weren't locked, so I went on in. He's asleep upstairs. I didn't want to wake him."

"Good of you," I said waspishly. "He's

been sleeping a lot. Charlie says he needs it. He also says he'll be just fine once he gets enough rest, so I'm letting him do it. I expect he'll be back at the office in a day or two. Can it wait, whatever you wanted with him?"

"Oh, yeah. I was just being a mother hen. But now that I'm here . . . Caro, have you had a chance to do what we agreed on? About Dayclear?"

I knew in that instant that that was why he had come. Not to check on Clay, but to see if I had been to Dayclear yet, to put the company's proposal to the village. I don't know why it made me so angry. From the beginning I had known that he was in a hurry for an answer.

"I've just come from there," I said, looking straight at him in the darkness. I could scarcely see his face, only the gleam of his pale blue eyes.

"I told them exactly what you told me. And essentially they told me it was up to me since I owned the island, and I told them that it wasn't going to happen. And it's not. I'm sorry, Hayes. I know that puts you all in a bind. But you redid the plans once. Surely there's an avenue you haven't explored yet. In any event, I cannot let it happen, and I won't."

He stood silently, looking at me, and then

down at his feet.

"I'm sorry to hear that, Caro," he said. "Clay will be, too."

"I know. Let me tell him, Hayes. I want him to hear it from me."

He shrugged. I could just make out the gesture.

"Better do it soon," he said, and padded away over the carpet of wet live oak leaves to the Porsche that crouched in the dark like a big cat.

I watched him out of sight, and then walked around the house and through the front yard, over the dunes and down to the beach. I had not known I was going to do that, but this time there was no heaviness, no darkness, no prickle of panic. I merely felt still and empty and very tired. I slipped off my sneakers and padded across the silky, snake-cold sand to the firmer, icy salt-slicked sand at the fringe of the surf and sat down on the trunk of the fallen palm tree that had been Carter's fort and Kylie's balance bar.

There was no moon, but the stars were huge and cold and near, and the sea itself seemed to breathe off a kind of radiance, like smoke. It made a long, infinitely gentle susurration: Hushhhhh. Hushhhhhh. There was almost no surf at all; what there was was white lace against the blackness of the beach.

There was no other sound, and no one at all on the beach. I knew that if I looked behind me I would see the lights of all the other houses that fringed our stretch of shore, see their windows lit for dinner and the coming evening. But I did not look back. I looked far out into the whispering sea, and I looked up into the sky.

"I wonder what you would make of all this?" I said to my daughter in the sky, or in the water, or wherever it was that held her. I felt her very near. "I wonder what you would do about the island if it were your decision to make."

But of course I knew the answer to that; she would make the decision that I had made. She was me and I was her. There had never been any question of that. It struck me then that it was time. It was, finally, time.

"I'm going to let you go," I said aloud. "I don't know how to do it, but I'm going to do it tonight. You need to be your own person now. If you were still with me, I'd be doing this about now . . . trying to learn to let you be yourself. So this is it, kid. You'll have to help me. I don't know what I need to do next."

I wriggled off the log and stretched out against it, leaning my head back, letting it take my weight. The damp cold of the sand seeped through the seat of my blue jeans, but it seemed a point of connection to the earth, not an uncomfortable intrusion. I closed my eyes and willed myself to think of nothing at all except her. I tried to empty my mind even of the image of her, and let just her essence, the warm, secret displacement of air and space that was Kylie in my soul, fill me.

It was a mystery, what happened then. I think everyone gets perhaps one to a lifetime. I know that I made it in my mind, but I know, too, that it was more than that, and I will always know that, no matter who tries to dissuade me. No one will, because I will never tell anyone. Not even Clay. This was my mystery, mine and Kylie's. I lay still on that empty beach with her filling me, and behind my eyes there began to appear golden prickles of light, like the ones that always come when you hold your eyes shut hard. And then one of the pinpricks began to grow larger and larger and brighter and brighter, so that it pressed hard against my lids, and I opened them to ease the pressure and the light drifted out of me and into the air, very slowly, and up into the sky. I watched it as it grew smaller and smaller, and finally I lost it among the winter stars.

I closed my eyes again and waited. And

then I saw behind my eyelids that very slowly, infinitely slowly, it disengaged itself from the body of stars and grew larger and more golden, and began to drift down again, down and down until it hovered in front of my face and bumped at my cheeks and lips with a cool sort of frisson, like the feeling a lit sparkler makes against your skin. A kiss, a nibble. I opened my eyes and it came in. I closed them. I felt it linger there just behind my lids, warm and cool at the same time, and then it slid down and down and came to rest in my chest, in what felt to be the absolute center of me. And there it stayed, until I finally opened my eyes for good and all and said, "Yes. Okay. You're safe and so am I. Thank you, darling. Go to sleep now."

And I believe that she did. And I believe that she sleeps there now and always, and will never again have to answer some sad, silly, frantic summons from me or anyone else. Wherever else she is I do not know, but I believe that the very living core, the essential flame of her, is inside me. I believe that.

When I finally got up off the beach and went inside my house, it was to find my husband still asleep on my daybed, his face looking, finally, cool and smoothed and full again. I kissed him on the forehead, and he stirred and mumbled, and then fell back into his long sleep.

"I just wanted to tell you that I have her home, and I think you can go back to your own bed," I whispered.

In the morning when I woke, I found a note on my bedside table that said, "Feel terrific for some reason & have gone into the office. Call me later. Thanks for hanging in there."

I lay there looking at the new morning on the face of the sea and thinking that if I was lucky there was time for coffee before I called him and blew his world to bits.

12

But I did not do that, after all, because when I finally had had enough coffee to jump-start my courage and called him at his office, it was to learn, from a Shawna whose smirk was almost visible over the wire, that he was gone again.

"Just ran out the door," she said happily. "Got a call about an hour ago from Atlanta and he and Hayes were out of here like scalded tomcats. He said for me to tell you when you called, and that he'd be away three or four days. The bigwigs are flying them to Texas to see some kind of Wild West theme park thing out there. Reckon we're all going to be wearing ten-gallon hats. Oh, and he said to tell you he was just fine, felt great, and to call Charlie and tell him. That's his doctor, isn't it? I could do that for you. I wouldn't mind talking to that doctor myself. I heard about Puerto Rico. Somebody needs to tell him just what's going on, and I know Clay isn't going to do it. . . ."

"Thank you so much, Shawna," I said through clenched teeth. It dawned on me that my head was pounding badly and my nose was stuffed up. Sinus infections are spring's first gift to me, and if I was in for one, the last thing I needed was to listen to Shawna chirp her love and ownership of my husband to me at ten o'clock in the morning.

"I'll call Charlie myself," I said. "We went over last week and saw him; he knows all he needs to know about Clay's condition. He's been our doctor for a long time. He was in our wedding. He would want to talk to Clay or me."

I heard her affronted little snort and realized that I had been cruel, and did not care. Shawna set herself up for rebuffs like a tenpin, over and over again. I wondered if she thought that if I were out of the picture Clay would sweep her into his arms? Look at her one afternoon, walk slowly to her, pull the pins out of her hair, and remove her glasses and whisper, "My God. I never realized."

Fat chance.

The sinus infection settled in by noon. I knew that I had done it to myself, sitting in the damp wind on the wet beach last night, and did not care at all. The infections make me sick and so dizzy that it is hard to walk, and the pressure in my eyes and cheeks feels like intense sleepiness. My face swells and my eyes close, and I am good for nothing but to burrow into bed and sleep. I know that they last approximately three full days and nights; if I take antibiotics, perhaps two and a half. When the fourth day dawns I am invariably as clear-headed and full of energy as I ever was, and so I have learned to give in to them, cancel whatever I can, and crawl into bed with hot tea and magazines.

And that is what I did. Estelle knows the drill now; she does not hover, but she keeps a carafe of hot tea beside my bed, and leaves soup and sandwiches for me, and goes on about her business. If Clay is at home he checks on me occasionally, but I really do prefer to be left alone, and it pleases me when one of the attacks happens to fall during one of his business trips. I don't feel so much that I am wasting time.

I will wonder the rest of my life what would have happened if I had not been at home in bed for the next three days. Or what would not have.

On the morning of the fourth day I awoke and the room did not spin and my eyes did not feel poached and my face was not swollen to the size of a cantaloupe, and I was ravenous. I showered and washed my hair and pulled on jeans and a T-shirt — for outside it was still warm and sweet with sun — and went downstairs. Estelle, smiling, made me sausage and cheese grits, and gave me a list of the calls that had come in while I was out of pocket. None were from Clay. One was from Shawna: Clay and Hayes were going on west with the SouthWard people, to see a gold rush theme park in northern California. Perhaps they would be in by Thursday. He would let Shawna know where he could be reached. They were on the move almost constantly; I probably couldn't reach him.

"I have my finger on him for you though, Caro," Shawna chirped. I made a rude noise at the answering machine and finished my coffee and thought about the soft golden week spinning out ahead of me. The light on the marshes would be wonderful: ineffable and radiant. I jumped up and rooted out my paints and camera and threw some clothes into my duffel and fairly flew to the island.

I was set up on the end of the dock, drowning in the gilt glitter off the water and the marshes, breathing in the clean old salt breath of the island, feeling the sun pouring like pale new clover honey over my arms and face, when I heard the shouts from the house. I knew without turning around that it was Luis Cassells, and that something was badly wrong.

By the time I had pounded halfway down

the dock, he came around the corner of the house, stumbling and running, and in his arms he carried Lita. Her face was buried in his neck and she did not move. My heart swooped into my stomach and back up, and I stumbled and nearly fell. "Dear Lord, goddamn it, you take care of this little girl," I whispered as I ran.

I met him at the steps up to the dock. He thrust her into my arms and I took her automatically and held her close. She scrubbed her face into my shoulder. I watched him as he stood there, head hanging, chest heaving for breath enough to speak. While I stood I was going over the sick-child checklist in my mind, as I had done a thousand times; I did it automatically. Breathing shallow but clear, skin cool, grip strong. She was obviously conscious and I had seen no blood. Her arms were so tight around me that I could hardly get my own breath. I waited.

He lifted his head and looked at me, and his face was white under the tan and mottled red over his cheeks. His eyes were opaque black and blazing with something: fear and anguish, I thought, and fury.

"Take her to Auntie, over in Dayclear," he rasped. "Tell her to keep her warm. Then get Janie to ring the bell; Ezra and Esau are fishing down at the bridge. When they come,

400

tell Ezra to bring a truck and meet me here, and to bring whoever else is around who can lift. And then go back and stay with Lita . . ."

"What is it, Luis?"

"It's the horses," he said sickly. "The mare and the colt. We found them about a half-mile down the creek. We were bringing apples for them. They've been poisoned, and I think it was the apples; there are half-digested apples all over the place. Tell Ezra that, too. I'm going to wait here for them. I'll need something to carry some of the apples in, and a tarp or something to cover the pile under the house. Don't go near those apples, and don't let anybody from Dayclear but Ezra and the men come back here. Especially no children."

"I'll call a vet, and the rangers," I said. Lord God, please. Not Nissy and the baby. I was afraid to ask.

"*Not the rangers!* I mean that, Caro. Just get Ezra and tell him what I said. We'll take the colt to the vet in the truck, it's faster."

"Nissy . . ." I whispered in dread.

"We can't help her, Caro. But the colt is still alive, I think. It would be good if somebody could walk the creek and see if any of the other horses are . . . sick. There's no way to know how many of the apples were eaten . . ."

"Who could do such a thing?" I said through stiff white lips; I had felt them blanch.

"Who, indeed?" he spat. "But I'll tell you who thinks she did. Lita does. She thinks she did it with her apples. She hasn't said one word since. I'm so afraid for her. My God . . . go on now. Get her out of here. Auntie has some kind of tea that she uses for sleep; tell her to give Lita some of that . . ."

"Luis . . ."

"GO, CARO!"

I helped him ease the limp child into the Cherokee and ran up for my keys and ran back down. Clashing the Jeep into gear, I said to him, "Did she see?"

"She found them," he said, and closed his eyes. Then he gave the car fender a smack and said, *"Vamanos,"* and turned and went under my house to find the tarp that stayed there, over the whaler. I screeched out of the yard and headed as fast as I dared for Dayclear and Ezra's Auntie Tuesday. Lita lay with her head in my lap, eyes closed, perfectly still. Her face was as white and empty as that of a dead child. There were no tear tracks on her bleached cheeks.

When I reached the store I held the horn down with the flat of my hand. Janie came out, muttering darkly, saw me and the child in my lap, and put both hands to her mouth.

"Ring the bell," I called, and she turned and ran. In a second I heard it speak with its great dark voice, like eternity. The sound seemed to roll on forever.

"Send Ezra and Esau down to Auntie's," I said. "Luis needs them over at my place. Oh, God, I never thought . . . Is Auntie at home, do you know?"

"She to home," Janie said. "I seen her this morning, and she say comp'ny comin' and she got to brew some tea. I give her some lemons an' sugar for it. . . . What the matter with the baby, Caro?"

"Somebody poisoned the horses," I quavered. I was finding it hard to speak past the dread that lay cold and knotted in my throat. Under it was a red anger of a magnitude I had never known. But I knew that I could not let it out yet.

"This baby didn't get none of it, did she?" Janie cried.

"No. But she found the horses. The mother is dead. Luis needs Ezra and Esau to bring a truck; he wants to take the colt to the vet in it. And he needs some people to walk the creek and see if any other horses got into the apples."

"I tell 'em when they come. An' I go walk that creek myself," she said. "You get that

403

baby on down to Auntie. I reckon she know what to do; she knowed you was coming, didn't she? Go on now . . ."

"Thank you, Janie," I said, and screeched off down the lane. Far off down the hidden creek I thought I heard the faint, stuttering drone of a faulty outboard engine.

Auntie Tuesday stood in her doorway. She looked from me to the child with her milky old eyes and shook her head.

"MMMMM, MMMMM," she said sadly. "Badness walkin' right up here in the world today, sho is. Bring that baby on in here. I 'spec we can find somethin' make her feel better."

I lifted Lita and brought her up the steps. She still did not remove her face from my shoulder, and she still did not speak. Occasionally she shuddered, a deep, racking tremor that ran all through her, but that was all. I started to put her down on the little cot in the corner, where Auntie slept, but she shook her head at me.

"Set down in that rockin' chair and rock her," she said. "I done built up the fire. You jus' get settled comfortable and rock her now. Keep on a'rockin' her. I got somethin' on the stove do her some good . . ."

"She's not sick or hurt," I said over Lita's head. "She saw something terrible and she thinks it's her fault. She's stopped talking again. But it's not physical . . ."

"I knowed it wasn't her body," Auntie said. "Look like it worse when it git the soul. Well, we do what we can. We do what we can. The Lord give us things from the earth help the soul as well as the body, and He tell those of us what'll listen how to use 'em. It the tackies, ain't it?"

"How did you know?" I could only whisper it.

"Seen 'em last night. Seen 'em in the fire. Knew somethin' dark was after them. If it's a happy thing coming I sees it in water. Here, see will she take this."

She brought a chipped cup of something steaming hot from the old stove in the corner of the dark little room. I took it, not questioning for an instant the wisdom of giving a child the arcane brew of whatever this strange old woman found in the woods. I held the cup to Lita's lips.

"Take a sip for me, baby," I said.

But she turned her head away.

"Give her to me," Auntie said. "I been gittin' that tea down chirrun's craws for lots of years now."

She indicated that I should get up and let her sit down in the rocker and put the child in her lap.

"Auntie, she's too heavy for you," I said. "I'm afraid she'll break one of your little old bones."

"Ain't no child gon' hurt me," she said, and I got up with Lita, and she settled herself stiffly into the rocker and held out her arms, and I put the child into them. Lita's face found the thin old shoulder and burrowed there. Her legs dangled almost to the floor, but Auntie held her firmly. She put her face down to the top of Lita's head and whispered something into her hair, and began to rock. Presently I heard her begin to sing softly, in a thin reedy old monotone:

"Fix me, Jesus, fix me right,
Fix me so I can stand.
Fix my feet on a solid rock,
Fix me so I can stand.
My tongue tired and I can't speak plain,
Fix me so I can stand,
Fix my feet on a solid rock,
Fix me so I can stand . . ."

She sang it over and over, more a faraway, atonal chant than a song, and presently the dim little room seemed to shimmer with it, and the flickering light from the lit stove rose up to meet it, and song and fire and woman and child seemed to sway in the room until my eyes grew heavy and I nodded. Whenever I forced them open I saw that she still sat, cradling the child, rocking, rocking. The last time I looked I saw Lita lift her head from Auntie's shoulder and sigh deeply, and relax against her into sleep.

"Thank you," I whispered, sliding into sleep myself, but I could not have said who it was I thanked.

When I woke it was after noon; I could tell from the square of pale sunlight that was creeping across the cabin's linoleum floor, from the open doorway. The sweet smell of high sun on pine and salt from the estuary blew into the room. Another smell, rich and green and savory, came from a big black iron kettle on the stove. Janie Biggins was stirring it and smiling over at me. Her gold tooth flashed in the sunlight from the doorway.

"That smells good," I said. "What are you doing here, Janie?"

And then I remembered, and whipped my head around toward the rocker. It was empty. I made an inadvertent sound of fear.

"She all right," Janie said. "She gon' be fine. She sleepin' hard. Auntie and I put her to bed in the spare room. She sleep a long time, I 'spec. Need to. Auntie say when she wake up maybe she talk some."

"Oh, God, I hope so. She . . . There was a

long time when she didn't talk at all, before she came here. Luis didn't know if she ever would again. I was so afraid that she'd lost it again . . ."

"Auntie sing her a healin' song. It a good one. I've seed it bring the tongue back to folks what had been struck and ain't talk for months. 'Sides, Auntie seen her talkin' in the well water. She gon' be all right. Her mama gon' take care of her."

"Her mama's dead, Janie. She's only got her grandfather . . ."

"Auntie seed her mama in the water, too," she said, and I could tell that for her, that ended the matter. I did not pursue it.

I got up and straightened my rumpled clothes and went into the tiny, shedlike room off the cabin's main one. A big, beautiful old rice bed stood against the far wall, the room's only furniture, looking like a great mahogany yacht in a tiny harbor. I wondered where Auntie might have come by it; it would have been at home on Legare Street. It gleamed with care and polish. Lita lay curled in the middle of it, covered with an exquisite ivory quilt so old that it was yellowed and brittle. Her fist was doubled under her chin, and her face was smooth and calm and flushed with sleep. I listened; her breath came slow and deep and even. For now, she seemed all right. For now . . .

"Where's Auntie?" I said.

"She down to the cemetery. She grow some things down there that help this child. Plant 'em there so the ancestors bless 'em. We gon' put 'em in this here soup when she git back, and they perk her up right good. You, too. You looks like the hind axle of hard times."

"I feel like it. It was so awful about the ponies. Has anybody heard from Luis and Ezra yet? I hate to think of that poor old mare just lying there in the sun . . ."

My eyes filled up and I fell silent. It seemed too cruel for the mind to encompass.

"She ain't lie there," Janie said. "Esau and two, three of the others took Esau's tractor and some log chains and move her to the woods over behind the creek, back of our cemetery. There a big hole there, go way down in the ground. Been there a long time; don't nobody know who dug it. Our good old animals goes there. It deep and cool and real quiet. Esau drops pine branches over them."

I put my face into my hands.

Sleep well, dear old Nissy, I said in my mind. Down there in the deep, cool, quiet ground with all the other good animals, under your green blanket.

"Here, you take some of this now," Janie said, handing me a bowl of the soup. I took it and sipped; it was wonderful, silky and thin and tasting of green things and sea salt.

"What is it? You could make a fortune in any restaurant in Charleston with this," I said.

"Fiddlehead soup. Found the first fiddleheads yestiddy, out in the woods. They real early this year. Auntie say they has power, but I just thinks they taste good."

They did. Gradually the cold, hard knot of grief and the red lick of submerged anger deep inside me loosened and cooled. I went and stood on the doorstep of the cabin, looking off across the bare garden plots to the edge of the marsh and the creek. The sky was a tender, washed blue and in it specks wheeled and dove. Ospreys. I wondered if they were nesting already in the dead cypresses along the distant river. If so, we could kiss this terrible winter good-bye. The ospreys never miscalculated.

Behind me I heard a thin little voice: "Caro? Caro . . ."

I turned and ran for the bedroom. Janie stood in the doorway, smiling.

"Somebody wake an' talkin'," she said.

I sat down on the bed and smiled at Lita. She was half sitting, tangled in the quilt and frowning with sleep and confusion. Her wiry curls spilled over her forehead and cheeks, and she had the imprint of a quilted square on one of them. Her skin was lightly pearled with perspiration. She reached her arms up for me even before her eyes were fully opened, and I gathered her against me.

"You had a nice long nap, didn't you?" I said into her hair. It did not feel at all like Kylie's, or I don't think I could have done it.

"Are you hungry?"

"I don't know. Where's Abuelo? Caro, I had the most awful dream . . ."

I sat her up and brushed the hair off her face and looked into it.

"I'm afraid it wasn't a dream, sweetie pie," I said. "You found the horses, and they were real sick, and it made you very sad. Your grandfather and Ezra have gone to take Yambi to the doctor so he can be well again. They'll be back before long, and they can tell you about it."

Please let it be so, I said to the distant God who took children and horses.

"They didn't take Nissy with them, did they?" she said in a tiny voice. I saw that she was screwing her face up with the effort not to cry.

"No, baby. They didn't. Nissy was too

sick, and she died. We didn't see any of the other horses sick, though, so maybe they didn't eat the apples . . ."

Her breath drew in, and I winced.

"You need to know that it was not your apples that made them sick, Lita," I said. "Somebody came and put something bad in the apples after you left them there. We know you would never hurt the horses. They know that, too. It was some bad people, and we'll find out who it was, don't you worry about that."

She was silent for a while, breathing deeply. Then she looked up at me. Her eyes were entirely ringed with white, remembering.

"Her teeth were sticking out all yellow," she said. "And there was flies in her eyes. I knew she was dead then. There was flies in my mama's eyes, too."

I pulled her back hard against me, my own eyes shut tight against the pain. I would have given anything on earth if I could have scrubbed the memories out of her head.

"You're a brave girl," I said. "It was a bad thing to see, but she isn't suffering now. Esau took her and put her with all the other good animals from Dayclear who have . . . died. They're all together."

She sighed deeply and relaxed against me a little.

"Yambi stayed with her," she murmured against my shoulder. "That was the right thing to do, wasn't it? He wouldn't leave his mama."

"That was just the right thing to do," I said, seeing in my mind the image of a small child huddled in a wrecked mountain hut, her shivering flesh pressed to the cold flesh of her mother. I did not think I was going to be able to bear this.

Suddenly she gave a great sob, and then pressed her fists against her mouth. Her whole body shook with the effort not to cry.

"It's all right," I said, beginning to rock her. "It's good to cry. It's the right thing to do. It's a way of honoring Nissy. She would be pleased with your tears."

And then they came, a great, wild storm of them, so hard and primitive and somehow ancient that I was, for a little while, frightened for her. She wept and howled, and sometimes lapsed into a phrase or two of anguished Spanish, and then howled again. I could almost hear this sound rolling out over a jungle somewhere, as old as time itself and as implacable. These were not a child's tears.

Presently she began to subside into simple

sobs and, after a long while, sniffles. When she finally pulled herself away from me and looked up, her eyes were swollen nearly shut, and her face was congested with red anguish. But her breathing was slow again, and deep.

"I think I'm hungry," she said.

Auntie was back by now, and she brought in a bowl of the soup, presumably bearing its cargo of herbs, and a piece of hot corn bread. She sat down on the bed beside Lita and began to feed the soup to her by the spoonful, crooning wordlessly. I stood and stretched and looked down. The front of my shirt was soaking wet with Lita's tears.

"You go in that drawer in the front room an' git one of them ol' undershirts," she said. "Th'ow that shirt of your'n in the wash pot. Don't do to sit around in it. That's poison there."

I looked at her.

"It's what come out of her," she said, smiling. "The song and the tea drawed it. Look like it got most of it, too, but you don't want it soakin' into you. I bile it with lye soap when I does my wash and Ezra bring it to you."

"Oh, Auntie, I don't care about the shirt," I said. "I'm just so glad she's better, and so grateful to you. . . . What was in that tea? What was in the soup?"

"This 'n' that. Little feverfew, some goldenseal, some seamuckle, jimsey, little life everlasting. You couldn't make it, chile. It's all in the words you says over it. I make some up before you go and you can give it to her if she git bad again, though."

"I don't think she'll be with me," I said. "I think she'll be staying with her grandfather, unless he's really late getting back. I'll be glad to stay with her until he comes, though."

"I give you some anyway," she said.

Lita fell asleep again, and we three women sat in chairs that Janie dragged out into the dooryard, talking idly of nothing much, taking the sun. It was slanting low when the noise of an old truck came down the road, followed by the angry burr of Ezra's Harley.

I met them up at the store. Luis's face was drawn and grim.

"Lita?" he said.

"Sleeping. She's been awake, and talked, and cried most of it out, I think. And she ate a good lunch. I doubt that she'll forget it, Luis, but I think she'll heal from it. Auntie . . . Auntie has been beyond wonderful."

"I don't think you've been so bad yourself, Caro," he said, relief making the tight muscles around his mouth sag into a tired smile. "You know, it was you she cried out for before she stopped talking."

"Oh, Luis . . ." I said softly.

I can't take the weight of this, I thought.

"It's okay," he said, understanding. "It's more than enough that you were here today."

I found some beer in the cooler and opened it for him and Ezra and Esau, who had come wearily into the store behind him. They all took deep swallows, but no one spoke.

Finally I said, "The colt?"

"The colt is alive," Ezra said, and his voice was hard and remote. I had not heard this voice before. His eyes were distant, too. I could not imagine what they saw.

"The vet thinks he'll make it. He didn't eat many of the apples, apparently."

"He likes sweet potatoes better," I said, and felt the tears sting again.

"Well, that saved him then, because those apples were full of it, whatever it is," Ezra said. "The vet isn't sure, but he's got a friend with his own lab who's running tox tests right now. He thinks probably botulism toxin. Nothing else is really powerful enough to down a grown horse so fast. He thinks that they ate the apples last night early. It would have been put in by injection. He found the holes in some of the apples."

"My God, you don't think it was a doctor!" I cried. Somehow the thought was horrifying beyond words.

"No, no. You can get the stuff; plastic surgeons use it, and other kinds of doctors, too. It's around. There's probably a real good black market for it, if you know where to go. And you can get hypodermics at any drugstore. I don't think whoever did it got the stuff himself, but I think somebody he knew did. We'll know more when the test comes in late tonight. If it's botulism toxin, I think I know where to start looking for the source."

"Where?"

"Better you just don't ask," he said. "I've got some friends in not very high places."

We were quiet again for a bit.

"Do you think any of the rest of the herd got into the apples?" I asked.

"Doesn't look like it right now," Luis said. "Simon Miller and his boys from Greenville rode and walked every inch of the creek and the bottoms where they usually are. They didn't see anything. And there were an awful lot of apples left. It looked to me like the pile we took day before yesterday was mostly still there. They're in a croker sack in the back of the truck. I'm going to drop them in the incinerator at the dump on Edisto when I go tonight."

"When you go?"

"Walk me down to Auntie's," he said. "I need to see Lita. We'll talk on the way."

We walked side by side down the rutted sandy road. The swift darkness was rolling in from the Inland Waterway, and the shadows of the Spanish moss laid long fingers across the road. The air was cooling rapidly. Luis walked with his hands in his pockets, his stride heavy and slow. I cradled my elbows in my hands against the chill. The old white Fruit of the Loom men's undershirt was decent and clean, but it was worn thin.

"I'm taking her over to Edisto," he said finally, not looking at me. "Ezra has a friend over there who's not using his trailer. He left the key with Ezra. I can't stay here with her, Caro. Everywhere she looked she'd remember . . . And who knows what's going to come next? I can't take the chance. I'm quitting your husband's company, too, as soon as I can give notice in the morning. I'm not going to make myself a sitting target; she's the one who's vulnerable."

I stopped dead in my tracks, looking at him.

"Dear God, surely you don't think that Clay . . ."

"Of course not. But I think that somebody acting in his name, if not with his knowledge or permission, stuck those needles in those apples. We'll probably never find out who, but I don't really care. I can't afford to take chances with her. You can see that, can't you?"

"But . . . we . . . you were winning! I've already told you I'm not going to turn over this land; there's no more fight to fight . . ."

He looked at me in disbelief.

"Winning what? The right to eat apples with botulism toxin in them? If that's a victory, I can't afford it, Caro."

I could not argue with that. Desolation settled over me. The night turned vast and cold. There were stars, the same ones I had seen over Kylie's ocean four nights before, but I could not see their light now. It did not seem to reach the earth.

"I'll miss both of you," I said as matter-of-factly as I could. My voice shook.

He took a great breath as if to speak in return, but then did not. Presently he said, "You could come by and see us sometime on your way to Charleston. It's not far off the highway. Lita would love that. I'll be around; I'm not going to look for anything for a while, till I know she's going to be all right. Maybe when we know about the colt. After that I'll find something and get her into preschool. Ezra knows a woman with a good little one near the trailer park."

"Well, of course," I said, thinking of it: this great, exuberant force of a man, with his wild darkness and his big shoulders, pent up in a double-wide in a trailer park. The living flame that was Lita battering at those enclosing walls . . .

I knew that I would not visit him on Edisto.

"So when will you go?"

"In the morning, I think. Or later tomorrow. If the colt comes along like the vet thinks he will, I'd like to take her by to see for herself. I think Esau and Janie will take him when he's well enough to leave; he'll be used to people then, and the vet doesn't think the herd will take him in after he's been away so long. They'll smell us on him. The Bigginses have a pen behind the store. I can bring Lita over in the summer and she can learn to ride him. You could come, too . . ."

The plans sounded positive, full of hope, but his voice was merely defeated.

"Luis . . ." I began, unsure what I would say but willing almost to say anything that would bring life back into that voice.

"Don't, Caro," he said, his head down so that I could not see his face. "You can't straddle two camps, and it's not possible for you to choose one. You've lost too much already. I would not permit it if you could."

I was silent. What were we speaking of, or rather, not speaking of, here?

"Abuelo! Grandpapa!" a small voice shrieked, a voice with relief and joy behind it, and we looked up to see Lita tearing out of the cabin door toward us, her arms outstretched, her face wreathed in smiles. He opened his arms and took two great strides forward, and she ran into them and was enclosed.

After that I painted. I painted for almost two straight days and nights, faster and more intensely than I have ever painted before, virtually scouring color onto the paper and then, when it tore, abandoning my watercolors and pulling out my old oils and the moldy canvases I found stacked in the utility closet and slashing at them with palette knife and stiff drypoint brushes. I put on my grandfather's old tapes of Beethoven and Mahler, great, crashing, apocalyptic music, and I built up the fire, and when I got so tired and hungry that I dropped the knife, I opened cans of Vienna sausage and tuna fish and ate them with soda crackers and rat cheese and washed them down with Diet Cokes and fell asleep on the sofa before the fire, and dreamed more paintings.

It was almost like automatic writing, I thought, watching as if from a distance the work unrolling from my fingers onto the canvases. It was not that I was unaware of what I did; indeed, I felt an almost preternatural control, an awesome kind of focus, that I have never felt before. It was simply that I did not quite know where my subject matter was coming from. I did not go out into the marshes and sketch or photograph and return to work, as was my habit. I did not leave the living room of the house. What I painted was the island: the marshes and the river and the creeks and the hammocks, and the secret groves of live oaks and the shrouding moss, but it was not an island I knew. It seemed to be an island out of another time, seen through other eyes. I painted stormy skies and nets flying like clouds, and dark people in fierce colors with their heads thrown back and their arms outstretched, shouts and songs stretching the cords of their shining throats. I painted fires in black woods and not quite human creatures out of an African night a millennium before. I painted baptisms in blood-dark rivers and burials in fire-lit woods. I painted wild horses, running, running. Running free.

When I finished painting, as suddenly as I had begun, morning was well along on the third day after Luis and Lita found the horses, and I was as cool and dry and depleted as if I had given birth. And perhaps I had.

I took a shower and cooked myself a real breakfast and took the paintings out onto the deck and propped them in the white sunlight and studied them. They were crude and hastily done and primitive past anything I had never even seen in my mind, and they had a power that almost frightened me. I could not even imagine where they had come from. Well, that was not entirely true; I knew or could sense that they sprang from the bottomless well of red anger I had discovered at the poisoning of the horses, and the fear I had felt for Lita and the colt and the island . . . and for Clay. But the images themselves . . . it was as if they had passed through me from somewhere else, not had their genesis in my mind. I poked around inside myself, prodding carefully, to see if that all-generating rage still lived there. I felt none at all. Just the emptiness.

As if they had been waiting until I finished my work, Ezra and Lottie Funderburke drove up in Lottie's little Subaru truck. I greeted them calmly, almost peacefully. I had not known that they knew each other, but it did not surprise me. Two such forces of nature on a small island: of course they would meet. Incuriously, I looked at each to see if the nature of the relationship was apparent, but it was not. They could be lovers or mortal enemies during a truce. The only thing I thought that they could not be was casual acquaintances.

"Coffee, for God's sake," Lottie said, stumping up onto the deck, and then, "Jesus, God, Caro! Are these yours?"

"I think so. Nobody else here but us chickens," I said. "You want coffee, too, Ezra?"

"Please. Whhhoooee, look at that stuff! You been hag-rode in the night, Caro?"

"I honestly don't know," I said, and padded inside, barefoot, to put on the coffee.

When I came back out with the coffee tray and some stale doughnuts, Lottie was sitting on the deck floor with her back against the railing studying the paintings. Ezra stood looking out at the morning dance of the light on the creek.

"Whatever got ahold of you, you treat it good, you hear?" Lottie said. "This stuff is dynamite. I don't know if you'll do much with them around Charleston or in the village center. Likely scare the bejesus out of the culturines and the retired admirals. I know some odd little galleries around that would love to hang them, though. I'll put some up in the studio, too. The kind of people who'll buy them stop by my place pretty often. You think you've got any more of that in you, or did you paint it all out?"

"I just can't tell yet," I said. "It's like somebody else that I don't know did it. I'm not going to show it or sell it, though. Not now. Maybe when I can tell whether or not it's a real direction, or just a twitch . . ."

"More an explosion, I'd say," Ezra said, grinning. "You get any madder than that and you gon' blow a hole in that canvas."

"I don't feel mad now," I said. "I know I was the other day, but I can't seem to find it again."

"I don't wonder," he said. "It's all in there."

He gestured at the paintings.

"So, what about the colt?" I said. "What about Lita . . . and Luis? Have you gotten the toxicology reports yet?"

"The colt is up and running around and eating," he said. "I'm going to take him over to Janie and Esau's in the morning. He's already let the vet slip a snaffle on him. Lita is talking a blue streak and pestering Luis to bring her back over here. He doesn't feel like he can do that right now. He's got her in preschool half a day. The other half he stays with her. He's looking for somebody over there to stay with her after school; he's got to get some work pretty soon. Meanwhile, mornings, he's doing some legwork for me around the Lowcountry. The vet was right; it was botulism toxin. I know a guy who knows a guy knows a guy who might be able to find out where it was bought. We do that, we know who bought it. Luis is visiting old . . . contacts of mine. Be a good thing to know, that."

"Is it . . . Could he be in any kind of danger?"

"Not much, I don't think. Not till he gets closer to home base on it, anyway. Luis knows how to take care of himself. He's in less danger than he would be if he stayed on this island. I agree with him about that."

"Have you been to the police?" I said. "Surely if illegal poison was used . . ."

"No. Somehow I can't imagine the authorities getting real upset over a dead marsh tacky. The rest is speculation. I think it's island business. I think the island ought to see about it."

"I just can't believe this," I said. "Who on this island would hurt Luis? Who would hurt that child? I know you think somebody in Clay's organization is behind this, but I think you're just plain wrong. That's . . . that's James Bond stuff. I don't know anybody in the company who's even capable of thinking like that."

"Don't you?"

I dropped my eyes.

"No. I don't."

But I did. I don't know how I knew, but I did know.

"Well, listen, Caro, I hope you can scrape some of that mad back up, because I think you might need it," Lottie said. "I have a message for you from that nitwit in your husband's office, Shiny, or whatever her name is. She called me saying she couldn't raise you either at the house or over here. Your phone's off the hook. Said to tell you Clay was coming in this morning; he's probably at the office now. I assume you're going to want to share the little tidbit about the horses with him, aren't you?"

"Maybe he knows," I said. I did not want to have to tell Clay about the horses. I did not want, now, to have the conversation that we should have had almost a week ago. I just wanted to go to sleep, and then to get up and paint some more.

"I doubt it," Lottie said. "Old motor-mouth would have blabbed it if he did. She practically told me what color his jockstrap was before I hung up on her."

"I'll go over there after lunch," I said. "I

really need to get some sleep now. I think I've painted through two nights."

Ezra looked at me.

"I think you ought to go now, Caro," he said.

I looked back at him. Somehow I did not want to ask him why.

They finished their coffee and left. Just before he got into the passenger side of Lottie's truck, Ezra turned and looked up at me.

"The paintings are terrific, Caro," he said. "You really got under our black hides. I didn't think you had it in you."

I didn't, either, I said to myself, watching the truck lurch down the rutted road under the live oaks. And then I went to dress and go back to Peacock's Island and speak to my husband of things that would, I thought, wound us forever.

The anger came back when I crossed the bridge onto Peacock's Island. It sprang up like a living flame when I saw the first Mercedes station wagon leaving the nursery, laden with mature bedding plants that would have cost a family in Dayclear a month's food money. It licked higher at the sight of two groups of square, tanned women in little golf skirts and T-shirts and sun visors, piloting their private golf carts across the road from the harborside villas to the golf club. It spurted into my nose and throat like lava as I threaded my way around the lushly planted traffic circle that led into the main street of the tiny village center and saw the green-uniformed Peacock's Island ground crew tearing out great clumps of blooming pansies and setting in their places flat after flat of rioting impatiens and mature ferns. Instant tropical paradise; why had I always thought it beautiful? My hot eyes wanted the tangled, littered coolness of the dank marshes and the forest; wanted, instead of this studied, expensive order, wildness and the vast amplitude of water and sky. By the time I pulled into the parking lot at the company's headquarters, I was shimmering all over with rage.

"Well, goodness, Caro, where you been? We been lookin' all over the place for you. Your wandering boy is back and rarin' to see you, and here we thought you'd run off with the hired help or something . . ."

Shawna was often familiar with me, when she thought she could get away with it, but she would not have dared go so far if she had not had an audience. It seemed to me that three-fourths of Clay's female office staff lingered in the front office where her desk sat, finding this and that to do while they waited

429

for me to come. Lottie was wrong, I knew; the office staff knew about the horses even if Clay did not. They must have known I would be furious.

"Shawna," I said, smiling savagely at her, "eat a shit sandwich."

I did not hear the gasps and the murmurs begin until I had reached Clay's door, opened it, and gone in.

". . . completely lost her mind," I heard Shawna squawk as I slammed the door shut behind me.

Clay was standing at the window wall that overlooked the little enclosed courtyard behind his office. It had been planned to look like an old Charleston garden, sheltered with tabby and old brick walls and lushly planted with vines and shrubs and brilliant oleanders and cape jessamine and camellias. The camellias were out now, hanging from the great bushes like ripe, perfect fruit. The twisted trunk of the massive live oak that grew in the center of the garden was brilliant green with resurrection ferns. The little wrought-iron table against the back wall held the remains of a coffee and pastry breakfast for three or four people. I did not wonder who had shared it with Clay. I did not care. I knew before he turned to face me that I was going to say something that would change us both, would divide time. I could scarcely breathe around the anger.

He swung around. He needed a shave and looked a little faded, as he always did when he was very tired, but there was nothing of the past holiday's joy or the pain of Puerto Rico on it. Just the habitual remoteness that the office called out in him, and a cool impatience. I knew that he hated slammed doors. I could not imagine that anyone had ever slammed this one before. He wore one of his immaculate gray tropical worsted suits and a fresh shirt. On the lapel of his coat was a gold pin shaped like a ten-gallon hat. It said, REMEMBER THE ALAMO.

I had never seen even a Rotary button on Clay's person before. I stared. For some reason this object made me want to rip it off his coat, rip the coat off him, shake him, scream.

He looked down at the button and then back at me and made a small, fastidious face.

"The SouthWard brass came back with us," he said. "They've gone over to the island with Hayes. I guess I can take this thing off now. How are you, Caro?"

He did not call me "baby," as he sometimes did. The smell of anger must be coming off me like smoke.

"I am not really very good right now, Clay," I said, and was appalled to hear that

431

my voice shook so that I could hardly get my words out. Where was all this rage coming from? This was Clay. . . . "While you were gone somebody poisoned the horses. The ones on the island. The mare — you know, Nissy, Kylie's mare — died. Her colt just barely lived. We don't know about the rest of the herd. It was botulism toxin. The vet is sure of that. Ezra thinks he's going to be able to find out who bought the stuff, or stole it. Then we'll know who . . . authorized it. You may know already, of course."

He sat down slowly in his chair and put his hands flat on his desk, and leaned forward, staring at me. The color went out of his face.

"What are you saying?"

I just looked at him.

"Do you mean to tell me that you think that I . . . that I . . . authorized somebody to kill those horses? Is that what you think? Have you lost your mind? I would never on this earth . . . I didn't know. God, Caro. *God* . . ."

He looked sick. It did not dampen the fire of my fury at all. The horrified face over that awful, silly Alamo pin made me angrier than I have ever been in my life. What right had he to mourn that old horse, if indeed that was what he was feeling, when what he planned for its island was so much worse than anything I could even imagine. . . .

"Don't be a fool, Clay. Of course I know that you did not authorize it. I don't think you had to authorize it. Do you remember, when we saw *Becket*, in Charleston? And Henry the Second said, 'Will no one rid me of this meddlesome priest?' and looked around at all his . . . his henchmen? He didn't say, 'Somebody go kill Thomas Becket'; he didn't have to. They all knew what he meant. And pretty soon a couple of them got up and kind of slid out of the room and you knew . . . Who said it here, Clay? Somebody did. Somebody poisoned those horses in the name of this company. If you didn't know about it, you ought to be able to figure out who did. I could give you a pretty good guess right now. He's back over there right now with that bunch of snake-oil salesmen you plan to sell my island to. Okay, I came to tell you what I decided about that. Listen up. There's not going to be any sale. There's not going to be any golf course, or marina, or shopping center, or Gullah World over there. I'm not giving it to you. And —"

He got to his feet and came around the desk.

"Caro, let's go home. We can talk about this at home. You're upset about the horses; God, I don't blame you. We'll straighten it out, I promise. I could use some rest, too. We'll have lunch out on the patio and then we'll —"

I took a deep breath. I don't want to say this, I thought, but I did say it. I only knew as I did that I meant it. At least for now, I meant every word of it. It almost broke my heart.

"I'm staying over at the island, Clay," I said. "I can't go . . . home . . . now. I don't know when I can again. It just feels all of a sudden like I don't belong here and never did. But the island . . . at least that's mine. My place. Maybe in a little while I'll feel differently, but right now . . ."

"No," he said.

I stopped and looked at him. There was something strange and terrible in his voice. He had turned to the window again. I could see that his neck and shoulders were held as rigidly as a statue's.

"No," he said again. "It's not your place. It never was, Caro. It's still in my name. Technically, I can do whatever I want with it."

I could not understand what he was saying.

"But I . . . I signed that thing," I said. "You know, the transfer of title. Remember, you brought it home and I signed it, and you said that all that was left was for you to file it at the county courthouse . . .”

My voice trailed off. He did not turn.

“You didn't file it, did you?” I said.

“I thought I did. Or at least I thought it had been filed,” he said. “I gave it to Hayes to do; he's the company lawyer, after all. He said he'd take care of it. But . . . he didn't. I didn't know that, Caro. All those years I thought it was yours, too. He only told me when the business about Calista came up and it looked like we were going under. He said . . . he said that something just told him not to file that thing, to hang on to that land for me. He said he knew he should have told me, but he didn't think it would ever come up, and that no harm would be done by you thinking it was yours. And it wouldn't have . . . if things had been different in Puerto Rico . . .”

My head swam as badly as I remembered it doing when I was first pregnant with Carter and could hardly take an unassisted step for three months. I sat down abruptly in Clay's visitor's chair. He still did not turn from the window.

“You should have told me,” I said.

“Yes. I should have. But by the time I knew, it looked as if we really might be able to come up with something you . . .

could live with . . . and I could tell you then. I still thought so until this trip. Even with SouthWard in the saddle, I thought my . . . vision for it could prevail. You always liked my vision for the Lowcountry land, Caro. Your grandfather understood it, and liked it . . ."

"My grandfather would die of shame if he knew about any of this," I said. "He would die. And your children. How do you think Kylie would feel about this? My God, I'm almost glad . . ."

I did not finish, but I saw the words hit home. He flinched slightly, but said nothing. Finally I got up and walked back to the door. I hoped dully that he would not turn around. I did not think I could bear to see the Alamo pin again. I did not think I could bear to see his face.

"Will you give it to me now?" I said, stopping at the door. I was amazed to hear that my voice was merely conversational.

"I . . . no. Caro, I can't. Don't you see? This will save us. This will save everything we've ever worked for, save everything I've ever built here, everything I've ever wanted for this land . . . Don't you see that? Don't you see that it's for your future, too? Can't you see that most of it won't even touch you over at your precious house?"

"I'll ask you again. Will you deed it back to me?"

"I can't do that," he said. It was a whisper, a terrible sound. "I can't just . . . not have anything. Not after having it all. Not after all this time. Not after what I've made here . . ."

"It was never yours," I said. "You were a guest here from the first time you set foot on this island. I asked you here. I let you come. My grandfather let you come because of me. It's a fine thing you're doing to repay us, Clay."

I went back out through the reception area. Neither Shawna nor any of the other women were there. The phones were ringing shrilly. I left them shrieking their frustration and went out into the sun. After the cool dimness of the office, it was blinding. Behind me, very faintly, I heard him calling me: "Caro! Caro!"

I don't remember thinking much at all while I drove back to the island except, I don't know how to be anything but Clay Venable's wife and Carter and Kylie's mother. That leaves one out of three. I wonder if it's enough.

Enough for what, I could not have said.

I drove over to Dayclear and asked Janie to find Ezra Upchurch for me. She looked into my face and said nothing, just went out back

437

and rang the big indigo bell. I sat out front and waited for him, and she did not join me. It was high noon; no one was about. I supposed that most of the people of Dayclear were having their lunches and perhaps their naps. A few, I knew, would be looking at the beginning soaps. Their stories, as they called them. For a moment I ached with the simple, one-celled wish to be one of them.

Ezra came from behind the settlement, grease on his hands and shirt. He still carried a wrench. I knew that something mechanical in Dayclear had to be fixed every day. I wondered what the settlement would do when Ezra concluded his business here and went back to Washington, or wherever his next crusade took him. I found that I could not imagine this stark, sunny little street without him.

He dropped down into the chair next to me.

"He told you about the deed," he said. It was not a question.

I did not ask him how he knew. He told me, though.

"A deed's a matter of public record," he said. "I went and looked it up at the courthouse when I first knew what was going on over here. You always check your facts before you start a fight. I always knew that you really thought it was yours, though; I never thought you were just blowing smoke at us, to save your husband's fanny. Nobody over here did. Most of them knew your grandfather. They knew you were his girl."

"So . . . even when I was over here spouting off about nobody ever having to worry about anything again you all knew . . . Clay still owned it?"

"Yeah. But we knew how you felt. We still hoped you could change his mind about it. I take it that's not the case, huh?"

"I don't think it is, Ezra," I said. I was so tired that I thought I would fall out of the chair and simply lie on the sun-warmed earth of the Bigginses' storeyard until it swallowed me into the damp coolness under its surface.

"Okay," Ezra said. "Now we ruin his ass."

13

When Ezra Upchurch set out to ruin an ass, he didn't waste any time. By afternoon of the next day he had a press conference of national proportions set up for high noon two days later. Because he was Ezra Upchurch, the national media listened when his people in Washington called to announce it. Because he was Ezra Upchurch, most of them planned to attend. *The Today Show* was in North Carolina filming a series on black church bombings and would send a crew. All three major evening news shows scheduled reporters. Virtually all the national news magazines and many of the dailies would at least have stringers and photographers present. They would all meet at the bridge from Peacock's over to the island. Ezra would meet them there with the residents of Dayclear, five or six other Gullah communities in the Lowcountry, and representatives of every significant environmental group that could mount a presence. They would march from Dayclear to the bridge, singing and holding hands as they had done, many of them, so many years before, in Selma.

Even in my fugue state of a pathetic grief, I knew that it would be irresistible. No matter if Clay could have managed to prevail over the natural tastelessness of SouthWard and create something approaching environmental genius for the island, he would be dead meat now in the eyes of the nation, a despoiler of priceless wetlands and a fragile, ancient culture. It might not matter at all to SouthWard, but it would, indeed, be the emotional ruin of Clay Venable.

Oh, Clay, I thought in such pure sorrow that it surprised me, when Sophia Bridges told me Ezra's plans. What did you think would happen? Did you think the Sierra Club would give you a lifetime achievement award?

While I was still sitting in the chair in front of the Bigginses's store the afternoon I confronted Clay, spent and silent, Auntie Tuesday came out of her cabin, toddled down the street on Janie's arm, and brought me a giant pickle jar full of her tea.

"You take you some of this when you gits home," she said, peering into my face. "Take you another cup befo' you goes to bed. You sleep through without no hagridin'. You gon' need yo' sleep for a while. I fix you some fiddlehead broth tomorrow and send it over. This time I put some St. John in it. You gon' need yo' courage, too."

"Auntie," I said tiredly, "please don't ever tell me whether you saw all that in fire or water."

"Didn't see nothin' this time," she said. "Ezra been talkin' all along about callin' in those news folks did he have to. I knowed from the look of you when I seen you out my window that he gon' have to now. That gon' be hard on you. Likely gon' split you right in two. This he'p. It really will."

I hugged her when I left with my pickle jar, holding her hard. She was almost a head shorter than I and so frail that I could feel her tiny bird's ribs, but there was a strength in her that I could feel in my own hollowed and watery bones. I wished that I could simply move in with her and be cosseted, as she had cosseted Lita. But I knew that there was no place for me now in Dayclear. I was not the enemy. They all knew that. But I was married to him. I could not blame them if they wondered which loyalty would finally prevail.

So I drove slowly back to my island house and before the grief that hung like heavy, rotted fruit over my head could fall, I heated the tea and drank a cup. I could not handle much more right now than drowsiness, sleep. The knowledge of the betrayal needed time to work its way deep into the fibers of my mind and heart so that I knew its whole scope, its essential truth. Until that could happen, I knew that I would spend my time veering wildly from despair to denial, and back again. I had done it with Kylie. I would do it, too, now, with whatever might be left of my marriage. Better to drowse. Better still to sleep.

And I did. The smoky, slightly bitter tea eased the ache in my heart and the snarl in my head just enough so that I could read, and I stretched out on the sofa and lit my fire and pulled out the crumbling, yellowed old copy of *The Jungle Book* that had been Kylie's favorite. The exotic, firelit world of Mowgli and Baloo and Bagheera and Shere Khan swallowed me totally. I fell asleep before the fire and dreamed, not of my own threatened river and forest, but of a gold-green jungle where animals spoke and a child lived in a profound and sustaining harmony with them. When I awoke, it was almost ten the next morning, and I was cold and stiff and hungry, and the razor-sharp new pain was infinitesimally dulled.

It seemed to me that I should make a plan, a blueprint for living a new way, a map for getting through the next days in a new and diminished territory. So I showered and washed my hair and put on clean jeans and shirt and sat down on the deck with coffee and a fossilized bagel. I brought a legal pad and a pen with me for the outlining of my new life, but nothing came to me. Nothing at all. I could not think of a life without this island and this house, and I could not imagine one without Clay. It was a strange, suspended time, that morning. I both had a husband and did not; both had a home and did not. I would think, Well, we can live very well over here if we lose the Peacock's house, and then think, But who is we? Or I would think, This is absurd; Clay will no more let me lose this place than he would let me go naked, or starve, and then realize that he was prepared to put the machinery of that loss into motion whenever he wished, and so far as I knew, would do it without delay. I felt nearly crazy, actually near insanity. I did not know how even to think of Clay in any terms but the ones in which I had always thought of him: my husband; the man I had always loved; the man I would grow old with; would, with luck, come to the end of my days with.

And yet, for all practical purposes, he had ended that life yesterday. Or had it been I? I did not know even the most basic truth of all this, and so I sat in the soft sun of late January and waited for what would come next.

It was Sophia Bridges, on Ezra's motorcycle. She came roaring into the clearing and slewed smartly to a stop, dismounting in one single fluid motion of her long, elegant legs and unpacking a small sweet-grass basket from the saddlebag. I stared at her. She might as well have ridden up on a Komodo dragon. Even in my strange, suspended state, I realized how profoundly Sophia had changed on this island. There was little of the chilly, distant woman I had met in the kitchen of the guest house before Thanksgiving. She seemed almost totally a creation of this wild island now.

"I brought you some of Auntie's magic soup," she said, dropping down beside me in the rickety chair that had been my grandfather's. "And I wanted to see how you are. You took a bad knock yesterday, Ezra says."

A Southern woman is raised from birth to say when someone asks how she is, "Oh, fine, thank you for asking." I remembered saying it even when the enormity of Kylie's death was still new, and remembered the strange looks it evoked from the asker.

But now I simply said, "I think I'm in bad trouble, but I don't know how I feel yet. It's like being shot or something, and it hasn't started hurting yet but you know it will any minute. I don't even know how to describe it. But thanks for asking."

She grinned wryly at that last, and stretched out her legs in the old faded jeans that were her island uniform.

"I think I know. I remember when Chris told me he was leaving me. It seemed like there ought to be some kind of book that would tell me how to feel and what to do about it. You just don't know who or what you are anymore, do you?"

"I guess that's it," I said. "Mainly, I just can't believe that what's happened . . . really happened. I just can't believe it."

"I know. In my case, I didn't know who I was anyway, so in the end it wasn't so much different from the way I usually felt. But it must be awful for you. You never much doubted who you were, did you?"

"I guess I never much doubted *what* I was. I think there must be a difference that I'm just learning about. So much for teaching old dogs new tricks."

"Well, I guess the main thing is not to do anything sudden," she said. "Nothing's cast in stone, is it? I mean, you haven't decided really to leave or anything, have you? Things change so fast, Caro. They really do. That's one thing I've finally learned. Things change."

"I guess I haven't decided anything," I said. "But, Sophia . . . I don't think I can live with . . . what will happen over here. I don't think I can be around for that."

"Then where would you go?"

I just looked at her. I had not gotten that far. She was right. Where would I go? The town house? And risk running into Hayes Howland or Lucy every time I put my head out my front door? See the line of green on the horizon that was the fringe of Peacock's Island every time I walked on the Battery? No. Not the town house.

"I never got around to residential options," I said.

"Neither did I, but one presented itself, anyway, and one will for you," she said. "Maybe the first thing we both needed to learn was just to let go and let life do it."

"Well," I said, feeling absurd laughter start deep in my stomach, "life has done gone and done it."

And we sat in the sun and laughed and laughed, like schoolgirls giddy with new spring and limitless possibility.

Presently she said, "I came to tell you what Ezra plans to do. He wanted to come tell you himself, he's so proud of it all, and he was just sure that the jewel in the crown would be to have you march with them to meet the media. It's the old Upchurch touch, doncha know. The piquant, poignant little coup de grace. When I got through telling him how many kinds of assholes he was he saw the wisdom of letting me come alone to tell you. It's a good plan and I think it could work, but I can also see how it would just finish you off if you thought you had to be part of it. My advice to you is to go somewhere off-island . . . like maybe Jamaica or the U.S. Virgins, or Bhutan . . . until this is over. It's going to hurt some folks you care about before it does any good, and whether it will stop the project or not is anybody's guess. Mine would be that it might stop Clay but it probably won't even make a dent in South-Ward's hide. But Ezra's good, I'll give him that. He's done more with less to work with than this. It's just that he is essentially a butthead and will never understand why you don't want to see Clay pounded through the ground."

"Do you understand?" I said.

"Of course I do, Caro," she said softly. "I've loved a man. You don't stop just because they've done a big awful. It may change the *way* you feel about them, but it doesn't necessarily lessen it."

I rubbed my eyes hard and said, "You better tell me what Ezra's got cooking," and she did.

When she was done, I said on a long breath, "My God. How could he do that in less than twenty-four hours?"

"His Washington staff did most of it," she said, and it was only then that I remembered that Ezra Upchurch did not always wear overalls without a shirt and work under the punishing Lowcountry sun with a hoe or a wrench, or even a mule team.

"You ought to know, too, that I've re-signed and that I'm going to be marching," she said soberly.

"What . . . did Clay say?" I said.

"I don't know. He'd gone to Charleston. I left a letter."

"What will you do next?"

She shrugged and smiled. It was a peaceful smile.

"It will emerge," she said.

"I feel like I've fallen down the rabbit hole," I said, smiling back at her bleakly.

"Yeah. I meant it when I said you ought to get out of here for a few days. Get some perspective. I don't see how you can, this close."

But I found that I could not do that. I could see perfectly well the wisdom of her advice, but I could not seem to leave the island house. I did not feel anxious or afraid, and I was not terribly aware of anything beyond the dull, disbelieving grief I felt whenever I thought of Clay, but I still could not wander far from the house. So I cleaned. I put on all the West Coast jazz I could find — somehow symphonic music threatened my precarious hold on peace and baroque music seemed as if it would break my heart — and waded into cleaning my grandfather's house.

I had not thought it really dirty, only cluttered with the residue of many years of island living, most of which I was loath to discard, since it had belonged to my grandfather. But with my microscopic new focus I saw years, decades, of the kind of dull, mucky patina that humidity and steady salt winds leave. I scrubbed and mopped and scoured and swept and vacuumed and changed ancient, sticky shelf paper and threw out jars of rock-hard garlic salt and clumped herbs and spices, and disinfected and polished and even did a little touch-up painting. I slept and started over the next day. When I was finally done, when I could find nothing else to rout out or touch up or scrub and my nails were broken to the quick and my muscles ached down to the bone and my body smelled of days-old sweat, I stopped and took a long shower and looked around me. The house shone. There was nothing more here that I could do. And the telephone had not rung.

I realized only then that for three days I had been waiting for Clay to call and say it was all a mistake.

I sat in the sunset of the night before Ezra's great march and felt the first sly, promissory fingerings of a great grief and a greater rage, and called Janie Biggins and found out where Luis and Lita Cassells were staying on Edisto. And then I got into the Cherokee and drove through the translucent, fast-falling dusk until I was there. If anyone had asked me why, the best I could have done would be to say, I need to be with people who know who I am.

The Creekview Court had no view of Milton Creek, which I assumed to be the nearest body of water off Edisto Oak Lane. But it did have a view of the island supermarket on one end and a nice panorama of woods and marsh on the other. I don't know what I had thought a trailer park would be like; the only image that came readily to mind at the words was the pitiful, flattened wreckage left behind by the South's frequent, vicious, trailer-eating tornadoes. But the Creekview was as neat and pretty as any small village whose inhabitants had considerable pride of place, and looked to me to be about as permanent as most. It was apparently a mature park; the plantings and trees were sizable and beginning to green up, and there were towering camellia bushes blooming fervently around many of them. Instead of rusted aluminum camp chairs and rump-sprung junkers, there were gaily painted wooden outdoor furniture and big umbrellas and well-tended sedans and midsize sports utility vehicles, and a good number of bikes and skates spoke of children. In the luminous green afterglow from the sunset, lights in windows were cheerful and welcoming, and joggers and walkers and in-line skaters thronged the clean streets. A thin white paring of a new moon rode high in the sky, waiting to bloom. It reminded me of a village scene painted by a minor Dutch artist of the eighteenth century, naive and idealized. For a long moment I paused at a cross street and simply drank it in. I would have given anything, at that moment, to belong to a place like this, my arena small and landlocked, my house as movable as a turtle's shell in case of calamity.

The small side street where Luis and Lita were staying had only four trailers, and since one of them had a huge, muddy black Harley-Davidson in front of it, I found it with no trouble. But I grimaced; I had not wanted to contend with Ezra Upchurch on this night. Only Lita. Only Luis.

I might have driven on past it, in fact, if at that moment Luis and Lita had not come around the side of the trailer from the back and spotted me. Lita had a big plastic bowl in her hands, which she tossed into the air when she saw me, and left to plop to earth while she streaked, squealing, toward the Cherokee. Luis held a cell phone to his ear, and when he saw me he smiled and said something rapidly into it and shoved it into his pocket and trotted behind her toward my car. So, feeling as shy as a teenager calling at a boys' dormitory, I got out of the Jeep and went toward them across the tiny lawn.

Lita hit me around the knees and almost knocked me over, gurgling with laughter, and Luis caught her by the back of her T-shirt and restrained her while he put a big arm around my shoulders and drew me close in an exuberant hug.

"*Ay, querida,* but you are a sight for sore eyes," he yelled. "And an answer to a prayer. And whatever else a brighter mind than mine could come up with. Come in. We've got real pizza from the real pizza place in the village. None of that frozen stuff for the likes of us."

He walked me into the trailer, and I looked around, Lita hanging from my hand and chattering so fast in Spanish that she sounded like an Alvin and the Chipmunks recording. The inside was much more spacious than I would have thought, and sparsely furnished, but with obviously new furniture and some taste. A huge television set had pride of place, with a tomato-colored recliner and a rocking chair drawn up to it, and on a big red-plaid sofa there was a litter of books and toys and crayon drawings. On the small pine dining table was a welter of maps and charts and books and a half-empty bottle of red wine: Luis's territory, obviously. The real pizza box sat on a shining Formica counter, smelling so good that I felt water gather in my mouth.

"We almost ate it before we went to feed the raccoons, but Lita wanted to wait," Luis said. "She knew something I didn't, obviously."

"Told you she'd come," Lita said, rolling her bright almond eyes at her grandfather. "Told you."

"So you did. Fourteen million times," he said. "She's wanted to call you for at least three days. She was afraid you wouldn't be able to find us. But I thought you might need a little time to yourself . . ."

Of course, Ezra would have told him about the deed to the island, and the march, all of it.

"Where's Ezra?" I said. "I saw his machine outside."

"He swapped it for my truck for the night," Luis said, grinning. "He's got stuff to haul for the big doings tomorrow, and I've always wanted to get that hawg off by myself."

"And have you?"

"Yep. Lita and I went to the beach this afternoon. It was great. Just like *Easy Rider*. So. Not that you need a reason, and I hope it's purely because you've missed us, but I suspect there's more to this than a social call. Can we do something for you?"

His words were light, but his voice was gentle and his face concerned, and I felt a prickle of weak tears in my eyes, and turned away.

"Not really," I said. "I just was . . . at loose ends, sort of, and I guess . . . I think I might have been a little lonesome out there in the marsh. I'm awfully used to seeing this monkey face around by now."

And I gave Lita's hand a squeeze. She squeezed back, hard.

"A bad time for you, Caro, and that's no joke," Luis said soberly. "A huge betrayal. A huge loss. A true evil. I would have given a lot to be able to prevent it."

"It wasn't really deliberate, Luis," I said, surprising myself. "I know Clay feels bad about it, too. I think . . . he just can't see any other way right now."

"Then he's a worse fool than I thought he was. But I wasn't talking about Clay. I know the poor stupid bastard's hurting. Look what he stands to lose . . . No, I meant our friend Hayes. Goebbels. Iago. He who smiles and smiles, and is a villain. Of course Mengele should have told you the minute he found out about that deed, and fired Iago's ass, and taken you over there with him to watch him personally fire that sucker. But his head's so fucked up by all those years of playing God that he really thinks he created the heavens and the earth, and now he's got to save his holy empire or he won't get to be God anymore. He might have come around, given time, but ol' Iago did him out of any leeway he had. He's no fool, Iago. He always knew who would inherit the earth."

"Who?"

"SouthWard. You start screwing around with the wilderness and SouthWard is two steps behind you, sure as gun's iron. I've always known that. Those folks over in Dayclear have always known that. We know that at best we're guests on that land. Nobody owns it but the gators and the crabs and the coons."

"And the panther," Lita piped. "Don't forget the panther, Abuelo!"

I look at Luis in surprise.

"We heard him, Lita and I. We heard him early in the morning, right before we found the mare and her baby. I'd heard *of* him, of course, but this time I heard that sucker. Lita did, too. You don't forget that. She's right. I reckon that's who owns this island. Pity Mengele forgot that."

I turned my head away, thinking of the night we had heard the panther, Clay and I. It had been the beginning of it all, of everything.

"Clay heard him, too, once," I said. It was almost a whisper. I thought my throat would burst with pain.

"He forgets fast then," Luis said. "That cat ought to put his snout right down Mengele's britches and roar. Look, Caro, let me put a proposition to you. Not that kind, though don't I wish. It's this. I just got a call from . . . a person in Columbia, somebody I've been looking for but wasn't sure existed. If he's willing to do what he says he will, we've got this botulism business nailed. Name of seller, name of buyer, dates, places, the whole nine yards. It could lift that march tomorrow right up into the stratosphere. It could put the blame right where it ought to be, too . . . and that ought to get ol' Clay baby off the hook a little with the media. But I'm going to have to leave right now and go meet him; he won't talk over the telephone, and he won't talk at all unless he sees the color of my cash first. I've been racking my brains trying to think of somebody to stay with Lita; I don't want her over on the island until this is all over, and I don't know anybody over here who could come on such short notice. Lottie will come get her first thing in the morning and take her to her studio; she's keeping Mark Bridges, too, until the crowd's dispersed, but Lottie's . . . tied up tonight. I'd get Auntie, but she, by God, wants to march and I think she should. So . . . do you think you could possibly baby-sit for me, just till Lottie gets here in the morning? I'll probably be going straight to the bridge from Columbia. I wouldn't ask you except that I don't like thinking of you over there by yourself in that house, just sitting there and waiting for us to barbecue Clay right under your nose. In fact, I think you ought to be off the island completely till tomorrow night. Somebody in that pack of press jackals is bound to get wind of where you are and come beating on your door. I was going to tell Lottie to go get you in the morning and take you over to her studio till the dust settles, anyway. Could you stay here, do you think? It's a lot to ask of you, I know, to help us sink your husband . . ."

He looked intently into my face and then looked away.

"It was a shitty idea," he said. "I'm sorry, Caro. Please forget I even mentioned it. I'm as bad as Ezra, trying to get you to march with us . . . . Fuck."

"No," I heard myself say. "I'd love to stay with Lita. You need to do this. Do it for the folks at Dayclear and the ponies; do it for Nissy and Yambi. You're right. If it was Hayes, God help him, then everybody ought to know it was. Apparently I don't know my husband as well as I thought I did, but I do know that he would never on this earth harm those horses, or let anybody do it for him. Do it for me if you can't do it for Clay. Please, Luis."

He took a deep breath and nodded. He turned to Lita.

"Will you stay with Caro and not give her any grief about going to bed, and not pester her for more than three stories?"

"I promise," Lita said. "She can have my bed and I'll sleep on the sofa, like you do. I'll be as quiet as a mouse. You said fuck, Abuelo."

"I did, and I should know better. I owe the jar a nickel. Go cut you and Caro a piece of pizza while she walks me out to the Harley. Look, Lita, I'm going to wear Uncle Ezra's helmet and leather jacket; will I look like James Dean, do you think?"

"Who's that?"

"Ay," he said, rolling his eyes. "I am too old for this. But I can't wait to straddle that hawg and eat that asphalt up. Think of it, Caro, a breath-held crowd waiting at the bridge, and I come thundering in on that thing with the proof of the pudding in my pocket . . . What more could a man ask?"

"Brains enough to be careful?" I ventured. "I don't like the sound of this clandestine stuff, Luis. If your guy knows that kind of stuff, he's a criminal himself. Are you meeting him in a safe place?"

"Deep in the sewers of Columbia at midnight," he said. "No, really. I'm meeting him at the VFW hut in the middle of the parking lot, with a fais-do-do going on inside. He's going to wear a red carnation in his navel and I'm going to carry a rose in my teeth. The worst danger is that he'll try to kiss me, and I can always claim sexual harassment."

"Then hit the road, fool," I said as we walked out into the night. Dark had fallen and the thin curl of moon had swollen and leaned closer. Someone nearby had planted Confederate jasmine; the sweet, tender smell almost took my breath. Even this far inland, the kiss of salt lay on the wet little night wind.

He pulled on the helmet and shrugged into the jacket. He should have looked ludicrous beyond words, but he did not; he looked enormous and rock-solid and somehow both boyish and dangerous, going off on this extravagant quest to save something not his own. But then, had that not been almost his whole life?

"Do you remember, you told me once to find what I would die for and then live for it?" I said. "What is it you would die for, Luis? What is it you live for? What is it you ride this silly thing to Columbia at night for?"

He was not smiling when he looked at me.

"For the quaint, old-fashioned notion that people ought to be able to live wherever the fuck they choose," he said. "I ought to be able to go back to Cuba if I want to. That little girl in there at least ought to have a choice. The people in Dayclear should, too.

You, too, for that matter. A great deal of this business is so that you can live on that island of yours if you want to. Didn't you know that?"

"I guess I didn't, really," I said, around the cold salt lump in my throat.

He reached out and touched my hair.

"I don't know what will happen with you," he said. "I do know that things change. I think things may change for you. I don't know what that means yet. But when I get back we will talk about it. Can we do that, Caro? Can we talk about that?"

"Yes," I whispered.

He stood still with his hand on my head, and then he leaned over and kissed me very chastely and softly on the forehead.

"Sleep well with my little girl," he said. "And I, I will ride like the wind until my great steed Rosinante brings me back to you."

"Get out of here." I laughed, choking on it.

He swung himself into the seat of the Harley and stomped down on the gas pedal. It roared into life, throbbing and bucking to get away, to ride out into the vast black night, to spit out the wind. He wiggled his eyebrows up and down like Groucho Marx, jerked back his thumb in the old WWII pilot's salute, and gunned the Harley. It leaped forward, roaring, and I watched it as he leaned into the turn at the bottom of the street, raised a hand, and was gone.

When I got back into the trailer, the pizza was waiting, smoking hot, on two flowered Melamine plates, and *The Lion King* was beginning on the TV screen.

"I always work the VCR," Lita said, settling herself into the rocking chair with her plate of pizza. "It makes Abuelo say fuck, and then he has to put a nickel in the jar. It's half-full now."

"I'll bet it is," I said, beginning to laugh. And that is what we had for our supper, Estrellita Esteban and I: pepperoni pizza from the real pizza place, with no anchovies, and laughter, and a golden lion cub growing through pain and despair into lordliness.

Lottie came so early the next morning that I was still in Luis's old seersucker robe, putting on coffee, and Lita was still asleep. She had had a restless night, muttering and whimpering, and I had heard her from the sofa bed in the little living room and gone in to her, and finally, when I could neither fully wake her nor quiet her, crawled in beside her. She had subsided then, but had rolled against me and clung there, and I was tired and sweaty when the first graying of the dark outside the high little windows came. I got up carefully, so as not to wake her, and found the robe hanging behind the bathroom door and put it on over my underwear, and went into the kitchen. The robe smelled of Luis and somehow of peat moss, an intimate, earthy smell. I drew it close around me in the morning chill.

When I had peered out to see who was banging so peremptorily on the trailer door and let Lottie in, she grinned, in spite of what was obviously one of her more advanced hangovers.

"Looks better on you than it does on me," she said, indicating the robe. I felt myself color, and she said, "Oh, for God's sake. I know he isn't here. He called me on his way out of town last night and told me you were staying, and to come over and get you all going early so you wouldn't run into reporters at the bridge. They're sure to know your car, and they know about Lita. He doesn't want them near either of you. You ought to know, too, that he and I are what they customarily call just good friends now."

"God, Lottie, I don't care . . ."

"Just so you know."

I gave her coffee while I went to wake Lita. She was fussy and petulant, and clung to me.

464

I had never heard her whine before, but her manner this morning was that of a much younger child, and I automatically felt her forehead to see if she had a fever. She did not. Well, she was only a small child after all; she was entitled to a small regression now and then. I had never really seen her in any state but her customary cheeky, sunny one.

"Got up on the wrong side of the bed, did we?" I said, and she looked in fretful puzzlement at each side of her double bed.

"It's just an expression that means fussy," I said. "That's okay. I do it, too, sometimes. Let's get some breakfast in you. Lottie's here to take you over to her studio with Mark. You all are going to have a great time. You might not know it, but it's a real honor. She doesn't invite many people over there. She's a famous artist, you know."

She was unimpressed.

"Don't want to go," she said, scrubbing fitfully at her eyes with her fists. "Want to go with you. And I want to go with Abuelo and ride the hawg in the march. I want to go home, too."

"Well, you can't do all three at the same time," I said in the tone I remembered employing with Carter and Kylie when total unreason ruled. "You were all excited about going to Lottie's last night, to play with

465

Mark. You can't come with me this morning, but we'll do something tomorrow maybe, or the next day. Where's home, Lita?"

I should not have had to ask, and felt a frisson of anger.

"Over there," she said sullenly, jerking her thumb back toward the road south. I knew that she meant the island. What would happen when Luis took her away from there, as he was bound to do sooner or later? Where would home be then?

"How about we go see Yambi tomorrow?" I said. "I hear he's been asking for you."

"Promise?"

"I'll do my best. It's up to your grandfather."

"He'll let me," she said, some of her sunniness returning. I thought that he would, too.

Lottie made appalling cinnamon toast while I got Lita into her miniature jeans and T-shirt and running shoes. When we were ready to go, Lottie said, "Why don't you pick out a few toys to take with you?" and Lita scampered off to gather her treasures.

Lottie turned to me.

"I heard about the island. The deed thing, I mean. I know somebody who does freelance hits, and in case you think I'm kidding,

I'm not. He would probably do Clay and Hayes for the price of one. Are you going to get through this, Caro? Why don't you come back with us today? It's not going to be pleasant, even over where you are. You're bound to hear some of it, and there's always the possibility that some of those assholes will track you down at the house. The patrician, betrayed, environmentalist wife . . . you're honey for the flies. Just for today? Luis and Ezra will keep them away from you after this, but they'll be tied up today . . ."

"I can take care of myself," I said. "I think I could easily shoot any son of a bitch who comes over there with a camera. I wouldn't mind a bit. I don't need Ezra and Luis to fight my battles for me."

"Well, don't shoot anybody. Ain't none of them worth jail. Save the bullets for Hayes. Somebody ought to do it, sure enough. That poor old mare . . . What will you do today then?"

"I think I might be ready to paint. If I can do that, I won't hear anything from the bridge, and I won't think about it."

"Okay, sweetie," she said, hugging me. She felt solid and warm and smelled of bourbon. It was somehow comforting, and then I realized it was my grandfather's smell.

"I'm coming by after I take the children

back to Dayclear tonight, though," she said. "I'm either going to spend the night with you or drag you back to my place. There are nights it's okay to be alone, but tonight is not one of them."

"We'll see," I said. The idea of Lottie's formidable presence on this looming night was oddly appealing. When it was over, something very basic to the fabric of my life would have changed. I knew that. I simply was not sure what.

It was still early when I pulled out onto 174 and drove south toward the bridge over to Peacock's. The sky was still pink behind the line of black pines to the east, and there was little traffic in the opposite direction. The islanders who worked in Charleston would just be leaving now. I thought that I would get home and take a long, hot, sulfurous shower and make myself some real coffee and dig out my camera and take the Whaler far up the creek. The eleven o'clock news last night had spoken of a powerful cold front working its way east through Alabama and Georgia, and predicted strong thunderstorms and high winds by the evening of the next day. I knew that meant a return, however briefly, of cold weather. We were not done with winter yet. This might be the last of the enchanted gold-green light on the marshes for several weeks. I remembered a poem Robert Frost had written about that first gilded green of spring. It ended, "Nothing gold can stay."

The line almost brought tears to my eyes as I drove. Why couldn't the gold stay? Was it too much to ask?

I crossed over to Peacock's Island and resolutely looked neither right nor left as I headed west, so that I would not have to see the company's offices or the artful stand of tropical plantings that led to the beach road and our house. I stepped on the gas when I got through the traffic circle; I had no wish to meet the first of the media gathered at the bridge over to the island. But when I approached it, it lay empty and dreaming in the first sun, only a couple of Gullah crabbers tossing their lines over into the black water. I lifted a hand and smiled, and they smiled back. I knew them but did not remember their names. I knew that they lived in Dayclear, though. I wondered how much longer they would be free to crab in this little estuary.

I flicked on the radio and found the station in Charleston that played baroque music in the early mornings. "Spring" from *The Four Seasons* uncurled into the Jeep, and I smiled. I turned off onto my dirt road and swept around the curve to the live oak hammock in a shower of glittering notes.

Clay's Jaguar was parked under the trees. Even as my lips framed the word "shit," my heart leaped like a gaffed mullet in my chest.

I stopped the Jeep a little way from the Jaguar and looked around. I saw no evidence that he was in the house; it was still dark, and no smoke came from the chimney. I did not see him on the hammock or out on the boardwalk to the dock, either. I sat still, trying to decide how I would think about this, how I would act when I saw him. I could not even imagine why he was here, on this of all days.

I decided on Dorothy Parker.

"What fresh hell is this?" I said aloud, in what I hoped was a coolly amused voice, as I got out of the Jeep.

No one answered me but an outraged squirrel in the live oak over my head.

I was almost up to the steps when I heard the faint putt-putt of the Whaler out on the creek. I went down to the edge of the board-walk over the reeds and dark water and stood watching as it came out of the glitter of the morning sun and glided to rest against the dock. He got out and stood looking toward me. He was bathed in the dancing light, as he had been the first time I saw him, and he was as tall and flame-tipped and lithe as he had ever been then. This was not fair. I felt a great, simple, abject grief start in my chest.

"I want that back," I whispered aloud. "Oh, I want that back."

I went to meet him.

I was perhaps fifteen feet away from him before his face came clear out of the dazzle, and I gasped aloud and stopped. Clay had been crying. His long face was as red and congested as Carter's when he was a toddler and just coming out of a spell of weeping; his eyes were bloodshot and slitted, and the silver scum of dried tears glittered in the silvery stubble on his chin and cheeks. His hair had not been combed, and was wildly tangled from the wind on the Whaler.

I had never seen Clay cry. Not like this. I simply looked at him.

"I couldn't find you," he said, and his lips shook, and his voice broke.

"I wasn't here," I said stupidly.

He shook his head hard, and tears flew out into the warming air. His face contorted and he turned it away.

"I know. I know you were over at Cassells's trailer. I went over there, but the lights were out . . ."

"He wasn't there, Clay," I said. "He went

to Columbia. I was staying with Lita."

"I know. I didn't mean I thought you . . . I just . . . I just wanted to see your car, to know you were safe somewhere. I thought you'd have called by now. . . . I came over here to wait for you."

As if by agreement, we began to walk back toward the house. The boardwalk squeaked and swayed under our weight. We walked side by side, but we did not touch. None of this felt at all real. I might have been watching a movie of myself, walking along a boardwalk on a spring morning with a man who could not stop crying. A man I knew only slightly, from another time.

"How did . . . how did you know where I was?" I said, more to break the silence than anything. I simply could not get a sense that this was my husband.

"Ezra Upchurch came to see me last night," he said. "He told me. Among other things. Christ, if that wasn't a scene . . . it's two in the morning and Ezra Upchurch is knocking on the door yelling for me to open up. I'm surprised somebody didn't call the cops."

"Ezra?" I said stupidly. "I didn't know you knew Ezra."

"I guess he figured it was time he introduced himself," Clay said, and to my sur-

472

prise began to laugh. It was not so far removed from tears, that laugh, but it was a laugh. I laughed, too. I could not imagine why.

At the beginning of the boardwalk my grandfather had built a pair of facing cypress benches, weathered now into a silky silver gray, and when we reached them he sagged onto one of them and I sat down on the other. We looked at each other across the boardwalk where we had met, all those years ago.

"Ah, God, Caro," he said presently. "So much shit. So much misery. So much . . . waste. I don't know what I was thinking. I really don't. Well, I *wasn't* thinking, of course . . . Listen, can we talk a little bit? Will you just listen to me without saying anything? I don't mean you should . . . change your mind about anything, but if you'd just listen . . ."

"Clay, I will always listen to you," I said. "When did I not?"

"Well, do you think . . . could you make some coffee? I couldn't find the cord to the pot . . ."

"Come on," I said. "Let's go to the house."

All the way across the grass and up the steps my heart was hammering as if it would explode in my chest. What was this? What could this possibly mean?

I made the coffee while he took a shower. I saw that he had slept on the sofa under a welter of quilts. The fire was cold and sour, and I relit it. It was really too warm for it, but I wanted the intimate hiss and snicker of it, and the dancing light. The living room was still in darkness, from the sheltering oaks. I turned on the lamps and brought out a tray of coffee and some of the Little Debbies that were Esau and Janie Biggins's sole gesture toward breakfast food.

He came into the room in an old pair of madras shorts and a sweatshirt. His feet were bare and his hair was wet and standing straight up in spikes from the towel. The sweatshirt was a horror of Carter's that said, RUGBY PLAYERS EAT THEIR DEAD. I was sure that Clay had no idea it said anything at all. I felt wild, braying laughter behind the tears in my chest. I bit my lips and waited.

"All right," he said on a long, exhaled breath. "Listen. The press thing at the bridge . . . the march, you know . . . that's off. Ezra's Washington people have been calling all night. And the project, the development, you know, the Dayclear thing . . . that's off, too. I pulled out of it. I called the

474

SouthWard guys at the guest house while Ezra was still at the house and told them to hit the road. He wouldn't leave until I'd given him the deed and he'd torn it up. Burned it, too. He's one tough cookie, Ezra Upchurch. And he still wouldn't leave until I'd called Hayes and fired him. That did it, though. After that we broke out the Glenfiddich and drank until about four, and then he left to get things straightened out with the press, and I went on over to Edisto, and then came back here. I hadn't been out on the water for fifteen minutes before you came."

He stopped and looked at me. I could not think of a single thing on earth to say to him.

"Why did you fire Hayes?" I said finally.

"Suspicion of equicide," my husband said, and began to laugh. I did, too. We sat in the growing light of this day I had dreaded and laughed and howled and wept and sobbed and laughed some more, and pounded our thighs with our fists, and when we finally subsided, Clay began to cry again.

I moved over to the sofa and sat down beside him and put my arm around his shoulder, very tentatively. I felt that I was trying to comfort a total stranger, someone I had met on an airplane or something, who had become suddenly inconsolable. It was almost . . . unseemly.

"Did you really do those things, Clay?" I said finally. "Did all that really happen?"

His face was buried in his hands, but he nodded.

I sat back and thought about that.

"Then . . . nothing is going to happen over here. There isn't going to be anything built on Dayclear?"

He nodded.

"Do you mean for now, or ever? You still own it; will you change your mind somewhere along the way? Will we go through this again?"

He raised his head and looked at me. It was painful to look at him.

"Caro," he said, "Last night, when I finally lay down to try to sleep, I thought Kylie was here. I could have sworn on a stack of Bibles that I heard her laughing, that I heard her walking outside; I'd know her step anywhere. I thought I heard her . . . talking, but I couldn't hear what she said. And when I got up to see, I heard . . . I heard the panther. And I knew then that if I did anything to this island I would be haunted for the rest of my life by it. I knew that it was theirs, not mine, yours and theirs, and your grandfather's, and the Dayclear folks . . . I knew that I never had belonged here and never would, not the way all of you did and do. They told me that, that panther and my dead baby. I know it's not possible, but that is what I heard. I started crying then. If I'm losing my mind . . . then so be it."

I felt joy and peace flood into my heart like an artesian well.

"If you're losing you mind, then I am, too," I said. "I've heard her here. I've talked to her. I've thought I saw her. And Luis and Lita heard the panther the morning . . . that Nissy died. I think . . . I think . . . that either that panther must be about one hundred and twenty-five years old or this island knows what we need to hear, and somehow . . . sees that we do. In any case, it doesn't matter. If you heard them, then maybe it can be your island, too."

He shook his head, no.

"But I'd like . . . I'd like to stay here on it with you, if you think you could let me do that. I thought you'd gone, Caro. I didn't think you would come back. I didn't think I could live with that."

I reached out and touched a tear track on his face. He covered my hand with his and pressed it into his bristled cheek.

"We'll lose everything, won't we?" I said, not pulling away. "If you don't do Dayclear? The company, the house . . . Is that why you're crying? Surely, Clay, there's something else you can do, some other way you can put your gift to work . . . and I don't care about the other stuff. I can live over here for the rest of my life. I was going to; I thought that was what I would do. I can sell my paintings. We could manage . . ."

He shook his head and grinned, a small, watery grin.

"We'll do okay," he said. "I'll find somebody decent to sell the company to, somebody who'll be generous; there have been good offers along the way. The Peacock Island Plantation Company is not chopped liver. I have a ton of stock. We could keep the house if you wanted to, but somehow I don't think I could live there now, and I was sure you wouldn't want to. Carter may want to be a part of it, and we can work that out with the new owners. I don't give a shit about any of that stuff; it's history. I want to see if I can earn my right to be part of this over here. That will be enough to hold me a few thousand years. No, what got to me was . . . I guess the thought of Kylie, and how she would feel about what I had become, and then that poor goddamned horse, and the colt . . . Kylie loved those horses . . . and Hayes. Hayes was my friend, Caro. Hayes was my first friend in this place, almost my first friend period . . ."

"Did he admit . . . that he had anything to do with the horses?"

"He didn't say he didn't. He just blustered and threatened and yelled; he really lost it when I told him there wasn't going to be any project. Said I was ruining him. Said I had betrayed him, after everything he'd done for me. I remembered what you said about Becket . . . I think he did it, or had it done. God help him for that."

"There may be proof by now that he was behind it, Clay," I said. "That was why Luis went to Columbia. He has a contact there who's going to tell him, who can name names and places and all that. He was going to bring it back with him for the press conference. You should have it soon . . ."

He turned his face away.

"I don't need it. I think I knew when you told me. Hayes . . . something has eaten Hayes up inside, like a worm. There's nothing left but rottenness. I don't know why I never saw it happening. He's going with SouthWard, by the way; it's been in the works for months. He hit me with that, too. He was to deliver the project and then go in as chief counsel and a managing partner. He'd have been out of Peacock's before the dust settled. The deal was that he'd be able to stay in Charleston, too; Hayes had it all figured out."

"Well, he'll have to refigure then . . ."

"No, I think they'll still take him. Oh, he won't be chief anything, and he'll have to move to Atlanta, and that will kill him and Lucy, and he'll never make anywhere near the money he stood to make this way . . . but Hayes is good about finding venture capital. He ought to be able to smell out enough for SouthWard so that they'll keep him. I think, for Hayes, living in a suburb of Atlanta near a strip shopping mall and being a middle-level money cruncher for SouthWard will be worse than jail. Maybe there's some justice in the world after all. I'd like to think there's a little, after what I've done . . ."

"But if you've pulled out of the Dayclear project, what harm *have* you done?" I said, reaching out to turn him around so that he faced me. His shoulder felt familiar again all of a sudden, muscle and bone that I knew.

He turned. His face shocked me. I felt my breath die in my chest.

"Ezra came for another reason," he whispered.

"Tell me," I said.

And that is when he took both my hands in his cold ones, and told me that Luis Cassells had spun the Harley off a long curve halfway between Edisto and Columbia near midnight the night before, and crashed into a tree, and died, the state patrol thought, on impact.

14

The storm the newscasts had promised us came a day early, screaming in from the west on a fast-running river of upper air. It hit about three o'clock that afternoon, out of a sky gone inky black and lurid with flickering lightning, and stalled out over the Lowcountry. It crouched there for twenty-four hours, alternately flooding the sea and marshes with torrential cold rains and scourging them with great, punishing winds. Sometimes there was the spatter of hail on the house's tin roof, and sometimes the light went queer and thick and green and Clay would stand me up and walk me hurriedly into the middle hall, where there were no windows, until the dull bellow high overhead passed and became ordinary rain again. Several tornadoes spun out of the low, flat clouds; I learned later that North Charleston had been nipped by one, and a couple of blocks were treeless and shingleless in Peacock Plantation, and the usual trailer park casualties had occurred. Much later Lottie told me that the trailer that Luis and Lita had borrowed was rocked off its foundation, though no real damage was done. It was as if the very air howled in grief and outrage for Luis Cassells.

I remember very little of the storm. For almost its day-and-night-long duration, I cried.

I began to cry at Clay's words that morning. I felt as though a lance had gone straight into a monstrous sac of pain deep within me and let it erupt. I cried great, shuddering sobs and moans that rose sometimes into real screams, and gasped for breath that would not come until my chest heaved and black specks danced before my eyes, and then sobbed again. I cried so much that I thought I would die of it; I did not think that the human heart and lungs could process that many tears, withstand that kind of savage, battering grief. When I stopped momentarily, gasping and rocking back and forth, I could feel a profound aching deep in the muscles of my stomach and under my ribs that felt mortal. I frightened myself badly with the velocity and duration of my grief and my inability to stop it, and I know that I frightened Clay. After an hour or so of rocking me in his arms on the sofa while the world outside blazed with lightning and boomed with thunder, and I wept, he picked me up and walked with me into the bedroom and laid me under the covers and crawled in beside me. For the rest of that roaring afternoon, he held me hard against him and I cried in my grandfather's old bed.

Sometimes, in a momentary lull, I would try to explain to him that it was not just for Luis Cassells that I cried, and I knew that that was true, although the thought of that lonely death on a dark country roadside would send me back into a fury of tears whenever it came, unbidden, into my mind.

"It's everything, Clay," I would hiccup. "It feels like it's just everything that ever happened to me. He was never . . . like that . . . to me. It's just . . . he gave me back Kylie, in a way. He showed me how to let her go so she could come back. And, Clay, he showed me how to stop the drinking; I haven't drunk anything since way before he . . ." And the tears would start again, endlessly, endlessly.

"I know," he would murmur against my hair. "I know. I know who you're crying for. You never did, did you? It's all right. Cry all you need to."

He didn't know, not really; I did cry for Kylie, of course, but through all of that vast storm of anguish I felt her, that fiery living kernel of her, within me, burning steadily. I cried, I think, for not having gotten her back sooner, and I cried for Nissy and her colt, and I cried for the awful, slinking thing that had ripped Clay away from me and had given me back this man who, even while I clung to him, was a stranger to me. I cried for the life that I had not even liked very much, perhaps, but that had been the one I knew. I cried for the fear that my foolishness had permitted the Gullahs of Dayclear. I cried for the gangling, vulnerable teenager who had grown to manhood waiting for me to really see him again. I cried for the man who had grown so nearly old waiting for the same thing. I even cried for Hayes Howland, for the young Hayes in tennis whites who had brought me my husband on a summer day.

All that I knew. Still, I could not stop.

Late in the afternoon the phone began to ring and people began to come to the house. Clay would leave me for a moment, to talk in low tones on the phone or to whisper hurriedly to whomever stood in the streaming doorway, but he always came back and got into bed with me again.

"Okay," he would say, pulling me against him. "Let 'er rip." And I did.

It was a strange state; in a way it was like the feverish fugue state in which I had painted that night before Ezra and Lottie had come. I seemed mired in the same fireshot old darkness, though I realized on some level that it was only the lightning outside, and the flickering of the fire in the little bedroom fireplace. I saw images and heard things with preternatural clarity: I heard Ezra's voice once, from the living room, talking about the funeral service for Luis, and I heard Sophia Bridges's cool clear voice saying, ". . . I'll take her, of course, but it isn't me she wants," and knew that she was speaking of Lita, and could not do anything at all about it. Lita . . . I found that I could not even think of Lita.

Later, in the full night, I heard Sophia again, telling Clay to give me a cup whenever I would take it, and knew that Auntie Tuesday had sent her magical tea, and actually smiled to myself before the tears started again. And I heard her telling him about Lita, about the horror that had taken her mother and baby brother and her journey to Luis, and about her silence. I gathered that she was silent again, once more at Auntie's house, and that the tea and the broth were not working, and that everyone was frightened for her. I was, too, but I could not make my muscles move me toward the edge of the bed.

"Ezra and I wanted to bring her over here,

but Auntie says let Caro be. She says a lot of poison has got to come out before she can help Lita or anybody else. She says give her the broth and the tea until tomorrow and then we'll see. It's Caro's time now. Auntie will tend to Lita."

Presently she went away, back into the storm, and Clay came into the room with a tray of Auntie's steaming fiddlehead broth, and I took it from him and drank it down greedily. I knew that it would spin me down into sleep. I thought if I cried anymore I would surely die.

Sleep came then. A sleep unlike any other I have ever known. In it fires burned and drums beat and animals flickered through forests of a primary greenness I had never known, and children ran laughing and shrieking, and hot blue seas beat on yellow sand, and great, hectic flowers hung from vines like boa constrictors. I remember thinking, as you do in dreams, that this was Eden, and I must be very careful or I would be cast out of it. It was not a peaceful Eden, not sweet, not idyllic, but it was so ravenously alive and exuberant in its fecundity that I could almost feel the fabric of a still-wet new world forming itself around me.

I woke the next morning with tears still

damp on my face, but this time they were tears of a fierce joy. I knew, without knowing how, that for a time I would not cry again.

I was alone in the tumbled bed. I stretched long and hard, feeling the soreness around my chest and diaphragm muscles from the storms of tears, and listened for the storm outside. It had slunk off in the night, leaving only a steady rain to patter on the roof. Even in my drowsing state I knew that it would be a cold rain. Spring had left us on the wings of the storm.

"Breakfast," Clay said, coming into the room with a tray, and I sat up. He was in the ratty old terry cloth robe he kept out here, and there were damp comb tracks in his hair. He was freshly shaved, too, but his eyes were wary and darkly shadowed, and the muscles of his jaw were as slack as if they had been pounded. I doubted that he had slept at all.

He brought coffee and pastries that I recognized as Janie Biggins's cream cheese turnovers, and orange juice. And he brought a damp washcloth and a mirror and comb and a long-sleeved flannel nightgown smelling of mothballs.

"Good morning," I tried to say, but my voice was a painful husk in my sore throat.

"Don't talk," he said. "You'll bust something for good."

He handed me the hot washcloth and I scrubbed my face with it, then looked into the mirror and flinched. A wild-haired, slit-eyed, mottled-cheeked witch looked back at me. I combed the snarls out of my hair and tied it back with the shoelace he had found, and took a long, scorching swallow of the coffee.

"My God," I croaked. "That was . . . extraordinary. I'm sorry, Clay. I had no idea . . . I don't know what . . ."

"You're entitled," he said. "As long as you give me an hour's notice if you think you're going to do it again. I thought you were dying. I thought you were just going to . . . cry up your insides and die. So did everybody else. Only Ezra's aunt seemed to know what to do for you. Is her name really Tuesday?"

"It really is. She's a conjure woman, they say. A healer. And she *can* heal. I'd take anything she gave me, even if it was green and smoking. She sent the tea and the broth, didn't she?"

"Yeah. I was afraid to give it to you, but Sophia said for me to."

"I thought I heard Sophia. I hope . . . I know she resigned, Clay. I hope there's no hard feelings between you. She's a good person. She's been a good friend to me."

"Caro, I didn't even think about that. I

don't think she did, either. She told me some more about Luis, and about the little girl. Did I know about her? I can't remember if you told me. God almighty, what is there left to happen to that child? We need to see if we can do anything for her . . ."

"I'll have to go," I said, feeling a great, listless white fatigue wash over me. "I'll have to go over there. Sometimes she'll talk to me when she won't to anybody else. I don't know if she can get over this, though . . . but oh, Lord, Clay, I am just so tired . . ."

"I know. You're not going anywhere today. Tomorrow, maybe. Carter's coming in tonight and will be out to see you and talk to me some about what happens next; he'll stay at the house and make the office his headquarters for a while. I don't think I'm going back in there. He can run it. Everybody's jobs are okay for a while, until something happens. I'm going to give him carte blanche to fire Shawna's ass if she mouths off to him, though. Caro, I'm just amazed at that boy. He's breathing fire to get hold of this; he really thinks he might be able to work something out with the investors so we can keep some of the Plantation. I'm going to let him try. I'm going to sign the whole thing over to him. If it goes under the onus will be on me, not him, and if he can salvage anything, he'll be a legend before he's thirty. Why didn't I know he could do this?"

"Why didn't I?" I whispered with my cracked voice. "He's very like you at that age, isn't he? I think I knew that, but not really . . . I haven't been very interested in Carter for a long time. I don't know if I can make that up to him or not."

"He understands. He'd heard about Luis, by the way; apparently he's some kind of folk hero among the Gullahs and the grounds staff."

I nodded. They would make a song about him now, I knew, about the big Latin man who rode out on the motorcycle to save their village and died for it.

Oh, Luis, you idiot, I thought, the tears rising again. Why couldn't you just have lived for it?

I shook the tears away. I knew that they would come back, but not yet, and perhaps never again in such a surf of anguish.

"Tell me about the funeral," I said, and Clay did.

They were going to bury Luis in the little old cemetery in the woods beyond Dayclear. There would be a graveside service only, and Ezra would preach it. I was invited to come, and Lottie Funderburke, but no other white people would be there. Clay was not invited.

"Well, I shouldn't be," he said. "I didn't know him. And yeah, they know by now that I'm not going ahead with the project, but I haven't given them much reason to trust me. I'm going to have to earn that, if I ever can. It wouldn't be right for me to be there. I wouldn't go if they asked me. But I want you to, if you're up to it. And Caro . . . afterward, you do whatever you need to do."

I looked at him.

"About what?"

"Anything. Anything at all."

For the rest of the afternoon, I slept again, off and on. The rain stopped and a cold wind blew the tattered clouds away, and a hard blue sky glittered like steel over the marsh. Clay built up the fire in the living room and we moved there on the sofa, and between my naps we talked. Not about much of import, and not for long, for the sleep would take me almost in mid-sentence, and I would go under. But we talked. It was a beginning.

Out of that afternoon came one thing that shines for me like a Christmas star. We decided that the entire island, "my" part of it, would become an irrevocable trust called the Elizabeth Kyle Venable Foundation, and that it would hold the land as it was, against any development, in perpetuity. It was Clay's idea. I did not doubt that it would happen. This was not the same man I had left in his office a few days back, calling angrily after me.

Early that evening Carter came. I was asleep on the sofa and could not seem to wake enough to do anything but smile at him and hold him as he bent over me. He looked so like the young Clay that it was almost laughable; the same messianic glint in his blue eyes, the same hunger as he looked out over the darkening marsh and creek.

"I hope you never lose the look in your eyes, but you can't have my island," I said sleepily to him.

"I don't want it, Ma," he said, kissing me on the forehead. "Gon' have my own island."

I slept again. When I woke it was to a cold, blowing blue morning, with the marsh grass rippling silver before the wind. The gold was gone. January was back, and Luis Cassells's funeral loomed like a great, dark rock.

I drove to Dayclear alone, and parked the car at the Bigginses's store. No one was there and it was locked. I knew that all of Dayclear would be at the cemetery except Auntie

Tuesday. Sophia had called that morning and told me that Auntie was staying with Lita, and asked that I stop by on my way to the service.

I walked down the rutted road, Clay's down jacket pulled tight against the cutting wind. I dreaded this visit. Sophia had said that Lita was very bad and Auntie was worried, but she had not said in what way the child was damaged. I knew, though: the great, dead silence would be back. Of course it would. Lita had lost the one great, fine, solid thing she had left in the world.

"Has she asked for me?" I said to Sophia, dreading the burden of Lita's need, for I still felt frail and hollow and as transient as milk-weed. But she had not.

"She hasn't spoken. She hasn't moved. And she hasn't slept. This is for two days now, Caro," Sophia said. "She lies in Auntie's bed all curled up like a fetus, and she just stares at the wall. Auntie says she doesn't think she's closed her eyes since Lottie brought her. She won't take the tea or the broth. She's like she's dead."

"What will happen to her?" I whispered in pain.

"I don't know. Auntie can't keep her for-ever; this is wearing her out, and she's God knows how old. Ezra doesn't know of anybody in Cuba, but he's going to get his people to look around in Miami and see if there's anybody who can take her. I might sometime in the future; Mark's crazy about her, but I don't know yet what we're going to be doing after this, and if there's anything she doesn't need it's more uncertainty, more dislocation. I could wring Luis's neck if he hadn't already done it. Anybody responsible for a child has no business running off in the middle of the night on a motorcycle . . ."

I agreed with her, but I did not want to hear any such talk about Luis.

"Well, she has a hero for a grandfather. That's no small thing, is it?" I said crisply.

She laughed a little.

"No. I guess not. It's just that a dead hero isn't going to take care of her right now, is he?"

So I walked the few muddy yards to Auntie Tuesday's house in pain and dread of what I would find. I did not know if I could get through the funeral without the endless salt surf of the tears breaking over me again, much less take the weight of this mute, shattered child.

Auntie was in her rocking chair before the roaring stove. The little shack was dim and warm to stuffiness, but it felt good. Auntie smiled up at me but did not get up, and I saw that she was weary down to the very bird's bones of her. I wondered how long she could withstand the sucking tiredness before she simply crumpled before it like tissue. Ezra would have to get her some help when this funeral was over; bring in a nurse or a girl from another village, something. She was simply too frail to tend this stricken child.

"How you doin', chile?" she said, and I sat down opposite her on the old rump-sprung Morris chair.

"I'm better than I was, thanks to your tea and your soup," I said. "I was in awful shape, Auntie. I should have been over here helping you, but I was . . . I don't know. Almost crazy, or something. I think you saved my silly life."

"No, you find the way to do that by yo'self," she said. "I just hurry it along a little. You need to git them tears out; I've knowed that ever since yo' baby died. And Luis, mmm, mmmm. He's one of God's good ones. We gon' miss him, yes, we are. You done right to cry for him. I cried, too. We all did. I just wish his grandbaby could cry for him, but she in there like a little stone baby. Don't look like any of the old things gon' work for her now."

"You want me to go see if she'll talk to me?"

"Not till after the service," she said. "You needs to go to that. You needs to bear witness with the others. After that you come on back here and we'll see does she want to talk to you. The thing is, she think you done gone, too. I say you's coming this afternoon an' she just look at me. I know what she thinkin'. She don't even want to go see that colt. I know she thinks he dead, too. An' why wouldn't she? Everything and everybody she love done gone and left her . . ."

I looked down into my lap. The tears were very near.

"Go on now. The cemetery's just through them wooden gates behind my house. You cain't see it from the road, but it there. The others are already down there, I reckon. Been workin' since early morning."

I followed her directions through the wet tangle of undergrowth behind her cabin. Sure enough, there were the old rail gates, weathered silver and half-collapsed. I went through them, and pushed through a thicket of vines, and the cemetery was there.

It was little more than a clearing in the woods, and I remembered that Ezra had said the woods around a Gullah cemetery were left thick so that the souls of the dead would not become confused and wander. Would Luis want to wander from here? I thought.

He knew little else but wandering. . . .

The headstones were small and listed in the wet earth, and some were very old. I could not read most of them for the encroaching moss. Most had the dried carcasses of wreaths and faded plastic flowers around them, and many were hung with what seemed to be photographs and small household objects. Hadn't Ezra said that the Gullahs often adorned the graves of their loved dead with the things they had cherished in life? There was a bleached and unraveling rag doll on a small grave, and a rotting pair of boots that had once been fine on another, and most of them had framed photographs that had gone yellow and brown and indistinguishable in the Lowcountry humidity. Around the perimeters of the little cemetery the sheltering moss hung down to touch the ground, like curtains that had been drawn to enclose it. How cozy it was, this tiny village of the dead of Dayclear, I thought. Nothing could reach you here.

Almost the entire village stood around a new oblong in the black earth at the far side of the cemetery, near the hanging curtain of moss. Beside the hole a raw yellow pine coffin stood beside a mound of fresh earth. My knees felt as if they would buckle. I don't know what I had thought, but somehow not that I would really stand and look at the box that held the still body of my friend who had never in his life been voluntarily still. Everyone looked up as I came into the clearing, and most of them smiled. The silence was as thick as air. They had been waiting for me.

Sophia Bridges stood in the small crowd. She held her hand out to me, and I went and stood beside her. She put her arm around me. I let her take part of my weight; my knees seemed reluctant to stiffen. As the silence spun out, I made myself look at the grave and the coffin beside it. "Bear witness," Auntie Tuesday had said, and I would do that. I would not forget this place where we were going to leave Luis.

The hole in the earth had dark water in the bottom of it. A bucket sat beside it, and I thought that they had been trying to bail it out, but I knew that it was groundwater and that bailing was useless. The water was never far from the surface of life on this island. That was all right. Let the clean, dark old salt water take him. Better that than the arid earth of some perpetual care field in an anonymous city. I had wondered if Luis would have wanted to lie here, so far from the country that he had never, after all, gotten back to, and had thought that perhaps Ezra should have looked into a burial in Miami, among other Cubans, some of whom Luis was sure to have known. But this, this felt right.

I looked more closely. There were a few florists' wreaths around the grave, which had cost their senders more than the florist would ever know, but most of the flowers were cut from the first of the marsh's blooming things: jasmine, and camellias, and great, drooping fronds of willow that were always the first to green up. In the middle of the coffin lid was a clock banked in flowers, stopped at eleven fifty-two. How did they know? I thought, and then, of course: his watch.

The tears threatened. I turned my head. Then I looked back.

On a small sapling that leaned over the grave someone had hung photographs. I saw one of Lita, obviously taken at some school event, solemn and alien in a dark dress with a white collar and a little wreath of flowers in her wild hair. There was one of a smiling young couple in front of a great wedding-cake church: Luis and his bride on their wedding day. Oh, dear God . . . the last one was a photograph of Lita on Nissy, taken at my house on the marsh. I recognized the steps up to the deck. Luis's dark-furred hand held a rope that had been slipped around Nissy's neck, and she had pulled it taut, but was standing, still and mulish, with the grinning child on her back. Behind them, almost out of focus, I stood, smiling, the light from the creek silhouetting my flyaway hair. I remembered that day: it had been New Year's Eve, the day we had all spent at my house, the day of the night when I first stayed alone at the house after the great fear had begun, and did not drink. The day that Luis had told me about finding what you would die for, and then living for it . . .

I felt my knees give again, and Sophia tightened her hold around my waist. I knew that she had taken the photograph and that she had probably placed it there with Luis's other sparse treasures. I did not think, after all, that I could do this.

As if at a signal, though I heard none, the people began to hum quietly, and to sway back and forth to the rhythm of the music. It had no words, and the tune was atonal and sounded very old in the cold, quiet glade. Outside the wall of trees the wind moaned, but in here it did not stir the bare branches. The people hummed and hummed, and I closed my eyes and let the sound take me where it would.

When I opened them again, the humming was slowing, and then it stopped. Ezra Upchurch came out of the small crowd and stood beside the open grave. He wore over-alls over a flannel shirt, clean but worn thin and faded almost patternless. He had a great, vivid camellia in his overall strap, and he looked down at the coffin of his friend and put his hand lightly on it. There were silver tear tracks on his dark face. He took a great breath and looked up at the crowd, and said, in a voice that rang out over the clearing and into the woods: "Our friend Luis felt that cycle leavin' him, and he say, 'Uh-oh, Lord, I think I'm coming home.' And the Lord say, 'I know you, Luis. Come on home . . .'"

And I knew that I could not stay. Murmuring to Sophia, I turned and stumbled back out of the clearing and through the vines until I stood again in the muddy road. Tears flooded my face and soaked into the collar of Clay's jacket, and my chest heaved and bucked. The big grief was back, but there was something else, too. It was a simple, one-celled gratitude. I had wondered if it was the right thing, laying him to rest here so far from anyone and anything that he had known. And I saw now that it was. He would be a part of them forever now. They would make him so. They would make a song of him and for him. They would make a great tale of him and for him. He would belong to them in a way that many of their own never did, and their children would sing of him, and their children, and as long as Dayclear stood, Luis Cassells would be at home.

And Dayclear would stand.

Looks like we're stuck with you, I said to him in my head. Looks like you're stuck with us. You're ours now. Sleep tight, Luis.

And I went back down the road to Auntie Tuesday's house.

"It ain't over, is it?" she said. She had been nodding by the stove. Its red was fading to gray, and I stooped and opened the door and poked at it until it leaped into life again.

"No. I . . . I just couldn't be there anymore."

"That all right. We knows you come. He knows, too."

We sat in silence for a bit, and then I sighed and said, "I'd better go see what I can do about Lita."

She nodded. "I tol' her you was on your way. She just turned her head. I 'spec it be all right now, though."

"Don't count on it, Auntie."

"Well, you know, I seed that it was."

I shook my head and got up and went into the bedroom where Lita was.

It was darkened, obviously in the hope that she would sleep, but she was not asleep.

503

She lay very still, curled on her side, facing the door. Auntie had covered her with the same beautiful quilt she had laid over her after the mare had died, but it seemed to me that the little body under it was vastly diminished now, much smaller than the one I had seen here before. I could not make out her face, both because of the darkness and the tangle of hair that had fallen into it. But I could see the gleam of the whites of her eyes. They did not seem to blink.

I sat down on the bed beside her. She did not move. I reached out to touch her hair, and she flinched slightly, so I let my hand fall to the quilt.

"Hello, baby bug," I said. "Auntie told you I'd come, didn't she?"

She did not move.

"I know that you don't feel like talking right now, and that's okay," I said. "It's all right to be sad. I'm sad, too. Your abuelo was the most wonderful man, and we'll miss him terribly. But there are still a lot of people who love you, and we're all worried because you won't talk to us. Do you think you might just try a word or two?"

Nothing.

"Well, then, I'll just sit here with you for a while. I think Auntie's making us some supper. In a little while I'll go get it and bring it in on a tray, and we can have it together right here. Like a picnic. Would you like that?"

She did not speak, but she put one hand out and clamped it onto my wrist. The strength in it was almost frightening.

"You don't want me to go?" I said, looking into her face.

This time she shook her head, very slightly, no. No.

"Then I won't. Auntie will bring in our supper. Would you . . ." And I knew that it was something I must do. "Would you like me to stay here with you tonight?"

She nodded her head, still not speaking. Yes. Her fingers tightened on my wrist.

"If I stay, will you try to close your eyes and sleep a little bit? After our supper, I mean."

No. Her head shook back and forth, harder and harder. No. There was fear in her white-ringed eyes. Well, I could not blame her. The last time she had shut her eyes her grandfather had died.

But we could not sit here like this forever, her hand fastened in a death grip on my arm, her eyes staring, staring.

Then I had a thought.

"Would you like to go see Yambi? He's right up there behind Janie and Esau's store, and every time anybody goes by he says,

'Where's Lita? Where's Lita?' I bet he's lonesome, too. He lost his mommy, just like you lost your abuelo."

She stared into my face intently for what seemed a very long time. Then, very slowly, she pulled her arms out from under the quilt and held them out to me. I could literally see them quivering with fear, but she did it.

I reached out and took her into my arms and held her close to me for a while, feeling the rabbitlike tremor of her heart, and then got up and carried her out into the living room. Auntie looked up and smiled.

"MMMM hmmm," she said. "Yes*sir*."

"We're going to walk up and see Yambi," I said over Lita's head. She had buried it in my neck, and was clinging for dear life. "I think we might like a bite to eat when we get back."

"Got me some vegetable soup and corn bread," she said. "And got a warm yam here for that colt. Been savin' it. He like to eat me out of yams, but this one's special. Wait a minute, let me put somethin' round her."

She pulled herself up out of the chair and tottered stiffly over to a hook behind the back door and took a thick old maroon cardigan from it and wrapped it close around the child. I settled her deeper into the circle of my arms and went out of the house into the wind.

She weighed almost nothing, but I was still breathing hard when we reached the store, partly because of the fear that gripped my heart. What if she did not speak? What if she never did again? Who was there that could heal this child?

We did not see the colt at first, but I called softly, "Yambi, Yambi," and then he came, trotting around a little lean-to that Esau had obviously made to shelter him from the weather. His legs had grown longer, and his mane and tail were more luxuriant than the little stiff brushes I remembered, and he looked altogether better than I could have expected. The Bigginses or someone had been currying him; his coat was as sleek as I supposed a marsh tacky's ever got, and on his narrow little head was a soft rope snaffle. He stopped and looked at us.

"Look, Lita," I said. "He's waiting for you."

Against my shoulder, she shook her head. But then slowly she turned it, and she looked. I felt a tremor go through the little body.

I reached into my jacket pocket and pulled out the yam. It was still warm and ashy from its tenure in the coals of Auntie's stove.

"Why don't you give him this?" I said, and she held her hand out very slowly, and I laid it in her palm.

She looked up at me, and then she held it out over the barbed wire fence.

The colt was still, his head cocked. We were not among the callers he was used to. On the other hand, we came bearing yams. I watched while he worked it out. The yam won.

He came trotting with his springy step up to the fence 'and put his black nose into Lita's palm and took the yam with his rubbery black lips. He gulped it with one great swallow, nosed at her hand, and then put his head over the fence and began to nose and sniff at her arm and neck and face and hair. I felt rather than saw the beginning of the smile on her face.

We stood there for a long time, the silent child and I, she smiling now, her eyes closed, as the colt nuzzled her face and neck with his wet black nose. Tears ran down my face in sheets, and I did not even realize it until much later, when my wet collar began to grow cold.

We must have stood there for ten or fifteen minutes when she turned her face back into my shoulder and gave a great sigh and said, so softly that I almost did not hear her, "It's time to go home now, Caro."

I stood very still, holding her. The colt began nosing at my arms and hands. I looked far into myself, feeling with my heart. Yes, she was still there, my daughter, the tiny, focused, radiant essence of her, burning steadily.

"Can we do this?" I whispered.

And as if she had said it, I knew that we could, knew that the point of flame that was Kylie Venable could warm both me and this cold child, and could do so forever. I put my chin down on the top of Lita's head.

"Yes," I said. "Yes, it is. So let's do it. There's somebody I want you to meet."